Human Sciences Research Council
Publication Series Number
86

paper books

Titles available in this series:

Lionel Abrahams
The Celibacy of Felix Greenspan

Michael Chapman and Tony Voss
Accents

Olive Schreiner
The Story of an African Farm

Olive Schreiner
The Woman's Rose

John Cleland
Fanny Hill

Bloke Modisane
Blame me on History

Sarah Gertrude Millin
God's Stepchildren

Russell Vandenbroucke
Truths the hand can touch

Sisa Ndaba
One Day in June

Dan Jacobson
The Price of Diamonds

Digby Ricci
Reef of Time

Michael Chapman
and Achmat Dangor
Voices from Within

Michael Chapman
The Paperbook of South African English Poetry

Stephen Gray
Market Plays

John Conyngham
The Arrowing of the Cane

Steve Jacobs
Diary of an Exile

Michael Macnamara
Meaning in Life

Joseph Conrad
Heart of Darkness and Typhoon

Jane Austen
Northanger Abbey

Henry James
Washington Square

Janet Hodgson
Princess Emma

Sheila Roberts
Jacks in Corners

Ridley Beeton
Facets of Olive Schreiner

Martin Orkin
Shakespeare Against Apartheid

Peter Walshe
The Rise of African Nationalism in South Africa

Peter Wilhelm
Some Place in Africa

Phyllis Altman
The Law of the Vultures

Martin Trump
Armed Vision

Phyllis Lewsen
Voices of Protest

Teresa Dovey
The Novels of J M Coetzee

Teresa Dovey

The Novels of J M Coetzee

Lacanian Allegories

AD. DONKER / PUBLISHER

AD. DONKER (PTY) LTD
A subsidiary of Donker Holdings (Pty) Ltd
P O Box 41021
Craighall
2024

First paperbook edition 1988

ISBN 0 86852 132 9

Typeset by Triangle Typesetters (Pty) Ltd.
Printed and bound by Creda Press (Pty) Ltd, Cape Town

It is the hermit crab, I remember from a book, that as it grows migrates from one empty shell to another . . . . Whose shell I presently skulk in does not matter, it is the shell of a dead creature. What matters is that my anxious softbodied self should have a refuge from the predators of the deep . . . .

In the Heart of the Country

The following abbreviations are used in the text:

HC – In the Heart of the Country
SAF – The Story of an African Farm
WB – Waiting for the Barbarians
L&T – Life & Times of Michael K

CONTENTS

1 Theoretical Framework: Lacan, Narration, Temporality

J.M. Coetzee is both novelist and critic. Between 1974 and 1986 he has published five novels; in the same period of time he has published more than two dozen articles and reviews, many of these in respected journals, and written on a wide range of topics. He is Professor of General Literature at the University of Cape Town, and regularly spends time at North American universities. This 'background information', which is all that will be offered in the way of biographical detail, is given, not by way of providing Coetzee's credentials as a writer, but as a means of introducing the kind of claims that will be made concerning his novels. In these five novels (if 'novels' is, indeed, the right term to use for them – the problem of correct terminology is not insignificant with a writer like Coetzee the novelistic and critical discourses fuse: like the *nouveau roman*, they are criticism-as-fiction, or fiction-as-criticism.[1] If one chooses to see the novel as defined precisely by its 'novelty', by its propensity to expose the codes of previous forms, then it might be argued that many novels function in this way. However, Coetzee's novels perform this function, of criticism-as-fiction, in a self-conscious and systematic fashion, engaging in the contemporary theoretical debate in a way that circumvents certain of the problems facing critics who adhere to more conventional forms of critical discourse. My purpose, then, is second degree criticism, of Coetzee's criticism-as-fiction within the context of contemporary theory, drawing attention to the theoretical issues the novels articulate and to the modes of novelistic discourse with which they engage. The theorists whose writing informs my reading of Coetzee's novels may, for the most part, be located within the broad context of post-structuralism. And with respect to Coetzee's novels, most notable amongst these theorists are Jacques Lacan and, to a lesser degree, Jacques Derrida.

In a paper on Sarah Gertrude Millin, Coetzee has said that

any reading of Millin must 'be tempered by a view of her as a practising novelist adapting whatever models and theories lie to hand to make writing possible ('Blood, Flaw, Taint, Degeneration: The Case of Sarah Gertrude Millin', p. 58). Now this describes the conditions under which any text is produced, as Stephen Heath (1972) says, opening 'in and from that complex formation of modes of articulation that gives, as it were, the theatre of its activity, a series of settings always already there as its very possibility' (p.24). However, what I am proposing is that Coetzee deliberately adopts and adapts the models and theories that lie to hand, inhabiting them in a way that closely approximates the Derridean strategy of deconstruction:

> The movements of deconstruction do not destroy structures from the outside. They are not possible and effective, nor can they take accurate aim, except by inhabiting those structures. Inhabiting them in a certain way, because one always inhabits, and all the more when one does not suspect it. Operating necessarily from the inside, borrowing all the strategic and economic resources of subversion from the old structure, borrowing them structurally, that is to say without being able to isolate their elements and atoms, the enterprise of deconstruction always in a certain way falls prey to its own work. (*Of Grammatology*, p.24)

Thus Magda, narrator of *In the Heart of the Country*, describes herself as a hermit crab, 'that as it grows migrates from one empty shell to another,' and, towards the end of the novel says: 'The host is dying, the parasite scuttles anxiously about the cooling entrails wondering whose tissues it will live off next' (*Heart of the Country*, pp. 43 and 119). The subgenres which I identify as those inhabited by Coetzee's novels are: in *Dusklands*, the anthropological/historical/fictional writing which may be grouped together under the heading 'journey of exploration'; in *In the Heart of the Country*, the romantic pastoral; in *Waiting for the Barbarians*, the liberal humanist novel; and in *Life & Times of Michael K*, the novel of the inarticulate victim. While the first four novels take as their starting point these sub-genres of white South African writing, the most recent novel, *Foe*, appears to locate itself within a far broader discursive arena, at the intersection of feminist, post-colonial and post-modern discourses.

Critical response to the novels thus far indicates that they have, in most cases, been read as offering a critique of the South African situation. My argument is that they offer a critique of various modes of writing, and that if, in the first four novels, these are modes of white South African writing, Coetzee is nevertheless concerned to locate these modes, or sub-genres, within the context of certain prevalent Western ideologies. Via the narrators of these novels – Eugene Dawn, Jacobus Coetzee, Magda, the Magistrate, the medical offer, and Susan Barton – we are able to trace a history of colonialism and neo-colonialism and, more importantly, of the forms of discourse which have provided the legitimising of representations of various phases of imperialism. Thus it might be argued that *Foe* differs only in degree from the previous novels, drawing attention to the general emergence of certain ideologies in Western discourses, rather than focusing upon their specific emergence in the sub-genres of white South African writing.

In the chapters which follow, I will show how Coetzee's novels recuperate the themes of each model they inhabit for a thematics of the Lacanian subject, which provides the means for a deconstructive reading and a self-deconstructive re-writing of these themes and genres. Thus it becomes necessary to describe Coetzee's strategy as, not simply criticism-as-fiction, but as (Lacanian) psychoanalytic criticism-as-fiction. Undertaking a study founded in Lacanian theory, I have experienced a fear of belatedness such as that expressed by Régis Durand, who makes the point that Lacanian theory over the last ten years,

> has become a broad cultural phenomenon, no longer
> restricted to the formation of analysts in training,
> but ranging over widely different fields. So that

> the situation, at present, for one who would turn or return to Lacanian theory for a specific purpose – say, a re-vision of narrative theory – is a fairly uncomfortable one. On the one hand, it may appear to be a questionable deflection of the original theory; on the other, it may appear to be part of an (already ebbing?) cultural trend – never a pleasant prospect. ('On Aphanisis', p.861)

The potential charge, of deflecting the original theory and of being part of an ebbing cultural trend, may be countered, in this case, by drawing attention to the nature of my reading of Coetzee's novels: this reading does not constitute Lacanian psychoanalytic criticism, but is based on the claim that the novels themselves constitute such criticism. This is not to deflect the charge of belatedness onto Coetzee, for his first novel was published in 1974, and this, and his subsequent novels, incorporate Lacanian theory in a way which is profoundly innovative, and which problematises rather than simply appropriates this theory.

Whereas Robert Con Davis points out that 'the literary appropriation of Lacan' involves 'experiments in the situating of narration as an effect (or product) of the unconscious – narration (in a sense) as already Lacanian even before or apart from, even in spite of, Lacan' ('Lacan and Narration', p.848), the claim I am making vis à vis Coetzee's writing is that it deliberately incorporates the paradigm of the Lacanian subject in a way which draws attention to its own genesis in the unconscious. In making this claim, it is at the same time necessary to point out that what is involved is not a 'simple' appropriation of the Lacanian paradigm, for the paradigm is itself not 'simple', not a unified theory, but a complex and paradoxical reading and repetition of Freud's texts. Discussing 'Freudian' and 'anti-Freudian' readings of Henry James's *The Turn of the Screw*, in the course of her own Lacanian reading of the James text, Shoshana Felman says:

> Whereas the two opposing critical sides believe themselves to be in spectacular disagreement over James's

> 'true meaning', they demonstrate in fact a spectacular agreement over Freud's 'true meaning', which, unlike that of James, is considered by both sides to be transparent, unequivocal, incontrovertible. But in reality the 'true Freud' is no more immediately accessible to us than the 'true James'. For 'Freud' is equally a text, known only through the difficulties and uncertainties of the act of reading and of interpretation. ('Turning the Screw', p. 116)

In the case of Coetzee's novels, it would, likewise, be mistaken to claim that one has access to their 'meaning' via the 'meaning' of the Lacanian subject, which itself resists reduction to a specific, unified 'meaning'. While it would be more accurate to say that the novels constitute a redramatisation of the paradoxes of the Lacanian subject, which is what my reading of the individual novels suggests, to claim these paradoxes and the ambiguity they generate as the 'meaning' of the novels would be equally mistaken. Felman asks:

> is a reading of ambiguity as such really possible? Is it at all possible to read and to interpret ambiguity without reducing it in the very process of interpretation? Are reading and ambiguity in any way compatible? ('Turning the Screw', p.117).

She provides a partial solution to the problem of ambiguity when she describes her own reading of *The Turn of the Screw* as attempting 'not so much to name and make explicit the ambiguity of the text, but to understand the necessity and the rhetorical functioning of textual ambiguity' (p.119). The rhetorical function of the Lacanian paradoxes dramatised in Coetzee's novels is, similarly, an issue which my reading of these novels must address. It is an issue which I believe can best be accounted for in terms of the deconstructive and allegorical nature of Coetzee's writing.

In these novels, then, Lacanian theory provides the means of translating an unwitting habitation of pre-existing forms into a deliberate dialogue, based on the model of the psychoanalytic dialogue, which, as Roy Schafer (1980) points out, 'is fundamentally a dialogue concerning the present moment of transference and resistance', and one in which 'the analyst takes the telling as performance as well as content' (pp.36 and 39). That is to say:

> Telling is treated as an object of description rather than, as the analysand wishes, an indifferent or transparent medium for imparting information or thematic content. The analyst has something to say about the how, when, and why of the telling. (Schafer, p.43)

My readings of the individual novels will demonstrate how they conduct an analysis of the 'how, when, and why of the telling' of previous texts, and how, by focussing on the repetitions and resistances of these texts, they draw attention to what has been repressed from their content, but nevertheless manifests itself in their manner of telling. Thus the 'how, when, and why' of these previous texts becomes the 'what', that is, the content, of Coetzee's novels. This does not, however, take into account the 'how, when, and why' of Coetzee's writing: playing the role of analyst in relation to the prior texts as analysands, Coetzee's novels must nevertheless assume the role of analysand in the ongoing analytic dialogue between text and reader. In this case we find that the 'what' becomes the 'how, when, and why,' the content of Coetzee's novels becomes the performance itself, as the traditional themes and the theme of the Lacanian subject intersect to produce allegories of the narrating self.

In a short piece titled 'A Note on Writing', Coetzee makes the point that writing in the 'middle voice' inevitably constitutes a commentary on the act of writing:

> Though modern Indo-European languages retain morphologically distinct forms for only the active-passive opposition, the phantom presence of a middle voice (a voice still morphologically present in Ancient Greek and Sanskrit) can be felt in some senses of

> modern verbs if one is alert to the possibility of the threefold opposition active-middle-passive. 'To write' is one of these verbs. To write (active) is to carry out the action without reference to the self, perhaps, though not necessarily, on behalf of someone else. To write (middle) is to carry out the action (or better, to do-writing) with reference to the self. Or—to follow Barthes in his metaphorical leap from grammar to meaning—'today to write is to make oneself the centre of the action of *la parole*; it is to effect writing in being affected oneself; it is to leave the writer (*le scripteur*) inside the writing, not as a psychological subject . . . but as the agent of the action.' The field of writing, Barthes goes on to suggest, has today become nothing but writing itself, not as art for art's sake but as the only space there is for the one who writes.[2]

Coetzee's writing is clearly conducted in the middle voice, and his novels all, in various ways, refer us to the fact that the narrator, as the representative of the writer, is not only affected but also effected by the writing: Magda speaks for all of Coetzee's narrators when she says 'I create myself in the words that create me' (*Heart of the Country*, p.8). The novels reveal their own status, and the status of the texts they deconstruct, to be the equivalent of performative speech acts, the function of these speech acts being to elicit the recognition of the reader as Other. According to Felman,

> Recognition is, indeed, for Freud as for Lacan, the crucial psychoanalytic stake both of the clinical and of the literary work . . . . In Lacan's different emphasis however, the psychoanalytic recognition is radically tied up with language, with the subject's analytic speech-act, and as such, its value is less cognitive than performative: it is, itself, essentially a speech-act, whose symbolic action modifies the subject's history, rather than cerebrally observing or recording it, at last correctly. ('Beyond Oedipus', pp.1026–27)

Coetzee's deconstructive diagnosis of previous modes of writing as speech acts is, at the same time, a self-deconstructive diagnosis effected by the novels upon themselves, and the Lacanian subject becomes the means of linking the two levels of the allegory, the means of avoiding the fallacy of assuming that one can take up a stance outside writing in order to comment upon another act of writing. However, what we have in Coetzee's novels is not only a diagnosis, but also a kind of cure: a curative re-writing of the pre-existing texts. As Felman says:

> The analytical speech-act by which the subject recognizes, and performatively names, his desire and his history (insofar as the misapprehension of the one has in effect structured the other), has to be completed, consummated, by an ultimate analytic act of speech which Lacan calls 'the *assumption* of one's history', that is, the ultimate acceptance – and endorsement – of one's destiny, the acknowledgement of responsibility for the discourse of the Other in oneself, but also the forgiving of this discourse. ('Beyond Oedipus', pp.1026-27)

Coetzee's novels, as I will demonstrate in the chapters which follow, deconstruct the previous genres both in terms of their desire for recognition and in terms of the various forms of their failure to acknowledge the responsibility for the discourse of the Other in themselves. Coetzee's novels themselves *do* make this acknowledgement of the discourse of the Other, but are articulated around the necessity and the impossibility of 'forgiving' this discourse.

It is here that the rhetorical function of the paradoxical Lacanian subject comes into play most strongly. The novels are 'Songs of the Narrating Self,'[3] songs predicated on the paradoxical movement which Durand refers to as *aphanisis*, a term appropriated by Lacan to describe the way in which 'the subject manifests himself in his movement of disappearance.'[4] Oscillating between appearance and disappearance, enunciation and utterance,[5] between the desire which is named and the desire which escapes all naming, these are the movements in which the subject arises and which ensure the continuation of the discourse. To 'forgive' the discourse of the Other would be to forego the novelistic discourse, which prolongs itself in the continued alternation between the assertion of a secret self, an assertion arising out of the very *inadequacy* of the discourse, and the acknowledgement that this secret self, too, has its genesis in the Other. This discursive movement is an aspect to which I will return at a later stage in this Introduction, as I discuss the particular nature of allegory in Coetzee's novels.

While I will elaborate upon the relevant Lacanian concepts as the need arises during my discussion of the individual novels, I will, at this point, draw attention to those paradoxical aspects of the Lacanian subject which appear to be most significant in Coetzee's novels. This will serve to establish the basis of the analysis which follows, and, at the same time, will serve to demonstrate that the novels constitute a profoundly unified body of work, despite the diversity of style necessitated by the adoption of previous modes of writing. The paradoxes of the Lacanian subject all arise out of the fundamental notion of division. As Robert Con Davis says:

> Most scandalizing about Lacan's paradigm . . . is a figure that can be described rather simply, that of a division, a *split*. For Lacan the pervasive figure of the split indicates a fundamental division in psychic life, in selfhood, and even within the things we know. In literary studies, it is a permanent division within the text and narration. ('Lacan and Narration', p.857)

This division is produced and re-produced at the significant developmental stages of the individual: birth, weaning, the perception of the self as other in the Mirror Stage, the symbolic castration in the Oedipal Stage, and, most significant with respect to the literary text, the accession to the Symbolic Order and language. The division which occurs at each of these stages institutes a loss, or lack of object, which the movement of speech attempts to recover. In Anthony Wilden's words:

> At the logical or epistemological level, says Lacan, the 'lack of object' is the gap in the signifying chain which the subject seeks to fill at the level of the signifier. This is the condition which makes it possible to discover the subject's truth in the linear movement of his discourse, since all other relationships, phantasies, and so forth will eventually be represented at this level of representation. Here Lacan is seeking to answer the question of the *movement* of the discourse. Whereas linguists tend to view speech as essentially static – that is to say, as subject to the mechanics of articulation and to time in a non-essential way – Lacan views speech as a movement toward something, an attempt to fill the gaps without which speech could not be articulated. In other words, speech is as dependent upon the notion of *lack* as is the theory of desire. (pp.163-64)

The movement of the discourse not only arises out of the condition of division, but gives rise to a divided subject: language confers 'subjectivity', but, at the same time, 'subjects' the self to the order of the signifier. Emile Benveniste describes the purely linguistic basis of this notion of subjectivity as follows:

> The 'subjectivity' we are discussing here is the capacity of the speaker to posit himself as 'subject', It is defined not by the feeling which everyone experiences of being himself . . . but as the psychic unity that transcends the totality of the actual experiences it assembles and that makes the permanence of the consciousness. Now we hold that that 'subjectivity', whether it is placed in phenomenology or in psychology, as one may wish, is only the emergence in the being of a fundamental property of language. 'Ego' is he who *says* 'ego'. That is where we see the foundation of 'subjectivity', which is determined by the lin-

guistic status of 'person'. (p.224)

Anika Lemaire elaborates upon the effects of the signifier, including the signifiers of 'person', when she says:

> The subject is in effect represented in symbolism by a stand in; a signifier which may be the personal pronoun 'I', the forename which devolves upon the subject, or the denomination 'son of . . . . ' What is more, the order of the symbol, of the signifier, an order supported only by its collateral relations – relations between the signifier and other signifiers – has definitively captured the subject in its nets. Mediated by language, the subject is irremediably divided, because he is at once excluded from the signifying chain and 'represented' in it. (p.68)

The *I* which is spoken is a stand-in for the self who speaks, and who is in turn 'determined retroactively, becomes a signification, engendered at the level of the statement, of what it produces at the level of the enunciation' (Lacan, *Four Fundamental Concepts*, p.139): in Magda's words, 'I make it all up in order that it shall make me up. I cannot stop now' (*In the Heart of the Country*, p.73). Of all Coetzee's narrators, Magda is the most explicit in articulating the dilemmas of a subject engaged in producing evidence of a self which, though lacking in the discourse, 'is not purely and simply absent from it',[6] but is, one might say, present in its absence.

Magda is, likewise, the narrator who constantly draws attention to her motivation in desire. She says, for example:

> What does one do with desire? My eye falls idly on objects, odd stones, pretty flowers, strange insects: I pick them up, bear them home, store them away. A man comes to Anna and comes to me: we embrace him, we hold him inside us, we are his, he is ours. I am heir to a space of natal earth which my ancestors found good and fenced about. To the spur of desire we have only one response: to capture, to enclose, to hold. But

> how real is our possession? The flowers turn to dust, Hendrik uncouples and leaves, the land knows nothing of fences, the stones will be here when I have crumbled away, the very food I devour passes through me. I am not one of the heroes of desire, what I want is not infinite or unattainable, all I ask myself, faintly, dubiously, querulously, is whether there is not something to do with desire other than striving to possess the desired in a project which must be vain, since its end can only be the annihilation of the desired. And how much keener does my question become when woman desires woman, two holes, two emptinesses. For if that is what I am then that is what she is too, anatomy is destiny: an emptiness, or a shell, a film over an emptiness longing to be filled in a world in which nothing fills . . . . It is the first condition of life for desire not to be fulfilled, otherwise life ceases. Fulfillment does not fulfil. (*In the Heart of the Country*, pp.113–114)

Or, one might say, 'It is the first condition of speech for desire not to be fulfilled, otherwise the discourse ceases'. Not only Magda's frantic endeavours, but the various activities of all of Coetzee's narrators, and of a figure like Michael K, may be read as metaphors of the act of narrating. Returning to Wilden's description of the function of speech, it is possible to rephrase his 'speech is as dependent upon the notion of lack as is the theory of desire', as: 'speech and desire are, in effect, inseparable.' Situating its cause in an absence, a lack, and showing it as incapable of being fulfilled, Magda provides us with an essentially Lacanian description of desire, as is evident when we compare it with the following passages from *Ecrits*:

> In the first instance, they [the effects of the presence of the signifier] proceed from a deviation of man's needs from the fact that he speaks, in the sense that in so far as his needs are subjected to demand, they return to him alienated . . . . That which is thus alienated in needs constitutes an *Urverdrängung*

> (primal repression), an inability, it is supposed, to be articulated in demand, but it re-appears in something it gives rise to that presents itself in man as desire (*das Begehren*). (Lacan, *Ecrits*, pp.285-86)

> Desire is that which is manifested in the interval that demand hollows within itself, in as much as the subject, in articulating the signifying chain, brings to light the want-to-be, together with the appeal to receive the complement from the Other, if the Other,. the locus of speech, is also the locus of this want, or lack . . . .
>
> It is also what is evoked by any demand beyond the need that is articulated in it, and it is certainly that of which the subject remains all the more deprived to the extent that the need articulated in the demand is satisfied. (*Ecrits*, p.263)

The demand is unequal to the need articulated in it, as this need is related to the desire for a fullness of being experienced by the infant as complement of the mother (as Other), but irretrievably lost once acceptance of the Father's veto of the desire to be the mother's complement has granted access to language and to sexual identity:[7]

> Demand in itself bears on something other than the satisfactions it calls for. It is demand of a presence or of an absence – which is what is manifested in the primordial relation to the mother, pregnant with that Other to be situated *within* the needs that it can satisfy. demand constitutes the Other as already possessing the 'privilege' of satisfying needs, that is to say, the power of depriving them of that alone by which they are satisfied. (*Ecrits*, p.286)

As we shall see, when I come to a consideration of the Lacanian model of reading and writing, the speech which is the text may itself be viewed as a demand that 'constitutes the Other as already possessing the "privilege" of satisfying needs.'

The notion of desire, then, is one of the central paradoxes dramatized in Coetzee's novels, a paradox which may be reduced to Lacan's characteristically aphoristic statement that 'it is precisely because desire is articulated that it is not articulable' (*Ecrits*, p.302). Tracing the sources of the Lacanian notion of desire, we go back, via Alexandre Kojève, to the Hegelian Master/Slave dialectic, which, as I will demonstrate, performs a particularly significant function in Coetzee's novels. Anthony Wilden draws attention to this aspect of desire when he says:

> Demand is . . . *for* something, whether that something is desired or not, whereas desire, as an absolute, is fundamentally the Hegelian desire for recognition, in that the subject seeks recognition as a (human) subject by requiring the other to recognize his (human) desire; in this sense one desires what another desires. And in the sense that desire is unconscious, one desires what the Other (here the unconscious subject) desires. (p.189)

Wilden points out that Lacan's use of the Hegelian notion of desire repeats the formulas of Kojève's reading of *The Phenomenology of Mind*, particularly of Section A of Chapter IV, titled 'Autonomy and Dependence of Self-Consciousness: Mastery and Slavery.'[8] According to Kojève, for desire to be human, it must be directed toward a non-natural object, toward something beyond objective reality, which, he claims, can only be desire itself:

> Man's humanity 'comes to light' only in risking his life to satisfy his human Desire – that is, his Desire directed toward another Desire. Now, to desire a Desire is to want to substitute oneself for the value desired by this Desire. For without this substitution, one would desire the value, the desired object, and not the Desire itself. Therefore, to desire the Desire of another is in the final analysis to desire that the value that I am or that I 'represent' be the value desired by

> the other: I want him to 'recognize' my value as his value. I want him to 'recognize' me as an autonomous value. In other words, all human, anthropogenetic Desire . . . is, finally, a function of the desire for 'recognition.' And the risk of life by which the human reality 'comes to light' is a risk for the sake of such a Desire. (p.7)

The desire for 'recognition' takes the form of a (symbolic) fight to the death, a fight in which one of the combatants forces the other to 'recognize him/her, and so assumes a position of mastery in relation to the other's servitude. For one to achieve 'recognition,' the other cannot die, but

> must give up his desire and satisfy the desire of the other: he must 'recognize' the other without being 'recognized' by him. Now, 'to recognize' him thus is 'to recognize' him as his Master and to recognize himself and to be recognized as the Master's Slave. (Kojève, p.8)

This, however, results in a situation in which there is not real 'recognition', because the Master 'is recognized by someone whom he does not recognize' (Kojève, p.19), by an inessential consciousness: Magda, narrator of *In the Heart of the Country*, obligingly cites the relevant passage from *The Phenomenology of Mind*:

> *It is the slave's consciousness that constitutes the master's certainty of his own truth. But the slave's consciousness is a dependent consciousness. So the master is not sure of the truth of his autonomy. His truth lies in an inessential consciousness and its inessential acts.*[9]

Jacobus Coetzee's encounters with the Hottentot tribe, Eugene Dawn's fantasies of the encounter between the American troops and the Vietcong, Magda's fantasies of aggression against the father and rape by the servant, the Magistrate's relationship with the barbarian girl, the medical officer's battle of words with Michael K, and Susan Barton's struggle with Foe and with Friday may all be read as forms of this struggle for recognition. In Coetzee's novels the Master/Slave dialectic functions at levels of varying complexity and abstraction: it serves to articulate the actual dynamic of racial domination represented in the novels, a dynamic in which the position of mastery held by the Whites is a hollow mastery, and, at the same time, it serves to articulate the desire for recognition in which Coetzee's novels and the texts they deconstruct have their genesis. The way in which the narrating self becomes involved in this dialectic, and the way in which the struggle for mastery is inscribed in the narrative, is best understood by means of reference to the crucial developmental moment of Lacan's Mirror Stage. In the Mirror Stage, the infant achieves its first perception of identity in the form of an alienating image of itself, a form of 'primary identification that structures the subject as a rival with himself' (*Ecrits*, p.22). The perception of an image of self as harmonious unity is the source of a form, an 'Ideal-I', which 'situates the agency of the ego, before its social determination, in a fictional direction' (*Ecrits*, p.2). The Imaginary construct internalised at this stage, the illusion of a potential 'identity', or state of 'Oneness', is the basis of all future constructs, including those produced in the act of narrating. The infant is structured as a rival with itself and occupies a position of servitude in relation to the image of self as object: thus begins what Wilden calls the 'Imaginary battle of mutual objectification', in which the child functions as 'a subject to be reduced to an object (a slave) in a Hegelian struggle for recognition' (p.167). The intrasubjective aggressivity generated out of this relationship between self as subject and self as object is perpetuated in the struggle for recognition in intersubjective relationships, which constitute the dialectic of identification in the Symbolic.

The field of narrative may be regarded as a form of intersubjective relationship: this is what Robert Con Davis calls 'a psychoanalytic anthropomorphism of the text', based on the premise that 'Since the operations of the psychoanalytic subject and the text are synonomous – rather, since textuality is an inscription of the subject – many of the same laws govern both' ('The Discourse of the Father', p.3). At the purely linguistic level, the combatants in the struggle for recognition perpetuated in the text are the *I* of the narrator and the *You* of the narratee. Continuing his definition of the linguistic 'subject', Benveniste says:

> Consciousness of self is only possible if it is experienced by contrast. I use *I* only when I am speaking to someone who will be a *you* in my address. It is this condition of dialogue that is constitutive of *person,* for it implies that reciprocally *I* becomes *you* in the address of the one who in his turn designates himself as *I*. Here we see a principle whose consequences are to spread out in all directions. Language is possible only because each speaker sets himself up as a *subject* by referring to himself as *I* in his discourse. Because of this, *I* posits another person, the one who, being, as he is, completely exterior to 'me', becomes my echo to whom I say *you* and who says *you* to me. This polarity of persons is the fundamental condition in language, of which the process of communication, in which we share, is only a mere pragmatic consequence. (pp. 224-25)

Coetzee has said, in response to a question concerning the psychology of power in *Dusklands* and *In the Heart of the Country*, that the situation in both novels is that of 'living among people without reciprocity, so that there's only an 'I' and the 'You' is not on the same basis, the 'You' is a debased 'You', ' Responding to the interviewer's further question, 'An 'It' in effect?' he said, 'Correct. And both of them [Jacobus Coetzee and Magda] feel, perhaps in different ways, that it's impossible to live that way, but lack the stature to transform that 'It' into a 'You', to, so to speak, create a society in which reciprocity exists; and therefore condemn themselves to desperate gestures towards establishing intimacy' (Watson Interview, p.23). It is a condition of language that the *I* cannot transform the *It* into a *You*: the *You* is always a 'debased

You' in relation to the *I*; in Hegelian terms as 'inessential *You'*, dependent for its existence upon the *I* which utters it. As Coetzee says, in an article on Achterberg's 'Ballade van de gasfitter':

> The *You* has little solidity to the gaze of the *I*. On the contrary, the *You* is absent; or is present only passively, as an object of the awareness of the *I*; or is incapable of action; or is capable only of involuntary action hypothesized by the *I*; or is capable only of an inactive locativity defined in relation to the *I*. In other words, the *You* is absent or evanescent or dependent on the *I*, and the relation of *I* to *You*, being barely transitive, cannot be reciprocal. (p.287)[10]

Within the context of the Lacanian theory of the subject, it is possible to say that any utterance is a 'desperate gesture towards establishing intimacy', is an attempt to establish a dual, immediate relationship modelled on the relationship of self and image in the Mirror Stage. Thus Lacan says:

> For the function of lanuage is not to inform but to evoke.
>
> What I seek in speech is the response of the other. What constitutes me as subject is my question. In order to be recognized by the other, I utter what was only in view of what will be. I order to find him, I call him by a name that he must assume or refuse in order to reply to me. (*Ecrits*, p.86).

As my reading of *Dusklands*, in particular, will indicate, the utterance which is the literary text may constitute either a gesture of mastery, or a gesture of submission to the mastery of the reader as Other. This is, likewise, the case with the utterance which is the interpretive text, which may claim mastery over meaning, or may locate the mastery of meaning within the literary text itself. Thus, for example, Spivak points out that:

> Derrida acknowledges that the desire of deconstruction may itself become a desire to reappropriate the text actively through mastery, to show the text what it 'does not know', And as she deconstructs, all protestations to the contrary, the critic necessarily assumes that she at least, and for the time being, means what she says. Even the declaration of her vulnerability must come, after all, in the controlling language of demonstration and reference. In other words, the critic provisionally forgets that her own text is necessarily self-deconstructed, always already a palimpsest. (Translator's Preface to *Of Grammatology*, p. lxxvii)

And, discussing the stance traditionally taken by psychoanalysis toward the literary text, Shoshana Felman says:

> While literature is considered as a body of *language* – to *be interpreted* – psychoanalysis is considered as a body of *knowledge*, whose competence is called upon *to interpret*. Psychoanalysis, in other words, occupies the place of a *subject*, literature that of an *object*; the relation of interpretation is structed as a relation of master to slave, according to the Hegelian definition: the dynamic encounter between the two areas is in effect, in Hegel's terms, a 'fight for recognition,' whose outcome is the sole recognition of the master – of (the truth of) psychoanalytical theory; literature's function, like that of the slave, is to *serve* precisely the *desire* of psychoanalytical theory – its desire for recognition; exercising its authority and *power* over the literary field, holding a discourse of masterly competence, psychoanalysis, in literature, thus seems to seek above all its own *satisfaction*. ('To Open the Question', pp. 5–6)

Felman proposes a reversal of this position, a reversal intended to 'disrupt altogether the position of mastery as such, to try to avoid *both* terms of the alternative, to deconstruct the very structure of the opposition, mastery/slavery' ('To Open the Question', p.7). Now Coetzee's novels, deconstructing themselves (in so far as this is possible) as they perform a psychoanalytic deconstruction of the texts of the tradition, *do* disrupt the position of mastery as such, and, furthermore, they show that the dual reciprocity of the Master/Slave relationship is founded in an illusion. It is, in effect, subverted by the Other as the Word which occupies the position of 'Thirdness' between two subjects'.[11] It is, as Lacan points out, the Other as the locus of speech, 'the locus in which is constituted the I who speaks to him who hears' (*Ecrits*, p.141), that holds the ultimate position of mastery:

> The Other as previous site of the pure subject of the signifier holds the master position, even before coming into existence, to use Hegel's term against him, as absolute Master. For what is omitted in the platitude of modern information theory is the fact that one can speak of code only if it is already the code of the Other, and that is something quite different from what is in question in the message, since it is from this code that the subject is constituted, which means that it is from the Other that the subject receives even the message that he emits. (*Ecrits*, p.305)

Thus even the one who would assume a position of mastery is subjected to the mastery of the Other; the position of servitude is a condition of language itself:

> When the slave is confronted with the choice of his freedom or his life, he decides, *no freedom without life* – life remains forever deprived of freedom. And, when we stand back to look at things, we will see that the alienation of the master is structured in exactly the same way. For if Hegel shows us that the status of the master is established in the struggle to the death of pure prestige, it is because it is to bring his choice through death that the master also constitutes his fundamental alienation . . . . The revelation of the

essence of the master is manifested at the moment of terror when it is to him that one says *freedom or death*, and then he has obviously only death to choose in order to have freedom. (*The Four Fundamental Concepts of Psycho-Analysis*, p. 219–20)

This death is the 'death' that results from the transformation of the subject into an object in its passage through the signifier: 'I identify myself in language,' says Lacan, 'but only by losing myself in it like an object' (*Ecrits*, p.86).[12] The dual relationship between subject and subject, or subject and object, an Imaginary relationship which has its origin in the Mirror Stage, is subverted in the Symbolic, where the individual has access to subjectivity, but where s/he is reduced to the status of object: and so there is 'no freedom without life', but 'life remains forever deprived of freedom'.

This introduces another of the paradoxes dramatized in Coetzee's novels, or rather, another in the set of inextricably inter-connected paradoxes, which are those of the function of the Imaginary and the Symbolic registers, the death instinct and temporality. Edmond Ortigues describes the passage from the Imaginary to the Symbolic as follows:

> This is the sense of J. Lacan's definition of the essence of the Imaginary as a 'dual relationship', an ambiguous redoubling, a 'mirror' reflection, an immediate relationship between the subject and its other in which each term passes immediately into the other and is lost in a never-ending play of reflections. Imagination and desire are the realities of a finite being which can emerge from the contradiction between self and other only by the genesis of a third term, a mediatory 'concept' which, by determining each term, orders them into reversible and progressive relations which can be developed in language. The whole problem of symbolization lies here, in this passage from a dual opposition to a ternary relation, a passage from desire to the concept.[13]

While the transition from the Imaginary to the Symbolic involves a loss, it also involves a simultaneous gain: as Frederic Jameson points out, 'the acquisition of the Symbolic is rather the precondition for a full mastery of the Imaginary as well' ('Imaginary and Symbolic in Lacan', p.360). Jameson is concerned primarily with the hermeneutic possibilities of plotting the interface, in the text, between the Imaginary and Symbolic registers, in a way which, rather than producing a dualistic treatment of one as 'bad' and the other as 'good', is able to 'articulate both, while preserving their radical discontinuity with each other' ('Imaginary and Symbolic in Lacan', p.378). This is an appropriate description of what is undertaken in Coetzee's novels, particularly in their own hermeneutic relationship to previous texts. More than this, however, while they reject the automatism of repetition arising out of a relative fixation in the Imaginary, Coetzee's novels resist the alienation of desire resulting from fixation in the Symbolic. The Symbolic Order is not alone responsible for the fixation of the subject, for the conditions which lead to fixation arise in the Mirror Stage, which Lacan describes as follows:

> The *mirror stage* is a drama whose internal thrust is precipitated from insufficiency to anticipation – and which manufactures for the subject, caught up in the lure of spatial identification, the succession of phantasies that extends from a fragmented body-image to a form of its totality that I shall call orthopaedic – and, lastly, to the assumption of the armour of an alienating identity, which will mark with its rigid structure the subject's entire mental development. (*Ecrits*, p.4)

Jane Gallop draws attention to the way in which retroactive and anticipatory effects are entangled in Lacan's description of the Mirror Stage, saying:

> The problem of rigidity seems to be linked to a certain sort of temporal succession, an irreversible chronology that one might call 'tragic'. It appears

> that the internal linear progression of the drama leads to rigidity. But given the effect of retroaction, one might also say that it is rigidity that produces irreversible chronology. (p.124)

Asking, 'Is the "rigid armor" an inevitable conclusion?' and tentatively answering this question in the negative by saying, 'This struggle against the ineluctable progress of chronology must stake its hopes upon the combined effects of anticipation and retroaction' (pp. 124 and 127), she articulates both the question addressed implicitly in Coetzee's writing, and the particular form the response takes in the novels.

The combined effects of anticipation and retroaction constitute the dialectic in which the subject arises, a dialectic which Lacan describes in the following terms:

> The symbolic function presents itself as a double movement within the subject: man makes an object of his action, but only in order to restore to this action in due time its place as a grounding. In this equivocation, operating at every instant, lies the whole process of a function in which action and knowledge alternate. (*Ecrits*, p.73)

Elsewhere he says:

> Being of non-being, that is how *I* as subject comes on the scene, conjugated with the double aporia of a true survival that is abolished by knowledge of itself, and by a discourse in which it is death that sustains existence. (*Ecrits*, p.300)

As we see from this last passage, this dialectic is essentially the equivalent of the paradoxical movements of the death instinct, based as it is on Freud's observation of the phenomena of transference and repetition, which might be described as the retroactive recreation of the anticipatory effects of an individual history. Roy Schafer points out that:

> In the traditional transference narration, one tells how the analysand is repetitively reliving or re-experiencing the past in the present relationship with the analyst. It is said that there occurs a regression within the transference to the infantile neurosis or neurotic matrix, which then lies exposed to the analyst's view. This is, however, a poor account. It tells of life history as static, archival, linear, reversible, and literally retrievable. Epistemologically, this story is highly problematic. Another and, I suggest, better account tells of change of action along certain lines; it emphasizes new experiencing and new remembering of the past that unconsciously has never become the past. More and more, the alleged past must be experienced consciously as a mutual interpenetration of the past and present, both being viewed in psychoanalytically organized and coordinated terms. (p.36)

According to Lacan, in the transference, 'the past which reveals itself reversed in repetition' (*Ecrits*, p.103) is the individual's accession to 'subjectivity', to life, in language; the past in which the individual was originally subjected to the desire of the Other and initiated into the role of servitude in relation to the mastery of the Symbolic Order. Lacan rejects the biological foundation of Freud's thesis, which is based on the formulation of an instinct as

> *an urge inherent in organic life to restore an earlier state of things* which the living entity has been obliged to abandon under the pressure of external disturbing forces; that is, it is a kind of organic elasticity, or, to put it another way, the expression of the inertia inherent in organic life. (*Beyond the Pleasure Principle*, p.36)

According to Freud, the compulsion to repeat, by means of which individuals 'can master a powerful impression far more thoroughly by being active than they could by merely experiencing it passively' (*Beyond the Pleasure Principle*, p.35), arises out of the need to master the painful experience whereby the organism was originally separated from the rest of inert matter. On the basis of these observations, Freud makes his momentous claim that 'the aim of all life is death' (*Beyond the Pleasure Principle*, p.38), by which he means to indicate that the living organism is motivated by the desire to return to the state of inertia 'inherent in organic life'. Freud's corollary to this is that the instincts of self-preservation

> are component instincts whose function it is to assure that the organism shall follow its own path to death, and to ward off any possible ways of returning to inorganic existence other than those which are immanent in the organism itself. (*Beyond the Pleasure Principle*, p.39)

Peter Brooks refers to the formulation of the death instinct in *Beyond the Pleasure Principle* as 'Freud's Masterplot',[14] and notes the importance of the notion of repetition in relation to the structuring of narrative, in which 'The sense of beginning . . . is determined by the sense of an ending' (Brooks, p.283). Brooks reads Freud's formulation of the death instinct, founded in the notion of repetition, as a metaphor of the way in which the repetitions of narrative constitute 'the cure which prolongs narrative', always threatened, as it is, by breakdown, 'on the verge of premature discharge, of short-circuit' (pp.297 and 296). Thus Brooks says:

> The organism must live in order to die in the proper manner, to die the right death. We must have the arabesque of plot in order to reach the end. We must have metonymy in order to reach metaphor.
>
> We emerge from reading *Beyond the Pleasure Principle* with a dynamic model which effectively structures ends (death, quiescence, non-narratability) against beginnings (Eros, stimulation into tension, the desire of narrative) in a manner that necessitates the middle as *detour*, as struggle toward the end under the compulsion of imposed delay, as arabesque in the

> dilatory space of the text. (p.295)

His argument that

> repetition speaks in the text of a return which ultimately subverts the very notion of beginning and end, suggesting that the idea of beginning presupposes the end, that the end is a time before the beginning, and hence that the interminable never can be finally bound in a plot (p.297),

provides a description of what I have been referring to as the combined effects of retroaction and anticipation. However, the fact that his argument is based on the Freudian, rather than the Lacanian formulation of the death instinct,[15] means that he derives from the death instinct a 'dynamic model', which has an unnecessarily metaphoric relationship to the effects of narrative temporality (or what he refers to as the transformation effected by plot). Lacan's *re*-formulation of the death instinct allows us to perceive the development of the narrative in time as a *manifestation* of the death instinct, rather than as having a somewhat incidental metaphoric relationship to it. According to Lacan's analysis of the death instinct

> There is . . . no further need to have recourse to the outworn notion of primordial masochism in order to understand the reason for the repetitive games in which subjectivity brings together mastery of its dereliction and the birth of the symbol. (*Ecrits*, p.103)

Transference involves the repeition of this experience of 'dereliction', a repetition in which the subject either claims a position of mastery, or accords to the partner the power of mastery, constituting the one who is addressed 'as already possessing the "privilege" of satisfying needs, that is to say, the power of depriving them of that alone by which they are satisfied' (*Ecrits*, p.186). This, then, describes the transferential relationship between text and reader, and allows us to perceive the field of the narrative as the playing out of the death instinct.

The death instinct is a two-way process, as Lacan indicates when he says: 'It still remains to be decided which death, that which is brought by life or that which brings life' (*Ecrits*, p.308). If the death instinct designates the movement by means of which the individual 'at every moment . . . constitutes his world by his suicide' (*Ecrits*, p.28), achieving 'life' via the 'death' resulting from the alienation of the self in the signifier, it also designates the movement by which the individual retreats from the field of the signifier, as

> The subject says 'No!' to this intersubjective game of hunt-the-slipper in which desire makes itself recognized for a moment, only to become lost in a will that is will [sic] of the other. Patiently, the subject withdraws his precarious life from the sheeplike conglomerations of the Eros of the symbol in order to affirm it at last in an unspoken curse. (*Ecrits*, pp.104–05)

Lacan describes this latter movement as 'that desperate affirmation of life that is the purest form in which we recognize the death instinct' (*Ecrits*, p.104). Now, both implicitly, at the level of structure, and explicitly, in the form of self-reflexive commentary, such as Eugene Dawn's claim that he is a story 'of life itself, life in obedience to which even the simplest organism represses its entropic yearning for the mud and follows the road of evolutionary duty toward the glory of consciousness', and Jacobus Coetzee's statement, 'On the other hand, if the worst comes you will find that I am not irrevocably attached to life. I know my lessons. I too can retreat before a beckoning finger through the infinite corridors of my self' (*Dusklands*, pp.29 and 114), Coetzee's novels draw attention to this two-way movement which is inscribed in the text as the death-in-life of the discourse, and the life-in-death offered by the possibility of a retreat from the discursive arena. And so we find in the death instinct the summation of the rhetorical function of the various paradoxes in which the theory of the Lacanian subject and, in turn, Coetzee's novels are founded. If the text provides evidence of a divided subject, of the concept of desire (not desire itself), of the Word intruding in the position of Thirdness in the dual Imaginary relationship, of the subject's servitude in the bonds of language as master, of time as a 'dead past' (as the subsequent discussion of narrative temporality will indicate) – in short, of death – at the same time it posits the possibility of fullness of being, desire fulfilled, the achievement of a dual, immediate relationship, of freedom and of unlimited time – of life – outside or beyond the text. Like Lacan, Coetzee's novels never omit the reminder that 'the dialectic is not individual' (*Ecrits*, p.105) but always engages the subject in a symbolic movement within the historical moment; and again like Lacan, they suggest that:

> the reader should recognize in the metaphor of the return to the inanimate (which Freud attached to every living body) that margin beyond life that language gives to the human being by virtue of the fact that he speaks, and which is precisely that in which such a being places in the position of a signifier, not only those parts of his body that are exchangeable, but this body itself. (*Ecrits*, p.301)

This brings us full circle, back to the notion of aphanisis, to the way in which the subject is manifested in the lethal movement of disappearance. Coetzee's novels are articulated around the recognition of the lethal effect of the discourse and, at the same time, of the margin beyond this death-in-life, a margin, paradoxically, inscribed in the discourse precisely because of the recognition and acceptance of this death. It is, as we shall see, the ongoing dialectical movement of this dual recognition which produces the successive ironic moments of these novels. The function of the death instinct here approximates the function which it has in the psychoanalytic relationship as Felman describes it:

> What is, then, psychoanalysis if not, precisely,

> *a life-usage of the death-instinct* – a practical, productive usage of the compulsion to repeat, through a *replaying* of the symbolic meaning of the *death* the subject has repeatedly experienced, and through a recognition and *assumption* of the meaning of this death (separation, loss) by the subject, as a symbolic means of his coming to terms not with death but, precisely, with his *life?* ('Beyond Oedipus', p.1034)

Coetzee's novels engage in the 'struggle against the ineluctable progress of chronology', against rigidity not only of the individual subject inscribed in the utterance, but of the literary history represented in the text. This struggle is produced in the 'combined effects of anticipation and retroaction' (Gallop, p.127), as the novels recognize themselves as a 'new experiencing and new remembering of [a literary] past that unconsciously has never become the past' (Schafer, p.36).

It is in this manner, too, that the novels cope with the problem of narrative temporality, a problem addressed at a structural and linguistic level in all the novels, and at an explicitly thematic level in *In the Heart of the Country* and *Life & Times of Michael K.* The problem of temporality is essentially the equivalent of the problem of subjectivity, for, as Ronald Schleifer points out, 'temporality itself as a concept . . . emerges and is recognized simultaneously with the emergence of the subject' (p.876). While temporality may be equated with the emergence of the Imaginary within the Symbolic, it 'is not a pole in a binary opposition, but arises out of such an opposition' (Schleifer, p.877). Schleifer goes on to say:

> Time exists between the *power* of its illusory felt presence and our articulated *knowledge* of it which, apprehending its radical insusceptibility to articulation, erases its presence: to articulate time is to represent it by something else. (p.881)

This is best understood by means of reference to Jameson's

description of the interdependence of the Imaginary and the Symbolic:

> Yet to speak of the Imaginary independently of the Symbolic is to perpetuate the illusion that we could have a relatively pure experience of either. If, for instance, we overhastily identify the Symbolic with the dimension of language and the function of speech in general, then it becomes obvious that we can hardly convey any experience of the Imaginary without presupposing the former. Meanwhile, insofar as the Imaginary is understood as the place of the insertion of my unique individuality as *Dasein* and as *corps propre*, it will become increasingly difficult to form a notion of the Symbolic Order as some pure syntactic web, which entertains no relationship to individual subjects at all. ('Imaginary and Symbolic in Lacan', p.350)

Thus, corresponding to the Imaginary, there is the time of enunciation, which is ' "outside of time", morphemic, and only becomes temporal when it is incribed – that is, structured and "symbolized" – in discourse' (Schleifer, p.879), and, corresponding to the Symbolic, there is the time of the utterance, articulated time, time represented by something else and therefore 'inscribed with death' (Schleifer, p.882). Schleifer cites St. Augustine as saying:

> If the present were always present, and would not pass into the past, it would no longer be time but eternity. Therefore, if the present, so as to be time, must be so constituted that it passes into the past, how can we say that it is, since the cause of its being is the fact that it will cease to be? Does it not follow that we can say that it is time, only because it tends towards non-being?[16]

This is essentially the same understanding of time as that articulated by Roman Ingarden when he says:

> the *perpetual transformation* of the actuality of something present into that enigmatic 'no-longer-being-present-any-more,' [which is] the ultimate essence of temporality, or better, of existence in time – naturally is not accidental, but is a certain kind of imperfection in something that exists in this mode – an imperfection which is closely connected with the *impossibility of its persisting in actuality* (*of maintaining actuality*) without sinking into the past.
> ....
> Gradually, the deeper it sinks into the unfathomable depths of the '*dead*' past, the fewer its traces in the present. (pp. 111–112 and p.117)

Coetzee has demonstrated his concern with the paradoxical nature of temporality, not only in the novels themselves, but also in a paper entitled 'Time, Tense and Aspect in Kafka's "The Burrow".' There he refers to a parable from Kafka's notebook of October 1917:

> a parable whose gist we might express as follows: We die at every moment, but blindly do not recognize our death and are spat back into life. Kafka goes on: 'From a certain point on, there is no more turning back. This is the point to be reached'. And then: 'The decisive (*entscheidende*) moment of human development is everlasting (*immerwährend).* Therefore those revolutionary spiritual movements that declare everything before themselves null are right, in that nothing has yet happened'. The next aphorism is: 'Human history is the second between two steps of a traveller'.
>
> The passage as a whole therefore contrasts two kinds of awareness of time. The first, which we can call historical awareness, imputes reality to a past which it sees as continuous with the present. The second, which we can call eschatological, recognizes no such continuity: there is only the present, which is always present, separated from Ingarden's 'dead past' by a moment of rupture, *the entscheidende Augenblick*.

> Hence the paradox that history is over in 'a second' while the present moment is 'everlasting'. (pp. 577–78)[17]

The first awareness of time, the historical awareness, produces the effect of the 'ineluctable progress of chronology' (Gallop, p.127), and corresponds to the narrative mode that Durand refers to as 'the successful achievement of the "family romance," a linear and non-contradictory discursive and symbolic mode' ('The Captive King', p.51). Operating within the second, eschatological awareness of time, as Coetzee claims Kafka does in 'The Burrow', 'There is no smooth course of narrative development that will lead from beginnings to the present moment of narration. Between then and now is always a break' (Coetzee, 'Time, Tense and Aspect', p.576). That is to say, likewise, that there is a break between the 'now' of enunciation and the 'now' of the utterance, a break that, according to Coetzee, produces the paradox of 'the apparent identity . . . of the texture of time in the narrated now . . . and the moment of narration' ('Time, Tense and Aspect', p.573). Kafka's response to the problematic opposition between these two awarenesses of time, in Coetzee's analysis, is an insistence upon the 'everlasting present [which] is nothing but the moment of narration itself' ('Time, Tense and Aspect', p.579). Schleifer, however, makes the point that it is the *intersection* between these two types of awareness that 'makes time itself perceptible [and] engenders temporality':

> temporality arises in difference that cannot be categorized within the logical categories of opposition yet is more than pure accident, pure contiguity. Narrative, Greimas writes, creates a temporal succession which is neither pure contiguity nor a logical implication, neither the contiguity of enunciation's 'schizophrenic' morphemes . . . nor the necessary succession of the statement's systematic, socialized and iterative speech. (pp. 879–80)

Coetzee's own response to the problem of the conjunction of

these two awarenesses of time might be viewed, like that of Kafka, as an insistence upon the present moment of narration, an insistence which is evident in the predominance of autodiegetic narrators and present verb forms.[18] However, the paradigm of the Lacanian subject means that this conjunction takes the form of an *intersection* rather than an *opposition:* the present moment of narration is a speech act, whose function is 'not to inform but to invoke' (*Ecrits*, p.86), and in which the past is retroactively determined by a present which it anticipated.[19] The separate moments of enunciation together constitute the dialectical movement of the discourse, 'in which it is death that sustains existence' (*Ecrits*, p.300). Thus we find Lacan's memorable description of the subject's constitution in time:[20]

> I identify myself in language, but only by losing myself in it like an object. What is realized in my history is not the past definite of what was, since it is no more, or even the present perfect of what has been in what I am, but the future anterior of what I shall have been for what I am in the process of becoming. (*Ecrits*, p.86)

The dialectical movement of the discourse is essentially the equivalent of the mode of irony as Paul de Man describes it in 'The Rhetoric of Temporality', and one might approach Coetzee's response to the problem of narrative temporality via de Man's analysis of the modes of irony and allegory. De Man refers to the problematic conjunction of two different awarenesses of time in the novel when he points out that it 'is caught within the truly perverse assignment of using both the narrative duration of the diachronic allegory and the instantaneity of the narrative present' (p.207). De Man's view of irony locates it within what Coetzee calls the eschatological awareness of time, while allegory engenders a narrative duration which approximates the historical awareness of time, but always only produces an 'illusion of continuity';

> . . . irony comes closer to the pattern of factual

experience and recaptures some of the factitiousness of human existence as a succession of isolated moments lived by a divided self. Essentially the mode of the present, it knows neither memory nor prefigurative duration, whereas allegory exists entirely within an ideal time that is never here and now but always a past or an endless future. Irony is a synchronic structure, while allegory appears as the illusion of a continuity that it knows to be illusionary. Yet the two modes, for all their profound distinctions in mood and structure, are the two faces of the same fundamental experience of time. (de Man, p.207)

This 'same fundamental experience of time' is the experience of a division in time, which produces a division in the self:

> it remains necessary, if there is to be allegory, that the allegorical sign refer to another sign that precedes it. The meaning constituted by the allegorical sign can then consist only in the *repetition* (in the Kierkegaardian sense of the term) of a previous sign with which it can never coincide, since it is of the essence of this previous sign to be pure anteriority . . . . Whereas the symbol postulates the possibility of an identity or identification, allegory designates primarily a distance in relation to its own origin, and, renouncing the nostalgia and the desire to coincide, it establishes its language in the void of this temporal difference. In so doing, it prevents the self from an illusory identification with the non-self, which is now fully, though painfully, recognized as a non-self. (de Man, pp.190–91)
>
> The ironic language splits the subject into an empirical self that exists in a state of inauthenticity and a self that exists only in the form of a language that asserts the knowledge of this inauthenticity. This does not, however, make it into an authentic language, for

> to know inauthenticity is not the same as to be authentic. (de Man, p.197)

Irony is a 'dialectic of self-destruction and self-invention' which 'engenders a temporal sequence of acts of consciousness which is endless' (de Man, p.202). Thus both in its mode of perception and in the metonymic discursive movement that it generates, de Man's irony is essentially the equivalent of the Lacanian death instinct. Allegory allows for narrative continuity between the separate moments of consciousness and provides a temporary resting place for the repetitive dialectical movement of irony. In Coetzee's novels, this resting place may be located between their allegorical readings of the texts of the tradition, and the allegorical writing of their own evocation of the response of the Other in a future of potential readings: their time is thus 'never here and now but always a past or an endless future'. The interminable, metonymic movements of irony, the repetitions within the text, are held within the totality of the allegory, which implies the text's metonymic relationship to and non-coincidence with prior texts which it repeats, so that the novels are (to appropriate de Man's description of Stendhal's novels) 'allegories of irony'.

In Coetzee's novels, the mode of allegory, a mode implying the recognition that to speak is to speak as Other, is conflated with the practice of psychoanalytic criticism to effect a kind of 'cure', as together they perform the text's

> ultimate analytic act of speech which Lacan calls 'the assumption of one's history', that is, the ultimate acceptance – and endorsement – of one's destiny, the acknowledgement of responsibility for the discourse of the Other in oneself . . . . (Felman, 'Beyond Oedipus', pp.1026–27)

Joel Fineman, who notes that 'allegory' derives etymologically from the Greek words 'other' and 'to speak' (p. 46), says;

> It is as though allegory were precisely that mode that makes up for the distance, or heals the gap, between

> the present and a disappearing past, which, without interpretation, would be otherwise irretrievable and foreclosed . . . . (p.29)

He bases this observation on an analysis of the relationship that allegory has, historically, established with the texts of the tradition, a relationship which he describes as 'defensively recuperative', and in the service of literary authorities, which it revives through 'critical revision' (p.28). In the case of Coetzee's novels, it would be more accurate to say that allegory and psychoanalytic criticism combine to produce a '*self*-defensively recuperative strategy', which, while it implies a recognition of the *inevitable* revival of literary authorities as a result of repetition, at the same time challenges the authority and the priority of the tradition, as the novels engage in the retroactive determination of the texts in which they are anticipated. In this simultaneous healing and rupturing of the gap between themselves and prior texts the novels effect their own cure. Fineman draws attention to the congruity between allegory and the psychoanalytic method when he says:

> This famous Lacanian barring of the subject – the loss of being that comes from re-presenting oneself in language as a meaning, correlative with the formation of the unconscious and the onset of desire, the Oedipeanization of the subject, and the acquisition of a place in the cultural order through the recognition of the Name of the Father – is what makes the psyche a critical allegory of itself and is what justifies psychoanalysis as the allegory of that allegory. For it is in search of the meaning of this division of the subject through the dialectics of desire, brought on by the structurality of the logos, that psychoanalysis finds its own initiatory desire. (p.47)

And so, as Fineman points out, 'Freud's hermeneutics are at one with the object of their inquiry' (p.47), and 'desire becomes in psychoanalysis, as in allegory, both a theme and a structuring principle' (p.27). Now, as the preceding discussion has suggested, and as my analysis of the individual novels will demonstrate, Coetzee's psychoanalytic allegories (or allegorical psychoanalysis) constantly refer to the way in which both their objects of inquiry (the texts of the tradition), and their own hermeneutic activity have their genesis in the dialectic of desire, which thus becomes both theme and structuring principle in these novels. The practice of psychoanalytic criticism in the form of deliberately fictional allegories implies a recognition of the literary and allegorical nature of psychoanalysis, and thus of the essentially equal status of the object and the practice of criticism: it allows, finally, for the disruption of the Master/Slave opposition between text and interpretation.

Accounting, in this manner, for the way in which Coetzee's novels resolve the issue of mastery and servitude in relation to prior texts, we are left with the problem of the relationship between the novels and the interpretive texts which *follow* them. Although the acknowledgement of the transferential and counter-transferential relationship between text and reader *in theory* subverts the position of dominance of either one, *in practice* criticism (or most criticism, my own included) operates *outside* the fictional framework, and so lacks the means of referring to its own desire as structuring principle.[21] Thus Spivak says:

> I do not see how literary criticism can do more than decide to deny its desire as master, nor how it can not attend to the conditions of intelligibility of a text.
>
> . . . .
>
> All precautions taken, literary criticism must operate as if the critic is responsible for the interpretation, and, to a lesser extent, as if the writer is responsible for the text. ('The Letter as Cutting Edge', pp.223–24)

While this refers to the problematic stance of interpretation in relation to texts in general, the particular nature of Coetzee's writing gives rise to more specific problems. The fact that the novels themselves engage in psychoanalytic criticism, and effect a kind of cure, in the manner I have suggested, would seem to make them invulnerable to psychoanalytic criticism, or, indeed, to any form of interpretation which would assume a position of mastery. Forcing to the surface the repressed material of the texts they deconstruct, deliberately structuring themselves in a way which produces breaks and divisions in the text, these novels draw attention to the repressions operative in their own speech but, precisely because of this self-deconstructive activity, seem to allow no glimpses of the repressed material that surfaces *in*voluntarily, *un*consciously: they seem to provide no evidence of

> the 'gaps' or 'lapses' that indicate the 'Other' scene of signification, the repressed scene of writing not a part of manifest narration but which (like a buoy, or series of buoys) holds it up and enables it to exist at all. (Davis, 'Lacan and Narration', p.853)

This self-deconstructive activity is an aspect of Coetzee's writing which is common to much contemporary writing, and which, as André Green points out, has resulted in 'a sort of *avoidance* on the part of psychoanalysis with regard to contemporary literature' (p.12). Green attributes this avoidance to the fact that, unlike classical texts, which provide evidence of a 'binding process' at work, contemporary texts perform a kind of 'unbinding', which seems to make them inaccessible to the 'unbinding' performed by psychoanalytic criticism. In the binding process, as Green describes it,

> free (unbound) energy seeking to be released, making use of the condensation and displacement compromises, forcing the co-existence of opposites while remaining unresponsive to temporalization, manages to transform itself into bound energy whose release is postponed, restrained, and limited in conformity with the laws of logic and temporal succession. (p.18)

The analyst, while recognizing that s/he is the '*analyzed* of the text', and that the interpretation is 'the interpretation that he must give *himself* of the effects of the text in his own unconscious', 'does not "read" [*lire*] the text, he "unbinds" [*delier*] it. He breaks open the secondarity in order to retrieve, upstream from the binding process, the state of bondlessness [*deliaison*] which the binding process has covered up' (Green, pp. 18 and 19; translator's interpolations in brackets). According to Green, the self-unbinding process of contemporary writing

> is tending to split between a writing of the body and a writing of the thought. On the body-writing side, representation no longer lays the foundation of a structured fantasy; it becomes fragmented into short-lived, evanescent bodily states, the writer failing repeatedly to communicate through the writing process this uncommunicable reality because neither the spoken nor the written word can yield a rendering of it . . . . The new object is the state of the body proper in its most violent manifestation.
>
> At the opposite pole we are witnessing the advent of literature which I shall call that of the sublimated text – a text devoid of any representation or meaning, a text which strives to say nothing beyond the mere statement of the writing process. This writing style is non-figurative in the same respect as the preceding one, which was not so much concerned with representing the body as in making it come alive in chips, in fragmented form and piecemeal. (pp.31–32)

Green, however, points out that writing at either of these poles fails to perform its function because of the inevitability of representation: in the case of 'body-writing', the body has to be *re*-presented in writing; and writing which would refer only to the process of writing betrays a form of presence in its dependence upon re*present*ation. In *Dusklands* both of these tendencies in contemporary writing are deconstructed.

Writing of the body, or pornography, is shown to be at the mercy of writing:

> The pornographer is the doomed upstart hero who aspires to such delirium of ecstasy that the surface of the print will crack beneath his words. We write our violent novelties on the walls of lavatories to bring the walls down. This is the secret reason, the mere hidden reason. Obscuring the hidden reason, unseen to us, is the true reason: that we write on lavatory walls to abase ourselves before them. Pornography is an abasement before the page, such abasement as to convulse the very page. (*Dusklands*, p.15)

And writing which would be a thing unto itself, represented in *Dusklands* by Eugene Dawn's metafictional, metahistorical project, is shown to be 'the subject of a revolting body' (*Dusklands*, p.7).

And so Coetzee's novels perform this unbinding of the texts of the tradition, of the polarized modes of contemporary writing, and of themselves, located, as they are, between these two historical poles which determine the 'theatre' of their activity. But what of the *binding* which they inevitably perform? Even writing which appears to perform this ultimate gesture of self-deconstruction involves the transformation of 'something sprung from the desiring body into a binding structure made up exclusively of language symbols bound together in a determinate chain responding to the laws of grammaticality' (Green, p.28). Any unbinding necessarily becomes the preliminary to another form of binding, a point which Green makes in relation to the psychoanalytic method,[22] and which he recognizes when he says:

> It seems as if the unveiling of the unconscious through the use of analysis has driven literature into an even more radical veiling process, which has resulted in an out-and-out foreclosure of representation. (p. 37)

Applying, for the moment, the diagnostic procedures of psychoanalysis, although I said at the outset that this was not my intention here, it seems that the novels' attempt at self-unbinding must be read as a form of resistance to mastery by interpretation. What we have in these novels is the speech of an analysand who is too thoroughly versed in psychoanalytic method, an analysand like Eugene Dawn, who says of his analysts:

> Toward these doctors whose task it is, with the scantiest of documentation, to explicate me, I feel nothing but sympathy. I do my best to help them; but I do not forget that I am a patient, for whom it is presumptuous to take too active a part in the diagnosis of his condition. (*Dusklands*, p.49)

While the novels appear to submit to the process of analysis, prefiguring their own mastery by interpretation in various images of reading, again like Eugene Dawn, they retain their secret through this very gesture of acquiescence:

> My secret is what makes me desirable to you, my secret is what makes me strong. But will you ever win it? When I think of the heart that holds my secret I think of something closed and wet and black, say, the ball in the toilet cistern. Sealed in my chest of treasures, lapped in dark blood, it tramps its blind round and will not die. (*Dusklands*, pp.49–50)

Having diagnosed Coetzee's self-deconstructive mode of writing as a form of resistance, it is necessary to point out that resistance is not necessarily a negative symptom which the analysand manifests in an unconscious, passive way, but that it may be read as performing an active and constructive function in the analytic relationship. Thus, as Roy Schafer says:

> There is another, entirely affirmative way to retell the story of resistance. In this account, the analysand is portrayed as doing something on his/her behalf,

> something that makes sense unconsciously though it may not yet be understood empathically by the analyst. The analyst may then press confrontations and interpretations on the analysand at the wrong time, in the wrong way, and with the wrong content. Kohut's account of narcissistic rage in response to such interventions presents the analysand as protecting a fragile self against further disintegration in response to the analyst's empathically deficient interventions. Or the analysand may be protecting the analyst against his/her own anticipated ruthless, destructive, or at least permanently alienating form of love . . . . Whatever the case and whatever the manifestly oppositional attitude, the analysand is portrayed as engaged in a project of preservation, even enhancement, of self or analyst or both. (pp.45–46)

Schafer gives, as an example of this type of resistance, the narrative of a young girl, whose persistent excoriation of her parents might be read, negatively, as a turning away from 'the unbearable horror of her imagined inner world', or, positively, as an assertion that 'the problem resided in the family as a system and not merely in her infantile fantasies and wishes' (p.46). Now in Coetzee's novels, resistance seems to function actively, positively, in precisely this manner. Engaged in a project of preservation and enhancement of text and critic, this mode of writing protects the critic from a false and falsifying gesture of mastery, and protects the text from a diagnosis which should be directed at the system in which the textual subject is constituted. This resistance, then, may be read as a positive strategy for concealment, and as a strategy which deconstructs the position of mastery *per se*, for this is a mode of writing which denies the critic the position of mastery, and at the same time makes it clear that the text itself cannot be master of its own unconscious meaning, of that repressed Other which no strategy of writing can bring to the surface. The resistance thus affirms the existence of a secret self, which is inaccessible to the conscious processes of writing and interpretation, but which re-surfaces in the unconscious processes of successive readings and re-writings. Concealment is necessary because where the subject appears, s/he disappears, and it is in the movement of disappearance, of *aphanisis,* that the self becomes manifest. Magda speaks for all of Coetzee's narrators when she says:

> Whose shell I presently skulk in does not matter, it is the shell of a dead creature. What matters is that my anxious softbodied self should have a refuge from the predators of the deep, from the squid, the shark, the baleen whale, and whatever else it is that preys on the hermit crab . . . . (*In the Heart of the Country*, pp. 43–44)

Taking up residence in the borrowed dwellings which are pre-existing genres and modes of writing, refusing to make a dwelling for themselves (although they inevitably do, as I have pointed out), always referring only to the process of construction of the dwelling, these novels, on the one hand, enact an ultimate kind of revelation, and, on the other hand, enact the most radical concealment.

This concealment performs, as it were, a secondary function, this function being an insistance upon the possibility of the subversion of the Other which is language, the locus in which the subject is constituted, by the Other which is repressed in the unconscious. Fineman points out that 'allegory seems regularly to surface in critical or polemical atmospheres, when for political or metaphysical reasons there is something that cannot be said' (p.28). This is an observation that, in the context of writing in South Africa, is relevant to Coetzee's use of allegory, and which might also be applied to his strategies for concealment. In *Life & Times of Michael K*, Michael K is made to comment:

> What a pity that to live in times like these a man must be ready to live like a beast. A man who wants to live cannot live in a house with lights in the windows. He must live in a hole and hide by day. A man must live so that he leaves no trace of his living.
> (*Life & Times of Michael K*, p. 135)

The novel itself thematizes the perpetual escape of meaning to what must be called a condition rather than a place, as it is a place which implies no fixed place: atopia. This is Roland Barthes' term for what were his own continually renewed attempts to avoid the fixation of meaning, to remain outside the constraints of the discursive context:

> *Pigeonholed*: I am pigeonholed, assigned to an (intellectual) site, to residence in a caste (if not in a class). Against which there is only one internal doctrine: that of *atopia* (of a drifting habitation). Atopia is superior to utopia (utopia is reactive, tactical, literary, it proceeds from meaning and governs it). (*Roland Barthes*, p.49)

To avoid fixation in a particular meaning, which inevitably bespeaks an ideology, the self has to conceal itself, and the site in which it achieves this concealment is an atopic 'drifting habitation', in Green's words, a 'potential space' that comes to exist between writer and reader, a 'metaphorical locus . . . inhabited by the nonrepresented and nonrepresentable unconscious fantasy' (p.26). It is here that the potentially subversive effect of these novels must be located.

Now in the context of the South African novel in English, some kind of subversive function would appear to be obligatory, and I recognize that my reading of Coetzee's novels is, at least to some degree, motivated by my expectations as a reader in this context. That this is one of the predominant expectations of readers of these novels is evident from existing critical commentary, which demonstrates a degree of consensus in the view that Coetzee does not go far enough in deploring the system, in delineating the historical and economic bases of oppression, or in projecting the ultimate triumph of the oppressed peoples of South Africa. Thus Michael Vaughan sets out by proposing that Coetzee's mode of writing poses 'a Modernist Challenge to Liberal Aesthetics', but finishes by concluding that:

> As a consequence of the prominence given to a state of agonised consciousness, material factors of oppression and struggle in contemporary South Africa achieve a subordinate attention . . . . It would seem, then, that in his novels Coetzee gives privileged attention to the predicament of a liberal petty bourgeois intelligentsia. (pp.126 and 137)

Paul Rich recognizes Coetzee's affinity to Postmodernism, but criticizes it as an art form which is

> probably destined to remain the vehicle for expressing the cultural and political dilemmas of a privileged class of white artists and intellectuals and at best . . . likely to lead to a more general loosening of contemporary South African writing away from a slavish imitation of the English liberal novel-writing tradition. (p.73)

Peter Knox-Shaw complains:

> It is regrettable that a writer of such considerable and varied talents should play down the political and economic aspects of history in favour of a psychopathology of Western life. (p.79)

and Nadine Gordimer says, of *Life & Times of Michael K*,

> A revulsion against all political and revolutionary solutions rises with the insistence of the song of cicadas to the climax of this novel. I don't think the author would deny that it is his own revulsion. ('The Idea of Gardening', p.6)

Common to all of these criticisms is a view of language as a transparent medium for transmitting the realitites of an empirical world, and a failure to see language itself as constitutive of those realities we are able to perceive. As Stephen Heath says:

> the 'realistic' is not substantial but formal . . . the generally received picture of what may be regarded as 'realistic' . . . being founded in our culture by, amongst other things, the novel itself. (p.20)

Coetzee himself consistently denies that his writing is intentionally subversive, as is evident in the following extract from an interview which he turns around on the interviewers. Having admitted that he is in sympathy with the endeavour of critical cinema, Coetzee goes on to say:

> And by a critical cinema I don't mean a cinema that is in the first place critical of conditions in South Africa, but a cinema that is in the first place critical of its own formal assumptions, which are reflections of an ideological position.
>
> *That seems fairly clearly also to be an intention of your novels.*
>
> Well, yes, I try to be aware of my own assumptions and the assumptions that I make in plugging myself into a particular form.
>
> *Would you not say that also, by implication, you cause the reader to become aware of his or her own ideological assumptions?*
>
> Well, I don't know. It may be.
>
> *If you . . . you must have some conception of what you're trying to do for yourself – you're questioning your own assumptions, and trying at all times to be aware . . . You're doing this in the form of a novel which is going to be read by other people . . .*
>
> What I would like to do at this point is to turn the discussion around. Because, what is actually going on?

> It seems to me that what you're trying to do is absorb certain novels, my novels, into a political discourse. . . . And it's perhaps a mark of all critical activity to try to swallow one kind of discourse into another kind of discourse . . . . And what I am now resisting is the attempt to swallow my novels into a political discourse. Because I'm not prepared to concede that the one kind of discourse is larger or more primary than the other. So that attempts to swallow up the intention that lies in or behind a book of mine – let's assume for the moment that there is an intention there – into some wider or more all-embracing, more swallowing, notion of social intention – I have to resist them because, frankly, my allegiances lie with the discourse of the novels and not with the discourse of politics. (Thorold and Wickstead Interview, p.5)

Via the Lacanian paradigm, it is possible to make claims concerning the subversive effect of writing which remain firmly within the novelistic discourse: both Frederic Jameson (in 'Imaginary and Symbolic in Lacan') and Coward and Ellis found their descriptions of subversive textuality on the Lacanian theory of the subject's constitution in language. While Jameson focuses on the possibility of reading the subversive eruptions of Imaginary material within the Symbolic structure of the text, Coward and Ellis make more sweeping claims, seeing the Lacanian subject as a means of resolving

> the ambiguity of traditional Marxism: the ambiguity of showing the place of the subjective moment in the transformation of society when subjective actions are initially posited as simply mirroring the objective processes of history. (p.8)

They put forward Julia Kristeva's theory that certain texts – Sollers, Joyce, Lautréamont – 'in opening onto [their] process of construction, and in fragmenting the unity of the subject . . . are no longer instruments of communication, but signifying practices which show the subject understanding and organising the real', and her insistence upon 'the correspondence of the signifying practices of these texts and revolutionary practice' (Coward and Ellis, pp.149–50). Kristeva draws attention to the need for escape, or concealment, when she says:

> Le sujet *n'est* jamais, le *sujet* n'est que le *procès de la signifiance* et ne se présente que comme *pratique signifiante,* c'est-à-dire lorsqu'il s'absente *dans la position* à partir de laquelle se déploie l'activité sociale-historique-signifiante. (*La Revolution due Language Poétique, p.188*)

(The subject does not exist, the subject is nothing but the process of signification and makes its appearance only as signifying practice, that is to say when it goes missing from the locus in which the social – historical – signifying activity is manifest.)

However, Kristeva, and, via her, Coward and Ellis, appear to view the unbinding process of what she calls the semiotic mode of signification, or poetic language, as subversive in itself, whereas the point I am making is that Lacanian theory allows us to locate the effect of subversion in a potential site of *readership.* It allows us to do this in a way which the Derridean notion of free-floating textuality does not. This is a crucial difference between Derridean and Lacanian theory which has been noted by both Coward and Ellis[23] and Robert Con Davis, who says:

> the Lacanian text differs from the deconstructionist (problematic) text, to which it bears a resemblance, in that the 'positions' of narration ('I' and 'you,' for example) are anchored, held down, by Freudian desire, which forces a curb on the infinite textual regress opened by *différance.* [24] The 'signifier' – subject to desire, as Lacan states – 'stops the otherwise endless movement (*glissement*) of the signification.' Hence the Lacanian text – to Derrida's outraged dismay – may speak its own 'truth' – the Other's 'truth' . . . . ('Lacan and Narration', pp. 854–55)

For Lacan, speech always signifies an attempt at communication:

> Even if it communicates nothing, the discourse represents the existence of communication; even if it denies the evidence, it affirms that speech constitutes truth; even if it is intended to deceive, the discourse speculates on faith in testimony. (*Ecrits*, p.43)

He concludes his seminar on Edgar Allen Poe's 'The Purloined Letter' by saying that 'a letter always arrives at its destination' ('Seminar on the Purloined Letter,' p.72). Derrida deconstructs this reading of the Poe story, saying that a letter *can* miss its destination and be disseminated (Derrida, 'The Purveyor of Truth'), and Barbara Johnson deconstructs Derrida's reading by showing how 'he reads "destination" as a place which pre-exists the letter's movement' (p.502). Johnson makes the point that:

> Everyone who has held the letter – or even beheld it – including the narrator, has ended up having the letter addressed to *him* as its destination. The reader is comprehended by the letter: there is no *place* from which he can stand back and observe *it*. Not that the letter's meaning is subjective rather than objective, but that the letter is precisely that which subverts the polarity subjective/objective, that which makes subjectivity into something whose position in a structure is situated by the passage through it of an object. The letter's destination is thus *wherever it is read*. (p.502)

The letter, or the text, 'subverts the polarity subjective/objective': in the same movement the text constitutes the reader and the reader constitutes the text, and it is this point of intersection that is the site of subversion, a subversion that must be described as potential rather than intentional. Bringing the panel discussion I have orchestrated here full circle, back to

Coetzee, I will cite his concluding comment in the interview from which I quoted earlier, a comment which situates the effect of the text in the same way that Johnson does:

> But let me make one last observation. Thus far we have not questioned it that intentions lie *behind* books, behind acts, etc. I would see this assumption as fundamental to the discourse of politics, where it is not meaningful (I think) to talk of acts with no intention behind them, acts which are themselves efforts to locate their intent. Well, then I would ask: isn't it in fact *useful* to think that there might be acts whose meaning lies before rather than after them? That's the kind of question I would want to ask before talking about intentions behind or before acts of writing. (Thorold and Wicksteed Interview, p.5)

The discourse of novels, then, comprises acts 'which are themselves efforts to locate their intent', speech acts in which 'in order to be recognized by the other [the writer] utter[s] what was only in view of what will be' (*Ecrits*, p.86). The discourse of criticism provides this recognition in a way which is 'less cognitive than *performative*: it is, itself, essentially, a speech-act,'[25] as Coetzee's critical/novelistic discourse demonstrates. Thus what we have is a transferential relationship in which writer and reader situate one another in the role of *sujet supposé savoir*: in Lacan's words,

> In so far as the analyst is supposed to know, he is also supposed to set out in search of unconscious desire.
>
> . . . .
>
> The transference is unthinkable unless one sets out from the subject who is supposed to know . . . . He is supposed to know that from which no one can escape, as soon as he formulates it – quite simply, signification.[26]

In the case of the relationship between writer and reader,

each grants to the other the position of mastery, the authority of the knowledge of the meaning which is inaccessible to him/herself.

Coetzee's reading and re-writing of the texts of the tradition involves a *displacement* of the ideological position available to the subject in language, rather than the passive *repetitions* involved in normative reading and writing.[27] It is a displacement that, by virtue of its own secrecy and success at concealment, would occupy no fixed place, would occupy only the metaphorical locus which is the link in the chain of potentially infinite displacements.[28] Indeed, it would appear that the potential for *further* displacements is proportionate, precisely, to the degree of secrecy, to the success of concealment. As I have already indicated, the insistence upon a secret self is a means of prolonging the novelistic discourse; however, secrecy, as a form of resistance, may also be read as a strategy for prolonging the critical discourse. Read in this way, secrecy is a form of seduction and deception, a form of love, which is, in Lacanian terms, the wish to be loved. Thus Lacan says:

> What emerges in the transference effect is opposed to revelation. Love intervenes in its function, revealed here as essential, in its function as deception. Love, no doubt, is a transference effect, but it is its resistance side. We are linked together in awaiting this transference effect in order to be able to interpret, and at the same time, we know that it closes the subject off from the effect of our interpretation. The alienation effect, in which is articulated, in the relation of the subject to the Other, the effect that we are, is here absolutely manifest. (*Four Fundamental Concepts*, p.253)

As I have indicated, Coetzee reads the 'meaning' of the texts of the tradition as the effect of certain rhetorical strategies; reads the 'what' of these texts as an effect of the 'how, when and why' of their telling. At the same time, the allegorical and fictional nature of his readings refers us to the fact that they are themselves performative speech acts, and so are dependent upon the rhetorical manoeuvres of their own manner of telling. The radical concealment effected by this focussing upon the performance itself must be read affirmatively, in the manner suggested by Schafer (this chapter, p.47), as a resistance which elicits interpretation, but closes the subject off from interpretation, in an attempt to protect the reader from claiming a position of mastery which is itself nothing more than a rhetorical effect. These novels thus simultaneously deny the mastery of both novelistic and critical discourse; in the same move dispossess us 'both of our mastery and of our Master'.[29]

I am, nevertheless, conscious that in the course of the foregoing discussion I *have* been engaged in pronouncing upon the 'meaning' of Coetzee's novels by means of reference to the 'how, when and why' of their telling; *have* been engaged in tracing their formal implications, even if this form is no more than the attempt to divest itself of form, and even if the meaning I read in it turns out to be no more than a commentary upon the conditions in which meaning is produced. And this brings me back to the untenable position which criticism occupies within this theoretical context: as Spivak says, it 'can do no more than *decide* to deny its desire as master' ('The Letter as Cutting Edge', p.223). Whether it articulates this denial in the form of a statement tacked onto a reading which itself enacts a kind of ruthless mastery, finding in the lies of the text under scrutiny the truths that it does not and cannot tell;[30] or whether this denial is a product of the reading itself, as in the case of the 'new' psychoanalytic readings of Felman and Johnson, granting the text the authority of prefiguring its misguidedly masterful misreadings,[31] criticism inevitably *acts* as master. Lacking the formal means of integrating any reference to its own desire, and thus to the status of its own speech, within its discourse, criticism 'can never be more self-subversive than to question the status of intelligibility, or be more or less deliberately playful' (Spivak, 'The Letter as Cutting Edge', p.223). And, lacking the means of *reproducing* the combined effects of anticipation and retroaction operative in these novels, one can talk about them, merely, and produce criticism which, while it emphasizes *either* the anticipatory *or* the retroactive effects, finds itself undermined by the *opposite* effect.

Apart from the brief application of the psychoanalytic method in reading the significance of resistance in these novels, my own critical procedure involves tracing Coetzee's allegories of reading and writing, and contextualizing them in terms of Lacanian and other post-structuralist theory. This results in criticism-as-pastiche, criticism which is synchronic rather than diachronic, and whose dimensions are spatial rather than temporal. It is criticism which risks becoming interminably circular, or labyrinthine, to use one of the favourite figures of contemporary criticism, and one which we find repeated in Coetzee's novels. Tracing the conditions of intelligibility of these novels, my discourse turns and re-turns to the novels and to myself, to the starting point which, by virtue of the journey of investigation, is not the same, but different, and so necessitates another journey out. And so I will conclude this Introduction – and in the context of Lacanian theory the conclusion of an introduction would appear to be the only kind of conclusion that is permissible – by means of another addition to the pastiche. It is a passage from Joel Fineman which refers to the way in which the nature of the critical discourse makes it difficult even to conclude with dignity:

> Because the things of poetry are words, poetry can, in a way that criticism cannot, conclude itself when it cannot continue. When poetry can find no new words with which to maintain the meaning of its longing, it can lapse into significant literary silence, thereby pro-longing its desire ad infinitum . . . . But criticism, whose things are not words but the meanings of words, meanings forever foreclosed by words, will find in silence only the impetus for further speech and further longing, which it will thereupon thematize as its own responsibility for the loss of meaning. Whereas a poem can be closed poetically even by a gesture of self-abandon, criticism, discovering the

futility of its pro-ject, can only go on and on, frustratingly repeating its own frustration, increasingly obsessed with its own sense of sin – unless, of course, in the psychoanalytic sense, it projects its own critical unhappiness onto literature whose self-deconstructions would then be understood as criticism. (p.50)

NOTES

1. Coetzee himself has described the enterprise of the *nouveau roman* as 'criticism in the form of . . . fiction' (J.M. Coetzee, 'The First Sentence of Yvonne Burgess's *The Strike*', p. 47).
2. J.M. Coetzee, 'A Note on Writing,' p. 11. Coetzee cites Roland Barthes, 'To Write: An Intransitive Verb?' in *The Languages of Criticism and the Sciences of Man*, ed. Richard Macksey and Eugenio Donato (Baltimore: John Hopkins, 1970), pp. 134–156.
3. Régis Durand, in 'The Anxiety of Performance', uses Whitman's *Song of Myself* as the starting point in his discussion of the staging of the self in the performative mode of certain contemporary writing.
4. Durand, 'On Aphanisis: A Note on the Dramaturgy of the Subject in Narrative Analysis,' cites Lacan, *The Four Fundamental Concepts of Psycho-Analysis*, ed. Jacques Alain Miller, trans. Alan Sheridan (New York: W.W. Norton and Co., 1978), pp. 207–08.
5. 'Utterance' is the translation of the French, *énoncé*, also frequently translated as 'statement,' and refers to the actual words uttered; 'enunciation' is the translation of *énonciation*, and refers to the act of uttering the words.
6. Anika Lemaire, p. 68, cit. J.A. Miller, 'La Suture', *Cahiers pour l'Analyse*, no. 1.
7. I capitalise the initial letter of 'Father' here to indicate that it is a term which has a specialized significance within the Lacanian discourse (the Father is not necessarily the genetic father, but the representative of the Law). This is a convention which I will use for other specialized terms of this nature, terms such as Symbolic and Imaginary.
8. 'Lacan's early use of the Hegelian notion of desire repeats Kojèvian formulas. There are in fact few contemporary readings of Hegel which do not owe a considerable debt to Kojève's commentary, and he himself owes an equal debt to Heidegger' (Wilden, p. 193).

9. This appears to be Coetzee's own translation of Hegel. It may be compared with Nichols' translation of Kojève's translation of Hegel (I have left out Kojève's interspersed commentary):

> 'Thus, the nonessential Consciousness is – for the Master – the object that forms the *truth* of the subjective certainty he has of himself. But it is obvious that this object does not correspond to its concept. For in the Master's fulfilling himself something entirely different from an autonomous Consciousness has come into being. It is not such an autonomous Consciousness, but all to the contrary, a dependent Consciousness, that exists for him. Therefore, he is not subjectively certain of his *Being-for-itself* as of a truth. His truth, all to the contrary is nonessential Consciousness, and the nonessential activity of that Consciousness' (Kojève, p. 20)

10. Coetzee's observations concerning the *You* are based on an analysis of the pronoun as it occurs in Achterberg's poem, and are congruent with Benveniste's linguistic analysis of the nature of pronouns. For Coetzee's translation of Achterberg's poem see Appendix One.
11. Wilden points out that: 'in view of the multiple ways in which Lacan employs "the Other," we might supplement the suggested translation of *l'Autre* as "the unconscious" or "Otherness" by the expression "Thirdness." Thus in a recent broadcast over French radio, Lacan defined the Other as follows: "The Other with a big 'O' is the scene of the Word insofar as the scene of the Word is always in third position between two subjects'. (p. 269)
12. The other much-cited aphorisms which convey the same concept are: 'the symbol manifests itself first of all as the murder of the thing' (*Ecrits*, p. 104), and 'the being of language is the non-being of objects' (*Ecrits*, p. 263).
13. Edmond Ortiques, *Le Discours et le symbole* (Paris: Aubier, 1962) p. 194, cited by Frederic Jameson in 'Imaginary and Symbolic in Lacan', p. 378.
14. Brooks describes *Beyond the Pleasure Principle* as 'Freud's own masterplot, the text in which he most fully lays out a total scheme of how life proceeds from beginning to end and how each individual life in its own way repeats the masterplot' (p. 285).
15. Although Brooks reveals his familiarity with Lacan when he says: 'That Jacques Lacan has equated metonymy and desire is of the utmost pertinence, since desire must be considered the very motor of narrative, its dynamic principle' (p. 281).
16. St. Augustine in *The Confessions of St. Augustine*, trans. John K.

Ryan (New York, 1960), p. 287, cited by Schleifer, p. 882.

17. Ingarden describes these two awarenesses of time as follows: 'according to *one* experience of time, everything that exists temporally is limited to only one 'now', conceived as non-dimensional, and beyond which there are, as it were, two abysses of absolute nonbeing. According to the *second* experience, however, the past exists in its own way, as does the future. Time is not a force that destroys being' (p. 104).

18. Gèrard Genette, in *Narrative Discourse*, uses the term 'autodiegetic narrator' to designate the narrator who is present 'as the star' in the story s/he tells (p. 245). I use the term here and in the subsequent chapters in preference to 'first-person' narrator, for, as Genette points out, 'the narrator can be in his narrative (like every subject of an enunciating in his enunciated statement) *only* in the 'first person' (p. 244).

19. According to Ingarden, 'the past, being radically transcendent in relation to [that, is absent from] an actual existent capable of acting in the present remains in the realm of being because it conditioned and generated the present existent. But the past something remains in existence only as – so to speak – a *retrogressively derivative* entity – namely, as secondarily derivative, proceeding 'backwards' from a certain actual existent subsequent to it.' (p. 117)

20. This appears to derive from Kojève: 'Desire directed toward another Desire, taken as Desire, will create, by the negating and assimilating action that satisfies it, an I essentially different from the animal 'I' . . . . This I will not, like the animal 'I', be 'identity' or equality to itself, but 'negating-negativity.' In other words, the very being of this I will be becoming, and the universal form of this being will not be space, but time. Therefore, its continuation in existence will signify for this I: 'not to be what it is (as static and given being, as 'innate character') and to be (that is, to become) what it is not.' Thus, this I will be its own product: it will be (in the future) what it has become by negation (in the present) of what it was (in the past), this negation being accomplished with a view to what it will become'. (p. 5)

21. This is an issue which Coetzee addresses when he asks: 'If the desire of literary criticism is to tell every truth, to unveil whatever is veiled, to expose very [sic] secret to sight, why does it not tell its own secrets? Or does it claim to have none?' (J.M. Coetzee, 'Truth in Autobiography').

22. Green says: 'The analyst, for his part, goes on with his decon-

struction—construction, often ruthlessly, sometimes – rather rarely one must admit – hitting it just right, when the censuring process does not thwart his own analysis. For this unbinding of the text is the necessary step toward a new binding, different from the one that occurs in the literary work'. (pp. 20–21).

23. Coward and Ellis point out that Derrida 'points to the spacing, the temporal constitution by which generation and transformation of language are achieved. But while the development of 'grammatology' enables the challenging of the dominant notion of 'sign-meaning-concept', it nevertheless is unable to account for language as a social practice, that is, meaningful communication between two subjects' (p. 126).

24. The Derridean notion of *différance* closely approximates the Barthesian notion of *atopia*, as is evident from Spivak's explanation of the term:

> 'I have spoken of the radically other, which is always different, nonidentical. Add to this the structure of the perennial postponement of that which is constituted only through postponement. The two together – 'difference' and 'deferment' – both senses present in the French verb 'différer,' and both 'properties' of the sign under erasure – Derrida calls 'différance.' (Translator's Preface to *Of Grammatology*, p. xliii)

25. Felman, 'Beyond Oedipus', p. 1026. Felman makes this point in relation to psychoanalytic recognition, which, she says, is 'essentially a speech-act, whose symbolic action modifies the subject's history, rather than cerebrally observing or recording it, at last correctly' (p. 1026).

26. I am indebted to Felman for her translation of this description of the psychoanalytic relationship into a description of the relationship between writer and reader. Discussing *The Turn of the Screw*, she says:

> 'If, by virtue of the storyteller's transference on the reader, the reader thus becomes the storyteller's *ghost* (the addressee of his unconscious), the reader, in his turn, transfers on the storyteller or the 'author,' to the extent that he invests the latter with the authority and prestige of the 'subject presumed to know'. ('Turning the Screw of Interpretation', p. 134).

She cites the passage from Lacan (*Four Fundamental Concepts of Psycho-Analysis*, pp. 235 and 253) in support of her observation.

27. This would be the equivalent of the passive voice in writing, identified by Coetzee as 'a linguistic metaphor for . . . writing in stereotyped forms and genres and characterological systems and

narrative orderings, where the machine runs the operator' ('A Note on Writing', p. 13).

28. Barbara Johnson, discussing Foe's 'The Purloined Letter', points out that 'The letter . . . acts as a signifier *not* because its contents are lacking, but because its function is not dependent on the knowledge *or* nonknowledge of those contents . . . . The signifier is an articulation in a chain, not an identifiable unit. It cannot be known in itself because it is capable of 'sustaining itself *only* in a displacement'. (Johnson, pp. 494–95, cit. Lacan, 'Seminar on the Purloined Letter', p. 59; Johnson's emphasis).

29. Felman, 'Turning the Screw', p. 207 sees this dispossession of mastery as definitive of literality *per se*.

30. In the lecture, 'Truth in Autobiography', Coetzee says: 'In some models of psychoanalysis, we might note, the analyst, listening for the truth of the patient, listens not for the patient's truths, the truths the patient finds or tells, but for the patient's lies and silences and evasions, believing that there lie the clues to the 'real' truth. The patient's lie becomes the analyst's truth.' He goes on to disclaim the 'truth' of his own reading of Rousseau:

> 'I say . . . that truth is merely heuristic, yet in the secret that secrets held close to the chest are valuable I find the truth which Rousseau cannot afford to come out with. I say that autobiography cannot tell its own truth, and tell the truth it cannot tell. Does that not make of criticism the only mode in which final truths can be told; and how sincere is *that*?' ('Truth in Autobiography', pp. 4 and 5)

31. Felman says of *The Turn of the Screw*:

> 'Indeed it is not so much the critic who comprehends the text, as the text which comprehends the critic. Comprehending its own criticism, the text, through its reading, orchestrates the critical disagreement as the performance and the 'speech *act*' of its own disharmony.' ('Turning the Screw', p. 115).

And Johnson, referring to the various readings of 'a letter always arrives at its destination', says, 'It is not any one of these readings, but all of them and others in their very incompatibility, which *repeat* the letter in its way of reading the act of reading' (p. 503).

2 Dusklands

Reading the title of this, Coetzee's first novel, as an allusion to Oswald Spengler's *Der Untergang das Abenlandes*,[1] one is alerted to the fact that what one has here is a history of sorts. Furthermore, the title suggests, it is a history founded in the notion of cyclicality, or repetition, in Vico's notion of *ricorso*, from which Spengler derives his theory of history as cyclical process.[2] However, it becomes evident that *Dusklands* is informed, not so much by the notion of history founded in the metaphor of organic cycles, as by the concept of repetition; a concept which, in this novel, functions at different levels, both thematically and structurally, to problematize the concept of history itself.

One would anticipate that, in this project of problematizing the historical discourse, Coetzee might demonstrate some affinity with writers such as Truman Capote, Norman Mailer, Tom Wolfe, and E.L. Doctorow, who claimed for themselves the freedom 'to compose false documents more valid, more real, more truthful than the true documents of the politicians or the journalists or the psychologists,'[3] and whose non-fiction novels of the sixties and seventies enacted a rupture of traditional discursive categories. The fact that much of *Dusklands* was written in the United States at this time,[4] and that a large section of the novel is articulated around American involvement in Vietnam, would seem to endorse this presupposition. Coetzee does appropriate certain strategies of the non-fiction novel, for example the incorporation and distortion of documentary material; he also adopts the self-reflexive mode of the metafiction, which was being produced at the same time by writers such as Barth, Gass, Barthelme, and Brautigan (and earlier, by Nabokov, Beckett and Borges), who playfully draw attention to their writing as performance, exposing the rhetorical strategies in which this performance is founded. And Coetzee does address the problem which is addressed by writers of non-fiction novels and metafiction alike: the problem of the truthful translation of the empirical world, of lived experience, whether this be the individual experience of the self, or the communal experience of history, into the text. Employing the strategies and modes of writing which are available to him in the historical moment in which he finds himself, entering into the contemporary theoretical debate concerning textuality, much of which is conducted in fictional form, Coetzee nevertheless takes the process of *aufhebung* a stage further, by re-inserting these fictional projects in which he participates into history. Thus we shall see that the self-reflexiveness of Coetzee's writing does not enact what he has described as an attempt 'to get behind (*aufheben*) fiction by incorporating into fiction a critical consciousness of the procedures of fiction' ('The First Sentence of Yvonne Burgess's *The Strike*', p.48), and that the re-writing of history which he undertakes does not constitute 'an anti-documentary polemic' which establishes a claim to a 'more potent truth',[5] as one of his critics would have it. These are simply the modes of writing available to him, the theatre of his activity as a writer, and they are not adopted passively, but actively, in a way that holds them up for scrutiny.

If these, then, are the modes of writing which establish the parameters of the 'theatre of activity' for a writer who is also a member of the international community of academics and critics, there are other parameters which are operative within the context of white South African writing, these being the generic forms which, as I indicated in the introductory chapter, Coetzee adopts and adapts. The genre adopted in *Dusklands* is a complex one in which anthropological and historical, documentary and fictional writing intermingle and overlap in a way that makes Coetzee's juxtaposition of documentary and fictional material more than just a superficial device borrowed from his contemporaries. *Dusklands* conflates the various forms of writing which have been articulated around the notion of a frontier to be traversed, a virgin territory to be opened up, an unknown interior against which the self can be pitted.[6] Charting the continuing themes of South African literature, Stephen Gray draws attention to the notion of a frontier – what he calls the frontier myth – within the context of this writing:

> The frontier myth has no clear beginning and no forseeable end, that is to say, it is not narrative; for the European in Southern Africa it starts as an uneasy xenophobia, continues as a social principle, and in South Africa today could be shown to be so deeply entrenched that all of the literature is to some extent explained in terms of the pressures at work within a continuing frontier mentality.
>
> The frontier myth itself, however, is devised not only to describe and assess a cultural gulf, but to bridge it. The history of 'Europeans' in South Africa cannot be reduced to a view of a mere private war having been continually waged from behind a border, because no matter how much the South African white enclave behind its frontier has resisted impregnation from Africa and its indigenous peoples, the frontier myth itself, even in its most negative aspects, is an expression of interdependence, of involvement across barriers. (p.38)

All of Coetzee's novels may, in effect, be read as expositions of the frontier mentality as it occurs in the existing forms of white South African writing, expositions which, as I suggested in the previous chapter, re-write the 'expression of interdependence' in terms of the Hegelian Master/Slave dialectic. In *Dusklands*, however, the notion of a frontier to be traversed is central to the allegorical structure of the novel, based, as it is, on the correspondence between the colonizing activities of the West, and the activity of a literature which would transgress the frontiers of known forms and annex areas of language which will allow it to speak the self, to establish an identity.

Gray claims that 'The essence of the hunter-explorer's world view has to remain an external one; it probes ever forward, it never probes inward', and makes the mistake of saying that 'No Southern African work of hunting and adventure has received its reverse image, as Ballantyne's *The Coral Island* did in Golding's *Lord of the Flies* in 1954'.[7] *Dusklands* provides precisely this reverse image, as it probes an interior rather than an exterior space in search of the sources of adventure/exploration writing and, ultimately, in search of its own historical and psychological sources. In this reversal of the orientation of the exploratory journey, Coetzee appears to take his cue from Mannoni's analysis of the psychology of colonization. Mannoni's thesis is that

> the personality of the colonial is made up, not of characteristics acquired during and through the experience of the colonies, but of traits, very often in the nature of a complex, already in existence in a latent and repressed form in the European's psyche, traits which the colonial experience has simply brought to the surface and made manifest.
>
> . . . .
>
> We can explore the retinas of our own eyes by looking at a piece of white paper; if we look at a black man we shall perhaps find out something about our own unconscious . . . . The negro, then, is the white man's fear of himself . . . . The rift between man and man which racialism indicates, with all its confused emotional force, thus reflects an inner conflict in which we are divided against ourselves. (pp.97 and 200)

Mannoni makes the further point that the unconscious desire in which the colonizing activity has its genesis is likewise the source of writing about situations which 'though imaginary, are typically colonial' (p.98), whence the title of his study: *Prospero and Caliban*. Considered in this way, it becomes evident that the terms of Coetzee's allegory are not distinct, but intimately connected; that the colonizing activity and the modes of writing it serves to allegorize have their source in the same quest for identity and the same historical trend toward individualism, individuation and selfhood, which manifests itself as an assertion of mastery.

In Coetzee's adoption and adaption of this genre, we find

repetition functioning at its most obvious and explicit level. It is as though, by means of this deliberate repetition of one of the models available within the context, Coetzee seeks to avoid the passive repetition, not only of a form, but of the ideology inherent in the assumptions of that form.[8] One might re-phrase the Derridean formula, 'one always inhabits [existing structures], and all the more when one does not suspect it' (*Of Grammatology*, p.24), as, 'one is always engaged in repetition, and all the more when one does not suspect it'. In Coetzee's novels, repetition as an inevitable effect of writing is transformed into a subversive strategy, and, continuing our analysis of *Dusklands*, it becomes evident that, in this novel, it is also translated into a structural principle. *Dusklands* comprises, under this single title, two apparently separate shorter works: these are 'The Vietnam Project', narrated by Eugene Dawn under supervision of one, Coetzee, who is in charge of the New Life Project, a project of psychological warfare conducted by America against the Vietcong; and 'The Narrative of Jacobus Coetzee', which is made up of three different accounts, all supposedly translated, not written, by J.M. Coetzee, of an actual journey into the Southern African interior made by one of his ancestors, Jacobus Coetzee, in 1760. The first section, 'The Vietnam Project', concludes with the narrator's statement, 'I have high hopes of finding whose fault I am,' (*Dusklands*, p.51), which may be regarded as the ontological query around which the novel as a whole is articulated. Situated here, at the end of the first section, this query occupies a focal point across which the two sections of the novel mirror, or repeat, one another, setting up a potentially infinite series of reflections, and making it difficult to find a way in, to establish an appropriate starting point for discussion.

In the absence of a conventional plot, which would provide narrative continuity and thereby hold the different sections of the novel together, we find this structure of repetitions, which allows us to move forward or backward in the space of the text in order to respond to Eugene Dawn's query. Moving forward in the novel, we go back in time, from the 1970s to 1760, in a way which produces the kind of temporal reversal implicit in conventional plot structure, in which 'The sense of beginning . . . is determined by the sense of an ending' (Brooks, p.283). As Brooks says:

> The beginning in fact presupposes the end. The very possibility of meaning plotted through time depends on the anticipated structuring force of the ending: the interminable would be the meaningless. We read the incidents of narration as 'promises and annunciations' of final coherence: the metaphor reached through the chain of metonymies. (p.283)

The repetitions which create the metonymic, 'dilatory space' (Brooks, p.295) of this novel carry us forward to an end which is an origin, and suggest that we should read the meaning of the beginning, of Eugene Dawn's narrative, in this ending. There is, however, a series of repetitions working simultaneously in the opposite direction, that is, backwards in the space of the text and forward in time, replicating the pattern of repetitions which inevitably sustains and maintains the process of writing as a reading effect. Reading in this direction, that is, beginning with the last section and progressing to the first, we find that the original document, the Deposition of Jacobus Coetzee (1760), does not represent an origin, but is a somewhat arbitrary starting point for a diachronic progression of readings which proliferate out of other readings. While a reading from front to back leads us to account for the provenance of the particular configuration of the *I* represented by Eugene Dawn's utterance in terms of repetition as a *return to* origins, a back-to-front reading suggests that the constitution of this particular linguistic subject can be explained in terms of repetition as a *return of* the repressed (a suggestion which is endorsed at a thematic level in Eugene Dawn's narrative). Once again, this deliberate ambiguity in the functioning of repetition would appear to represent an ambiguity which is inherent in narrative. As Brooks says:

> Narrative must ever present itself as a repetition of events [or a repetition of other narratives] that have

> already happened, and within this postulate of a generalized repetition it must make use of specific, perceptible repetitions in order to create plot, that is, to show us a significant interconnection of events. Events gain meaning by repeating (with variation) other events. Repetition is a *return* in the text, a doubling back. We cannot say whether this return is a return *to* or a return *of*: for instance, a return to origins or a return of the repressed. Repetition through this ambiguity appears to suspend temporal process, or rather, to subject it to an indeterminate shuttling or oscillation which binds different moments together as a middle which might turn forward or back. (p.288)

This suspension of temporal process in an oscillatory movement is the equivalent of the combined effects of anticipation and retroaction, which, as I suggested in the previous chapter, constitute the dialectic in which the subject arises, and also the strategy by means of which Coetzee's novels attempt to avoid rigidity of individual and literary history. The middle which might turn forward or back is Eugene Dawn's query, 'I have high hopes of finding whose fault I am' (*Dusklands*, p.51); it is also, as we shall see, the allegorical history of the narrating self that occupies the centre of this novel, wedged between 'The Vietnam Project' and the Afterword of S.J. Coetzee.

If, as I suggested at the outset of this chapter, *Dusklands* problematizes the concept of history by means of the notion of repetition, it is a notion of repetition in which the effects of anticipation and retroaction are inextricably and inevitably combined. While the readings from front to back and from back to front would appear to represent the historical and anti-historical perspectives respectively, they are, in effect, representative of two opposed views of history, each of which emphasizes the effects of either anticipation or retroaction.[9] Read in the conventional direction, the ordering of the sections represents the historical project's search for documentary material which will provide a validating context, and so allow for the stabilization of meaning. Eugene Dawn's narrative arises out of the situation of the American occupation of Vietnam, which can be accounted for historically as a continuation of the colonizing activity of the West, revealed in its incipient stages in 'The Narrative of Jacobus Coetzee'. This, in turn, receives its explication in the Afterword of S.J. Coetzee, which is substantiated by means of copious endnotes and an original document included in the form of an Appendix. A reading in this direction takes us on a search for origins, and locates the mastery of truth, or meaning, in factual documentation that anticipates the historical moment in which the act of reading, or interpretation, is located. In Derridean terms, this approximates the archaeological project:

> As always this archeology is also a teleology and an eschatology; the dream of a full and immediate presence closing history, the transparence and indivision of a parousia, the suppression of contradiction and difference. (*Of Grammatology*, p.115)

According to a reading in the opposite direction, the ordering of the sections of the novel demonstrates the effect of difference produced by successive readings, and so demonstrates the impossibility of closing off meaning by means of reference to a determining context. The ordering of the sections from back to front of the novel enacts a progressively radical decentering of the subject, thus dramatizing the impossibility of achieving a 'full and immediate presence'. We move from the authentic Jacobus Coetzee, to S.J. Coetzee, 'father' of the implied author, to J. M. Coetzee in the role of translator, and thence to 'The Vietnam Project', in which Coetzee is a peripheral character, a *he,* who is resented and defied by the narrator, Eugene Dawn. And, if we grant the act of translation its full significance, J.M. Coetzee's stance as translator of the three accounts of Jacobus Coetzee's journey becomes an additional means of drawing attention to the work of reconstruction going on here. Coetzee has said that,

> . . . just like the process of translation, the process

> of reading is a process of constructing a whole for oneself out of the datum of the printed text, of constructing one's own version of the poem. In a clear sense, all reading is translation, just as all translation is criticism. ('Achterberg's "Ballade van de gasfitter" ', p.294)

What we have in *Dusklands*, then, is translation as simultaneously a reading and a re-writing, translation in the Derridean sense, as 'a regulated transformation of one language by another, of one text by another'.[10] A reading in this direction locates meaning in the work of construction itself, an approach which achieves its apotheosis in Eugene Dawn's mythographic method, and in the extravagance of his claim to be able to bring 'meaning to light in that blinding moment of ascending meta-historical consciousness in which we begin to shape our own myths' (*Dusklands*, p. 28).

These two opposed views of history are correlative to the historical and the eschatological awareness of time:[11] correlative to the historical awareness of time is a view of history which sees past events as determining the present, which is continuous with, and therefore causally connected with, that past; correlative to the eschatological awareness of time is a view of history as a strategy which, proclaiming a rupture between its own stance in the present and the past which it reconstructs, claims to *produce* the meaning of the past by means of active interpretation. This latter view is history as meta-myth,[12] as an interpretive procedure which, by means of a deliberate *aufhebung*, locates itself on the periphery of the myths which constrain meaning in the present. Each of these views of history is undermined by the opposite view, but their *intersection* within the novel as a whole produces a view of history as,

> not so much a text, as rather a text-to-be-(re-) constructed. Better still, it is an obligation to do so, whose means and techniques are themselves historically irreversible, so that we are not at liberty to construct any historical narrative at

> all . . . (Jameson, 'Imaginary and Symbolic in Lacan', p.288)

Each section and sub-section of *Dusklands* presents us with a new phase of this reconstruction in progress, and shows how the mode of this reconstruction has, in some measure, been prescribed by texts which come before it in time and after it in the space of the novel. I will begin with the last sub-section, the Appendix, which, as I have indicated, is the somewhat arbitrary starting point of these readings which proliferate out of one another, and of which my own reading of this novel is the latest. The document presented in the Appendix, the Deposition of Jacobus Coetzee (1760), is the only authentic document in a set of narratives all posing as historical documents:[13] according to one view of history it is a source document, but we find that it is, in effect, just another narrative,

> *Narrative given at the order of the Right Honourable Rijk Tulbagh, Councillor Extraordinary of Netherlands India and Governor of the Cape of Good Hope and all Dependencies thereof, etc., etc., by the burgher Jacobus Coetsé, Janszoon, concerning the journey undertaken by him in the Land of the Great Namaquas.* . . . (*Dusklands*, p.131),

which has been dictated to a Company Scribe, O.M. Bergh. Thus the nature of this original document, rather than establishing a definitive context, establishes the model on which the narratives which follow it (although preceding it in the novel) are based. This model provides us with a view of narrative as comprising a relationship between a teller and a receiver; it is the first link we are shown in what Felman (in her reading of *The Turn of the Screw*) calls a 'chain of readings . . . readings which re-read, and re-write, other readings'. Felman points out that

> In the chain transmission of the story, each narrator to relay the story, must first be a *receiver* of the

> story, a *reader* who at once records it and *interprets* it, simultaneously trying to make sense of it and *undergoing* it, as a lived experience, an 'impression,' a *reading-effect.* ('Turning the Screw', p.124)

While this may be seen as describing the nature of narrative in general, as I suggested in the introductory chapter, Coetzee's novels constitute *deliberate* readings and re-writings of pre-existing texts, with the writer, in this case, playing the role of analyst; analyst as reader, and, in Lacan's words, analyst as scribe:

> As a witness called to account for the sincerity of the subject, depositary of the minutes of his discourse, reference as to his exactitude, guarantor of his uprightness, custodian of his testament, scrivener of his codicils, the analyst has something of the scribe about him. (*Ecrits*, p.98)

If the figure of the scribe serves to problematize the notion of an 'original' document, to deconstruct the concept of the origin *per se*, at the same time it introduces the notion of a context which, while it is not definitive, is present as the Other, as 'the locus in which is constituted the I who speaks to him who hears' (*Ecrits*, p.141), the locus in which the partnership between teller and listener is circumscribed. O.M. Bergh is a *Company* Scribe: so, one might say, is Eugene Dawn, employed, as he is, by the United States Government, and so, to a greater or lesser extent, is any writer of any history. Coetzee's retreat to a peripheral position in 'The Vietnam Project' simply invokes what is inevitable: that is, the way in which the self is usurped by an image and an utterance which is Other. This is a response to a situation in which, as Kritzman says,

> The writer has been evicted from his locus as origin of his work, and instead becomes a public scribe whose re-writing of the *topoi* of critical fashionability problematizes the very production of the self-image. (p.205)

Coetzee's response to this problem of the subject's disappearance at the moment of its inscription in the public discourse, is, both here and as a general strategy in all of his novels thus far, a deliberate withdrawal from the scene of writing, a withdrawal which Barthes describes as,

> the vacancy of the 'person', if not annulled at least rendered irretrievable – absence of *imago* – the suspension of judgement, of due process – displacement – the refusal 'to keep oneself in countenance' . . . (*Roland Barthes*, p. 132)

As I pointed out in the introductory chapter, referring to the Lacanian notion of *aphanisis*, the secrecy of the subject, the 'absence of *imago*', is, paradoxically, the means by which the self attempts to maintain some kind of identity, attempts to manifest itself in the 'movement of disappearance' or fading (Lacan, *Four Fundamental Concepts*, p.208).

Now, the writing of history has traditionally been thought of as having nothing to do with the production of a self-image: in its standard form it effaces the identity of the narrator in favour of a neutral and objective presentation of factual data. This is the stance we see represented in O.M. Bergh's transcription of Jacobus Coetzee's narrative, and also in the numbered segments of Eugene Dawn's scientific mythographic discourse (Section II of 'The Vietnam Project', titled Introduction, pp.19–31). This is a mode of writing history which Hayden White calls narrativizing discourse, a mode whereby real events are made to speak themselves in the form of a story. White argues that in this way the historical narrative appropriates for itself both the authority of the Real,[14] and the attraction of the Imaginary:

> The history, then, belongs to the category of what might be called the 'discourse of the real,' as against the 'discourse of the imaginary' or the 'discourse of desire'. The formulation is Lacanian,

> obviously, but I do not wish to push the Lacanian aspects of it too far. I merely wish to suggest that we can comprehend the appeal of historical discourse by recognizing the extent to which it makes the real desirable, makes the real into an object of desire, and does so by its imposition, upon events that are represented as real, of the formal coherency that stories possess. (pp.23–24)[15]

White goes on to say that,

> The demand for closure in the historical story is a demand, I suggest, for moral meaning, a demand that sequences of real events be assessed as to their significance as elements of a moral drama. Has any historical narrative ever been written that was not informed not only by moral awarenss but specifically by the moral authority of the narrator? (p.24)

Now, the Afterword of S.J. Coetzee (fictitious historian and father of the 'translator'), as a parody of what Coetzee has elsewhere referred to as the Afrikaans writer's 'mythographic revision of history' ('Man's Fate in the Novels of Alex la Guma', p.17), manifests the methods and motivation of narrativizing discourse, although the naive and blatant form in which these methods and motives reveal themselves means that it differs in style from the more insidious manipulations of classic narrativizing discourse as it is described by White. Thus, while it claims for itself the objective status of historical discourse, this Afterword states its moral purpose quite explicitly:

> The *present* work ventures to *present* a more complete and therefore more just view of Jacobus Coetzee. It is a work of piety but also a work of history: a work of piety toward an ancestor and one of the founders of our people, a work which offers the evidence of history to correct certain of the anti-heroic distortions that have been creeping into our

> conception of the great age of exploration when the White man first made contact with the native peoples of our interior. (*Dusklands*, p.115, my emphasis: note the insistence on 'presence'.)

It is evident from this passage that this Afterword is intended to perform the function of traditional historical commentary, which is that of correcting and controlling adjacent texts: as Hayden White says, 'Unless at least two versions of the same set of events can be imagined, there is no reason for the historian to take upon himself the authority of giving the true account of what really happened' (p.23).

The historical discourse of S.J. Coetzee invokes the effects of the Real in the form of notes, which draw upon existing historical documents for substantiation, and in the form of increasingly absurd lists of empirical data, such as the following:

> At one of their halts (August 18) the expedition left behind: the ashes of the night fire, combustion complete, a feature of dry climates; faeces dotted in mounds over a broad area, herbivore in the open, carnivore behind rocks; urine stains with minute traces of copper salts; tea leaves; the leg bones of a springbok; five inches of braided oxhide rope; tobacco ash; and a musket ball. The faeces dried in the course of the day. Rope and bones were eaten by a hyena on August 22. A storm on November 2 scattered all else. The musket ball was not there on August 18, 1933. (*Dusklands*, p.126)

At the same time, however, S.J. Coetzee makes it clear that his discourse, of necessity, draws upon the effects of the Imaginary, as he says, 'To understand the life of this obscure farmer requires a positive act of the imagination' (*Dusklands*, p.116). He goes on to say:

> I wish I had hunting adventures to relate . . . .
> Hunting adventures lend excitement, however

> spurious, to history. Their structure is dramatically satisfying: complacency (I have a gun), discomfiture (my gun is not loaded, you have teeth/tusks/horns), relief (you jump the wrong one and/or I shoot you despite all). (*Dusklands*, p.124)

Having confessed that 'Coetzee was not alas the kind of hunter whom such adventures frequented', S.J. Coetzee goes on to fabricate a story, which he concludes by saying, 'I trust you have enjoyed this adventure' (*Dusklands*, p.124). The purposive nature of S.J. Coetzee's discourse, which invests him with moral authority in the 'work of piety toward an ancestor and one of the founders of our people', clearly hinges around the establishment of an identity, the identity of the Afrikaans people. The authority of history is invoked in order to justify the Afrikaner's presence in Africa and the entrenchment of colonial attitudes in relation to the indigenous population. Bringing his history to a close, S.J. Coetzee says:

> Herewith we have come to the end of that part of Coetzee's narrative which belongs to the annals of exploration. His journey and sojourn north of the Great River, his return, his second expedition with Hendrik Hop, full of incident though they are, are nevertheless somewhat of an historical irrelevance. Man's thrust into the future is history; all the rest, the dallying by the wayside, the retraced path, belongs to anecdote, the evening by the hearth-fire. (*Dusklands*, p.128)

The past is yoked into the service of a thrust into the future, and history, here, performs the function of legitimating an ideological project founded in a notion of the superiority of white civilization.

Now, 'The Narrative of Jacobus Coetzee' as a whole is a narrative of 'the retraced path', tracing, as it does, the chain of readings and re-writings which constitute the ongoing historical project. 'What is important is the philosophy of history', the epigraph to this section tells us (*Dusklands*, p.57);

and, indeed, what we have, not only in this section but in the novel as a whole, *is* a philosophy of history, in which

> the various plots of the various histories which
> tell us of merely regional happenings in the past
> are revealed for what they really are: images of
> that authority which summons us to participation in
> a moral universe that, but for its story form, would
> have no appeal at all. (Hayden White, p.24)

Hayden White's objection is not to narrative as such, which he recognizes as an inevitable and 'panglobal fact of culture' (p.5), but to a historical method which denies the fact that it *is* narrative, while it reaps the benefits of the *attraction* which narrative as an Imaginary construct offers. The alternative to narrativizing discourse would be a historical narrative which, explicitly or implicitly, acknowledges its source in the Imaginary, thereby acknowledging its concomitant function of providing an identity, or self-image, for the writer. It would be, in Paul Ricoeur's terms, a narrative which functions 'to establish human action at the level of authentic historicality, that is, of repetition'.[16] According to Ricoeur, the historical narrative which is potentially able to function in this way is the interpretive history,[17] which, it would seem, approximates the philosophy of history. Basing his claim on Hannah Arendt's analysis of action in *The Human Condition* (Chicago, 1958), Ricoeur says:

> Arendt distinguishes among labor, work, and action.
> Labor, she says, aims merely at survival in the
> struggle between man and nature. Work aims at
> leaving a mark on the course of things. Action
> deserves its name when, beyond the concern for
> submitting nature to man or for leaving behind
> some monuments witnessing to our activity, it
> aims only at being recollected in stories whose
> function it is to provide an identity to the doer,
> an identity that is merely a narrative identity.
> (p.187)

'The Narrative of Jacobus Coetzee', as opposed to the Deposition or the Afterword, is a narrative which has abandoned any pretence at scientific objectivity in the recording of events, and which has given itself over entirely to the project of providing an identity for the doer, in this case, the writer, J.M. Coetzee. It is, furthermore, a narrative founded in repetition, a 'retraced path', a journey of exploration which, rather than moving outwards, moves inwards to the origin of this identity. This account of the journey of Jacobus Coetzee becomes the means of articulating an allegorical history of the narrating self; a history of a certain endeavour to establish an identity in narrative, which is, simultaneously, a history of Eugene Dawn's identity as narrator, and, beyond this, of the 'absent identity' of the writer of *Dusklands.* It is the allegorical history of a particular narrative tradition, which has insisted with increasing urgency upon the possibility of establishing an autonomous identity in narrative, and which Coetzee outlines briefly but succinctly in his article on Achterberg:

> The poem that incorporates a denunciation of itself (sub specie aeternitatis or however) paradoxically acquires the ontological self-sufficiency, and therefore extends the ontological challenge, of the self-consuming artifact: Can language reach outside itself? The tradition, represented by *Don Quixote* and *Tristram Shandy*, of self-reflexive undercutting of the mimetic pretensions of fiction, which finds its apotheosis in Flaubert's dream of 'a book about nothing, a book without external attachments' raises the same question.
>
> The hide-and-seek of the *I* in Sterne has become a serious game, with dangers to the psyche, in Eliot's 'Love Song of J. Alfred Prufrock' (1917). What has intervened has been the rise and decline of the romantic-liberal notion of the self. The self in Eliot is struggling with problems of authentic being. The self in Beckett is struggling with problems of being at all, unable to get from Descartes' *cogito* to Descartes' *sum.* I hint so skimpily at an entire history

> because I intend no more than to point to what lies behind the metamorphosis of fiction from the adventures of the self in nineteenth-century classic realism to the metafictional commentary on the fictionality of self that precipitates such fictions as Nabokov's *Pale Fire* and Barth's *Lost in the Funhouse* and that forms the whole of Beckett's *The Unnamable*. The poetics of these works is a veritable poetics of failure, a program for constructing artifacts out of an endlessly regressive, etiolated self-consciousness lost in the labyrinth of language and endlessly failing to erect itself into autonomy. ('Achterberg's "Ballade van de gasfitter" ', p.293)

The structural device of the journey, which, in the traditional quest narrative, projects the hero forward in space, sustaining the movement of the narrative as it produces the effect of linear temporality, is subverted in the case of Jacobus Coetzee's journey. He is diverted from the path which would take him forward and outward into the wilderness by 'a plan of diabolical indirection' (*Dusklands*, p.72); that is, by his capture by the Hottentot tribe.[18] This disruption of the journey brings the narrative back to what Ricoeur calls 'a primordial space and time that is more akin to the realm of dreams than to the sphere of action'.[19] Thus we find Jacobus Coetzee saying:

> I meditated and perhaps even dreamed on the subject of dreams. Might I hope that all the misfortune that had befallen me since I set eye on the Namaqua was a bad dream? Were the Namaqua merely demons? Was I become a prisoner of my own underworld? If so, where was the passage that led back to daylight? Was there a charm I had to know? Was the charm simply 'I am dreaming' ejaculated with conviction? If so, why did I lack conviction? Did I fear that not only my sojourn among the Namaqua but all my life might be a dream? But if so, where would the exit from my dream take me? To a universe of which I the Dreamer

was sole inhabitant? (*Dusklands*, p.83)

What began as the narrative of a journey is transformed into Jacobus Coetzee's meditations from his sickbed in the Hottentot camp, and, once he has been expelled from the camp in disgrace, becomes the narrative of a retreat, or a return. Appropriately, since it traces what Coetzee calls 'the poetics of failure', it becomes a quest narrative marked by yielding and losing, rather than by fighting and victory,[20] and one in which first stasis and then regression generate the narrative movement. It becomes one of those narratives in which repetition generates the quest itself. As Ricoeur says:

> In these stories, repetition is constitutive of the temporal form itself. The paradigmatic case of such stories is Augustine's *Confessions.* Here the form of the travel is interiorized to such a degree that there is no longer any privileged place in space to which to return. It is a travel 'from the exterior to the interior, and from the interior to the superior' . . . . The model created by Augustine is so powerful and enduring that it has generated a whole set of narrative forms down to Rousseau's *Confessions* and Proust's *Le Temps retrouvé.* If Augustine's *Confessions* tells 'how I became a Christian,' Proust's narrative tells 'how Marcel became an artist.' The quest has been absorbed into the movement by which the hero – if we may still call him by that name – becomes *who he is.* Memory, therefore, is no longer the narrative of external adventures stretching along episodic time. It is itself the spiral movement that, through anecdotes and episodes, brings us back to the almost motionless constellation of potentialities that the narrative retrieves. The end of the story is what equates the present with the past, the actual with the potential. The hero *is* who he *was.* (p.186)

Dusklands tells, not how J.M. Coetzee became an artist, or writer, but how a narrator like Eugene Dawn whose narrative is representative of a kind of extreme self-reflexivity, came into being, and, by extension, how J.M. Coetzee came to write in the way that he does. If J.M. Coetzee as a writer *is* who he *was*, the structure of the novel allows us to see that the history which reveals who he *was* is, likewise, a product of who he *is* in the present. And, if this allegorical history enacts a deliberate return to origins, the stages in this quest will demonstrate that this return to origins is simultaneously marked by a return of the repressed, as we are taken on a retrogressive journey through the stages in the constitution of the linguistic subject.

Tracing the stages of Jacobus Coetzee's account of his journey, we see that his narrative, whose commencement is unobtrusively marked by means of a sub-heading, 'The narrative' (*Dusklands*, p.67), is preceded by a passage of discourse which establishes his identity as a member of a clearly defined group. Thus the opening paragraphs of this account comprise a series of ethnocentric observations concerning the Bushmen and the Hottentots, and serve to locate the narrator in relation to the contemporary discourse (that is, the discourse of 18th Century white settlers at the Cape) concerning the indigenous population. The narrating self is articulated as a *we* or a *you* (the impersonal *you*, implying *one*), accepting its position within the discourse of the group which, in turn, is defined in relation to another group: 'Everywhere differences grow smaller as they come up and we go down . . . . The one gulf that divides us from the Hottentots is our Christianity' (*Dusklands*, p.61). The *I* is subsumed under the collective pronouns of the discourse which conveys the attitudes of the white frontiersmen toward other racial groups, the only instances of the *I* serving to substantiate the shared discourse, thus:

> The only sure way to kill a Bushman is to catch
> him in the open where *your* horse can run him down.
> On foot *you* haven't a chance, he knows all about
> guns, he keeps out of range. The only one *I* ever
> caught on foot was an old woman up in the mountains:
> I found her in a hole in the rocks abandoned by her

> people, too old and sick to walk. *For they are not like us*, they don't look after their aged, when *you* cannot keep up with the troop they put down a little food and water and abandon *you* to the animals. (*Dusklands*, p.63, my emphasis)

It is significant that the ethnographic description of this prolegomenon refers chiefly to the Bushmen, rather than the Hottentots, and that the Bushmen are presented in terms which imply their classification as animals: 'The Bushman is a different creature, a wild animal with an animal's soul . . . . Heartless as baboons they are, and the only way to treat them is like beasts' (*Dusklands*, p.62). This would appear to have two functions in relation to the narrative. First, the animal prey of the traditional hunting narrative is replaced by human prey (albeit humans classified as animals), in this way suggesting the connection between hunting and ethnography, a connection that J.M. Coetzee makes in his paper, 'Idleness in South Africa':

> The science of Man is itself a discipline, one of what Foucault calls the disciplines of surveillance; among its tasks are the tracking down and investigating of obscure societies in all quarters of the globe, the photographing and recording and deciphering of their activities. (p.11)

In Eugene Dawn's narrative we find that ethnography – or mythography – has replaced hunting, and that the camera has replaced the gun. The second function of this prolegomenon is, it would seem, to establish a hierarchy which specifies the role of the Hottentots in this narrative, in contradistinction to the Bushmen. If, on a hierarchical scale, the Bushman is classified as animal and the Hottentot as human, it becomes clear that Jacobus Coetzee's encounter with the tribe of Hottentots does not represent a nature/culture confrontation, as one might otherwise suppose. Instead it represents a confrontation with a culture that is situated at the furthest remove along the scale of civilization, but which, paradoxically, provides nothing to confront. This is the attitude which J.M. Coetzee describes as characterizing the Discourse of the Cape (his term for late 17th and early 18th Century writing about the Cape):

> The Hottentot is Man but not yet Anthropological Man; and what keeps him in his backward state is idleness. Thus his idleness has the status of an *anthropological scandal*: despite the fact that nothing remoter and more *different* from European Man can be imagined than the Hottentot, the Hottentot generates an extremely impoverished set of differences to inscribe in the table of categories. ('Idleness in South Africa', pp.5–6)

As Coetzee says, the idleness of the Hottentot represents 'a way of life so indolent that, in its extreme form, it presents the writer with *nothing to say*' ('Idleness in South Africa', p.11). In the context of the narrating self's confrontation with the Other, the strange Hottentot tribe functions as a kind of cultural silence, a nothingness, a void. In its apparent absence of organization and ritual, it is one with the infinitely receding space which offers no resistance to Jacobus Coetzee's advance, and so provides no proof of his identity: it is one with 'the wilderness without polity called the land of the Great Namaqua where everything . . . was possible' (*Dusklands*, pp.70–71).

Having established that, in the initial phases of the narrative, Jacobus Coetzee gains his identity from a group whose Symbolic structures he does not challenge in any way, we find that, initially, the progression of both the journey and the narrative is, likewise, produced according to a set of procedures derived from a pre-existing code. As he rides out to meet the strange Hottentot tribe, he anticipates the encounter in terms of the narrative formulae available to a narrator in this genre:

> Tranquilly I traced in my heart the forking paths of the endless inner adventure: the order to follow,

> the inner debate (resist? submit?), underlings rolling their eyeballs, words of moderation, calm, swift march, the hidden defile, the encampment, the graybeard chieftain, the curious throng, words of greeting, firm tones, Peace! Tobacco! . . . the order to follow, the inner debate, the casual spear in the vitals (Viscount d'Almeida) . . . the order to follow, the inner debate, the cowardly blow, the dark hut, bound hands . . . victory, an amusing but tedious reign as tribal demigod, return to civilization with numerous entourage of cattle . . . (*Dusklands*, p.70)

This list of narrative sequences appropriate to the genre constitutes a set of expectations correlative to Jacobus Coetzee's expectations concerning the correct way of approaching a strange people. Witness the way in which he addresses the Hottentots via the linguistic rituals of a system which is negated by their response:

> I spoke slowly, as befitted the opening of negotiations with possibly unfriendly powers . . . . My words were heard with attention by the man on the ox; but followers of his began to sidle away while I spoke, drifting out of my firm but friendly line of vision. Prudence compelled me to drop the diplomatic manner and wheel from my interlocutor to shout a clipped warning in Dutch to my men to be on their guard (*Dusklands*, p.71);

> The irony and moralism of forensic oratory, uneasily translated into Nama, were quite alien to the Hottentot sensibility. They did not flare into action, nor indeed did my speech receive any reply. The oxrider, lacking both pipe and spark, was chewing his tobacco. The silence grew. It began to embarrass me. (*Dusklands*, p.75)

Incapacitated by diarrhoea (which he suspects is caused by Hottentot poison), forced to abandon his journey, Jacobus

Coetzee initiates his meditative history from his sickbed in the Hottentot camp, saying:

> I inhabited the past again, meditating upon my life as tamer of the wild. I meditated upon the acres of new ground I had eaten up with my eyes. I meditated upon the deaths I had presided over . . . . Thus I progressed, sending myself out from the shrunken space of my bed to repossess my old world . . . (*Dusklands*, p. 82)

His life as 'tamer of the wild' is a metaphor for a particular narrative tradition, and he narrates this history in terms which conflate the attempt to penetrate the interior of an unknown country with the attempt to explore his own psyche; terms that make us see that this interior is as much the unconscious as it is the virgin territory of unexplored Africa:

> The stone desert shimmered in the haze. Behind this familiar red or grey exterior, spoke the stone from its stone heart to mine, this exterior jutting into every dimension inhabited by man, lies in ambush a black interior quite, quite strange to the world. Yet under the explorer's hammerblow this innocent interior transforms itself in a flash into a replete, confident, wordly image of that red or grey exterior. How then, asked the stone, can the hammer-wielder who seeks to penetrate the heart of the universe be sure that there exist any interiors? Are they not perhaps fictions, these lures of interiors for rape which the universe uses to draw out its explorers? (Entombed in its coffer my heart too had lived in darkness all its life. My gut would dazzle if I pierced myself. These thoughts disquieted me). (*Dusklands*, p.83)

The image of the 'lures of interiors for rape' establishes the terms of the sexual metaphor whereby the figure of the explorer riding out (and, by implication, the writer exploring an interior space) is presented as an erect Phallus, proclaiming its mastery over space. That is to say, as a Lacanian Phallus, which has been described as 'a copula, a hyphen – in the evanescence of its erection – the signifier par excellence of the impossible identity'.[21] Lacan says:

> It [the Phallus] is the signifier intended to designate as a whole the effects of the signified, in that the signifier conditions them by its presence as a signifier.
>
> It can be said that this signifier is chosen because it is the most tangible element in the real of sexual copulation, and also the most symbolic in the literal (typographical) sense of the term, since it is equivalent there to the (logical) copula. (*Ecrits*, pp.285 and 287)

The explorer as Phallus is a metaphor for a literary project whose aim is to *be* the Phallus, rather than just being in possession of the Phallus; a literary project which challenges the effects of the signifier in an attempt to attain the condition of 'impossible identity', or full presence, to achieve unmediated expression of desire. Thus Jacobus Coetzee's meditative history traces a series of subject/object relationships in which the eye, conflated with the *I* of narration, the penis and the gun are subsumed under this 'signifier of the impossible identity'. Jacobus Coetzee says:

> In the wild I lose my sense of boundaries . . . . Only the eyes have power . . . . I become a spherical reflecting eye moving through the wilderness and ingesting it. Destroyer of the wilderness, I move through the land cutting a devouring path from horizon to horizon. There is nothing from which my eye turns, I am all that I see. Such loneliness! Not a stone, not a bush, not a wretched provident ant that is not comprehended in this travelling sphere. What is there that is not me? I am a transparent sac with a black core full of images and a gun. (*Dusklands*, p.84)

He articulates an extreme version of the Romantic position, in which the reciprocal relationship between self and nature has been superseded by a claim of 'ontological priority of the one over the other', and by 'an intersubjective, interpersonal relationship that, in the last analysis, is a relationship of the subject toward itself' (de Man, p.180). The attempt at fusion between self and nature in Romantic symbolism is presented in psychological terms as an attempt to achieve identity by means of ingestion of the lost object; it is presented as a drive, as a displacement of the instincts in which the basic vital function of feeding becomes the desire to ingest, or incorporate, nature in its entirety.[22]

This claim of ontological priority over nature ultimately fails to provide proof of identity, as the incorporated object becomes part of a purely subjective identity, and if there is no Other, there can be no evidence of a self distinct from that Other. And so Jacobus Coetzee continues:

> The gun stands for the hope that there exists that which is other than oneself. The gun is our last defense [sic] against isolation within the travelling sphere. The gun is our mediator with the world and therefore our saviour. The tidings of the gun: such-and-such is outside, have no fear. The gun saves us from the fear that all life is within us. It does so by laying at our feet all the evidence we need of a dying and therefore a living world. I move through the wilderness with my gun at the shoulder of my eye and slay elephants, hippopotami, rhinoceres, buffalo, lions, leopards, dogs, giraffes, antelope and buck of all descriptions, fowl of all descriptions, hares and snakes; I leave behind me a mountain of skin, bones, inedible gristle, and excrement. All this is my dispersed pyramid to life. It is my lifes work, my incessant proclamation of the otherness of the dead and therefore the otherness of life. (*Dusklands*, p.84)

This path of destruction which Jacobus Coetzee describes is

essentially the equivalent of Kojève's description of the action which arises out of desire:

> Born of Desire, action tends to satisfy it, and can do so only by the 'negation', the destruction, or at least the transformation, of the desired object: to satisfy hunger, for example, the food must be destroyed or, in any case, transformed. Thus, all action is 'negating.' . . . But negating action is not purely destructive, for if action destroys an objective reality, for the sake of satisfying the Desire from which it is born, it creates in its place, in and by that very destruction, a subjective reality . . . . Generally speaking, the I of Desire is an emptiness that receives a real positive content only by negating action that satisfies Desire in destroying, transforming, and 'assimilating' the desired non-I. (p.7)

However, Jacobus Coetzee goes on to say:

> The death of the hare is the logic of salvation. For either he was living out there and is dying into a world of objects, and I am content; or he was living within me and would not die within me, for we know that no man ever yet hated his own flesh, that flesh will not kill itself, that every suicide is a declaration of the otherness of killer from victim (*Dusklands*, p.85),

demonstrating in his fallacious reasoning that this claim to mastery is a hollow one: the self is shown to be dependent for proof of its existence upon an object, whether this be the dead, and therefore 'inessential' hare, or upon an image of self as Other, and therefore as object; Like Magda, in *In the Heart of the Country*, Jacobus Coetzee is a 'hero of enumeration' (*Dusklands*, p.85), and his hunting activity is a metaphor for the narrative project which, likewise, attempts to erect an identity for the self by means of a compilation of numbered items, 'a project which must be vain, since its end can only be the annihilation of the desired'.[23] While Jacobus Coetzee claims: 'Every territory through which I march with my gun becomes a territory cast loose from the past and bound to the future' (*Dusklands*, p.85), the opposite is, in effect, true, as the progression of the narrative means that 'territories' from the future are cast loose and bound to the past.[24] This destructive action can never satisfy desire, as the subject is continually transformed into an object, or the assimilated object becomes part of a purely subjective reality, and so cannot provide proof 'that there exists that which is other than oneself' (*Dusklands*, p.84). As Kojève says, 'this proving oneself by death does away with the truth [or revealed objective reality] that was supposed to come from it; and, for that very reason, it also does away with the subjective-certainty of oneself as such' (pp.13–14).

Jacobus Coetzee's meditations present the explorer's encounter with the 'savage' in terms of the Hegelian confrontation of Master and Slave (see pp. 22–23, my Chapter One):

> Across this annulus I behold him approach bearing the wilderness in his heart. On the far side he is nothing to me and I probably nothing to him. On the near side mutual fear will drive us to our little comedies of man and man, prospector and guide, benefactor and beneficiary, victim and assassin, teacher and pupil, father and child. He crosses it, however, in none of these characters but as representative of that out there which my eye once enfolded and ingested and which now promises to enfold, ingest, and project me through itself as a speck on a field which we may call annihilation or alternatively history. He threatens to have a history in which I shall be a term. Such is the material basis of the malady of the master's soul. So often, waking or dreaming, has his soul lived through the approach of the savage that this has become an ideal form of the life of penetration. (*Dusklands*, p.86)

The explorer's encounter with the 'savage' here becomes an

'ideal form' of the poetic attempt to penetrate language; in Magda's words, 'to burst through the screen of names' (*In the Heart of the Country*, p.18), in order to establish an identity beyond words. The 'savage' occupies the position of a subservient *You* which is to be coerced into recognizing the *I* of the explorer/writer:[25]

> He must give up his desire and satisfy the desire of the other: he must 'recognize' the other without being 'recognized' by him. Now, 'to recognize' him thus is 'to recognize' him as his Master and to recognize himself and to be recognized as the Master's slave. (Kojève, p. 8)

However, the fact that Jacobus Coetzee's illness places him at the mercy of the Hottentots, combined with the fact that they fail to respond to him in any systematic way, means that he does not achieve 'recognition' as Master. Their apparent absence of ritual means that he is deprived of even the satisfaction which a sacrificial killing would bring, the sense of 'having belonged to a satisfying aesthetic whole' (*Dusklands*, p. 88). On his return journey he reflects upon their treatment of him in the following terms:

> What evidence of disdain for life or delight in pain could I point to in their treatment of me? What evidence was there, indeed, that they had a way of life of any coherence? I had lived in their midst and I had seen no government, no laws, no religion, no arts beyond the singing of lewd songs and dancing of lewd dances. Aside from their greed for the trash in my wagon, had they exhibited any consistent attributes but sloth and an appetite for meat? And once stripped had I been anything but an irrelevance to them? To these people to whom life was nothing but a sequence of accidents had I not been simply another accident? Was there nothing to be done to make them take me more seriously? (*Dusklands*, p.104)

The failure to achieve 'recognition' by the Hottentots represents the failure of the Romantic quest, the failure to erect into being a *You* beyond words,[26] which would provide proof of the existence of the *I*. This marks a turning point in the poetic history we are tracing via the adventures of Jacobus Coetzee: it marks the point at which the writer turns inward, to the text itself, for proof of identity. The attempt at intersubjective communication in the Symbolic is abandoned for an intrasubjective Imaginary relationship, as Jacobus Coetzee turns to the eruption on his buttock, which becomes the centre of his masturbatory attention:

> I imagined the swelling in my buttock as a bulb shooting pustular roots into my fertile flesh. It had grown sensitive to pressure, but to gentle finger-stroking it still yielded a pleasant itch. *Thus I was not quite alone.* (*Dusklands*, p.88, my emphasis)

The subject/object relationship projected in the text becomes a relationship between the self as subject and the self as object, between the self of enunciation and the subject of utterance. This is presented as regression to the narcissistic aggressivity of the Lacian Mirror Stage, in which the self is structured as a rival with its image, as the act of lancing the carbuncle is described in terms which make it, simultaneously, a violation of the self (in the sexual sense) and an act of procreation:

> I gathered the pus-knob between the knuckles of my thumbs and readied myself for the *violation*. With growing might I pressed, *bearing down* with the full fury, more or less, allowing for posture, of an adult male in the pride of his years, through *climax* after *climax* of pain and even through the first whispered consolations of failure. 'It is the diet', said the whispers. I called off. A tocsin of revolt beat in my crushed tissues. I was divided between pride in my *offspring's* stubbornness and a prayer that for a brief while my heart would stop. Cold sweat stood

out on my face. My bowels had turned to water again. I scrambled up and squatted over the stream. *A paroxysm of yellow ooze drifted downstream. I washed and readied myself for labour anew.*

The skin must have been weakened by my exertions; for at once, with exquisite surprise, I heard, or if not heard felt in my eardrums, the tissues give way and bathe my fingers in *a spurt and then a steady dribble of wet warmth.* My body relaxed, and while I continued to *milk the fistula* with my right hand I could afford to bring my left hand up to the sense-organs of my face for the indulgences of inhalation and scrutiny. Such must be the gratifications of the damned. (*Dusklands*, p.95, my emphasis)

The lancing of the carbuncle is a metaphor for what Coetzee has described as the poetic gesture of 'ontological self-sufficiency' (see p. 83, this chapter). It represents the initial phase in what becomes an increasingly radical declaration of textual independence, and which, as I have indicated, reaches its apotheosis in Eugene Dawn's stabbing of his son, an act which Dawn describes as 'injuring one's own . . . flesh and blood' (*Dusklands*, p.45). Historically, it marks the point at which Western philosophy turns inward for confirmation of existence, or consciousness, in the Cartesian *cogito ergo sum*, which Lacan claims 'is at the centre of the mirage that renders modern man so sure of being himself even in his uncertainties about himself . . . (*Ecrits*, p.165).

If the narratives of Jacobus Coetzee and Eugene Dawn oppose exotic and Western consciousness,[27] they do this in order to historicize contemporary philosophies of the self and the corresponding projects of contemporary writing, in order to dereify them. This juxtaposition of archaic and contemporary Western cultures at the same time introduces a historical critique of narrators such as Jacobus Coetzee and Eugene Dawn, in a way which is similar to Lacan's view of the development of the Western psyche, as Wilden describes it:

Since the early Lacan viewed both the paranoid

> character of the *moi* and its master-slave relationship to others as characteristics of modern civilization developed since the end of the sixteenth century (correlative to the discovery of the Cartesian subject whose primacy Lacan rejects), the implication seems to be that the Imaginary death struggle between egos is how things are, rather than how they have to be, whereas the subject's profoundest desire to be 'one' again (to control the Other to whom he becomes subjected) is totally and absolutely irreducible. It is this desire for what is really annihilation (non-difference) that makes human beings human. (pp. 190–91)

In *Dusklands* the difference between archaic and contemporary Western societies is presented in terms of opposing notions of identity: in the former, identity as such is not an issue, in that the individual has a taken-for-granted identity within the group, while in the latter, the achievement of a unique and individual identity and the expression of unmediated desire has become a burning imperative.[28] The difference between these two attitudes toward identity is made explicit in Eugene Dawn's analysis of the reasons for the failure of American propaganda programmes in Vietnam:

> It is a mistake to think of the Vietnamese as individuals, for their culture prepares them to subordinate individual interest to the interest of family or band or hamlet. The rational promptings of self-interest matter less than the counsel of father and brothers . . . . But the voice which our broadcasting projects into Vietnamese homes is the voice of neither father nor brother. It is the voice of the doubting self, the voice of René Descartes driving his wedge between the self in the world and the self who contemplates that self. The voices of our Chieu Hoi (surrender/reconciliation) programming are wholly Cartesian. Their record is not a happy one . . . . they have failed because they speak

> out of an alienated *doppelgänger* rationality for which there is no precedent in Vietnamese thought. We attempt to embody the ghost inside the villager, but there has never been any ghost there. (*Dusklands*, p.21)

Jacobus Coetzee also refers to this difference when he claims that savagery may be defined as 'enslavement to space, as one speaks obversely of the explorer's mastery of space' (*Dusklands*, p.86). In the context of the spatial metaphor of the journey, Jacobus Coetzee, as explorer/writer challenges space, which is the linguistic space allocated him on the signifying chain, 'the *locus* in which is constituted the I who speaks to him who hears' (*Ecrits*, p.141, my emphasis). Conversely, the 'enslavement to space' implies that the archaic personality does not challenge the symbolic confines which are constitutive of identity: thus Mannoni says,

> Archaic personalities . . . exist only by virtue of the well-defined place they occupy in an unchanging whole, and it is that place which is instrumental in the first instance in giving them their form. They cannot contemplate leaving that place for another, except on very rare occasions, and that only with the help of magical ceremonies powerful enough to loosen the affective bonds. (p.209)

Or, in Wilden's words, a member of a so-called primitive society 'cannot pose the question of identity, because he has already been identified (as the mother's brother, for example)' (p.177). Both Mannoni and Wilden would appear to derive their observations from Marie-Cécile and Edmond Ortigues' *Oedipe Africain*, of which Jameson says:

> The methodological recourse to . . . sociologically different contexts . . . has the merit of freeing the psychoanalytic model from its dependency on the classical Western family, with its ideology of

> individualism and its categories of the subject and (in matters of literary representation) of the character. It suggests in turn the need for a model which is not locked into the classical opposition between the individual and the collective, but is rather able to think these continuities in a radically different way. Such is indeed the promise of Lacan's conception of the three orders (the Imaginary, the Symbolic, and the Real) . . . ('Imaginary and Symbolic in Lacan', pp.348–49)

Now Lacan re-phrases the *cogito* as 'I am not wherever I am the plaything of my thought; I think of what I am where I do not think to think' (*Ecrits*, p.166), giving us a version of the self which in its insistence upon *duality*, clearly derives from the Cartesian philosophical tradition, but which nevertheless *subverts* this tradition by means of an insistence upon *non-presence* rather than presence: the self cannot be present to itself in an immediate way because it always produces itself as Other, as a function of the collectivity which is language.[29]

Returning to the metaphor of the lancing of the carbuncle, and the masturbatory view of linguistic practice which it implies, we find that the Lacanian and Derridean views of language overlap in this respect, as is evident in Derrida's insistence upon the equivalence between the movement of language and sexual auto-affection:

> From the moment that nonpresence comes to be felt within speech itself – and there is at least a foreboding of it from the very threshold of articulation and diacriticity – writing is somehow fissured in its value. On the one hand . . . it is the effort of symbolically reappropriating presence. On the other, it consecrates the dispossession that had already dislocated the spoken word. In both senses, one may say that in one way or another, it had already begun to undermine and shape 'living' speech, exposing it to the death within the sign. But

the supplementary sign does not expose to death by affecting a self-presence that is already possible. *Auto*-affection constitutes the same (*auto*) as it divides the same. Privation of presence is the condition of experience, that is to say of presence.

In as much as it *puts into play* the presence of the present and the life of the living, the movement of language does not, one suspects, have only an analogical relationship with 'sexual' auto-affection. It is totally indistinguishable from it, even if that totality is severely articulated and differentiated. (*Of Grammatology*, pp.166–67)

Auto-affection 'constitutes the same as it divides the same', just as the signifier, which constitutes the subject, marks the division between conscious utterance and unconscious self. In the Lacanian paradigm, the Phallus is, as I have indicated, 'the signifier intended to designate as a whole the effects of the signified, in that the signifier conditions them by its presence as signifier' (*Ecrits*, p.285). It performs this function because it is a signifier whose presence signifies an absence: possessing the Phallus (as symbol), one cannot *be* the Phallus, cannot attain full presence or identity. Derrida, however, accuses the Lacanian Phallus of being a transcendental signifier, saying that 'Thanks to castration, the phallus always stays in its place in the transcendental topology . . . . It is indivisible and indestructible there . . . . ' ('The Purveyor of Truth', p.63). And, as Spivak points out, he offers an alternative metaphor to the one of castration:

Within this sexual fable of the production of meaning, Derrida's term is dissemination. Exploiting a false etymological kinship between semantics and semen, Derrida offers this version of textuality: A sowing that does not produce plants, but is simply infinitely repeated. A semination that is not *in*semination but *dis*semination, seed spilled in vain, an emission that cannot return to its origin in the father. Not an exact and controlled polysemy, but

> a proliferation of always different, always postponed meanings . . . . Castration, the lack of superintendence by phallic authority, is what transforms the 'author' or the 'book' into a 'text'. Presence can be articulated only if it is *fragmented* into discourse; 'castration' and dismemberment being both a menace to and the condition of the possibility of discourse. Somewhat extravagantly, the phallus may itself be seen as the knife that severs itself to perpetuate its dissemination. ('Translator's Preface' to *Of Grammatology*, pp. lxv–lxvi)

Now, despite Derrida's objections, it must be pointed out that the Lacanian Phallus, likewise, 'cannot return to its origin in the father', for as Barbara Johnson points out:

> What Lacan means by saying that the letter cannot be divided is thus not that the phallus must remain intact, but that the phallus, the letter, and the signifier are *not substances*. The letter cannot be divided because it only functions *as* a division. It is not something with 'an *identity* to itself inaccessible to dismemberment' as Derrida interprets it; it is a *difference*. It is known only in its effects. The signifier is an articulation in a chain, not an identifiable unit. It cannot be known in itself because it is capable of 'sustaining itself *only* in a displacement.' It is localized, but only as the non-generalizable locus of a differential relationship. (Johnson, p.495, cit. Lacan, 'Seminar on the Purloined Letter', p.59)

The Derridean notion of the Phallus as a knife 'that severs itself to perpetuate its dissemination' is, nevertheless, a useful one in the context of Coetzee's novel: this extravagant figure allows us to read the knife turned against the self in the lancing of the carbuncle and the stabbing of the child, also somewhat extravagantly, as gestures of ontological self-sufficiency which, paradoxically, result in the dissemination of meaning.[30]

Having myself suggested an interpretation of Jacobus Coetzee's and Eugene Dawn's acts of auto-erotic incision via Derrida's fable of castration and dissemination, I came across an anonymous paper,[31] titled 'Litcrit and the Novels of J.M. Coetzee', in which the lancing of the carbuncle is interpreted by means of reference to the same passage from Spivak's Preface:

> Jacobus Coetzee's dualism, the split between his self-in-the-world and his self-observing-and-acting-on-that-self, is instrumentalized in his sexual/surgical operation on himself, in which he is both violator and violated, and enjoys both roles. The terms he uses suggest that the phallus as a symbol lends itself to both roles: it is both the knife and the carbuncle. In one act the knife *is* the penis (breaking the hymen of the carbuncle) and the penis is castrated *by* the knife. This strange act becomes a metaphor for the text's abolition of its own authority. (p.16)

I would like to suggest, however, that the metaphor functions in a way which is more complex than this. First of all, the act of lancing the carbuncle (as opposed to the act of stabbing the child) is simultaneously an act of procreation and violation, and as such describes the movement whereby the self gives birth to the subject while violating the extra-linguistic self: it is the equivalent of the Lacanian death instinct, of which 'it might be said that at every moment he [man] constitutes his world by his suicide' (*Ecrits*, p.28). While auto-erotism, from both the Lacanian and Derridean perspective, would appear to be a property of language and sexuality in general,[32] in the context of Coetzee's novel it is presented as, most specifically, a property of self-reflexive writing, which, in its 'undercutting of the mimetic pretensions of fiction' ('Achterberg's "Ballade van de gasfitter" ', p.293), does abolish its own authority. The metaphor of stabbing the son, however, describes a movement which turns around on itself not once, but twice: referring to its own fictional devices, the text not only abolishes its own authority, but enacts a form of deliberate *aufhebung*, which would also disinvest the reader of authority, as the text cuts itself off from further interpretation. This is a gesture which must fail, as the text is inevitably 'cut off' and subjected to the process of interpretation. As Coetzee says in his discussion of Nabokov's *Pale Fire*:

> By incorporating the exegesis into the fiction we do not escape history, we merely pre-empt its first stage. The double irony of *Pale Fire* does no more than pre-empt two stages. *Pale Fire* is after all only another version of the same Romantic myth (a version whose clearest expression is J. Alfred Prufrock): that an ironic consciousness permits transcendence of a bad infinity of exegesis. The ideal of *Pale Fire* is a Symbolist ideal: a state of being in which, having incorporated into itself all possible interpretations of itself, the work of art has, like a closed system of mirrors, shut itself off forever from interpretation and become a monument of unageing intellect. ('Nabokov's *Pale Fire* and the Primacy of Art', p.6)

Thus the stabbing of the child would seem to be a metaphor for a kind of terminal self-reflexivity, while the lancing of the carbuncle initiates a kind of productive regression. It is this regression which generates the narrative of the return, and which is able to turn the failure of the quest, marked by Jacobus Coetzee's expulsion from the Hottentot camp and undignified retreat, into a form of qualified success.[33] Jacobus Coetzee's expulsion by the Hottentots following his act of mutilating a child repeats Eugene Dawn's confinement to an institution following the stabbing of his own child, as is evident in the exchange between Coetzee and the Hottentots:

> 'Have you no children of your own? Do you not know how to play with children? You have mutilated this child!'
>
> 'It was not my fault'.
>
> 'Of course it was your fault! You are mad, we can no longer have you here. You are not sick any more.

> You must go'. (*Dusklands*, p.97)

This is indicative of certain limits, of prohibitions operative even in a culture which, in its apparent absence of ritual, presents itself as a void, as a 'wilderness without polity' in which everything is possible.

Heading South with only his servant, Klawer, and a minimum of equipment, Jacobus Coetzee says: 'I was casting off attachments' (*Dusklands*, p.99), echoing Flaubert's dream of 'a book about nothing, a book without external attachments.'[34] Then, having given us two versions of the death of Klawer (seemingly as a reminder that the narrative is not bound by connections to the external world, and therefore can, potentially, narrate any number of versions of a particular event), Jacobus Coetzee says:

> I was alone. I had no Klawer to record. I exulted like a young man whose mother has just died. Here I was, free to initiate myself into the desert. I yodelled, I growled, I hissed, I roared, I screamed, I clucked, I whistled; I danced, I stamped, I grovelled, I spun; I sat on the earth, I kicked it, I hugged it, I clawed it. Every possible copula was enacted that could link the world to an elephant hunter armed with a bow and crazed with freedom after seventy days of watching eyes and listening ears. I composed and sang a little ditty:
>
> *Hottentot, Hottentot,*
> *I am not a Hottentot.*
>
> .... I bored a sheath in the earth and would have performed the ur-act had joy and laughter not reduced me to a four-inch dangle and helpless urination. 'God', I shouted, 'God, God, God, why do you love me so?' I frothed and dribbled .... 'I love you too, God. I love everything .... But God, don't let them love me. I don't like accomplices, God, I want to be alone' ....

> I threw off my clothes and swaddled myself in blankets. My feet rubbed each other in ecstasy, my thighs lay together like lovers, my arms embraced my chest. I contemplated the miracle of the heavens and slid into a dream in which a slow torrent of milk, warm and balmy, poured out of the sky down my eager throat. (*Dusklands*, pp.101–102)

Here the 'Imaginary death struggle between egos' is abandoned for a regression to the 'profoundest desire to be 'One' again (to control the Other to whom he [the subject] becomes subjected)', a desire which Wilden claims is 'totally and absolutely irreducible' (pp.190–91). The image of the babe in swaddling clothes with a torrent of milk pouring down its throat clearly represents the return to a condition of primary narcissism (which, as Laplanche points out, 'as a physical reality, can only be the primal myth of a return to the maternal breast', p.72), as opposed to the secondary narcissism which we witnessed in the stabbing of the carbuncle. However, the image of the young man exulting at the death of the mother suggests that the image of the babe at the breast does not invoke the primal union with the mother: it represents, instead, a casting off of *all* attachments, including the attachment to the mother (who is the first representative of the Other to which the child is subjected), and as such constitutes a repetition of the attitude expressed in Eugene Dawn's statement: Thirty-three is the mythologically correct age for cutting ties. Marilyn can wither, I withdraw my investment in her. Coetzee can also die, though that is less likely' (*Dusklands*, p.37). And, if Jacobus Coetzee expresses a desire for initiation into the world, this world must be understood as the world of his own, or of the text's own making: this is the megalomania of primary narcissism, in which one is apparently free to fashion oneself and the world as one pleases. According to Mannoni, it is this desire which motivates the colonizing activity, and, by implication, writing about the colonial experience:

> We waver between the desire for a society, quite different from our own, in which the attachments

> will be preserved with the maximum of emotional comfort and stability, and the desire for complete individuation where the individual is radically independent and relies wholly on his courage, technical skill, and inventive powers. When the child suffers because he feels that the ties between himself and his parents are threatened and at the same time feels guilty because after all it is he who wants to break them, he reacts to the situation by dreaming of a world where there are no real bonds, a world which is entirely his and into which he can project the images of his unconscious, to which he is attached in the way which is to him the most satisfying. Now, it is this imaginary world which is, strictly speaking, the only 'primitive world' and it serves, so to speak, as the model of all other worlds . . . . It is this 'primitive' image of the world which we have in mind when we become explorers, ethnographers, or colonials and go amongst societies which seem to us to be less real than our own. (pp.206–207)

Now, Jacobus Coetzee's jubilant proclamation of independence, of One-ness, is fraught with contradictions. First of all, the erect Phallus which claims mastery over (linguistic) space as it penetrates the wilderness on the journey out, is reduced, here, to a condition of child-like impotence, to 'a four-inch dangle and helpless urination', as the copula between self and world cannot, finally, be enacted. Ejaculation becomes evacuation, as in the case of Eugene Dawn's penetration of Marilyn:

> Before the arrival of my seed her pouch yawns and falls back, leaving my betrayed representative gripped at its base, flailing its head in vain inside an immense cavern, at the very moment when above all else it craves to be rocked through its tantrum in a soft, firm, infinitely trustworthy grip. The word which at such moments flashes its tail across the heavens of my never quite extinguished consciousness

> is *evacuation*: my seed drips like urine into the futile sewers of Marilyn's reproductive ducts. (*Dusklands*, p.8)

Furthermore, Jacobus Coetzee's ditty, 'Hottentot, Hottentot /I am not a Hottentot,' indicates that his declaration of independence cannot grant him a completely autonomous identity, for, as Wilden says, 'one requires two' (p.191), and he is still bound to identify himself in relation to another, in relation to that which is Other. In addition to this, the rejection of complicity with the external world is addressed to God: 'I don't like accomplices, God, I want to be alone', in a way which reveals his ultimate dependence on the Word, and which reminds us that, no matter how radical the attempt to sever all ties, the act of writing is always a speech act, whose function it is to evoke the response of the Other. The dream of primary narcissism can achieve the status of a gesture only, for as Wilden points out:

> . . . the absolute subject is an inexpressible, asubjective entity, since the absolute subject is a contradiction in terms, whether it be the primordial monad or the goal of the Hegelian *Phenomenology*. And it is not the fact that the child at the stage of primary narcissism 'feels' all-powerful (another contradiction) which is significant for him, but rather his discovery of the absolute power of the whim of the Other who he is totally unable to control. (p.190)

The gesture of ultimate independence on the part of the text, rather than granting Phallic authority, betokens impotence: cutting itself off from all extra-linguistic phenomena (whether these be the phenomena of the empirical world, or of the unconscious), the self is brought face-to-face with its ultimate dependence upon language, and thereby with its ultimate subjection to the Other.

There is, furthermore, no core of selfhood to which the text can retreat, no interior for penetration. As Coetzee points out, again with respect to Achterberg's 'Ballade van de gasfitter':

> All versions of the *I* are fictions of the *I*. The primal *I* is not recoverable. Neither of the Words *I* and *You* can exist pure in the medium of language. Indeed, after the experience of the Word in relation to one's own existence, life cannot go on as before. 'Self-annihilation (i.e. annihilation of the self) is the essential form for the God-relationship', writes Kierkegaard (*Concluding Unscientific Postscript*, p.412). The fate of the gasfitter is precisely self-annihilation, a dwindling away of selfhood. (p.288)

The anthropological-cum-historical exploration of the self which we are tracing in Jacobus Coetzee's narrative arrives, likewise, at the point of self-annihilation, or death, as the final stages of the return journey involve, if not a dwindling away of selfhood, then a deliberate withdrawal of the self. This withdrawal is the equivalent of the Lacanian death instinct, and so, paradoxically, implies survival, or, more than survival, 'that desperate affirmation of life that is the purest form in which we recognize the death instinct' (*Ecrits*, p.104). Jacobus Coetzee likens himself to a little black beetle, 'a true creature of Zeno', which, feigning death, is prepared to lose its legs without wincing:

> 'Now I am only half-way dead. Now I am only three-fourths dead. Now I am only seven-eighths dead. The secret of my life regresses infinitely before your probing finger. You and I could spend eternity splitting fractions. If I keep still long enough you will go away. Now I am only fifteen-sixteenths dead'. (*Dusklands*, p.102)

Just as there is, theoretically, an infinitude of points through which Zeno's arrow must pass before it reaches its target, so there is a potentially infinite number of divisions which the self may undergo before reaching the end-point of self-annihilation, or no narration. The figure of the beetle, and the game nominated by Jacobus Coetzee, 'the Zenonian case in which only an infinitely diminishing fraction of [the] self survived, the fictive echo of a tiny 'I' whispered across the void of eternity' (*Dusklands*, p.105), signify the attempt 'to attain in the subject what was before the serial articulations of speech, and what is primordial to the birth of symbols' (*Ecrits*, p.105). The line of retreat produced by these infinitely diminishing fractions cannot, however, arrive at a destination in the self which is, by definition, beyond articulation. And articulation, however fractional, translates interiority into exteriority:

> Under the Hottentot captivity I had not failed to keep the Zeno beetle in mind. There had been legs, metaphorical legs, and much else too, that I had been prepared to lose. In the blindest alley of the labyrinth of my self I had hidden myself away, abandoning mile after mile of defences. The Hottentot assault had been disappointing. It had fallen on my shame, a judicious point of attack; but it had been baffled from the beginning, in a body which partook too of the labyrinth, by the continuity of my exterior with the interior surface of my digestive tract. The male body has no interior space. The Hottentots knew nothing of penetration. For penetration you need blue eyes. (*Dusklands*, pp.102-103)

This labyrinthine figure is the equivalent of the structure by means of which Lacan describes the dialectical process of the death instinct:

> To say that this mortal meaning reveals in speech a centre exterior to language is more than a metaphor; it manifests a structure. This structure is different from the spatialization of the circumference or of the sphere in which some people like to schematize the limits of the living being and his milieu: it corresponds rather to the relational group that symbolic logic designates topologically as an

> annulus.
>
> If I wished to give an intuitive representation of it, it seems that, rather than have recourse to the surface aspect of a zone, I should call on the three-dimensional form of a torus, in so far as its peripheral exteriority and its central exteriority constitute only one single region.
>
> This scheme satisfactorily expresses the endless circularity of the dialectical process that is produced when the subject brings his solitude to realization, be it in the vital ambiguity of immediate desire or in the full assumption of his being-for-death. (*Ecrits*, p.105)

Jacobus Coetzee's journey has traced a labyrinthine route, producing a movement which is spiral rather than circular, as it returns to an end point which is not identical with the starting point, if only by virtue of the intervention of the narrative in the space between. This is the spiral movement of the Imaginary journey, which, as Ricoeur says, 'brings us back to the almost motionless constellation of potentialities that the narrative retrieves' (p.186).

The quest has failed to provide proof of mastery, or even of identity, failed to achieve penetration of an interior space, has failed on all counts but one: it has succeeded in generating the narrative. Nominating games in order to overcome the dreariness and sense of obligation in bringing the journey to an end, Jacobus Coetzee turns defeat into victory, as he claims mere survival, or the continuation of narrative, as sufficient *raison d'être* for the quest: 'In each game the challenge was to undergo the history, and victory was mine if I survived it' (*Dusklands,* p.105). This, then, is the position of the narrating self to which this phase of the quest-as-history (or history-as-quest) brings us. It is a position which we find repeated in the narrative of Eugene Dawn, with Coetzee's retreat to a 'voiceless' peripheral position, a position which itself repeats the stance of contemporary writing in which irony has become 'a style of mind in constant metamorphosis [and] the ironic statement hides no definite meaning but merely designates the author's absence from his statements' (Bersani, p. 197).

The structure of the quest means, however, that the narrative cannot be left off at this point: the hero must return home and the narrative generated out of this Imaginary voyage must be re-inserted in the Symbolic. And so Jacobus Coetzee tells us:

> Only on the borders of settlement did I revive . . . . I glutted myself on a day of bloodlust and anarchy whose story would fill another book, an assault on colonial property which filled me out once more to a man's stature and whose consequences were visited on the unfortunate heads of the Bushmen.
>
> On 12 October 1760 in the evening I reached the markers of my own land. Unseen I donned my clothes and buried my bow. Like God in a whirlwind I fell upon a lamb, an innocent little fellow who had never seen his master and was thinking only of a good night's sleep, and slit his throat . . . . Bearing the liver, my favourite cut, I burst open the door. I was back. (*Dusklands*, p.106)

The manner of Jacobus Coetzee's return repeats the pattern of the traditional quest, in which 'the repetition of the origin has to be superseded by an act of rupture (like, for example, the episode of the woodcutters breaking open the belly of the wolf with an axe in "Little Red Riding Hood")' (Ricoeur, p.185), (with the difference that here it is the innocent lamb that is slit open to allow for the return of the 'villainous' narrator). The final sentence is a punning reminder of the victory of survival (bearing the liver); a victory whose proof is the existence of the narrative, but a victory which is achieved only at the price of a 'cut', or incision, as this narrating self finds itself cut off again with the inevitable *termination* of the narrative.

Jacobus Coetzee nominates another game, which he describes as 'an entirely different contest between myself and the circumjacent universe in which I might be required to call up an expeditionary force and return in triumph to punish my depredators and recover my property' (*Dusklands*, pp. 104–105). It is this game that is enacted in the account of the 'Second journey to the land of the Great Namaqua', which is subtitled, '*Expedition of Captain Hendrik Hop*; *16 August 1761–27 April 1762*', and which, as Knox-Shaw points out, 'corresponds, if only in date, to a fact finding expedition under the official command of Captain Hof but effectively led by Jacobus Coetzee which retraced his steps of the previous year'.[35] The account of this journey functions to resurrect the narrating self, as Jacobus Coetzee indicates when he says: 'Through their deaths I, who after they had expelled me had wandered the desert like a pallid symbol, again asserted my reality' (*Dusklands*, p.113). Following on from the narrative of self-annihilation, this second journey is an allegory of a self bent on revenge against an indifferent universe, intent on achieving, once more, a position of mastery. It is a *second* journey, a repetition of the first, failed quest, and as such represents the attempt to translate the experience of passivity into an experience of mastery. As Peter Brooks says, citing Freud:

> 'Choice stands in the place of necessity, of destiny. In this way man overcomes death, which he has recognized intellectually.' If repetition is mastery, movement from the passive to the active; and if mastery is an assertion of control over what man must in fact submit to – choice, we might say, of an imposed end – we have already a suggestive comment on the grammar of plot, where repetition, taking us back again over the same ground, could have to do with the choice of ends.[36]

This second journey takes us 'back again over the same ground' in an attempt to re-assert the reality of the self, to prolong the narrative and to choose another end. In addition to this, it represents a further phase in the history of strategies for 'self-realization', a further attempt on the part of the narrating self to challenge the space allocated it on the signifying chain. It is what André Green calls 'writing of the body', writing whose 'new object is the state of the body proper in its most violent manifestation' (p. 31; see my Chapter One, p. 47); in its detailed and unrelenting depiction of carnage and brutality, the account of the second journey is a pornography of violence.

If the second journey is an allegory of a particular narrative project, the *narrative* of the journey is itself a deliberate statement of transgression, a refusal of the taboos which prohibit certain areas of experience from articulation, and thereby establish the (fluctuating) limits of the linguistic code. As Bataille points out, 'violence belongs to humanity as a whole and is speechless, and . . . thus humanity as a whole lies by omission and language itself is founded upon this lie' (p. 186). That this narrative is, indeed, perceived as transgressing certain codes is evident in the critical response to the novel: there is, for example, Knox-Shaw's complaint that

> Nothing offsets the sadistic agency of the narrator: in so far as the suffering of Coetzee's victims is recorded it is through the gloating eyes of their killer . . . . Controlled certainly – the effect deliberately produced, but in the absence of any other resource it must be said that the writing itself furthers the claims of true savagery. This is an art that can only re-enact. (pp.73–74)

This, and the objection that Jacobus Coetzee hunts, not for pecuniary gain, but 'to satisfy a refined bloodlust' (p.68), suggests that Knox-Shaw would find the depiction of violence acceptable if it were shown to be motivated by something other than bloodlust,[37] and if it were pronounced morally reprehensible by a distanced narrator, him/herself removed from the field of violence. But it is precisely this that Coetzee's text refuses to do. Bataille says:

> As a general rule the torturer does not use the language of violence exerted by him in the name of an established authority; he uses the language

> of the authority, and that gives him what looks like an excuse, a lofty justification. (p.187)

In the account of the massacre we do not encounter the language of authority, which would explain and condemn violence (thereby justifying its presence in the text) in economic terms, for example as the by-product of a punitive raid to recover stolen cattle. The reason we do not encounter it is that this is a representation of violence which confronts the language of authority (and the authority of language) and would refuse complicity with it at any point; furthermore this is a text which confesses, rather than denies, its complicity with the violence that 'belongs to humanity as a whole'.

Pornography involves, as it were, a three-pronged confrontation with the Other, a confrontation whose emphasis varies according to the weight one grants to any particular signification of this problematic term, the Other.[38] In that pornography involves a transgression of taboos, it may be viewed as an attempt to penetrate *beyond* the Other as language, or the Symbolic. However, if the Other is granted its complementary signification as the unconscious, then the text of violence, in uttering that which is normally repressed from speech, becomes an endeavour to *attain* the Other. And thirdly, as a particular form of speech act, pornography bespeaks the desire to *by-pass* the Other which is in a position of thirdness between two subjects; in that its specific aim is arousal, it would effect a direct, un-mediated connection with the desiring reader. In all cases we have a projected return to a fullness of speech and thereby to a fullness of being; in all cases a refusal of the divided condition and of the restrictions and absences which the Other both imposes and implies.

We find, however, that all three components of this assault on the Other are doomed to failure. Jacobus Coetzee says:

> For months I had nourished myself on this day, which I had populated with retribution and death. On this day I would return as a storm-cloud casting the shadow of my justice over a small patch of earth. But this abject, treacherous rabble was telling

> me that here and everywhere else on this continent there would be no resistance to my power and no limit to its projection. My despair was despair at the undifferentiated plenum, which is after all nothing but the void dressed up as being . . . . I was undergoing nothing less than a failure of imagination before the void. I was sick at heart. (*Dusklands*, pp. 108–109)

The quest for mastery again leads to the paradoxical situation in which the realization of one's capacity to transgress all limits (one's capacity to say anything at all) brings with it a sense of ultimate powerlessness. The linguistic subject cannot traverse the boundaries of language, of the Other, because in effect the boundaries cannot be localized and pinned down: as J.M. Coetzee says, 'In language there are no stable and positive elements. Elements achieve definition only through their reciprocal differences, and all shift their boundaries continually with the passing of time' ('The First Sentence of Yvonne Burgess's *The Strike*', p.48). The moments of transgression are ultimately constitutive of the system,[39] as the attempts to traverse boundaries are swallowed up and incorporated into the 'corpus' of language, of the Other. In Lacan's words:

> Let us set out from the conception of the Other as the locus of the signifier. Any statement of authority has no other guarantee than its very enunciation, and it is pointless for it to seek it in another signifier, which could not appear outside this locus in any way. Which is what I mean when I say that no meta-language can be spoken, or, more aphoristically, that there is no Other of the Other. (*Ecrits*, pp.310–11)

Furthermore, although they exist in a state of fluctuation, limits and laws make meaning possible; the repression of certain meanings allows other meanings, authorized by the particular discourse, to stand. In so far as the Other (as the unconscious) is the repository of these repressed meanings, it is not possible to attain or to speak the Other, as this would result in the abolition of all meaning.

The text of violence cannot get outside or beyond the Other, cannot attain or speak the Other, and cannot, finally, by-pass the Other as 'the scene of the Word [which] is always in third position between two subjects' (Wilden, p.269). As is frequently the case in this novel, Eugene Dawn provides the relevant insights:

> Print, on the other hand, is sadism, and properly evokes terror. The message of the newspaper is: 'I can say anything and not be moved. Watch as I permute my 52 affectless signs'. Print is the hard master with the whip, print-reading a weeping search for signs of mercy. Writer is as much abased before him as reader. The pornographer is the doomed upstart hero who aspires to such delirium of ecstasy that the surface of the print will crack beneath his words. We write our violent novelties on the walls of lavatories to bring the walls down. This is the secret reason, the mere hidden reason. Obscuring the hidden reason, unseen to us, is the true reason: that we write on lavatory walls to abase ourselves before them. Pornography is an abasement before the page, such abasement as to convulse the very page. Print reading is a slave habit. (*Dusklands*, p.15)

Pornography is an abasement before the page because it reveals its ultimate dependence upon language to articulate something which is beyond language and which properly belongs to the zone of silence, as Bataille indicates in his commentary on de Sade:

> The Marquis de Sade, rebellious in his imprisonment, had to give his rebellion a voice. He spoke out, as violence itself never does . . . . De Sade's expression of violence changes violence into something else, something necessarily its opposite: into a reflecting and rationalised will to violence. (pp.190–91)

The Word is always there in the position of thirdness, and affectless signs are the only means of mediating between the desiring writer and the desiring reader; for this reason pornography fails as a copula, fails to achieve the delirium of ecstasy by means of which an immediate communication would be effected. As André Green points out, 'Even in the body-orientated writing mode, the mode that spurns literature in order to attain a certain living reality, one is bounced back to the writing act, since it is through the writing act that one has chosen to attain it' (p.34). In its dependence upon signs, pornographic writing has the same status as the erotic object:

> . . . eroticism which is a fusion, which shifts interest away from and beyond the person and his limits, is nevertheless expressed by an object. We are faced with the paradox of an object which implies the abolition of the limits of all objects, of an erotic object. (Bataille, p.130)

In the case of pornographic writing, the erotic object is simultaneously a linguistic object, which brings us back to the inevitable translation of the subject into an object, as the subject of this section, the *I* of the 'Second Journey to the land of the Great Namaqua', becomes another of the discarded objects strewn along the path of self representation.

That the repetition of this journey has indeed had to do with the choice of ends (see p. 113, this chapter) is evident from Jacobus Coetzee's flourish of bravado as he concludes this section:

> I too am frightened of death. I too have spent wakeful nights computing the percentage of three-score years and ten already devoured and projecting myself into the day after my decease when the undertaker's understudy will slit open and pluck from their tidy bed the organs of my inner self I have so long cherished . . . .
>
> Yet the truer truth is that my death is merely a winter story I tell to frighten myself, to make my

> blankets more cosy. A world without me is inconceivable.
>
> On the other hand, if the worst comes you will find that I am not irrevocably attached to life. I know my lessons. I too can retreat before a beckoning finger through the infinite corridors of myself. I too can attain and inhabit a point of view from which, like Plaatje, like Adonis, like Tamboer & Tamboer, like the Namaqua, I can be seen to be superfluous. At present I do not care to inhabit such a point of view; but when the day comes you will find that whether I am alive or dead, whether I ever lived or never was born, has never been of real concern to me. I have other things to think about. (*Dusklands*, p.114)

Withdrawing from the field of narrative, from the death-in-life which the discourse has granted him, to the life-in-death of silence, Jacobus Coetzee makes a gesture which amounts to 'the suicidal renunciation of the vanquished partner, depriving of his victory the master whom he abandons to his inhuman solitude' (*Ecrits*, p.104). And, with his closing words, his claim that whether he 'ever lived or never was born, has never been of real concern' to him, he 'rediscovers in negation a final triumph' (*Ecrits*, p.104).

Continuing with our back-to-front reading, we come to yet another resurrection of the linguistic subject, in the figure of Eugene Dawn, narrator of 'The Vietnam Project', who is working on the New Life Project under the supervision of an enigmatic manager, Coetzee. Eugene Dawn says of this Coetzee:

> I would have expected more understanding from Coetzee, who should be used to handling creative people. Once upon a time a creative person himself, he is now a failed creative person who lives vicariously off true creative people. He has built a reputation on the work of other people. (*Dusklands*, p.1)

By this it is implied that Coetzee is the writer, the self of enunciation, who, sustaining himself via the endeavours of various narrators, retreats from each utterance, leaving a trail of abandoned (linguistic) subjects in his wake. Again commenting on Achterberg's gasfitter, J.M. Coetzee says:

> For the *I* as wordfitter/*dichter* to survive, the *I* as failed *dichter* (gasfitter) must be split off. Failed *I* becomes false *I*, alienated *I*, or *he*. In fact, all the failed *I*-projects are successively split off as *he's* . . . phantoms nesting promiscuously within and upon each other, watched over by a murderous warden-*I*. ('Achterberg's "Ballade van de gasfitter", p.292)

What is happening here, however, is somewhat different, in that the fictional *I*, the narrator, Eugene Dawn, is asserting his autonomy in relation to a self which remains on the periphery of the narrative, relegated to the pronoun *he*. The use of the past historic in 'The Narrative of Jacobus Coetzee' automatically creates a situation in which *I's* are split off from one another, as a narrating *I* in the present comments upon past *I*'s which could, without disrupting the syntax, be converted to *he*'s. Eugene Dawn's narrative, by contrast, is given in the present definite, in a way which asserts his 'presence' in defiance of Coetzee: this is a challenge by the *I* of the utterance to the narrating self, a renewed and intensified gesture of ontological self-sufficiency. At the same time, however, in retreating to the sideline, Coetzee asserts his presence by virtue of his absence, as he 'manifests himself in this movement of disappearance', in Lacan's *aphanisis* (see my Chapter One, p. 16) which is the equivalent of the 'Zenonian case', in which only an infinitely diminishing fraction of the self survives.

In drawing attention to certain parallels between the 'Narrative of Jacobus Coetzee' and 'The Vietnam Project', I have already commented upon several aspects of Eugene Dawn's narrative. It remains to talk about the function of this section in relation to the whole, and about the way in which it extends the analysis of the impetus toward 'self realization' and self-sufficiency, and introduces a commentary upon reading and the act of interpretation. As manager of the New Life Project, Coetzee pronounces upon Eugene Dawn's work in terms which could be equally well applied to the text of *Dusklands* as a whole: 'I never imagined that this department would one day be producing work of an *avant-garde* nature .... You are working in a novel and contentious field and must expect contention .... this is the first time round for you' (*Dusklands*, pp.2–3). And he advises Eugene Dawn to modify his style in a way which approximates the approach which the novel itself takes to the problem of a potentially repressive and resistant readership:

> 'As you know from your dealings with them, the military are, as a class – to put it frankly – slow-thinking, suspicious, and conservative. Convincing them of something new is never easy .... I want you to rewrite your proposals so that people in the military can entertain them without losing self-respect .... if you stress continually, not only explicitly but through the very genuflexions of your *style*, that you are merely a functionary with a narrow if significant specialism, a near-academic with none of the soldier's all-round understanding of the science of warfare; that, nevertheless, within the narrow boundaries of your specialism you have some suggestions to offer which may have some strategic fallout – then, you will find, your proposals will get a hearing.' (*Dusklands*, pp.3–4)

All of this is self-reflexive commentary, functioning to control the meanings which may be attributed to this text, just as Coetzee-as-manager attempts to control the work of Eugene Dawn.

Coetzee gives Eugene Dawn some further advice, again drawing attention to the explanatory function of this section of the novel. He says:

> 'There is one more thing I would like you to think

> about. As you must know, you carry out your analysis of the propaganda services in terms which are alien to most people . . . . Let me suggest, therefore, some kind of introduction in which you explain in words of one syllable the kind of procedure you follow – how myths operate in human society, how signs are exchanged, and so forth; with lots of examples and for God's sake no footnotes.' (*Dusklands*, p.4)

'The Vietnam Project' is the introduction suggested by Coetzee; we shall see, however that it is not Eugene Dawn's 'scientific' mythographic discourse, but the violent familial drama which disrupts and eventually takes over his work as mythographer, that shows us 'how myths operate in human society'. The 'analysis of the propaganda services' to which Coetzee refers may be read as the project of deconstructing existing fictional forms, which, in their failure to scrutinize their own formal assumptions, unconsciously perform a subtle kind of propaganda, endorsing colonial attitudes: this is the work performed by Coetzee's novels, exploring as they do the myths – described by Eugene Dawn as the fictions a tribe coins to maintain its own powers (*Dusklands*, p.26) – of white South African writing. However, in giving us a narrator like Eugene Dawn, J.M. Coetzee deconstructs his own stance as mythographer, and deconstructs the mythographic discourse *per se*. At the same time he provides a critique of the sciences of humankind (which, as is evident from Eugene Dawn's narrative, encompass the discursive fields of history, anthropology, ethnography, and psychology, amongst others), demonstrating as fallacious the attempt to take up a neutral stance outside myth in order to comment upon an area of human experience. Thus when Eugene Dawn says, 'The highest propaganda is the propagation of a new mythology' (*Dusklands*, p.26), he refers to the tendency of the analytic exercise, or meta-commentary, to conceal its status as myth, and function of control, while in fact it cannot avoid propagating a new mythology. As Shoshana Felman says:

> Science is the drive to *go beyond*. The scientist's

> commitment is at once to acknowledge myth and to attempt to *go beyond the myth*. Only when this (mythical, narrative) movement of 'going beyond' stops, does science stop. Only when the myth is not acknowledged, is *believed to be a science*, does the myth prevail at the expense of science. It is precisely when we believe we are *beyond* the myth that we are (indulge in) fiction. There is no 'beyond' to myth – science is always, in one way or another, a new (generative) myth. ('Beyond Oedipus', p.1051)

S.J. Coetzee's claim that 'Man's thrust into the future is history' (*Dusklands*, p.128) finds its counterpart in Eugene Dawn's claim:

> I am the embodiment of the patient struggle of the intellect against blood and anarchy. I am a story not of emotion and violence – the illusory war-story of television – but of life itself, life in obedience to which even the simplest organism represses its entropic yearning for the mud and follows the road of evolutionary duty toward the glory of consciousness. (*Dusklands*, p.29)

Both Eugene Dawn and S.J. Coetzee manifest the self-delusions of the scientific discourse which proclaims itself beyond myth, and perceives itself as engaged in evolving consciousness for the good of humankind. When Eugene Dawn says:

> He [Coetzee] has no natural sympathy with a mythographic approach to the problem of control. He starts with the axiom that people act identically if their self-interests are identical. His career has been built on the self and its interests (*Dusklands*, p.34),

he reminds us of Freud's conclusion to his exposition of the death instinct in *Beyond the Pleasure Principle*, in which Freud claims that the drive toward perfection is a product of instinctual repression, and therefore a matter of 'self interest':

> It may be difficult . . . for many of us, to abandon the belief that there is an instinct towards perfection at work in human beings, which has brought them to their present high level of intellectual achievement and ethical sublimation and which may be expected to watch over their development into supermen. I have no faith, however, in the existence of any such internal instinct and I cannot see how this benevolent illusion is to be preserved . . . . What appears in a minority of human individuals as an untiring impulsion towards further perfection can easily be understood as a result of the instinctual repression upon which is based all that is most precious in human civilization. The repressed instinct never ceases to strive for complete satisfaction, which would consist in the repetition of a primary experience of satisfaction. No substitutive or reactive formations and no sublimations will suffice to remove the repressed instinct's persisting tension; and it is the difference in amount between the pleasure of satisfaction which is *demanded* and that which is actually *achieved* that provides the driving factor which will permit of no halting at any position attained, but, in the poet's words, '*ungebandigt immer vorwarts dringt*'. The backward path that leads to complete satisfaction is as a rule obstructed by the resistances which maintain the repressions. So there is no alternative but to advance in the direction in which growth is still free – though with no prospect of bringing the process to a conclusion or of being able to reach the goal.[40]

Eugene Dawn's story is not, as he claims, a story of life, but a story of death and destruction, motivated by an instinct 'whose function it is to assure that the organism shall follow its own path to death, and to ward off any possible ways of returning to inorganic existence other than those which are immanent in the organism itself' (*Beyond the Pleasure Prin-*

ciple, p.39): hence Eugene Dawn's statement, 'I do not intend to be cut off prematurely' (*Dusklands*, p.2). Eugene Dawn is an armchair explorer, for whom the camera has replaced the gun as the agency of power over the human territory he explores, which means that there is a great difference between the amount of (destructive) 'pleasure of satisfaction which is *demanded* and that which is actually *achieved*.' Thus he says:

> Mythography, my present specialism, is an open field like philosophy or criticism because it has not yet found a methodology to lose itself forever in the mazes of. When McGraw-Hill brings out the first textbook of mythography, I will move on. I have an exploring temperament. Had I lived two hundred years ago I would have had a continent to explore, to map, to open to colonization. In that vertiginous freedom I might have expanded to my true potential. If I feel cramped nowadays it is because I have no space to beat my wings. (*Dusklands*, p.33)

In this case, advancing in the direction in which growth is still free means retreating into the self, turning his destructive drives against himself or his offspring, the child or the text; and so he asks: 'Is it the blocked imperative of action that has caused the war, and my discourse of the war, to back up and poison me? Would I have freed myself if I had been a soldier boy and trod upon the Vietnam of my scholar fantasy?' (*Dusklands*, p.40).[41]

Eugene Dawn's mythographic programme for victory in Vietnam is made to intersect with his personal family drama in a way which shows how both result from the operation of the repressed instinct. What we have here is repetition as a return *of* the repressed, rather than as a return *to* origins (see p. 72, this chapter), as the myth which constitutes Eugene Dawn, which establishes his unconscious as a function of 'the collectivity which . . . creates and sustains it' (Wilden, p.265), is shown to be both the source of, and the reason for the failure of his attempt to make his own myths. The founding myth, in this case, is the myth of Captain America (of *Captain*

America and the Falcon, published by Marvel Comics). Thus Eugene Dawn says:

> He [Coetzee] cannot understand a man who experiences his self as an envelope holding his body-parts together while inside it he burns and burns. I was brought up on comic-books (I was brought up on books of all kinds). Enthralled once to monsters bound into the boots, belts, masks, and costumes of their heroic individualism, I am now become Herakles roasting in his poisoned shirt. For the American monster-hero there is relief: every sixteen pages the earthly paradise returns and its masked saviour can revert to pale-faced citizen. Whereas Herakles, it would seem, burns forever. (*Dusklands*, p.34)

In a paper titled 'Captain America in American Mythology', J M Coetzee describes Captain America as

> a great flag-wrapped phallus striding out, like all heroes of adventure since Achilles, in quest of a foe worthy of all that bulging displaced potency . . . . Captain America is the image of the stable ego . . . . Masked, he puts himself outside and above family and law: as a Protestant hero he will now heed only the authority of an inner voice.
>
> Captain America . . . is a hero not because he is an outlaw but because . . . he has responded to a call, the Calvinist categorical imperative of absolute urgency and absolute stringency. (pp.33–34)

The 'pale-faced citizen' to which Eugene Dawn claims the 'masked saviour' of the comics can revert is Steve Rogers:

> Captain America has a twilight double life as Steve Rogers, harried young patrolman. When Steven Rogers dons a drab windbreaker and resumes his cowed

> relationship with his blonde teenage girlfriend Sharon Carter, the heroic musculature fades quite away. The hero-costume, the tumescent body, the shield of virtue, the emblematic 'A' ('America', but also 'Adam', 'Alone'), are all of a piece. Captain America is the wish-fulfilment alter-ego of colourless citizen Rogers, anxious husband in embryo. ('Captain America in American Mythology', p.33)

Claiming to be 'the embodiment of the patient struggle of the intellect against blood and anarchy' (*Dusklands*, p.29), Eugene Dawn, like Captain America, is responding to a call, is operating within the myth of the Protestant ethic of work and obedience:

> Beyond courage there is the humble heart, the quiet garden into which we may escape from the cycles of time. I am neat and polite, but I am the man of the future paradise.
>
> Before paradise comes purgatory.
>
> Not without joy, I have girded myself for purgatory. If I must be a martyr to the cause of obedience, I am prepared to suffer. (*Dusklands*, pp.28–9)

While he dons the mask, not of the man of action, but of man of intellect, proclaiming, 'I am still the captain of my soul' (*Dusklands*, p.10), and, 'I am a hero of resistance. I am no less than that, properly understood, in metaphor. Staggering in my bleeding armor, I stand erect, alone on the plain, beset' (*Dusklands*, p.29), Eugene Dawn, too, leads a twilight double life as henpecked, mothered husband. However, the mask of heroic individualism has become a shirt of Nessus, which he cannot throw off, even in private life. He cannot revert to 'pale-faced citizen', and the imperative toward autonomous identity must be seen as motivating both his mythographic prescriptions for Vietnam and his deliberate disruption of the family constellation, both of which, in turn, function as metaphors for a particular textual strategy. As I have indicated, this strategy is one of terminal self-reflexivity, of extreme self-sufficiency on the part of the text, a strategy whose source in myth is shown to be identical to that of the plans for action which function as metaphors for it.

Outlining his programme for psychological warfare in Vietnam, Eugene Dawn assumes Phallic authority, acting as the Father. He says: 'We are the father putting down the rebellion of the band of brothers' (*Dusklands*, p.26), and 'the father cannot be a benign father until his sons have knelt before his wand. The plotting of the sons against the father must cease. They must kneel with hearts bathed in obedience' (*Dusklands*, p.28). His fantastical mythographic plan for victory in Vietnam is an attempt to counter what is essentially the myth put forward by Freud in *Totem and Taboo*, the myth of the band of brothers who would usurp the father's place. This myth is to be countered by an assertion of complete autonomy on the part of the all-powerful father, an autonomy which would allow him to stand outside myth to create his own myths:

> But has the master-myth of history not outdated the fiction of the symbiosis of earth and heaven? We live no longer by tilling the earth but by devouring her and her waste products. We signed our repudiation of her with flights toward new celestial loves. We have the capacity to breed out of our own head. When the earth conspires incestuously with her sons, should our recourse not be to the arms of the goddess of *techne* who springs from our brains? Is it not time that the earth-mother is supplanted by her own faithful daughter, shaped without woman's part? The age of Athene dawns. In the Indo-China Theater we play out the drama of the end of the tellurian age and the marriage of the sky-god with his parthonogene daughter-queen. If the play has been poor, it is because we have stumbled about the stage asleep, not knowing the meaning of our acts. Now I bring their meaning to light in that blinding moment of ascending meta-historical consciousness in which we begin to shape our own myths. (*Dusklands*, p.28)

Pronouncing upon the meaning of American action in Vietnam

from 'the impregnable stronghold of the intellect' (*Dusklands*, p.30), Eugene Dawn, like S J Coetzee, invests his statements with moral authority, while the numbered segments and mathematical formulae of his Introduction, like S J Coetzee's endnotes and empirical data, are an attempt to invoke the effects of the Real. However, in the case of Dawn's Introduction, the effects of the Imaginary, rather than lending credence to the discourse of the Real, *undermine* this discourse, as Dawn concludes by referring to his own precarious state of mental health:

> I am in a bad way as I write these words. My health is poor. I have a treacherous wife, an unhappy home, unsympathetic superiors . . . But I see things and have a duty toward history that cannot wait . . . You must listen. I speak with the voice of things to come. I speak in troubled times and tell you how to be as children again. I speak to the broken halves of all our selves and tell them to embrace, loving the worst in us equally with the best. (*Dusklands*, p.31)

Eugene Dawn's plan for Vietnam is translated into action within his family, as he abducts the child, Martin, and says of his wife, Marilyn: 'Thirty-three is the mythologically correct age for cutting ties. Marilyn can wither, I withdraw my investment in her' (*Dusklands*, p.37). Attempting to act as the father, to assert his independence, ironically, Eugene Dawn becomes as a child again; so that as we see him putting into action what he claims to be the myth of his own making, we see that he is, in effect, being overtaken by the myth which makes him. The triangular structure of father, mother, son is linked by recurrent images of fish and of an underwater world,[42] and by Dawn's description of Marilyn as 'Flesh of my flesh, bone of my bone' (*Dusklands*, p.35), and of Martin as his 'own flesh and blood' (*Dusklands*, p.45), suggesting that the woman and the child are *imagos* or internalized components of the self, present within Eugene Dawn's unconscious. Viewed from this perspective, the attempt to disrupt the family constellation, and its correlative, the plan for Vietnam – and of course the textual strategy for which these stand as metaphors – become the exteriorization of an interior drama of the unconscious; become the desperate repetitions of a son who would turn his powerlessness into mastery, the desperate response of the 'excluded orphan' before the 'barred gate' of his 'true home' (*Dusklands*, pp.35 and 36).

In the context of these metaphors of the metafictional project, Marilyn, as mother and embodiment of desire, which, in Lacanian terms, is always the desire of the Other's desire,[43] must be seen as representing the reader. The text, as speech act, is motivated in desire, which is, likewise, the desire of the Other's desire, the desire of the reader's desire. Seeing Marilyn as a figure representing the reader, we can account for Dawn's voyeuristic delight in her on her return home from what he likes to imagine are her assignments with other men:

> As an exercise I watch her through a strange man's eyes. New perspectives excite me . . . . I am plainly addicted to my marriage, and addiction is in the end a surer bond than love. If Marilyn is unfaithful she is so much the dearer to me, for if strangers prize her she must be valuable, and I am reassured . . . . It is most of all on Wednesday nights [the nights following her imagined assignments] that I have to own to myself that without Marilyn I would have no reason to go on; and thereby surely begin to know what it must be like to love. (*Dusklands*, p.12)

That Marilyn represents, not simply the reader in general, but a particular form of reading, is evident in Dawn's mention of her remorseless 'urge to unveil the mysteries' (*Dusklands*, p.11) and in his description of her attempts to uncover his secret:

> She believes I have a secret, a cancer of shameful knowledge. She attributes it to me for her own consolation, for to believe in secrets is to believe the cheery doctrine that hidden in the labyrinth

> of the memory lies an explanation for the haphazard present. She would not believe disclaimers, nor would her friends. They flex their talons: be it ever so deeply rooted, they promise her, we will dig it out. (*Dusklands*, pp.10–11; note the sexual *double entendre* in 'rooted')

It is in response to this kind of reading activity, which would lay bare all secrets, that Eugene Dawn enacts his self-deconstructive gesture, withdrawing his investment in Marilyn, cutting the text off from the reader's desire.

However, having left Marilyn and taken the child, he says from his motel room 'I ought to be happy in this place. I have cut my ties. There is no one breathing over my shoulder. My time is my own. Yet I am still unliberated' (*Dusklands*, p.40). Attempting to save the secret, interior self from appropriation by an avidly destructive readership (Dawn says: 'I saved the child from a woman of unstable, hysterical character', *Dusklands*, p.39), Eugene Dawn finds this self usurped in its place by another; finds himself invaded from the exterior by the language of authority, by the discourse of the war, by a hideous mongol boy:

> I call down death upon death upon the men of action. Since February of 1965 their war has been living its life at my expense. I know and I know and I know what it is that has eaten away my manhood from inside, devoured the food that should have nourished me. It is a thing, a child not mine, once a baby squat and yellow whelmed in the dead centre of my body, sucking my blood, growing by my waste, now, 1973, a hideous mongol boy who stretches his limbs inside my hollow bones, gnaws my liver with his smiling teeth, voids his bilious filth into my systems, and will not go. I want an end to it! I want my deliverance! (*Dusklands*, p.40)

Threatened by Marilyn and the officers of the law, who come to reappropriate the child, Eugene Dawn sees himself as the father guarding the child (the writer guarding the meaning of the text): 'I am the faithful father at his post, the watchdog guarding the sleeping babe. I am pierced by the desolation of my plight' (*Dusklands*, p.41). However, we have seen that even this babe, the text, cannot be regarded as his own, so that the stabbing of the boy must be seen as both the killing of the mongol boy within, that is, the denial of self as Other; and as a form of 'narcissistic rage . . . protecting a fragile self against further disintegration in response to the analyst's empathically deficient interventions' (Schafer, p.46). We have here the kind of aggression which J M Coetzee refers to, writing about Nabokov:

> Nabokov's protagonists (Kinbote, Humbert . . .) react aggressively (satirically) toward all systems (literally-critical, psychoanalytic) that seek to explicate (reduce) them. Why this aggressivity?
>
> Passage (a) below is from Jacques Lacan's *Discours de Rome* and discusses the frustration of the patient before the silence of the psychoanalyst. Passage (b) is from the end of Kinbote's commentary.
>
> (a) Is . . . not . . . [such] frustration inherent in the very discourse of the subject. Does the subject not become engaged in an ever-growing dispossession of that being of his, concerning which – by dint of sincere portraits which leave its idea no less incoherent, of rectifications which do not succeed in freeing its essence, of stays and defenses which do not prevent his statue from tottering, of narcissistic embraces which become like a puff of air in animating it – he ends up by recognizing that this being has never been anything more than his construct in the Imaginary and that this construct disappoints all his certitudes? For in this labor which he undertakes to reconstruct this construct *for another*, he finds again the fundamental alienation which made him construct it *like another one*

> [sic], and which has always destined it to be stripped from him *by another*.

> (b) God will help me, I trust, to rid myself of any desire to follow the example of two other characters in this work. I shall continue to exist. I may assume other disguises, other forms, but I shall try to exist. I may turn up yet, on another campus, as an old, happy, healthy, heterosexual Russian, a writer in exile, sans fame, sans audience, sans anything but his art.

By the end of his commentary, Kinbote ('Kinbote') faces not the authentic self-satisfaction of retiring into a version of the self created for and inserted into a real and authentic world, but the desperation (and resignation is but confirmed desperation, says Thoreau) of a being who finds that his being, gabbled for so long into an omnivorous silence, has never been anything more than his construct in the Imaginary. Without the bedrock of a real sense of the real, or alternatively of the reality of the imaginary, the process of self-elaboration must be felt not as an act of creation but as act of *decreation*, a shedding of exhausted self-constructs, a peeling of walnut shells in an endless search for the kernel.

> The aggressivity which the subject will experience at this point has nothing to do with the animal aggressivity of frustrated desire. Such a reference, which most people are content with, actually masks another one which is less agreeable for each and for all of us: the aggressivity of the slave whose response to the frustration of his labor is a desire for death.[44]

In our back-to-front reading of the novel, we have witnessed the subject becoming 'engaged in an ever-growing dispossession of that being of his'; we have witnessed, too, his insistence upon survival, his resolve to 'continue to exist'. In the stabbing of the child we see, finally, the subject's response to having his offspring (the text) created *like another* (the mongol boy as Other) and stripped from him *by another* (Marilyn as reader, and the particular discursive system which she applies to the text). Claiming to be the 'embodiment of the patient struggle of the intellect,' Eugene Dawn reveals himself to be 'the subject of a revolting body' (*Dusklands*, p.7); posing as the Phallic father, he acts as the son, cutting himself off deliberately in order to master a form of castration which he would otherwise experience passively. This self-castration is a desperate attempt to master, by repetition, the 'unmastery . . . the impotence, and . . . the unavoidable castration which inhere in *language*' (Felman, 'Turning the Screw', p.192).

Having tried, at all costs, to avoid being 'cut off prematurely' (*Dusklands*, p.2), Eugene Dawn finds himself effectively cut off: 'Amazing. I have been hit a terrible blow. How could that happen? I am utterly out of control' (*Dusklands*, p.44). Placed in an institution, he acquiesces in his being as language, or words:

> It has all come down to this (I ease myself in and tell over the clear, functional words): my bed, my window, my door, my walls, my room. These words I love . . . Around them I dance my slow, fat, happy dance of union, around them and around. I live in them and they in me. (*Dusklands*, p.45)

The text yields itself up to the process of supplementarity,[45] but continues to seek an anchoring point for meaning in the analyst-as-reader. Thus Eugene Dawn transfers onto his analysts the knowledge of the meaning of his aberrant act, saying:

> . . . I approve of the enterprise of exploring the self. I am deeply interested in my self. I should like to see in black and white an explanation of this disturbed and disturbing act of mine. (*Dusklands*, p.48)

The analysts-as-readers are Marilyn's counterparts. Eugene Dawn says of them:

> I watch their eyes and think: you want to know
> what makes me tick, and when you discover it
> you will rip it out and discard me. My secret is
> what makes me desirable to you, my secret is
> what makes me strong. (*Dusklands*, pp.49–50)

Like Marilyn, they wish to ferret out his secret; like Marilyn they make the connection between the brutalizing effects of the war and Eugene Dawn's work and behaviour. Their analysis and treatment is to be based on a knowledge of his personal history: '. . . their argument is that my treatment ought to start at my beginnings far in the past and work up gradually toward the present' (*Dusklands*, pp.45–46). This is the type of analysis which Lacan deplores, in a passage which, significantly, follows on directly from the passage cited by J M Coetzee:

> It is therefore readily conceivable how this aggressivity may respond to any intervention which, by denouncing the imaginary intentions of the discourse, dismantles the object constructed by the subject to satisfy them. This is in effect what is called the analysis of resistances, the dangerous aspect of which is immediately apparent . . . .
>
> Such an individual who, not hesitating to plead for a 'causalist' analysis that would aim to transform the subject in his present by learned explanations of his past, betrays well enough by his very intonation the anxiety that he wishes to spare himself – the anxiety of having to think that his patient's freedom may be dependent upon that of his own intervention. (*Ecrits*, pp.42–43)

This mode of analysis is the equivalent of the reading-as-archaeology to which I referred at the beginning of this chapter, reading as a search for origins in an attempt to establish meaning by means of reference to a determining context. While denying the effects of their own intervention, Eugene Dawn's analysts nevertheless demonstrate the counter-transferential structure of the reading process,[46] locating the knowledge of the 'secret' within the analysand-as-text itself. Arguing against the sequential narrative form of the case history, Roy Schafer suggests an alternative mode of interpretation:

> It soon becomes evident that, interpretively, one is working in a temporal circle. One works backward from what is told about the autobiographical present in order to define, refine, correct, organize, and complete an analytically coherent and useful account of the past, and one works forward from various tellings of the past to constitute that present and that anticipated future which are most important to explain . . . .
>
> I said that the analytic life history is a second-order history. The first-order history is that of the analytic dialogue. (This history is more like a set of histories that have been retold from multiple perspectives over the course of the analysis and that do not actually lend themselves to one seamless retelling . . . .) This history is situated in the present: it is always and necessarily a present account of the meanings and uses of the dialogue to date or, in other words, of the transference and resistance. (pp.52–53)

This describes the combined effects of anticipation and retroaction, and, as such, is the form of history that *Dusklands* as a whole gives us: a history of the ongoing dialogue inherent in the reading and re-writing process, a history that is 'more like a set of histories that have been told from multiple perspectives . . . and that do not actually lend themselves to one seamless retelling'.

And so we come full circle, back to the starting point of this reading, to Eugene Dawn's statement' 'I have high hopes of finding whose fault I am'. Reading 'fault' here as something that has gone wrong, a mistake, or an aberrance, we become caught up in a linear, causalist history, as we attempt to account for the 'fault' of this particular narrator in terms of a developmental history of modes of narration. If, however, we grant 'fault' its complementary (geological) significance as a rift or schism, or the significance it derives from the French '*faute*', meaning a lack, need or want, we are brought back to our own divided condition as readers, and to the lack at the source of our search for meaning. Meaning itself is the product of a schism between repressed, unconscious meanings and those meanings which are allowed to surface – which is not to say that those repressed meanings always stay in place: in French '*faute*' also signifies a transgression, and in Coetzee's novels we witness a reading and re-writing which constantly transgresses the meanings inherent in the forms they inhabit. Clearly, the 'fault' of the *I* must, in some measure, be located anew in each successive reading of the text, in the *I* of each critic who adopts this hollow shifter in order to pronounce upon the meaning of the novel. And so it becomes as difficult to find a way out of this reading as it was to find a way in to the novel, for what we have here is 'a story that begins in the middle, which is the present: the beginning is the beginning of the analysis . . . . The time is always present. The event is always an ongoing dialogue'. (Schafer, pp.52 and 53)

NOTES

1. Don Maclennan points out that the title of the novel carries echoes 'of *fin de siècle* works like Spengler's *Der Untergang das Abenlandes* and Nietzsche's *Twilight of the Gods*' (pp. 175–176).
2. H. Stuart Hughes, tracing the sources of the biological metaphor by means of which Spengler describes each culture's passage through childhood, youth, manhood, and old age, points out that Vico charted the typical course of history for each phase of a cycle as follows:

'Starting with a warrior or "heroic" age, they passed through a major phase of true civilization, arriving eventually at a second barbarism. This new "barbarism of reflection" was actually worse than the primitive 'barbarism of the senses", since it was mean-spirited and over-subtle, where the character of the heroic age had been generous and imaginative. With the advent of an intellectualized barbarism, civilized society had reached its limits, and the cycle ended.' (p. 9)

3. E.L. Doctorow cited by Mel Gussow, p. 12.
4. In the interview with Stephen Watson, Coetzee said: 'I came back to this country in 1971 with half of what later turned into *Dusklands*' (p. 23). Coetzee spent approximately ten years in the United States before returning to South Africa in 1971.
5. Peter Knox-Shaw says of *Dusklands*: 'The documentary presentation serves, of course, as an ironic mask to what is essentially an anti-documentary polemic . . . . Fact and fiction are subtly intermeshed in the narrative but we soon learn to distinguish fiction from historical report by the claim it establishes to a more potent truth' (p. 66).
6. Stephen Gray provides the most comprehensive description of these forms of writing, tracing their beginnings in the documentation of travel writers such as Sir Thomas Herbert (1638), François le Vaillant (1790), John Barrow (1806), and Cowper Rose (1829), through the novel of the imaginary voyage into Southern Africa – *The Travels of Baron Munchhausen* (1786 and 1792), *The Travels of Sylvester Tramper* (1813) and Jules Verne's *The Adventures of Three Russians and Three Englishmen in South Africa* (1872) and *L'Etoile du Sud* (1884) – to the adventures of the colonial hunter, of William Harris (1840), R. Gordon Cumming (1850) and William Baldwin (1852 and 1860). These latter are followed by hunting fictions, whose genealogy Gray traces 'from Kendall through Captain Marryat and R.M. Ballantyne, Haggard and Bertram Mitford and G.A. Henty through John Buchan to Stuart Cloete and Wilbur Smith' (p. 111).
7. Gray, pp. 106 and 111. In a work as comprehensive as this, and in which both *Dusklands* and Mannoni's *Prospero and Caliban* are mentioned, it is surprising that Gray fails to perceive *Dusklands* as constituting this reverse image.
8. See the interview in which Coetzee describes critical cinema as 'a cinema that is in the first place critical of its own formal assumptions, which are reflections of an ideological position' (my Chapter One, pp. 54–55).

9. It is interesting to find Catherine Belsey expressing the view that history has two meanings. Commenting on a paper by Tony Bennett, 'Texts in History: the Determinations of Readings and their Texts,' Belsey says:

'The history Bennett invokes appears to be more and more firmly the present-as-process, the process of which the present is a part, in which we exist at a specific moment that is understood to be both the product and the location of certain determinations. This meaning of history is important, and Marxist, but there is another important and Marxist meaning of history which needs emphasis, and this is history-as-the-past, the past which we produce from the present in order to show the present not only as its product but also as its difference, the past from which the present is differentiated. The history of the reception of literary texts shows how the present appropriates the text for itself. We need to study this history. But there are other histories to which both literary texts and their readings may give us access, enabling us to reproduce the past from the present, to identify its discontinuity with the present.' (p. 138)

10. Jacques Derrida, cited by Spivak in her Translator's Preface to *Of Grammatology*, p. lxxxvii.
11. See J.M. Coetzee, 'Time, Tense and Aspect in Kafka's 'The Burrow', pp. 577–78, and my Chapter One, p. 35.
12. Commenting upon the metafiction's attempt to pronounce upon its own meaning, Coetzee points out that this attempt will itself 'be open to the endless exegesis of the meta-myth we call history' ('Nabokov's *Pale Fire* and the Primacy of Art', p. 6).
13. Peter Knox-Shaw points out that 'Of the four documents that comprise the second part of *Dusklands* only the last is authentic', and that this document, the Deposition or *Relaas*, 'Together with an English translation by Dr. E.E. Mossop, appears in *The Journal of Wiker, Coetsé and Van Reenen*, edited , with an introduction and footnotes by Dr. E.E. Mossop (Van Riebeeck Society no. 15, Cape Town, 1935), pp. 276–291. The text given in *Dusklands* (pp. 131–133) is a translation by the author' (p. 66 and note 1, p. 80).
14. Of the three Lacanian orders (Imaginary, Symbolic, Real), the Real is the least mentioned and the most difficult to define. Alan Sheridan, in the Translator's Note to *Four Fundamental Concepts* provides a fairly comprehensive description of the term:

'The "real" emerges as a third term, linked to the symbolic

and the imaginary: it stands for what is neither symbolic nor imaginary, and remains foreclosed from the analytic experience, which is an experience of speech. What is prior to the assumption of the symbolic, the real in its "raw" state (in the case of the subject, for instance, the organism and its biological needs), may only be supposed, it is an algebraic *x*. This Lacanian concept of the "real" is not to be confused with reality, which is perfectly knowable: the subject of desire knows no more than that, since for it reality is entirely phantasmatic.

The term "real", which was at first of only minor importance, acting as a kind of safety rail, has gradually been developed, and its signification has been considerably altered. It began, naturally enough, by presenting, in relation to symbolic substitutions and imaginary variations, a function of constancy: "the real is that which always returns to the same place". It then became that before which the imaginary faltered, that over which the symbolic stumbles, that which is refractory, resistant. Hence the formula: "the real is the impossible". It is in this sense that the term begins to appear regularly, as an adjective, to describe that which is lacking in the symbolic order, the ineliminable residue of all articulation, the foreclosed element, which may be approached, but never grasped: the umbilical cord of the symbolic.' (p. 280)

15. This may be compared with Coetzee's commentary upon the way in which certain of the early travel writers, documenting their findings in Southern Africa, 'try to have the best of both worlds – the immediacy of narrative, the synopticism of description – by disguising the latter as the former' ('Idleness in Africa', p. 2)

16. Although Ricoeur uses Heidegger's notion of repetition, it overlaps, to a large degree, with the Freudian or Lacanian notion of repetition, as is evident from the following definition:

'Repetition, for Heidegger, means more than a mere reversal of the basic orientation of care toward the future; it means the retrieval of our most basic potentialities inherited from our past in the form of personal fate and collective destiny . . . . Through repetition, the character of time as stretching-along is rooted in the deep unity of time as future, past, and present, the backward move toward the past is retrieved in the anticipation of a project, and the endlessness of historical time is grafted on the finite structure of being-toward-death'. (pp. 180–82).

What appears to be Ricoeur's positive, and White's negative attitude toward narrative is merely a difference in the orientation of their arguments. What they both object to is an approach which considers 'history to be an explanatory endeavour that has severed its ties with storytelling' (Ricoeur, p. 171).

17. As opposed to sequential or explanatory history, a classification which Ricoeur derives from Maurice Mandelbaum, *The Anatomy of Historical Knowledge* (Baltimore, 1977), pp. 39–44.
18. Instead of the correct terms, Khoikhoin and Khoi-san, I use the terms Hottentot and Bushman throughout this chapter, as these are the terms used in 'The Narrative of Jacobus Coetzee'. They are the names which were given to the indigenous tribes by the European settlers at the Cape, and reflect the ethnocentric attitudes of these settlers.
19. Referring to certain temporal aspects that have been overlooked by structuralist models of the traditional quest narrative, Ricoeur says:

    'Before projecting the hero forward for the sake of the quest, many tales send the hero or heroine into some dark forest where he or she goes astray or meets some devouring beast (as in 'Little Red Riding Hood') or where the younger brother or sister has been kidnapped by some threatening force (like the birds in 'The Swan-Geese Tale'). These initial episodes do more than merely introduce the mischief that is to be suppressed; they bring the hero or heroine back into a primordial space and time that is more akin to the realm of dreams than to the sphere of action' (p. 185).
20. According to the model of the heroic quest, the hero 'is confronted with a series of trials which require that he choose to fight rather than to yield or flee, and which finally end in victory. The paradigmatic story ignores the nonchosen alternatives, yielding and losing. It knows only the chain of episodes that that leads the hero from challenge to victory' (Ricoeur, p. 184).
21. S. Leclaire, 'Les elements en jeu dans une psychanalyse,' *Cahiers pour l'Analyse*, no. 5, 1966, cited by Anika Lemaire in Jacques Lacan, p. 86. Lemaire explains the effects of the Phallus as signifier as follows:

    'Originally, the *infans* subject wishes *to be* the Phallus, the object of his mother's desire . . . . Castrated, that is, removed from his mother by the paternal interdiction, the child must renounce the omnipotence of his desire and accept a Law of limitation: he must assume his lack. Through the paternal metaphor, the child names his desire and renounces it. His true desire and the multiple phantasmatic forms it took are pushed back into the unconscious. This is the primal repression which determines accession to language and which substitutes a symbol and a Law for the Real of existence . . . . By assuming the Law of his father the child passes from the register of being (being the all-powerful phallus) to the register of having (having a limited and legitimate desire which can be formulated in an utterance) and enters into a quest for objects which are further and further removed from the initial object of his desire . . . . The desire to be the phallus which is lacking in the mother, the desire for union with the mother, is repressed and replaced by a substitute which names it and at the same time transforms it: the symbol.' (p. 87)

22. The drives are founded in the instinct, which, as Laplanche points out, is a 'bodily function essential to life', the most important function being that of feeding. The drives constitute a displacement of the instinct, so that the original ingestion extends to 'an entire series of possible relations; ingestion is no longer limited to food, since one can conceive of incorporation occurring in other bodily systems than the digestive apparatus; reference is thus made in psychoanalysis to incorporation at the level of other bodily orifices, of the skin or even, for instance, of the eyes' (pp. 16 and 20).
23. *In the Heart of the Country*, p. 114. Magda also says: 'I pick up and sniff and describe and drop, numbering the universe steadily with my words' (p. 27).
24. This property of narrative emerges from my discussion of time and narrative temporality in Chapter One. *Vide* Ingarden:

    ' . . . it is of the essence of what is future that it *does not have to be actualized* in a present, while, on the o han hand, the past cannot in general be conceived as something which would not have been actualized in some present. Then it would not be the past. It is only this actualization, realization, in a *certain entirely specific way*, which makes it *become* the past. Transience as a mode of being is contingent not only upon something else's becoming present, but above all on the *perpetual transformation* of the actuality of something present into that enigmatic 'no-longer-being-present-any-more,' while, at the same time, it *subsists in some mode of being* in the past as something of the past.' (p. 111).
25. *Vide* Benveniste: 'Consciousness of self is only possible if it is experienced by contrast. I use *I* only when I am speaking to

someone who will be a *you* in my address. It is this condition of dialogue that is constitutive of person, for it implies that reciprocally *I* becomes *you* in the address of the one who in his turn designates himself as *I*' (pp. 224–25).

26. Analyzing the poetics of failure which he finds in Achterberg's 'Ballade van de gasfitter', Coetzee says:

> 'The *I* fails in his goetic-poetic attempt (disguised as an attempt to restore the *I-You*) to constitute the *You* out of nothing. Having failed, this I is split off and discarded by a "real" I (in fact only the second in a theoretically infinite progression) who asserts his mere survival – that is to say, the mere existence of the "Ballad" – as the opposite of failure. Thus we find a three-level structure of left-hand failure and right-hand success (but I use the word "success" in a purely contrastive sense, so that "failure" shall not be vacant of meaning) with a bar of unknowing between them:

Left	*Right*
As unreflective, unreflexive gasfitter, I fail to meet the *You* of my life.	As absurd quester I fail to find You. But it is the nature of quests to confront me finally with myself alone.
I split off and kill the failed questing *I*. Only by splitting myself do I seem able to live.	Not only can I survive my failures, but I have created a way of sacrificing myself endlessly to quest-as-process
Seeking, as Romantic poet, to bring into being, through words, a *You* beyond words, I fail.	Prepared, as post-Romantic poet of failure, to construct a poetry that is no more than the processes of poetry, I am finished.

('Achterberg's "Ballade van de gasfitter",' p. 293)

27. Knox-Shaw points out that 'the bifurcated structure of *Dusklands* . . . opposes the exotic and Western (as victim and aggressor).' The gist of his complaint concerning the novel is that, in presenting 'a psychopathology of Western life', Coetzee confers the 'status of a categorical imperative upon violence', and thereby 'seriously depreciates the force of context' (pp. 76 and 79). The

point I am making is the opposite one, that Coetzee is concerned, precisely, to contextualize violence, in particular the violence of contemporary textual strategies.

28. Discussing René Girard's notion of mediated desire, Coetzee points out that:

 'Girard writes in a philosophical tradition stretching from Hegel to Sartre which attaches crucial importance to the ability of the subject to choose his own desires. In fact, in Hegel the stage of self-consciousness does not arrive, the 'I' does not come into being, until the subject becomes aware of itself as the locus of a lack, a desire. Thus the being of the 'I' is wholly implicated in its desires; and for the 'I' to yield its autonomy as a desiring subject is to yield its being. This yielding is what Girard calls an 'ontological sickness': in turning his desire toward the desiring mediator, the subject yields his ontological autonomy . . . . The question arises at once, of course: Why is the self so mistrusted that it cannot desire its own desires? Girard does not give a single answer to this question, but the argument that appears scattered over his discussion of the romanesque *novelists* is an essentially historical one . . . . It arises as a consequence of post-religious humanism and multiplies as social differences are levelled.' ('Triangular Structures of Desire in Advertising', pp. 36–37).

29. As Wilden points out:

 'What is surely essential to keep in mind about Lacan's use of the terms 'unconscious' and 'Other' is their relationship to the concept of *trans-subjectivity* that he emphasizes in the Discours [*Discours de Rome*, translated as *The Language of the Self*], which entails a correlative: the position of both unconscious and Other as third terms in any dual situation. Like Lévi-Strauss, Lacan seeks to rebut the notion of the unconscious as an individual, intrapsychic entity, and to restore it as a function to the collectivity which in fact creates and sustains it'. (pp. 264–65)

30. We find this image of auto-erotic incision repeated in *Life & Times of Michael K*, this time with positive connotations, as Michael K (representing the extra-linguistic self) joyfully cuts off his first pumpkin (representing the text) in a sacrificial ceremony:

 'Then came the evening when the first pumpkin was ripe enough to cut . . . K had marked it out as the first fruit, the firstborn. The shell was soft, the knife sank in without a struggle. The flesh, though still rimmed with green was a deep orange'. (p. 155)

31. This paper was passed on to me by Dr. Nick Visser at Rhodes University, Grahamstown (South Africa), but he has not been able to trace the author.

32. As Laplanche points out, 'For sexuality, it is the reflexive (*selbst* or *auto-*) moment that is constitutive: the moment of a turning back towards self, an 'autoerotism' in which the object has been replaced by a fantasy, by an object *reflected* within the subject' (*Life and Death in Psychoanalysis*, p. 88).

33. See note 26, p. 143, of this chapter for Coetzee's analysis of the way in which the failed Romantic quest is translated into the 'success' of the poetics of failure.

34. Flaubert, *Correspondence* (Paris: Conrad, 1929), II, 345, cited by Coetzee in the Achterberg paper, p. 293.

35. Knox-Shaw continues: 'An uneventful though fairly detailed dairy of this expedition, kept by Carel Frederik Brink, survives', and gives the details of this diary in a footnote: *The Journal of Carel Frederik Brink of the Journey into Great Namaqualand (1761–2) made by Captain Hendrik Hop* in *The Journals of Brink and Rhenius* . . . . trans. Dr. E.E. Mossop (Van Riebeeck Society no. 28, Cape Town, 1947), pp. 6–71. (p. 66 and note 2, p. 80)

36. Brooks, p. 286, cites Freud, 'The Theme of the Three Caskets' (1913), *Standard Edition*, 12, 299.

37. Knox-Shaw's objection to the novel is that it confers 'the status of a categorical imperative upon violence' (p. 79). The thrust of his argument implies that the presentation of violence would be acceptable if it were shown to be motived by economic gain. Thus, for example, he notes what he sees as significant departures from the original documents:

> 'The copper mine which Jacobus Coetzee has noted in his deposition and over which Brink on his way back expended his most detailed entry appears in *Dusklands* merely as a date carved on the rocks. The fictional narrative is distinguished throughout by a virtual effacement of economic motive. Nothing is made of the gold dust which Jacobus Coetzee gathered on the banks of the Great River and later displayed at the castle . . . . Moreover the poverty-stricken burgher of history hunts in *Dusklands* to satisfy refined bloodlust . . . rather than to procure the ivory for which he had been granted a permit by the Governor.
>
> In place of the mercenary concerns that predominate in most early colonial travelogues John Coetzee foregrounds his explorer's encounter with primitives' (p. 68)

38. Anika Lemaire gives a useful summary, supported by quotations from Lacan, of the various concepts covered by the term Other:

> The Other is:
>
> (i) language, the site of the signifier, the symbolic. 'The Other, by which name we designate a place essential to the structure of the symbolic.'
>
> (ii) the site of the intersubjectivity of patient and analyst, and hence the analytic dialogue. 'The Other is the locus in which is constituted the I who speaks to him who hears.'
>
> (iii) the unconscious in that it is constituted by signifying elements and that it is the subject's other. 'A conceptual junction must be established between this Elsewhere and the place where it (ça) thinks: another scene . . . this Other of the subjects.'
>
> If *it* (*ça*) speaks in the Other it is because it is there that the subject, by means of a logic anterior to any awakening of the signified, finds its signifying place. The discovery of what it articulates in that place, that is to say, enables us to grasp at the price of what split (Spaltung) it has been constituted.
>
> (iv) the third party witness invoked in analysis as soon as it is a question of formulating a truth. 'The Other is the guarantor of the good faith one evokes in the pact of speech.'
>
> (v) it is the Father or the Mother.
>
> Desire whose signifier is the phallus of which the giving and receiving are equally impossible for the neurotic, whether he knows that the Other does not have it, or knows that he does have it, because in either case his desire is elsewhere: it belongs to being.

Lemaire, p. 157. Lemaire cites from the French edition of *Ecrits*, and does not give page numbers for the citations.

39. As Coward and Ellis point out in their critique of Lévi-Strauss: 'These moments [of discrepancy which straddle the division between Nature and Culture] are treated as transgressions of an already-constituted system, rather than as evidence of its very process of constitution, which then would have to be analysed as a continuous process of contradiction' (p. 22).

40. Freud, *Beyond the Pleasure Principle*, p. 42, citing, in German, Mephistopheles in Faust, Part I [Scene 4]. The translation is given as 'Presses ever forward unsubdued.'

41. Claiming that the violence of war is a form of organized transgression, whose function is akin to that of religion, in that it controls violence *within* the society, Bataille says:

'Organised war with its efficient military operations based on discipline, which when all is said and done excludes the mass of the combatants from the pleasure of transgressing the limits, has been caught up in a mechanism foreign to the impulsions which set it off in the first place; war today has only the remotest connection with war as I have described it; it is a dismal aberration geared to political ends. Primitive war itself can hardly be defended: from the outset it bore the seeds of modern warfare, but the organised form we are familiar with today, that has travelled such a long way from the original organised transgression of the taboo, is the only one that would leave humanity unsatisfied.' (p. 80)

42. For example: 'like a pale stunned deep-sea fish I float' (p. 7); 'The frozen sea inside me thaws and cracks' (p. 14); 'Marilyn sat on the bed . . . in the cool silence of her aquarial world' (p. 35); 'Marilyn floats face down through my nights. I chop in my hook and pull. Flesh flakes off bloodless and she floats away' (p. 36); 'Grateful for the simple honesty of this dream . . . I drift in and out, drowning and waking' (p. 36); 'poor little Martin squirms in my arms like a fish' (p. 43); 'I am also sweating a lot and turning white, in a fishy way' (p. 43). All page numbers refer to *Dusklands*.

43. Lacan says:

'For it is clear that the state of nescience in which man remains in relation to his desire is not so much a nescience of what he demands, which may after all be circumscribed, as a nescience as to where he desires.

This is what I mean by formula that the unconscious is '*discours de l'Autre*' (discourse of the Other), in which the *de* is to be understood in the sense of the Latin *de* (objective determination) . . . .

But we must also add that man's desire is the *désir de l'Autre* (the desire of the Other) in which the *de* provides what grammarians call the 'subjective determination', namely that it is *qua* Other that he desires (which is what provides the true compass of human passion).' (*Ecrits*, p. 312)

44. Coetzee, 'Nabokov's Pale Fire and the Primacy of Art', p. 4. The passage from Lacan is to be found on p. 42 of *Ecrits*, in which the *Discours de Rome* appears under the title 'The function and field of speech and language in psychoanalysis.'

45. Derrida describes the process of supplementarity as follows:

' . . . the indefinite process of supplementarity has always already *infiltrated* presence, always already inscribed there the space of repetition and the splitting of the self. Representation *in the abyss* of presence is not an accident of presence; the desire of presence is, on the contrary, born from the abyss (the indefinite multiplication) of representation, from the representation of representation, etc. The supplement itself is quite exorbitant, in every sense of the word.' (*Of Grammatology*, p. 163)

46. Felman describes reading as counter-transference when she says: 'If it is precisely out of *lack of knowledge* that the reading-process springs, the very act of reading implies at the same time the assumption that knowledge *is*, exists, but is *located in the Other*: in order for reading to be possible, there has to be knowledge in the Other (in the text, for instance), and it is that knowledge in the Other, of the Other, which must be *read*, which has to be appropriated, taken from the Other.' ('Turning the Screw', p. 157)

3 In The Heart of the Country

When I was a baby, I fancy my parents left me out in the frost one night, and I got nipped internally – it feels so!

Oliver Schreiner, *The Story of an African Farm*, p.187

I move through the world not as a knifeblade cutting the wind, or as a tower with eyes, like my father, but as a hole, a hole with a body draped around it, the two spindly legs hanging loose at the bottom and the two bony arms flapping at the sides and the big head lolling on top. I am a hole crying to be whole.

J M Coetzee, *In the Heart of the Country*, p.41

Coetzee's second novel takes the form of a monologue conducted by Magda, a woman located on an isolated Karroo farm, where the only figures with whom she might communicate – her stern and distant father, and the servants, Hendrik and Klein-Anna – do not reciprocate her desire for an exchange of words. Magda recounts the details of her father's seduction of Klein-Anna, and of her own outrage, which prompts successive fantastical scenes of patricide, followed by scenes of her rape by Hendrik.

While in *Dusklands* the erectile and penetrating Phallus is the metaphor operative in defining the enterprise of adventure/exploration writing, in *In the Heart of the Country* it is the female cavity, the hole, which functions as a metaphor for the pastoral mode, a mode which traditionally articulates a sense of loss, or nostalgia, for a former, more pleasurable state of being. It can be argued that the Lacanian Phallus, as the 'signifier intended to designate as a whole the effects of the signified' (*Ecrits*, p.285), is itself a '*manque à être* – a lack which is brought into being' (Wilden, p.188), and that therefore the lack of external genitalia cannot provide a more appropriate metaphor for the condition of absence or loss;

it is, however, as a means of reference to the function of two distinct genres within a particular phase of the colonization of South Africa that these metaphors of sexual identity are relevant. Adventure/exploration writing corresponds to the historical phase of opening up an unknown territory, and the Phallus stands for the hero who strides out and forward to conquer a potentially unlimited space. Pastoral, by contrast, corresponds to the phase of agrarian settlement, when the simple, natural values of farm life are already being threatened by encroaching urbanization: the land has been fenced in, boundaries established, and the forward gaze and active penetration of the explorer is replaced by the longing backward look and the sterility and stasis of rural life in the colony.

In the context of South African writing in English, the pastoral and liberal modes overlap to a large degree, and the imported liberal tradition, too, may be seen as the source of the lack or void which characterizes the genre, and which makes the metaphor of the cavity an appropriate one. *In the Heart of the Country* is, I believe, most specifically a re-writing of Olive Schreiner's *The Story of an African Farm*, a novel which combines the liberal and pastoral modes, and from which the liberal tradition in English South African writing derives. Stephen Gray remarks of this novel:

> The adventure novel offered easy solutions to every African dilemma. The tradition of the liberal realist novel in South Africa offers few.
>
> Thus the centre of Schreiner's novel is quite elsewhere from where the critics to date have looked for it. In a George Eliot or a Hardy one finds the focus of the entire moral and aesthetic universe at the core of their fictions; in Schreiner one finds – nothingness. It is only once one feels the South African novel in the imitative liberal mode to be a game played about a void, a vacuum, that it can be seen to emerge as a fundamentally different type of novel from those with which it, to its discredit, is constantly forced to bear

comparison. (p.155)

If Magda and, via her, both Coetzee's and Schreiner's novels, are presented as holes crying out to be whole, the significance of this metaphor can be explained, at least in part, by reference to their anticipation of a failure to find fulfilment within the 'moral and aesthetic universe' of South African writing and readership. The arid, semi-desert setting of the Karroo farm and the isolated, semi-orphaned situation of the protagonists, Lyndall and Magda, are parallels which are immediately apparent and which function as further metaphors of this condition of textual isolation. Thus Magda says:

> I live neither alone nor in society but as it were among children . . . . That is why my words are not words such as men use to men. Alone in my room with my duties behind me and the lamp steadily burning, I creak into rhythms that are my own, stumble over the rocks of words that I have never heard on another tongue. (*HC*, pp.7–8)

She refers to her literary predecessors[1] when she says: 'I am the one who stays in her room reading or writing or fighting migraines. The colonies are full of girls like that, but none, I think, so extreme as I' (*HC*, p.1), and, it would seem, to Schreiner and the pseudonym of Ralph Iron which she initially adopted when she says:

> There is no doubt about it, what keeps me going . . . is my determination, my iron determination, my iron intractable risible determination to burst through the screen of names into the goatseye view of Armoede and the stone desert, to name only these, in despite of all the philosophers have said (and what do I, poor provincial blackstocking, know about philosophy, as the lamp gutters and the clock strikes ten?). (*HC*, o.18)

The metaphor of the cavity, or hole may be seen to be

relevant to the pastoral mode, and to Schreiner's novel in particular, with respect not only to content and context – that is to say, with respect to the void created by the absence of a moral and aesthetic universe – but also with respect to structure. Whereas the adventure novel, or novel of exploration, generates the linear, sequential movement of the discourse, in the pastoral genre there is no in-built factor which can generate this necessary momentum. While in *Dusklands* the continuity generated by the journeys within the major sections of the novel co-exists alongside the discontinuous structure of the novel as a whole, Magda's discourse does not attain the continuity of narrative at all. Indeed, following W J T Mitchell, who, in his editor's note to the special issue of *Critical Inquiry* on 'Narrative: The Illusion of Sequence', asks, 'How much distortion can a narrative endure before it becomes something else?' (p.3), one might question whether the term narrative may legitimately be applied to the numbered segments of speech which constitute this novel.[2] Whereas in the novel of exploration it is, of course, movement in space (whether this movement be in the nature of an advance or a retreat, and whether the space be an interior or exterior space) which is the structuring principle of the narrative, in *In the Heart of the Country* we have a form of discourse which cannot, or will not, produce the 'illusion of sequence', and which is therefore articulated around the very principle of stasis: it is a desiring hole which cannot achieve the 'whole-ness' of narrative continuity.

The metaphor of the cavity, the hole, the absence, informs Coetzee's psychoanalytic reading of *The Story of an African Farm* in the same way that the metaphor of the Phallus informs his reading of the adventure/exploration novel.[3] In *Dusklands*, which is also a deconstructive reading and re-writing of the historical-cum-anthropological discourse, Coetzee produces a narrative structured according to a form of regenerative repetition; repetition as a return to origins which is able to inform, and indeed, generate, the movement into the future. In terms of the project of the narrating self, *Dusklands* presents us with a series of challenges conducted from a position *within* the Symbolic against *fixation* in the

Symbolic; a series of attempts to confront, transgress or retreat out of the forms of communication prescribed within the Symbolic. As I indicated in the previous chapter, the various sections of the novel stand as metaphors of the attempt on the part of the narrating self to avoid mediation in the Symbolic, and to return to an immediate, dual relationship between the self and its image in the text: in this case the erect Phallus stands for an attitude of (fallacious) mastery toward the text itself and toward language in general. In *In the Heart of the Country* the orientation of the challenge is reversed, as Coetzee's reading and re-writing of Schreiner's novel implies that it constitutes a thoroughly ambivalent 'challenge' to the Symbolic undertaken from a (metaphorically) pre-Symbolic position in the Imaginary. This challenge is ambivalent because, as we shall see, it expresses a desire to accede to a position in the Symbolic, in order to achieve an identity and engage in communication there, and expresses a simultaneous desire to avoid fixation in the Symbolic, enacting a revolt against the language of authority and the forms of the tradition.

From one perspective, the hole which is Magda represents the gap, or lack, in which desire has its genesis, and in which these novels, in turn, have their source. Thus Magda asks, 'What does one do with desire?' (*HC*, p.113), and, addressing the servant, Anna, says:

> 'Weet jy hoe ek voel, Anna? Soos 'n groot leemte, a great emptiness filled with a great absence, with an absence which is a desire to be filled. Yet I know that nothing will ever fill me. It is the first condition of life for desire not to be fulfilled, otherwise life ceases. Fulfilment does not fulfil . . . .'
>
> I lean over her, I caress her arms, I hold her limp hands in mine. That is what she gets from me, colonial philosophy, words with no history behind them, homespun, when she wants stories . . . . But these words of mine come from nowhere and go nowhere, they have no past or future, they whistle across the flats in a desolate eternal present, feeding

no one. (*HC*, p.114)

However, there is also a sense in which the hole can be seen as representing the *non-achievement* of sexual identity, the failure to accede to an identity in the Symbolic, and from this perspective the sexual metaphor refers to a nascent mode of writing, a mode of writing which has not achieved recognition and has not established an identity for itself in relation to its literary paternity. When Magda says, 'these words of mine come from nowhere and go nowhere, they have no past or future', she describes the situation of the colonial writer, caught in a kind of void, a hollow space, between the overpowering literary tradition of the country of origin, and the absence of tradition in the country of residence. This is a mode of writing which wishes to achieve recognition within the tradition of English literature, while seeking to avoid subservience to this tradition; it appears to have no past or future because it perceives itself as cut off from the tradition, and cannot anticipate evoking a response, either within the tradition, or within the new setting of the colony, which has no literature, no tradition of its own.

With respect to *The Story of an African Farm*, this is an ironic diagnosis of a novel which has come to be regarded as the seminal text in the tradition of white South African writing in English,[4] although it expresses no sense of its capacity to inseminate a tradition, or to achieve fruition of any kind. Schreiner's ambivalent attitude toward the English literary tradition becomes evident when one considers that, as Dan Jacobson points out in his Introduction to the novel, her 'first, adolescent attempt at a novel, *Undine*, was for the most part set in England: a never-never England taken entirely from books, where, when the characters are not drinking tea on the lawn or walking through vaguely described woods, the snow is incessantly falling'. Jacobson continues:

> From the hundreds of pages of *Undine* devoted to that fantasy-land we can judge just how difficult it was for her to make plausible to herself the material around her as a source of fiction: her

> snow-less, wood-less, lawn-less Karroo, about which not a word had ever appeared in any novel. To anyone who reflects seriously on what it must be like to grow up within a society that has never been given any kind of a voice of its own, there must appear something almost heroic about the opening of *The Story of an African Farm*, with its first fine sentence: 'The full African moon poured down its light from the blue sky into the wide, lonely plain . . . ' (Introduction to *The Story of an African Farm*, p.18)

Stephen Gray points out that *The Story of an African Farm* is the equivalent of Emerson's declaration of independence from British culture:[5] as such it is articulated around the theme of powerlessness – Lyndall says, 'When that day comes, and I am strong, I will hate everything that has power, and help everything that is weak' (*SAF*, p. 93) – and around the successive attempts to challenge the power to which Schreiner, as writer, sees herself subjected. These attempts are, however, presented as abortive, as is the project of the novel as a whole. In the dedication, Schreiner describes the novel as 'This little firstling of my pen' (*SAF*, p.25), but Gray points out that, 'According to her husband, one of the many working titles Schreiner adopted for *The Story of an African Farm* during the writing of it was *Mirage*, to which was to be added the epigraph: 'Life is a series of abortions' (Gray, p.153). Lyndall's child dies soon after birth, Waldo's machine and his carving, each nine months in the making, are destroyed or taken from him, and the novel ends with the death of both Lyndall and Waldo, male and female counterparts of what may be regarded as a single protagonist.

As I have indicated, Coetzee re-writes this series of abortions in terms of a failure to anticipate a future for the novel, either within the tradition it is challenging, or within its new context of readership. What we have in *In the Heart of the Country*, then, is a psychoanalytic reading and re-writing of *The Story of an African Farm* as a struggle conducted from within the Imaginary (metaphorically speaking, because, as a linguistic struggle, it must necessarily be conducted within the Symbolic); a struggle aimed at achieving the necessary recognition and identity in the Symbolic, while at the same time it resists insertion in the Symbolic, and the repressions and restrictions this would involve. Thus in the figure of Magda we have a narrating self who 'seems arrested in a narcissistic stage of the kind that takes over the psychic economy after a severe injury or loss to the self . . . . a sense of loss which will not be transcended into something else, but perversely explores its own mechanism, its own productivity.'[6] In a passage like the following, Magda articulates an ambivalent attitude toward self-transcendence, and explores the mechanism and productivity of her loss in a way which suggests that this is a deliberate parody of Schreiner's literary enterprise:

> Aching to form the words that will translate me into the land of myth and hero, here I am still my dowdy self in a dull summer heat that will not transcend itself. What do I lack? I weep and gnash my teeth. Is it mere passion? Is it merely a vision of a second existence passionate enough to carry me from the mundane of being into the doubleness of signification? Do I not quiver at every pore with a passion of vexation? Is it that my passion lacks will? Am I an angry yet somehow after all complacent farmyard spinster, wrapped in the embrace of my furies? Do I truly wish to get beyond myself? The story of my rage and its dire sequel: am I going to climb into this vehicle and close my eyes and be carried downstream over the rapids, through the broken water, to wake refreshed on the quiet estuary? What automatism is this, what liberation is it going to bring me, and without liberation what is the point of my story? Do I feel rich outrage at my spinster fate? Who is behind my oppression? You and you I say, crouching in the cinders, stabbing my finger at father and stepmother. But why have I not run away from them? As long as

> an elsewhere exists where I can lead a life, there are heavenly fingers pointing at me too. Or am I, hitherto unbeknown to me, but now alas known, reserved for a more complex fate: to be crucified head downward as a warning to those who love their rage and lack all vision of another tale? But what other tale is there for me? Marriage to the neighbour's second son? I am not a happy peasant. I am a miserable black virgin, and my story is my story, even if it is a dull black blind stupid miserable story ignorant of its own meanings and of all its many possible untapped happy variants. I am I. Character is fate. History is God. Pique, pique, pique. (*HC*, pp.4–5)

The loss which Schreiner, as novelist, experienced was the loss of a literary 'father', of a literary tradition upon which she could rely both as a point of departure and as a destination; it was also the loss of a 'mother' country, of a physical environment and a cultural milieu which could function as taken-for-granted subject matter. The fact that Lyndall is an orphan is not without significance, nor is the fact that her guardian, a kind of 'stepmother', is Tant Sannie, a coarse and ignorant Afrikaner woman. The equivalent of Tant Sannie in *In the Heart of the Country* is the 'new wife', Magda's stepmother, 'a lazy big-boned voluptuous feline woman with a wide slow-smiling mouth' (*HC*, p.1). Magda will not talk to this woman, saying:

> I ask myself: Why, since the moment she came clip-clop across the flats in the dog-cart . . . have I refused speech with her, stubbornly exerting myself to preserve the monologue of my life? . . . . Is it possible that I am a prisoner not of the lonely farmhouse and the stone desert but of my stony monologue? (*HC*, p.12)

It would seem that Magda's refusal to engage in speech with the stepmother represents Schreiner's refusal to recognize the inhabitants of the colony as an audience whose response she might evoke. Via the figure of Magda, Coetzee shows us the novelist trapped in her stony monologue, unable to make her speech achieve the condition of dialogue; and shows us a mode of writing which remains locked in the Oedipal struggle, a struggle in which the daughter, while refusing paternal authority, nevertheless demands the father's recognition, refusing, also, to transfer the demand for recognition to the mother.

Via the figure of Magda, we are shown a narrator alternately engaging in a violent confrontation with the father, and in a narcissistic relationship with its image in the text. This attitude of narcissistic self-sufficiency in Schreiner's novel is evident in the scenes in which Lyndall addresses her image in the mirror:

> The large dark eyes from the glass looked back at her. She looked deep into them.
>
> 'We are all alone, you and I', she whispered; no one helps us, no one understands us; but we will help ourselves'. . . . 'We shall never be quite alone, you and I,' she said; 'we shall always be together, as we were when we were little.'
>
> The beautiful eyes looked into the depths of her soul.
>
> 'We are not afraid; we will help ourselves!' she said. She stretched out her hand and pressed it over them on the glass. 'Dear eyes! we will never be quite alone till they part us; – till then!' (*SAF*, pp.242–43)

On her deathbed Lyndall again looks into the mirror:

> Then the white face on the pillow looked into the white face in the glass. They had looked at each other often so before. It had been a child's face once, looking out above its blue pinafore; it had been a woman's face, with a dim shadow in the eyes, and a something which had said, 'We are not afraid,

> you and I; we are together; we will fight, you and I', Now tonight it had come to this. The dying eyes on the pillow looked into the dying eyes in the glass; they knew that their hour had come. She raised one hand and pressed the stiff fingers against the glass. They were growing very stiff. She tried to speak to it, but she would never speak again. (*SAF*, pp.283–84)

Magda's discourse contains several references to the mirror, which appear to function as allusions to these passages from Schreiner's novel. Thus Magda says, for example:

> The mirror. Inherited from my long-lost mother, whose portrait it must be that hangs on the wall of the dining-room over the heads of my silent father and my silent self, though why it is that when I conjure up that wall I find below the picture-rail only a grey blur, a strip of grey blur, if such is imaginable, traced out by my eye along the wall . . . . Inherited from my long-lost mother, whom one day I shall find, the mirror fills the door of the wardrobe opposite my bed. It gives me no pleasure to pore over reflections of my body, but when I have sheathed myself in my nightgown . . . . I sometimes leave the light burning and recline abed sustained on my elbow and smile at the image that reclines abed facing me on an elbow, and sometimes even talk to it, or her. (*HC*, p.21)

If, as this passage suggests, 'The precursor of the mirror is the mother's face', the (Lacanian) mirror must, in turn, be seen as the precursor of the child's entry into the world of the Father, of the Symbolic. As Lemaire says, the mirror stage is 'the first articulation of the 'I', it preforms that I through the entry into the imaginary which precedes the symbolic' (p.177). Magda has been separated from the mother, but has not yet been granted admission to the Father's world:

> My father creates absence. Wherever he goes he leaves absence behind him. The absence of himself above all – a presence so cold, so dark, so remote as to be itself an absence, a moving shadow casting a blight on the heart. And the absence of my mother. My father is the absence of my mother, her negative, her death. (*HC*, p.37)

Within the Lacanian paradigm, the Father creates the absence of the mother through his interdiction of the infant's desire to be the mother's complement, to be the absent phallus; an interdiction which, as Lemaire points out, takes the form of the commandment: 'thou shalt not sleep with thy mother' (p.82). In this way the symbolic Father performs the symbolic castration on which is founded the assumption of sexual identity: instead of 'being' the phallus, the child becomes the one who either 'has the phallus or . . . does not have it, or . . . who can give or receive it in a full sexual relationship' (Lemaire, p.83). While the boy represses castration, the girl denies it:[8] perceiving the mother to be castrated, she rejects her, and turns to the father for recognition.[9] Perceived as a rival for the father's love, the mother of the Oedipal stage is inevitably regarded as distinct from the tender, loving mother of the pre-Oedipal stage, is inevitably perceived as a 'stepmother'. Thus Magda says of the woman her father brings home:

> She is the new wife, therefore the old one is dead. The old wife was my mother, but died so many years ago that I barely recall her. I must have been very young when she died, perhaps only a newborn babe. From one of the farthest oubliettes of memory I extract a faint grey image, the image of a faint grey frail gentle loving mother huddled on the floor, one such as any girl in my position would be likely to make up for herself. (*HC*, p.2)

And of the father she says:

> The land is full of melancholy spinsters like me, lost

> to history, blue as roaches in our ancestral homes, keeping a high shine on the copperware and laying in jam. Wooed when we were little by our masterful fathers, we are bitter vestals, spoiled for life. The childhood rape: someone should study the kernel of truth in this fancy. (*HC*, p.3)

She refers here to the fantasy of seduction by the father, which Freud has identified as 'the expression of the typical Oedipus complex in woman' ('The Psychology of Women', p.155).

In *In the Heart of the Country* the Oedipal struggle is articulated, thematically, in the form of a violent disruption of the family romance, in which Magda's repeated killings of the father replicate the pattern of Schreiner's novel, which has disposed of the father from the outset (Lyndall is an orphan), and which produces and gets rid of father figures in the form of Waldo's father, old Otto, and Bonaparte Blenkins, who, in wooing Tant Sannie, usurps the father's position. The triangular structure of the Oedipal drama is made explicit in Magda's reference to herself 'crouching in the cinders, stabbing [her] finger at father and stepmother' (thereby alluding to the archetypal structure of the fairytale), and in the opening segment of her speech, in which she says:

> I am the one who stays in her room reading or writing or fighting migraines . . . My father is the one who paces the floorboards back and forth, back and forth in his slow black boots. And then, for a third, there is the new wife, who lies late abed. Those are the antagonists. (*HC*, p.1)

Lyndall's powerlessness is located in her position as a woman and as a child: she says to Waldo, 'we will not be children always; we shall have power too, some day' (*SAF*, p.127), and expatiating on the fate of women she says:

> We see the complexion we were not to spoil, and the white frock, and we look into our own great

> eyes. Then the curse begins to act on us. It finishes its work when we are grown women, who no more look out wistfully at a more healthy life; we are contented. We fit our sphere as a Chinese woman's foot fits her shoe, exactly, as though God had made both – and yet He knows nothing of either. In some of us the shaping to our end has been quite completed. The parts we are not to use have been quite atrophied, and have even dropped off; but in others, and we are not less to be pitied, they have been weakened and left. We wear the bandages, but our limbs have not grown to them; we know that we are compressed, and chafe against them. (*SAF*, p.189)

Both here and in the passage which I have used as an epigraph to this chapter we find images of castration, images which, in *In the Heart of the Country*, are translated into Magda's insistence upon her own incomplete condition: 'I am incomplete, I am a being with a hole inside me' (*HC*, p.9), she says, referring to her sense of loss, and to the failure to achieve sexual identity via the Father's recognition.

As in the case of Lyndall, Magda's situation as a woman and as a child implies a position of powerlessness, or servitude, in relation to the all-powerful language of the Oedipal Father. In the father's speech she is not named, but is always only '*kind*' (child), and, as in the following passage, she repeatedly reflects upon her status as child:

> Now those booted feet come up the passage. I close the door and push against it. I have known that tread all my life, yet I stand with mouth agape and pulse drumming. He is turning me into a child again! The boots, the thud of the boots, the black brow, the black eyeholes, the black hole of the mouth from which roars the great NO, iron, cold, thunderous, that blasts me and buries me and locks me up. I am a child again, an infant, a grub, a white shapeless life with no arms, no legs, nothing even to grip the earth with, a

sucker, a claw . . . . (*HC*, p.51)

Magda demands recognition that will give her a 'Name, a place in the family constellation, an original signifier of self and subjectivity' (Lemaire, p.83): she calls upon the father, saying:

> Do you not see that it is only despair, love and despair, that makes me talk this way? Speak to me! Do I have to call on you in words of blood to make you speak? What horrors more do you demand of me? Must I carve out my beseechings with a knife on your flesh? Do you think you can die before you have said Yes to me? (*HC*, pp.71–2)

At the same time, the killings of the father represent the attempt to subvert the power of the Father as representative of the Law; they mark the resistance of these texts (both Schreiner's and Coetzee's) to the repressions and restrictions which the acceptance of the father's interdiction – the great NO – would impose. In Schreiner's novel this resistance is manifest in Lyndall's proclamation of sexual freedom in her relationship with her unnamed lover, a relationship which she embarks on because, as she says, 'I like to experience, I like to try' (*SAF*, p.238). Schreiner does not, however, succeed in casting off the restrictions imposed by the tradition, for all she can do is allude, in veiled terms, to the sexual aspects of the liaison, and make a gesture of freedom in having Lyndall refuse to marry the man, thus resisting his desire to master her (she says: 'I have seen enough to tell me that you love me because you cannot bear to be resisted, and want to master me,' *SAF*, p.238).

The killings mark the attempt to speak a new language, to effect a metamorphosis, or new birth, out of the language of the Father. Having axed the father and the stepmother in their bed, Magda says: Until this bloody afterbirth is gone there can be no new life for me' (*HC*, p.15). Then, having once again killed the father, this time by shooting him as he lies in bed with the servant, Klein-Anna, she says:

> The bundle, hauled out again, lies like a great grey larva at the graveside, and I, its tireless mother, instinct-driven, set again about stowing it in the safe place I have chosen, though for what hibernation, with what cell-food, toward what metamorphosis I do not know . . . (*HC*, p.92)

This is one of numerous images of herself as insect,[10] images which function to suggest that her speech is instinct-driven in the same manner as the blindly compulsive activities of the lowest forms of life, in which the instincts are minimally displaced into drives,[11] and persist in their most elementary form. (This suggestion is endorsed by Magda's reference to her 'dull black blind miserable story ignorant of its meaning and of all its many possible untapped happy variants', *HC*, p.5). This would also appear to be an additional way of implying that Magda has not gained access to the Symbolic, and is therefore not yet fully 'human', that is to say that the form of discourse which she represents remains locked in the Imaginary. Citing Lacan, Jameson points out

> 'That a name, no matter how confused, designates a particular person – this is precisely what the passage to the human state consists in. If we must define that moment in which man [sic] becomes human, we would say that it is at that instant when, as minimally as you like, he enters into a symbolic relationship'. It would seem fair to observe that Lacan's attention to the components of language has centered on those kinds of words, primarily names and pronouns, on those slots which, like the shifters generally, anchor a free-floating syntax to a particular subject, those verbal joints, therefore, at which the insertion of the subject into the Symbolic is particularly detectable . . . . Such names thus provide a liberation from the here-and-now of the Imaginary; for the separation, through language, of the paternal function from the biological father is precisely what permits the child to take the father's place in his turn. The Law, as

> Lacan calls it, the order of abstraction, is thus also what releases the subject from the constraints of his immediate family situation and from the 'bad-immediacy' of the pre-Symbolic period.[12]

What Jameson describes here is the process by means of which the Paternal Metaphor is installed in the subject.[13] The paternal Metaphor necessitates the 'death' of the father in that the biological father (or the person who plays this role in relation to the child) is replaced by the internalized symbol of the father, a signifier of the Law and of sexual identity. The violent and repetitive nature of Magda's killings of the father, however, implies that what is represented here is not the normal process whereby the child accedes to sexual identity, to subjectivity, but the symptom of a fixation: evidence that this necessary transition has not been successfully effected. Clearly, this is not the kind of repetition which involves the vital recuperation of the past for the purpose of the subject's re-insertion in a re-negotiated future: this latter is repetition of a positive kind, which occurs within the transferential relationship of a dialogue. As Schafer says:

> If analysis is a matter of moving in a direction, it is a moving forward into new modes of constructing experience. On this account, one must retell the story of regression to the infantile neurosis within the transference; for even though much of its matter may be defined in terms of the present version of the past, the so-called regression is necessarily a progression. (pp.36–37)

The repetitions of Magda's speech provide an analysis of Schreiner's situation as writer; an analysis which implies that Schreiner's writing, in its failure to anticipate evoking a response of any kind, cannot translate itself from monologue to dialogue, and therefore cannot achieve even the temporary satisfaction of repetition accomplished within the transferential relationship: it is incapable of 'moving forward into new modes of constructing experience', although it is presented as desperately desirous of doing so. Thus Magda says:

> For the day will come when I must have another human being, must hear another voice, even if it speaks only abuse. This monologue of the self is a maze of words out of which I shall not find a way until someone else gives me a lead. I roll my eyeballs, I pucker my lips, I stretch my ears, but the face in the mirror is my face and will go on being mine even if I hold it in the fire till it drips. No matter with what frenzy I live the business of death or wallow in blood or soapsuds, no matter what wolfhowls I hurl into the night, my acts, played out within the macabre theatre of my self, remain mere behaviour. I offend no one, for there is no one to offend but the servants and the dead. How shall I be saved? (*HC*, p.16)

Magda represents a mode of writing which, in Jameson's words, fails to release itself 'from the "bad-immediacy" of the pre-Symbolic period;' fails to emerge from the dual Imaginary relationship of the self and its image, an emergence which can be achieved 'only by the genesis of a third term, a mediatory 'concept' which, by determining each term, orders them into reversible and progressive relations which can be developed in language'.[14] 'How shall I be saved?' she asks, implying that without the presence of another human voice there is no Other which can intervene as the third term and translate her 'mere behaviour' into a speech act. There is a sense in which Magda's alternative killings and resuscitations of the father resemble the games played by the infant in the isolation of its cot, the games which Lacan refers to as

> the repetitive games in which subjectivity brings together mastery of its dereliction and the birth of the symbol.
>
> These are the games of occultation which Freud, in a flash of genius, revealed to us so that we might recognize in them that the moment in which desire becomes human is also that in which the child

> is born in language. (*Ecrits*, p.103)

The translator's note describes these games as follows:

> The child would associate the appearance and disappearance of a toy that he alternately threw away and drew back again with the vowel sounds 'o' and 'a', which Freud interpreted as those of the German words for 'gone!' (*Fort*!) and 'here!' (*Da*!). The repetition of this game was apparently evidence of the child's beginning to master his environment actively through speech, for the active repetition seemed clearly to replace the passivity of the situation where the child's mother was alternately present and absent. (Sheridan, note 113, p.112)

Disposing of the father and then bringing him back, Magda represents Schreiner's attempt 'to master [her] environment actively through speech', but this mastery of her dereliction in the (apparent) absence of an interlocutor means that her speech cannot progress beyond these games. Her repetitions, rather than constituting a consciously co-ordinated return to origins, are a blind and instinctive return of the repressed. And, rather than enacting a form of regression which allows for a progression, the killings of the father are repetitions which mark time: they constitute what Durand refers to as

> . . . the return of the narcissistic ego, its stasis, its empty time, and its suspension from the very knowledge [sic] of the lack of the absent father. It is a form of 'eternal recurrence' in which there is no circularity, but rather a paradoxical combination of linearity and circularity, of form and formlessness. . . . ('The Captive King', p.63)

This notion of a paradoxical combination of linearity and circularity and of form and formlessness is one which may fruitfully be applied to Schreiner's novel (Gray makes the point that the view of life operative in *The Story of an African Farm* is 'one that needs the conventions in order to be felt unconventional, and needs the built-in sense of form in order to express formlessness', p.143); later in this chapter I will show how in Coetzee's novel this notion is translated into a structural principle.

The 'eternal recurrence' which Durand speaks of is evident in Magda's ongoing attempts to speak a new language, to engage in a dialogue, to achieve a name and an identity of some kind. Magda's attempt to establish a relationship with the servants, Hendrik and Klein-Anna, would appear to represent Schreiner's liberal attitude toward the indigenous people of the colony,[15] but here again the triangular structure of the Oedipal drama is repeated. The congruence, in structural terms, between the primary and secondary triangles is evident in the duplication of images in sections 1 and 38:

> Today my father brought home his new bride. They came clip-clop across the flats in a dog-cart drawn by a horse with an ostrich-plume waving on its forehead, dusty after the long haul. Or perhaps they were drawn by two plumed donkeys, that is also possible. My father wore his black swallowtail coat and stovepipe hat, his bride a widebrimmed sunhat and a white dress tight at waist and throat. (*HC*, p.1)

> Six months ago Hendrik brought home his new bride. They came clip-clop across the flats in the donkey-cart, dusty after the long haul from Armoede. Hendrik wore the black suit passed on to him by my father with an old wide-brimmed felt hat and a shirt buttoned to the throat. His bride sat by his side clutching her shawl, exposed and apprehensive. (*HC*, p.17)

Disposing of the father at the apex of the triangle, Magda creates a gap which is filled by Hendrik, thus replicating the liberal fantasy of replacing the old authority with the new.

This fantasy is presented as an attempt by Magda to realize her sexual identity, and she asks:

> Am I now a woman? Has this made me into a woman? So many tiny events, acts, movements one after another, muscles pulling bones this way and that, and their upshot is that I can say, I am finally a woman, or, Am I finally a woman? (*HC*, p.107)

This question must be answered in the negative, for she succeeds only in reproducing the relationship of servitude in which she suffered the father's authority. The repeated fantasies of rape by Hendrik replicate the fantasies of childhood rape by the father, and the attempt at relationship becomes a fantasy of submission to another master, and of invasion by another version of the Law, repeating the earlier description of her invasion by the Law of language, as we see from the correlation between the following two segments:

> The law has gripped my throat, I say and do not say, it invades my larynx, its one hand on my tongue, its other hand on my lips. How can I say, I say, that these are not the eyes of the law that stare from behind my eyes, or that the mind of the law does not occupy my skull, leaving me only enough intellection to utter these doubting words, if it is I uttering them, and see their fallaciousness? How can I say that the law does not stand fullgrown inside my shell, its feet in my feet, its hands in my hands, its sex drooping through my hole . . . (*HC*, p.84)

> A body lies on top of a body pushing and pushing, trying to find a way in, motion everywhere. But what does this body want inside me? What is this man trying to find in me? Will he try again when he wakes up? What deeper invasion and possession does he plot in his sleep? That one day all his bony frame shall lie packed inside me, his

> skull inside my skull, his limbs along my limbs,
> the rest of him crammed into my belly? What will he
> leave me of myself? (*HC*, p.107)

The projected relationship is marked by ambivalence, for despite Magda's fantasies of mastery by Hendrik, and despite the gesture of bringing Hendrik and Klein-Anna into the ancestral farmhouse and dressing them up in the finery of her ancestors, she nevertheless maintains an attitude of mastery toward them. Having been the victim of her father's interdiction, of the great NO with which he blasts her, and having failed to make him pronounce the Yes which, as a token of his recognition, would grant her an identity, she now becomes the one who pronounces the *No* in response to Hendrik's *Yes*: ' "Nee!" I say. "Ja!" he grunts an inch from my ear, "Ja! . . . Ja! . . . Ja! . . . " ' (*HC*, pp.104–5). Addressing herself to the 'sky gods' in the segments which follow, she says:

> As for inventing enemies, the pitiful warrior in
> the hills was never as formidable as the enemy who
> walked in our shadow and said *Ja baas* [Yes master].
> To the slave who would only say *Yes* my father
> could only say *No*, and I after him, and that was
> the start of all my woe. (*HC*, p.128)

Like her father, she is dependent for her position of mastery upon the inessential consciousness of slaves. In response to the passage from Hegel's *The Phenomenology of Mind*, uttered by the sky gods

> *It is the slave's consciousness that constitutes*
> *the master's certainty of his own truth. But the*
> *slave's consciousness is a dependent consciousness.*
> *So the master is not sure of the truth of his*
> *autonomy. His truth lies in an inessential*
> *consciousness and its inessential acts* (*HC*, p.129)

Magda asks: 'Was my father crucified on the paradox the voices expound: that from people who bent like reeds to his whims he was asking, in his way, for an affirmation of his truth in and for himself?' (*HC*, p.130).

The passage which I cited from Jameson (p. 164, this chapter) makes reference to Lacan's emphasis upon 'those kinds of words, primarily names and pronouns . . . those verbal joints . . . at which the insertion of the subject into the Symbolic is particularly detectable' ('Imaginary and Symbolic in Lacan', p.362). Now, it is possible to say that Coetzee, following Lacan, makes Magda's attempts to enter the Symbolic centre on these same kinds of words: names and pronouns. Just as Magda, in the role of daughter, is not named in the father's speech, and is not able to pronounce the *Jy* (You) to the father, so Hendrik and Klein-Anna are not able to call Magda by her name, or pronounce the *Jy* in response to her *Ek* (I). The Afrikaans language provides terms of address, absent in modern English, which forbid the use of the *U* (You) or the *jy* (intimate you) by a subordinate, and require the use of a title in its place, thus 'Kan ek vir pa help om in die bed te klim?' (Can I help Daddy to get into bed?)[16] (*HC*, p.67), 'Nee mies, ek verstaan. As mies sê ons moet wag dan wag ons. Mies sê mos ons sal ons geld kry' (No, miss, I understand. If miss says we must wait then we must wait, if miss promises us our money) (*HC*, p.95). In an article on Pauline Smith and the Afrikaans language, Coetzee points out that

> As a generalization it is fair to say that a linguistically particularized rendering of the speech and thought of non-natives is rare in fiction. A corollary is that when foreign speech is rendered in a particularized manner, this is usually done for well-defined reasons . . . . ('Pauline Smith and the Afrikaans Language', p.199)

In the case of his own translation of the Afrikaans dialogue in *In the Heart of the Country* into English, Coetzee does not, on the whole, try to convey the peculiarities of the Afrikaans lexicon or syntax; the exception to his, as we see in the translations I have cited, is the use of the title in place of the *you*.

This usage must therefore be regarded as significant, its function being to emphasize the way in which those in the subservient position cannot pronounce the *you*, and thus cannot confirm the existence of those in the position of mastery.

To Magda's question, 'Toe, wie is ek?' (Well, who am I?), Klein-Anna can answer only 'Mies is die mies' (Miss is the miss) (*HC*, p.30); and, to Magda's plea to the girl to call her by her name, 'Kan jy Magda sê? Kom, sê vir my Magda' (Can you say Magda? Come, call me Magda), Klein-Anna replies, 'Nee mies, kan nie' (No miss, can't) (*HC*, p.102). This amounts to a refusal, or an inability, to recognize the other's selfhood: for Klein-Anna, the only identity Magda has is that of mistress. She recognizes Magda only from her own dependent position as servant, which is, in Hegelian terms, no recognition at all. Magda's discourse represents the attempt to change this: 'The medium, the median – that is what I wanted to be! Neither master nor slave, neither parent nor child, but the bridge between, so that in me the contraries should be reconciled' (*HC*, p.133), she laments at the end, having failed to free herself from the father's language 'of hierarchy, of distance and perspective' (*HC*, p.97). As Coetzee has said, the figures of Jacobus Coetzee and Magda 'lack the stature to transform [the] 'It' into a 'You', to, so to speak, create a society in which reciprocity exists; and therefore condemn themselves to desperate gestures towards establishing intimacy' (Watson Interview, p.123). When Magda is finally able to project a dialogue in which Hendrik addresses her as *you*, his speech signals his rejection, and the *you* merely functions to denote the outsider in opposition to whom the *we* is defined:

> 'Ek sê vir jou, een van die dae is hulle terug,
> sommer kort-kort, hulle en ander mense ook, al die
> boere! Dan vind hulle dat jy saam met die volkies
> in die groot huis woon! Dan ly ons, *dan* ly ons –
> nie jy nie, sy en ek!
>
> (I am telling you, one of these days they will be
> back, sooner than you think, along with other people,
> all the other farmers! Then they will see that you

> are living with the servants in the big house. Then we will be the ones to suffer, not you, she and I!) (*HC*, p.117)

The *you* which would reciprocate the address of the *I*, and so fill the hole to make her whole, does not eventuate. Magda says: 'There has been no transfiguration. What I long for, whatever it is, does not come' (*HC*, p.113), and

> I am pressed but not possessed, I am pierced but my core is not touched. At heart I am still the fierce mantis virgin of yore. Hendrik may take me, but it is I holding him holding I (*HC*, p.116)

indicating that the attempt to project a dialogue has failed either to provide proof of the existence of the self, or to allow for transcendence of this self.

The attempt is not abandoned however, for in her isolation Magda turns to the words from the 'sky gods' as a substitute for human intercourse, saying:

> I also hear voices. It is my commerce with the voices that has kept me from becoming a beast. For I am sure that if the voices did not speak to me I would long ago have given up this articulated chip-chop and begun to howl or bellow or squawk . . . . It is not speech that makes man but the speech of others. (*HC*, p.125)

The vehicles of the sky gods 'look like narrow silver pencils with two pairs of rigid wings', and 'fly from north to south on the first and fourth days and from south to north on the second and fifth days' (*HC*, p.126), which suggests that they are aeroplanes on bi-weekly passenger flights between Cape Town and Johannesburg, and that they function as heralds of the technological revolution, in the same way that the railway line in *The Story of an African Farm* signals a threat to pastoral values in the form of encroaching industrialization and urbanization. The words from the sky gods, given in italic print and drawn from what appears to be the discursive tradition of Hegel, Kierkegaard, Blake, and Nietzsche, articulate the philosophical dicta to which Coetzee's novel addresses itself. As such, these passages function to refer us to the way in which Schreiner, in her isolation, pondered those few texts which were available to her (certain texts of Mill, Darwin, Emerson, and Spencer), and, as Gray points out, incorporated them as part of the superstructure but not part of the essence, of her novel (Gray, p.149).

The fact that the sky gods speak Spanish, not 'a local Spanish but . . . a Spanish of pure meanings such as might be dreamed of by the philosophers', and which she finds 'immediately comprehensible' (*HC*, p.125), would appear to be a parodic reference to Schreiner's belief that she can comprehend the philosophical texts which she reads in isolation from their historical context, and can apply them *per se* to her lived experience on an African farm. Magda's own messages to the sky gods become increasingly urgent, increasingly importunate expressions of desire: 'How can I move them?' she asks, spelling out with stones (in Esperanto), CINDRLA ES MI and FEMM – AMOR POR TU (*HC*, pp.132 and 133), and finally resorting to pure figuration:

> . . . descending to ideographs, I spent all my stones on a sketch of a woman lying on her back, her figure fuller than mine, her legs parted, younger than myself too, this was no time for scrupulosity. (*HC*, p.133)

But the fairy tale prince does not descend to answer her desire, to fill her up, and this attempt at dialogue ends with Magda asking:

> Are not all these dicta from above blind to the source of our disease, which is that we have no one to speak with, that our desires stream out of us chaotically, without aim, without response, like our words, whoever *we* may be, perhaps I should speak only for myself? (*HC*, p.135)

The philosophical dicta are not able to occupy the position of thirdness which would release her from the dual Imaginary relationship of self to self, for, as she says, 'One cannot pursue a hopeless infatuation . . . without courting the fate of Narcissus' (*HC*, pp.134–5).

Coetzee's novels all prefigure the reader, or the act of interpretation, in some way, and *In the Heart of the Country* is no exception, even though Magda's speech is characterized by the *failure* to anticipate evoking a response. The readers here are the visitors, of whom Magda says:

> I have had visitors, more visitors than I can name. I did not know, in my aboriginal innocence, that there were so many people in the world. Every inch of the farm has been searched for my father, who rode out one ill-fated day and never came back.
>
> The name cannot be crossed off the list, they explain to me, until the remains are discovered. (*HC*, pp.120–1)

These are the generations of critics who have searched for the 'lost father', for the sources of Schreiner's novel, in the belief that they have not come to terms with the novel until they have excavated and laid bare these sources. Then there are the others, of whom Magda asks:

> When they came to search for my father, those bearded men, those boys with the rosy cheeks and the strict little mouths and the marksmen's blue eyes, were they truly searching for the absent master or were they after the truant slave and his mate? (*HC*, p.121).

Seeking the 'truant slave and his mate', these are the critics who seek in Schreiner's novel the sources of a truant liberal tradition: in either case it is implied that these visitors are not interested in Magda herself, that is to say, that Schreiner's readers have been less interested in her act of writing than in the tradition out of which it arises and the tradition to which, in turn, it gives rise. The last visitor is a boy who comes to deliver a letter requesting the payment of taxes for 'road maintenance, vermin eradication, and other marvels [Magda] had never heard of' (*HC*, p.124), again signalling a threat to pastoral values with the growth of bureaucratized forms of control, and with a network of roads which will open up the country. The boy is caught stealing fruit, and runs off in terror when Magda indicates her desire in a direct and graphic way: 'I made a circle of the thumb and first finger of my left hand and plunged the first finger of my right hand back and forth through it' (*HC*, p.125). This would appear to suggest that the readings of Schreiner's novel which might have found fruit ready for the picking there, have instead maintained and repeated the repressions operative in the novel itself, preferring to look for its 'meaning' elsewhere than in the desiring self of the writer.

In Magda's ongoing attempts to signal her desire and to establish a dialogue of some kind, we have witnessed a succession of fruitless repetitions which constitute a kind of drawing out of the fundamental repetition evident in her (oft-repeated) claim, 'I am I.' This is essentially the equivalent of the Fichtean claim of *Ich bin Ich*, or Ego = Ego, and, as such, is a self-positing, self-establishing, primordial act.[17] Fichte's system for establishing identity is based on the narcissistic premise of 'pure thinking that thinks itself, the identity of subject and object, in the form Ego = Ego;' however,

> The principle, the Subject-Object, turns out to be a subjective Subject-Object. What is deduced from it thereby gets the form of a conditioning of pure consciousness, of the Ego = Ego; and pure consciousness itself takes on the form of something conditioned by an objective infinity, namely the temporal progression *ad infinitum*. (Hegel, Preface to *The Difference Between Fichte's and Schelling's System of Philosophy*, p.81)

This comparison with Fichte's system, and the critiques of his system, enables us to see that Magda's claim, 'I am I', allows for no resting point: the first *I* is a subjective *I* which is dependent upon the second *I*, an objective entity, itself dependent upon the first, positing, subjective *I*, thus necessitating the potentially infinite progression of I am I am I am I . . . . As the foregoing discussion has indicated, the *I* achieves release from this situation only by positing a *You* exterior to, and independent of, the self, so that the '*I* becomes *you* in the address of the one who in his turn designates himself as *I*' (Benveniste, pp. 224–25; see my chapter one, p. 25).

Magda, however, is a prisoner of her monologue, trapped by her own declaration of independence. She represents the double-sided dilemma of a narrating self which can neither realize the independent existence of the self, nor *transcend* the self; which is trapped in the ongoing dialectic in which the self is dependent for its existence upon an object (the linguistic utterance) which is other than the self, but which, in turn, cannot escape its origins in this self. Thus Magda, on the one hand lamenting the translation of the self into the objective condition of words, says 'Words are coin. Words alienate. Language is no medium for desire . . . . The frenzy of desire in the medium of words yields the mania of the catalogue' (*HC*, p.26). On the other hand, lamenting her failure to achieve self-transcendence, she says:

> . . . tonight I have beaten the waters too long, I am weak, I am tired of telling myself things, tonight I am going to relax, give up, explore the pleasures of drowning, the feel of my body sliding out of me and another body sliding in, limbs inside my limbs, mouth inside my mouth. I welcome death as a version of life in which I will not be myself. There is a fallacy here which I ought to see but will not. For when I wake on the ocean floor it will be the same old voice that drones out of me, drones or bubbles or whatever it is that words do in water. What tedium! When will it ever stop? . . . . The words that whisper

> through those blue lips are mine. Drowning, I drown into myself. A phantom, I am no phantom. I stoop. I touch this skin and it is warm, I pinch this flesh and it hurts. What more proof could I want? I am I. (*HC*, pp.53–4)

This is essentially the same dilemma that Lacan refers to when, arguing against Descartes' *cogito*, he says:

> Is the place that I occupy as the subject of a signifier concentric or excentric, in relation to the place I occupy as subject of the signified? – that is the question.
>
> It is not a question of knowing whether I speak of myself in a way that conforms to what I am, but rather of knowing whether I am the same as that of which I speak . . . .
>
> Furthermore, if, turning the weapons of metonymy against the nostalgia that it serves, I refuse to seek any meaning beyond tautology, if in the name of 'war is war' and 'a penny's a penny' I decide to be only what I am, how even here can I elude the obvious fact that I am in that very act?
>
> And it is no less true if I take myself to the other, metaphoric pole of the signifying quest, and if I dedicate myself to becoming what I am, to coming into being, I cannot doubt that even if I lose myself in the process, I am in that process. (*Ecrits*, pp.165–66)

Having introduced the notion of metaphor and metonymy, via this passage from Lacan, I wish to leave it there, in order to come back to it via a somewhat circuitous route, which will allow me to elaborate upon these two aspects of the signifying process in relation to Coetzee's writing project in this novel. For it is at this point that Schreiner's writing project, as I see it inferred here, and Coetzee's writing project begin to diverge, although enacting the same basic revolt –

a revolt which I have not mentioned until now, except in so far as it is part of the revolt against the Symbolic – a revolt against time. In the opening pages of *The Story of an African Farm*, we find the hero, Waldo, in agonies over the ticking of his father's watch:

> It never waited; it went on inexorably; and every time it ticked *a man died*! He raised himself a little on his elbow and listened. He wished it would leave off . . . .
>
> 'Dying, dying, dying!' said the watch; 'dying, dying, dying!' (SAF, p. 37)

Magda, likewise, is made to pronounce upon her problematic relationship to time in one of the opening segments of *In the Heart of the Country*:

> In the shadowy hallway the clock ticks away day and night. I am the one who keeps it wound and who weekly, from sun and almanac, corrects it. Time on the farm is the time of the wide world, neither a jot nor a tittle more or less. Resolutely I beat down the blind subjective time of the heart, with its spurts of excitement and drags of tedium; my pulse will throb with the steady one-second beat of civilization. One day some as yet unborn scholar will recognise in the clock the machine that has tamed the wilds. But will he ever know the desolation of the hour of the siesta chiming in cool green high-ceilinged houses where the daughters of the colonies lie counting with their eyes shut? (*HC*, p.3)

Schreiner's response to the problem of time and human mutability is the Romantic response, whereby the self borrows 'the temporal stability that it lacks from nature' (de Man, p.181). The Romantic appropriation of temporal stability from nature in order to compensate for individual transience, is achieved via the symbol, in which the mind and nature are fused in an analogical unity, and in which the subject-object snythesis can therefore take place. The corollary to this is the 'tendency to transfer into nature attributes of consciousness and to unify it organically with respect to a centre that acts, for natural objects, as the identity of the self functions for a consciousness' (de Man, p.184). We find, at the centre of Schreiner's novel, the philosophical digression titled 'Times and Seasons', which describes the child's awakening into the awareness of human mutability, and goes on to resolve this temporal predicament in terms of a typically Romantic relationship of the self to nature. Thus, rejecting the notion of God's divine will, her narrator says:

> From our earliest hour we have been taught that the thought of the heart, the shaping of the rain-cloud, the amount of wool that grows on a sheep's back, the length of a drought, and the growing of the corn, depend on nothing that moves immutable, *at the heart of all things*; but on the changeable will of a changeable being, whom our prayers can alter. Nature has been but a poor plastic thing, to be toyed with this way or that, as man happens to please his deity or not . . . . Was it possible for us in an instant to see Nature as she is – the flowing vestment of an unchanging reality? (*SAF*, p.150; my emphasis)

And, exclaiming over the similarity of the patterns which she perceives in nature, she asks:

> How are these things related that such deep union should exist between them all? Is it chance? Or, are they not all the fine branches of one trunk, whose sap flows through us all? . . .
>
> This thing we call existence; is it not a something which has its roots far down below in the dark, and its branches stretching out into the immensity above, which we among the branches cannot see? Not a chance jumble; a living thing, a *One*. (*SAF*, p.153)

In Schreiner's novel, however, the Romantic view of nature,

and the form of resolution it offers to the temporal dilemma, is, as it were, tacked on to the rest: borrowed chiefly from Emerson, it forms part of the novel's superstructure, as I indicated earlier. Thus we find this view expounded in narratorial digressions which are not integrated in the form of a dialectic between the developing consciousness and the actions of the protagonists. Lyndall and Waldo die meaningless deaths, one in an attitude of revolt, the other in an attitude of temporary acquiescence in the unity of nature and humankind: it is only

> when the old idol is broken, when the old hope is dead, when the old desire is crushed, then the Divine compensation of Nature is made manifest. She shows herself to you. So near she draws you, that the blood seems to flow from her to you, through a still uncut cord: you feel the throb of her life. (*SAF*, p.298)

Thus this resolution is, in effect, no resolution, for it cannot allow for the continued narration of action; cannot, indeed, allow for the continuation of the narrative.

Magda alludes to Schreiner's Romantic heritage when she asks:

> Does an elementary life burn people down to elementary states, to pure anger, pure gluttony, pure sloth? Am I unfitted by my upbringing for a life of more complex feelings? Is that why I have never left the farm, foreign to townslife, preferring to immerse myself in a landscape of symbol where simple passions can spin and fume around their own centres . . . . (*HC*, p.12)

The title of Coetzee's novel, too, carries an allusion to this tendency to anthropomorphize nature, granting it a 'heart' which would unify it organically, and extending this unity to encompass human life, as Schreiner does in the passage which I have just cited. The notion of the *heart* of the country is translated, in Coetzee's novel, into the notion of a novelistic discourse which arises out of the heart of the *cunt*-ry;

out of the divided and desiring self, whose awareness of the divided condition sets it apart from the natural world, and makes the endeavour to overcome the pain of this awareness by means of an analogy between nature and consciousness a spurious one. Thus Magda does not have access to the state of unity which she perceives in nature, and she says:

> . . . the stones and bushes of the veld hum with life . . . because I am here to set them vibrating with their own variety of material awareness that I am forever not they, and they not I, that I can never be the rapture of pure self that they are but am alas forever set off from them by the babble of words within me that fabricate and refabricate me as something else, something else. The farm, the desert, the whole world as far as the horizon is in an ecstasy of communion with itself, exalted by the vain urge of my consciousness to inhabit it. (*HC*, pp.48–9)

While repeating the Romantic dilemmas of Schreiner's novel (although articulating the problem of time in a different way), Magda's discourse refuses the Romantic resolution of these dilemmas, to which it responds by means of a structure founded in irony (as de Man defines it) rather than in symbolism. At the same time, Coetzee's novel takes up the oscillation between resolution and non-resolution, between form and formlessness, operative in Schreiner's novel, and reproduces it in the form of a clear-cut opposition between what are normally implicit and complementary aspects of the novelistic discourse. The poles of the novelistic discourse are a feature of what de Man describes as 'the truly perverse assignment of using both the narrative duration of the diachronic allegory and the instantaneity of the narrative present' (p. 207): they may be seen in terms of the intersection of the lived experience of time and the *concept* of time produced when time is translated into narrative temporality; in terms of the intersection of metaphor and metonymy, or, broadly speaking, of the Imaginary and the Symbolic.

Schreiner's Waldo and Lyndall are parent-less, child-less protagonists who are not permitted to 'outlive' the termination of the narrative. Lyndall refuses marriage and her child dies shortly after its birth: in Coetzee's novel this is all read as an extended gesture toward the disruption of patrilineal authority, which, as I have indicated, is replicated in Magda's violent killings of the father. In *In the Heart of the Country*, this refusal of the illusion of temporal sequence generated out of the diachronic duration of the narrative; the simultaneous refusal of both narrativity and temporality, which, as both Schleifer and Ricoeur point out,[18] are reciprocally constitutive. It is a metaphor of a narrative mode which is 'opposed to linear coherence, emphasizes discontinuity, oscillation, and non-differentiation', and, as Durand points out, it implies a particular relation to the Symbolic Order, the opposite relation being 'the successful achievement of the "family romance", a linear and non-contradictory discursive and symbolic mode' ('The Captive King', p.51).

At this point I wish to digress in order to suggest that *In the Heart of the Country* constitutes a reading and re-writing not only of Schreiner's novel, but of the South African pastoral novel in general, including the Afrikaans pastoral novel, the *plaasroman* (farm novel) of the 1930's. In a paper titled 'Lineal Consciousness in the Farm Novels of C. M. van den Heever', Coetzee makes the point that in van den Heever's novels transcendence of the 'awareness of being doomed to die while the world lives on . . . is attained via conscious acceptance that the unit of life is the lineage, not the individual', He also makes the point that

> into the myth of the good farmer and his marriage with his farm are drawn many of the energies of European Romanticism, many of the feelings of cosmic identification and engulfment which in the first place were attributed to the relation not of farmer to farm but of man to the wilderness, to forest and moor and mountain. (p. 8)

With this in mind, it is possible to read Magda's killings of the father as a refusal of this lineal consciousness and the conservative ideology which it implies, and as a refusal of the stultifying effects of the pastoral mode in the South African context, to which Coetzee refers in his paper on Pauline Smith:

> The mode of Smith's work is elegy, its overall tone nostalgic. It looks back to a lost world (in terms of Smith's life, to her childhood in the Oudtshoorn district; in terms of history, to rural South Africa before the internal combustion engine). The mode is common in South African literature, particularly among Afrikaans writers; it is the mode of the generation that left the land, under various economic pressures, to live in cities. No doubt it has its parallels in scores of other national literatures of this century. The ramifying effects on cultural development that a national literature may have which is dominated, for the space of a crucial generation or two, by the theme of the longing backward glance, are very likely vast. ('Pauline Smith and the Afrikaans Language', p. 205)

Returning now to the mode of narration of *In the Heart of the Country*, we find that each segment of Magda's discourse stands for a separate moment of narration, so that the novel is structured according to what Coetzee calls the eschatological awareness of time, in which 'There is no smooth course of narrative development that will lead from beginnings to the present moment of narration. Between then and now is always a break' ('Time, Tense and Aspect in Kafka's "The Burrow" ', p. 576; see my Chapter One, p. 39). In Kafka's story, Coetzee claims, this awareness of time produces an insistence upon the 'everlasting present [which] is nothing but the moment of narration itself' (p. 579), and we find Magda, likewise, saying:

> . . . these words of mine come from nowhere and go nowhere, they have no past or future, they whistle across the flats in a desolate eternal present, feeding

> no one (*HC*, p. 114);
>
> How idyllic the old days seem; and how alluring, in a different way, a future in a garden behind barbed wire! Two stories to comfort myself with: for the truth is, I fear, that there is no past or future, that the medium I live in is an eternal present in which . . . I am the reluctant polestar about which all this phenomenal universe spins (*HC*, p. 116).

The segmented structure of her speech represents the attempt to make the *now* of narration coincide with the narrated *now*, and as such it constitutes a refusal to translate lived time into narrative temporality, and produces what Schleifer refers to as 'the contiguity of enunciation's "schizophrenic" morphemes' (p. 879). While this results in the metonymic sliding of desire from segment to segment, Lacan's 'incessant sliding of the signified under the signifier' (*Ecrits*, p. 154), it does not yield a smoothly sequential linear narrative, but 'the mania of the catalogue', that is to say, the discontinuous structure of lists of items, each separated from the other by a break in the signifying chain.

The signifying chain, here, is made up of vertical units which constitute 'punctuations' in the spatial dimension, rather than 'articulations' in the temporal dimension. Thus Magda says:

> . . . perhaps there is no time, perhaps I am deceived when I think of my medium as time, perhaps there is only space, and I a dot of light moving erratically from one point in space to another, skipping years in a flash, now a frightened child in the corner of a schoolroom, now an old woman with knobbly fingers, that is also possible, my mind is open, and it would explain some of the tentativeness with which I hold my memories. (*HC*, p. 123)

This recalls the example given by Ingarden in his discussion of temporal processes. Referring to the difficulty of conceiving of a process when operating within the awareness of time in which 'everything that exists temporally is limited to only one "now", conceived as non-dimensional, and beyond which there are, as it were, two abysses of absolute non-being' (*Time and Modes of Being*, p. 104), Ingarden says:

> 'Transience' would be nothing but the 'coming into being' of certain events in a determinate *order* of succession. Strictly speaking, there would be, not a continuous series, but merely a determinate (potential) manifold of separate ('discrete') *events* which, under appropriate conditions would *imitate* or simulate the course of a process, although it would be essentially different from it. Similarly, for example, a series of lamps appropriately arranged in space, when lighted one after another in succession, can produce the *appearance* of the *continuous* motion of a *single* lamp shining for a certain period of time, but can never be *identified* with it. Moreover, the appearance of a continuous motion is successfully produced, as we know, only because a continuous process, both physiological and psychological is taking place. It depends – especially psychologically – on the 'picture' of a previously lighted lamp's remaining preserved through a certain period of time after its lighting as a so-called after-picture that blends with the 'picture' of the lamp just being lighted. An illusion of the existence of a continuous process in the objective occurrence of a number of events in succession is successfully produced only when the very thing is realised that we have to *exclude* from the conception of time now being considered: namely, that something past, although it has ceased to be strictly actual, has not been completely annihilated, but retains, in spite of everything, some distinct, special mode of existence; it does not *break off* with each new instant of time, but *extends* into the continuation of that same process. (p. 110)

In the case of narrative, the appropriate condition which

would allow discrete events to simulate the course of a process is the consciousness, first of the narrating self, and then of the reader. However, Magda's speech, representing a mode of writing which would break from the past and cannot anticipate a future, cannot transfer to the reader the responsibility for re-constituting the segments of speech into the process of narrative, and so remains locked in the 'eternal present', repeatedly trying to bring the self into being.

As Schleifer points out, temporality, as a concept, 'emerges and is recognised simultaneously with the emergence of the subject' (p. 876), and in Coetzee's novel this insistence upon the 'eternal present' is both a refusal of narrative temporality and of the condition of subjectivity imposed upon the self with entry into the Symbolic. The vertical units of Magda's speech, as separate, successive attempts to signal her desire, are 'anchoring points', or '*points de capiton*', which may be identified with the metaphoric pole of the field of the signifier, in which, according to Lacan, signification as such arises.[19] It is as though the metaphoric signifying function is made to intrude in the domain of the metonymic function, refusing to allow the repression of the signified; a repression which is maintained with its elision from signifier to signifier. Lacan says:

> . . . what does man find in metonymy if not the power to circumvent the obstacles of social censure? Does not this form, which gives its field to truth in its very oppression, manifest a certain servitude inherent in its presentation? (*Ecrits*, p. 158),

and it would appear that the isolation and exaggeration of the metaphoric and metonymic poles in Coetzee's writing are attempts to avoid precisely this oppression of truth, this servitude.

Lacan goes on to say that

> The diachronic function of [the] anchoring point is to be found in the sentence, even if the sentence completes its signification only with its last term,

> each term being anticipated in the construction of the others, and, inversely, sealing their meaning by its retroactive effect (*Ecrits*, p. 303),

and Wilden elaborates upon this, and upon Lacan's diagrammatic representation of the anchoring point, as follows:

> In other words, for the complete message of the conscious subject to be understood (by the emitter or by the receiver) at any level at all, there must be an unconscious reading in reverse at the *end* of the message, a reference to the locus of the code *after* the complete message has been received (the message consisting if necessary of a series of significant 'bits'). (p. 275)

Thus metaphor and metonymy collaborate in the passage of the message through the code of the Other, the metonymic function allowing the discourse to develop diachronically in the temporal dimension, and the metaphoric function, or anchoring point, bringing the 'otherwise endless movement (*glissement*)' (*Ecrits*, p. 303) to a stop. The structure of Coetzee's novel, in attempting to prevent this collaboration of metaphor and metonymy, in refusing to give the 'last term' of the sentence, or of the discourse, which will complete its signification, seeks to avoid the translation of the *message* via the *code*, and thereby seeks to bypass the Other. Thus although Magda claims that she wants her story 'to have a beginning, a middle, and an end' (*HC*, p. 43), in the final segment we find her asking:

> At moments like the present, filled with lugubrious thoughts, one is tempted to add up one's reckoning, tie up loose ends. Will I find the courage to die a crazy old queen in the middle of nowhere, unexplained by and inexplicable to the archaeologists, her tomb full of *naif* whitewash paintings of sky-gods; or am I going to yield to the spectre of reason and explain myself to myself in the only kind of confession we

> protestants know? To die an enigma with a full soul or to die emptied of my secrets, that is how I picturesquely put the question to myself. (*HC*, p. 137)

Now, Schreiner does not have the courage to resist tying up the loose ends of her novel, and, although she terminates it with Waldo's death, she allows him to bow out amidst a blissful vision of Romantic harmony. Before going on to elaborate upon Coetzee's project of bypassing the Other, I want to talk about the way in which *In the Heart of the Country* allows for the resolution of the temporal dilemma without the imposition of an inauthentic solution in the manner of Schreiner's novel. As I suggested in Chapter One (p. 41), the eschatological awareness of time is the equivalent of the perception of time inherent in de Man's view of irony. To repeat the passages I cited earlier,

> . . . irony comes closer to the pattern of factual experience and recaptures some of the factitiousness of human existence as a succession of isolated moments lived by a divided self. Essentially the mode of the present, it knows neither memory nor prefigurative duration . . . (p. 207);

and

> The ironic language splits the subject into an empirical self that exists in a state of inauthenticity and a self that exists only in the form of a language that asserts the knowledge of this inauthenticity (p. 197).

This view of irony approximates the temporal dilemma articulated by Magda, and involves a rejection of the Romantic fusion of self and non-self, of self as subject and self as object; a rejection which is evident in Magda's insistence upon her divided condition:

> . . . perhaps I never had animal integrity, or lost it

> before I was six, perhaps by the age of six I was already a little corporate machine trotting around the werf . . . . watched over gravely by a little ghostly double . . . . (*HC*, p. 40)

Again as I indicated in the introductory chapter, this dialectical movement between authenticity and inauthenticity is also the equivalent of the Lacancian death instinct, which produces a movement whereby 'man makes an object of his action, but only in order to restore to this action in due time its place as a grounding' (*Ecrits*, p. 73). Brooks sees the repetitions of the death instinct as 'the cure which prolongs narrative', which is always threatened by breakdown, 'on the verge of premature discharge, of short-circuit' (pp. 297 and 296); that this is indeed one of Magda's concerns is evident in the admonishment which she addresses to herself: 'Prolong yourself, prolong yourself, that is the whisper I hear in my inmost' (*HC*, p. 5). However, the failure to anticipate a response means that the repetitions of Magda's speech do not represent a productive return to origins, but simply a static return of the repressed:

> The past. I grope around inside my head for the mouth of the tunnel that will lead me back in time and memory past images of myself younger and younger, fresher and fresher, through youth and childhood back to my mother's knee and my origins, but the tunnel is not there. Inside my skull the walls are glassy, I see only reflections of myself drab and surly staring back at myself. (*HC*, pp. 37–38)

In the absence of an interlocutor, the transference is not accomplished, and the repetition which is a manifestation of the death instinct does not achieve a form of release for the narrating self. There is no resolution, no resting point, and the act of prolonging the self must go on into infinity. Magda indicates that her repeated killings of the father represent the purely destructive aspect of the death instinct when she says: 'Labouring under my father's weight I struggle to give life to a world but seem to engender only death' (*HC*, pp. 10–11). Although these repetitions allow her to prolong her speech, they cannot become, in Felman's words, a '*life-usage of the death-instinct*' ('Beyond Oedipus', p. 1034); they do not provide 'new modes of constructing experience' (Schafer, p. 36).

If the death instinct is a 'cure which prolongs narrative', it does not, in this case, provide the 'cure' which allows for the termination of speech without submitting this speech to the norms of novelistic discourse, which requires 'a beginning, a middle, and an end;' without, therefore, succumbing to the mastery of the Other in the form of an imposed, rather than a freely chosen end. In the case of *The Story of an African Farm*, there is no movement into the future via the assumption of the past (the past as literary history), and so Schreiner does not achieve a fully innovative response to her environment. Clearly, Coetzee's project must be distinguished from the project which it represents, and, again as I have indicated in my first chapter, it is possible to do this by referring to the allegorical structure of his novel. In *In the Heart of the Country* it is allegory which effects the 'cure', allowing not only for the termination of the potentially infinite progression of ironic acts of consciousness, but also for the conjunction of the discontinuous metonymic segments of speech within the all-encompassing structure of the extended metaphor which constitutes allegory. Allegory allows the writer to transcend 'irony without falling into the myth of an organic totality or bypassing the temporality of all language' (de Man, p. 204). It does not provide a false resolution, because it maintains the self's knowledge of the temporal predicament, and maintains the structure of repetition:

> . . . it remains necessary, if there is to be allegory, that the allegorical sign refer to another sign that precedes it. The meaning constituted by the allegorical sign can then consist only in the *repetition* (in the Kierkegaardian sense of the term) of a previous sign with which it can never coincide, since it is of the essence of this previous sign to be pure anteriority . . .

> Whereas the symbol postulates the possibility of an identity or identification, allegory designates primarily a distance in relation to its own origin, and, renouncing the nostalgia and the desire to coincide, it establishes its language in the void of this temporal difference. (de Man, pp. 190–91)

This, then, is the 'void' which Coetzee's novel occupies. While the individual ironic moments of narration remain locked in an eternal present, the novel as a whole is situated in an 'ideal time that is never here and now but always a past or an endless future' (de Man, p. 207); in the space between the past made up of the texts of the tradition, and an endless future of potential readings. Thus, via its allegorical relationship to Schreiner's novel in particular, and to the South African pastoral mode in general, Coetzee's novel engages in a productive return to origins, as it simultaneously recuperates and subverts its origins in the tradition.

Turning now to the allegory of the narrating self which is to be read via the figure of Magda, it becomes apparent that her view of herself as cut off from past and future is *a gesture* merely, a gesture of negation on the part of the self of enunciation. According to Freud, negation is, in fact, a form of affirmation, in that it makes manifest that which would otherwise remain repressed:

> The content of a repressed presentation or thought can thus make its way through to consciousness on the condition that it lets itself be negated. The *Verneinung* is a way to take cognizance [*Kenntnis*] of what is repressed; indeed is already a 'lifting and conserving' [*Aufhebung*] of what is repressed.[20]

According to Lacan, negation is 'that desperate affirmation of life that is the purest form in which we recognise the death instinct', and through negation 'the immediate particularity of desire . . . rediscovers . . . a final trimph' (*Ecrits*, p. 104). In Lacanian terms, negation involves 'the suicidal renunciation of the vanquished partner' as 'The subject says "No!" to this intersubjective game of hunt-the-slipper in which desire makes itself recognised for a moment, only to become lost in a will that is the will of the other' (*Ecrits*, pp. 104–5). Magda is a subject who renounces the 'vanquished partner', denying the presence of an interlocutor, denying the status of her utterance as a speech act, denying the entry into the Symbolic, denying the repression of desire in the 'necessary sucession of the statement's systematic; socialised and iterative speech' (Schleifer, p. 879). It is possible to say that negation functions as a structural principle in this novel, and that the polarization of the elements of Magda's discourse constitutes the equivalent of the 'signifying game' which Lacan describes as follows:

> This signifying game between metonymy and metaphor, up to and including the active edge that splits my desire between a refusal of the signifier and a lack of being, and links my fate to the question of my destiny, this game, in all its inexorable subtlety, is played until the match is called, there where I am not, because I cannot situate myself there. (*Ecrits*, p.166)

In *In the Heart of the Country*, the game is played in a way that constantly reproduces the 'active edge that splits . . . desire between a refusal of the signifier and a lack of being', as Magda's discourse alternates between speech and silence, between the place where the *I* is, and where the *I* is not, and the gaps between her speech become *significant* blanks. We have, in the alternation between speech and silence, what Lacan describes as the 'temporal pulsation' (*Four Fundamental concepts of Psycho-Analysis*, p. 207), which marks the disappearance of the self in the signifier, and the paradoxical 'appearance' of the self in the 'lethal movement' of its retreat from the field of the signifier. Once again, the allegory of the Lacanian subject functions to insist upon the existence of a secret self, in Magda's words, a 'true deepdown I beyond words' (*HC*, p.16), and, once again, this insistence upon a secret self is a means of prolonging both the novelistic and the critical discourse (see my Chapter One, p. 59), as is evident from Magda's claim:

> To explain is to forgive, to be explained is to be forgiven, but I, I hope and fear, am inexplicable, unforgivable. (Yet what is it in me that shrinks from the light? Do I really have a secret or is this bafflement before myself only a way of mystifying my better, questing half? Do I truly believe that stuffed in a crack between my soft mother and my baby self lies the key to this black bored spinster? Prolong yourself, prolong yourself, that is the whisper I hear in my inmost.) (*HC*, p. 5)

As I indicated in my first chapter, the allegorical structure allows the secret self to inhabit the borrowed form of the genre it deconstructs, and we find Magda saying: 'Whose shell I presently skulk in does not matter, it is the shell of a dead creature. What matters is that my anxious softbodied self should have a refuge from the predators of the deep . . . ' (*HC*, pp. 43–44).

As in the case of Jacobus Coetzee, however, the revolt enacted by Magda gradually loses momentum, as she is made to recognize the futility of the attempt to attain, to bypass, or to transcend the Other. Thus Magda says to Hendrik:

> The lips are tired . . . they want to rest, they are tired of all the articulating they have had to do since they were babies, since it was revealed to them that there was a law, that they could no longer simply part themselves to make way for the long *aaaa*, which has, if truth be told, always been enough for them, enough of an expression of whatever this is that needs to be expressed, or clench themselves over the long satisfying silence into which I shall still, I promise one day retire. I am exhausted by obedience to this law, I try to say, whose mark lies on me in the spaces between words, the spaces or the pauses, and in the articulations that set up the war of sounds, the *b*

> against the *d*, the *m* against the *n*, and so forth, as well as in other places which I would be too weary to set out for you even if I felt that you understood, which I doubt, since you do not so much as know the alphabet . . . . How can I say that the law does not stand fullgrown inside my shell, its feet in my feet, its hands in my hands, its sex drooping through my hole; or that when I have had my chance to make this utterance, the lips and teeth of the law will not begin to gnaw their way out of this shell, until there it stands before you, the law grinning and triumphant again, its soft skin hardening in the air, while I lie sloughed, abandoned on the floor? (*HC*, p. 84)

Paradoxically, the secret self here becomes the shell, which is invaded by the law of language and is sloughed off as the law once again asserts its presence. The mark of the law lies on Magda even in the spaces and pauses between words, and, like Jacobus Coetzee, she finds that there is no interior to which the self can retreat; that the interior is continuous with the exterior, that the self is Other. This is essentially the situation which Durand describes in his discussion of the performative mode in contemporary writing:

> This secret place haunts our culture. Endless efforts are made, subtle strategies conceived to ensure either its uncovering or its concealment. Its presence/absence lies behind most of our intellectual constructions: to go behind, to strain toward interpretation, to dream of a return to a core, a node, a *hortus conclusus* where words and deeds would be one.
>
> This, as Whitman intuited, involves conflict with articulated speech, a resistance to its imperialism, its leveling and limitless expansion. Concern with the silent, secret self is in that sense a reactive, regressive gesture, one that would return the subject to the inchoate, the nascent. We recognize here, of course, certain unspoken theoretical foundations of performance in general, a regressive narcissism in

particular, which would make the self the principle of all things, equating the private 'prophetic scream' with the creative act iself.

> This vision of the performing self as a self-creating demiurge considers the living presence as the most valued form of knowledge and endows it with quasimagical intensity and power. Yet the irony is that this stance is based at the outset on the illusion that the self – its discourse and its secret – originate from the subject, when in fact they find their determination in the Other. ('The Anxiety of Performance', pp. 169–70)

We have seen how Magda's speech is characterized by a regressive narcissism, and she makes her desire for a return to 'the inchoate, the nascent' explicit when, as in the preceding passage, she promises to retire into a long satisfying silence, and when she says:

> Oh father, father, if I could only learn your secrets, creep through the honeycomb of your bones, listen to the turmoil of your marrow, the singing of your nerves, float on the tide of your blood, and come at last to the quiet sea where my countless brothers and sisters swim, flicking their tails, smiling, whispering to me of a life to come! (*HC*, p. 71)

Now, Magda's insistence upon the 'eternal present' would appear to represent a perception of time which is essentially anti-pastoral, and is endorsed by passages such as the following:

> Out of the blankness that surrounds me I must pluck the incident after incident after incident whose little explosions keep me going. For the other kind of story, the weave of reminiscence in the dozing space of the mind, can never be mine. My life is not past, my art cannot be the art of memory. What will happen to me has not yet happened. I am a blind spot hurtling with

> both eyes open into the maw of the future,
> my password 'And then?' (*HC*, p. 43)

> What was once pastoral has become one of those stifling stories in which brother and sister, wife and daughter and concubine prowl and snarl around the bedside listening for the death-rattle, or stalk each other through the dim passages of the ancestral home. It is not fair! Born into a vacuum in time, I have no understanding of changing forms. My talent is all for immanence, for the fire or ice of identity at the heart of things. Lyric is my medium, not chronicle. (*HC*, pp. 70–1)

This last passage would appear to refer to Schreiner's literary endeavour, to her failure to understand changing forms, to the way in which her writing occupies a 'vacuum in time', and to the way in which the pastoral mode in *The Story of an African Farm* is confusedly related to the Romantic lyricism of her assertion of an identity at the heart of things. As Jonathan Culler points out, the lyric is 'a monument to immediacy', and it is not heard but overheard, as the poet turns his back on his listeners and pretends to be talking to himself or someone else (pp. 152 and 137). As such, it may be identified with Magda's mode of narration, with her insistence upon immediacy and her refusal to invoke an audience. However, there is a sense in which the lyric moments of Magda's speech, expressing a sense of irremediable loss, and what Durand calls the 'dream of a return to a core', may be seen as articulating another version of pastoral. Marinelli claims that 'The Fall is the major pre-condition of pastoral poetry, the greatest loss of all. Hence pastoral's double concern for the primitive beginnings of the entire race, and with the primitive beginnings in childhood of the individual' (p. 20). The fall as it is articulated by Magda may be defined as a fall into language, and the resulting postlapsarian condition produces what Coetzee has referred to elsewhere as a 'yearning . . . for an unmediated world, that is, a world without language' ('Triangular Structures of Desire in Advertising', pp. 40–1). This yearning for a world without language is, simultaneously, a yearning for a retreat out of time:

> I long for the end. I long to be folded in someone's arms, to be soothed and fondled and told I may stop ticking. I want a cave, a hole to snuggle in, I want to block my ears against this chatter that streams endlessly from and into me, I want a home somewhere else, if it has to be in this body then on different terms in this body, though there is one I would far prefer, I cannot stop these words unless I cut my throat . . . (*HC*, p. 108)

This echoes a passage from Schreiner's novel, in which the narrator laments the postlapsarian condition produced by a loss of faith:

> Whether a man believes in a human-like God is no small thing. Whether he looks into the mental and physical world and sees no relation between cause and effect, no order, but a blind chance sporting, this in the mightiest fact that can be recorded in any spiritual existence. It were almost a mercy to cut his throat, if indeed he does not do it for himself.
>
> We, however, do not cut our throats. To do so would imply some desire and feeling, and we have no desire and no feeling; we are only cold. We do not wish to live and we do not wish to die. (*SAF*, p. 150)

'We do not wish to live and we do not wish to die' becomes, in Magda's terms, the ambivalence of a subject that does not want the life offered by the discourse, which is a kind of death, and yet cannot bring itself to die out of the life of the discourse into the life offered by a retreat into silence.

There is a passage of Magda's speech in which pastoral's 'double concern for the primitive beginnings of the entire race, and with the primitive beginnings in childhood of the individual' is evident, as Magda links the primitive beginnings of the indigenous peoples of the country with her own beginnings in childhood:

> I grew up with the servants' children. I spoke like one of them before I learned to speak like this . . . . I sat at the feet of their blind old grandfather while he whittled clothespegs and told his stories of bygone days when men and beasts migrated from winter grazing to summer grazing and lived together on the trail. At the feet of an old man I have drunk in a myth of a past when beast and man and master lived a common life as innocent as the stars in the sky, and I am far from laughing. How am I to endure the ache of whatever it is that is lost without a dream of a pristine age, tinged perhaps with the violet of melancholy, and a myth of expulsion to interpret my ache to me? And mother, soft scented loving mother who drugged me with milk and slumber in the featherbed and then, to the sound of bells in the night, vanished, leaving me alone among rough hands and hard bodies – where are you? (*HC*, pp. 7)

Phylogenesis and ontogenesis are conflated here to produce a 'myth of expulsion' which suggests an alternative path that might be taken by writing in the pastoral mode in South Africa: instead of expressing nostalgia for the rural life of the farm, with all its connotations of proprietorship,[21] it might lament the expulsion from the unspoiled natural environment, and might recognize, rather than deny, a childhood and a culture shared with the descendants of the country's first pastoralists, the Khoi-khoi and the Khoi-san. And so it would seem that the figure of Magda stands in opposition, not to the pastoral mode *per se*, but to the conservative nationalistic ideology reflected in the form as it occurs in the South African context.

For Magda, who represents the individual attempt to enact a revolt against the imperialism of language, a revolt which derives its impetus from the desire to return to a past condition of wholeness, to retrieve a lost 'paradise', the recognition that she is situated on an 'island out of space, out of time' where 'all things must be possible' (*HC*, p. 122), brings with it a sense of the futility of this revolt. Her existence in language, *as* language, means that she is forever separated from the time and space of the empirical world, and makes it possible to transgress with impunity:

> I have been through everything now and no angel
> has descended with flaming sword to forbid it. There
> are, it seems, no angels in this part of the sky, no
> God in this part of the world. (*HC*, p. 108)

We shall see that in *Life & Times of Michael K* the fact that the act of narration is directed toward a future potentiality, rather than an irretrievable past, means that Michael K's escape to a 'pocket outside time' (p. 82), to 'one of those islands without an owner' (p. 84), is presented positively as a metaphor of the potential regeneration of the narrative in the act of reading. Magda, however, echoes Jacobus Coetzee's lament that 'here and everywhere else on this continent there would be no resistance to [his] power and no limit to its projection' (*Dusklands*, p. 108) when she says:

> I am cantankerous, but only because there is infinite
> space around me, and time before and after from
> which history seems to have retreated, and evidence
> in these bowed faced of limitless power. Everywhere I
> beat my fists on air. What is there for me but dreary
> expansion to the limits of the universe? (*HC*, p. 74)

If no angel descends with flaming sword, it is, in part, because language itself knows no bounds, and anything may be said; but it is also because Magda locates herself 'in a district outside the law, where the bar against incest is often down' (*HC*, p. 138), the bar against incest being the prohibition via which the individual is granted access to the Symbolic, and via which the repressions are instituted that make meaning possible. Magda refers, here, to writing which is minimally inhibited by the repressions of a well-defined code, so that virtually anything is possible, but nothing 'means', because of the absence of the shared 'moral and aesthetic universe' to which Gray refers.

The subject's constitution in language means that it is perpetually involved in a no-win situation with respect to time, as we see from Magda's lament: 'once I lived in time as a fish in water, breathing it, drinking it, sustained by it. Now I kill time and time kills me. Country ways! How I long for country ways' (*HC*, p. 80). Magda 'kills time' because the realization of time in speech translates it into something else, into the concept of temporality, and because each moment of time that is 'realized' in this way moves from being into non-being, as it sinks further and further into what Ingarden calls the 'dead past' (see my Chapter One, p. 39). On the other hand, time kills Magda: that is to say, unarticulated lived time 'kills' her as subject of the utterance, in that it forces ever widening gaps between the segments of her speech. She says:

> I suspect that the day the day was missing I was
> not there; and if that is so I shall never know
> how the day was filled. For I seem to exist more
> and more intermittently. Whole hours, whole
> afternoons go missing. (*HC*, p. 80)

She cannot prolong herself indefinitely, and the blank spaces come to represent progressively longer periods of time, so that eventually even 'summers and winters come and go' (*HC*, p. 123); (this may be read as a parodic allusion to Schreiner's chapter, 'Times and seasons', which is her way of coping, structurally, with the passage of large segments of time).

And so, all else failing, the father is trundled out again, now 'a mannikin of dry bones held together by cobwebs' (*HC*, p. 135), and Magda lapses into the mode of reminiscence, into the 'Do you remembers' which are all the more poignant for having been resisted for so long. The revolt is not finally abandoned however, for Magda, like Jacobus Coetzee, bows out with a last statement of affirmation-in-negation:

> I have never felt myself to be another man's creature . . . I have uttered my life in my own voice throughout, what a consolation that is, I have chosen at every moment my own destiny, which is to die here in the petrified garden, behind locked gates, near my father's bones, in a space echoing with hymns I could have written but did not because (I thought) it was too easy. (*HC*, p. 138)

Here, again, Peter Brooks's commentary on the relationship between repetition, the death instinct, and the appropriate termination of the novelistic discourse is relevant:

> If repetition is mastery, movement from the passive to the active; and if mastery is an assertion of control over what man must in fact submit to – choice, we might say, of an imposed end – we have already a suggestive comment on the grammar of plot, where repetition, taking us back again over the same ground, could have to do with the choice of ends. (p. 286)

Magda's repetitions have had to do with the choice of ends, but at the end, though she claims to have chosen her own destiny, she has *not* chosen her own end, which is fated by the form of the novel and the requirement that, as narrating self, she must 'die' with the termination of the discourse. That is to say, she has not chosen her own end except in so far as she has chosen to conclude with a gesture of impossible autonomy, of ultimate closure, dying in a petrified garden behind locked gates. The petrified garden, and Magda's description of herself admonishing the young boy she catches stealing fruit –

> 'En wie is dit way my vrugte steel?' [And who is this stealing my fruit] I said, the words dropping heavily from my lips, like stones, how strange if was to speak real words again to a real listener, however

> petrified (*HC*, p. 124)

constitute a reminder of the way in which 'The signifier, producing itself in the field of the Other . . . functions . . . to petrify the subject in the same movement in which it calls the subject to function, to speak, as subject' (*Four Fundamental Concepts of Psycho-Analysis*, p. 207). However, if the text itself is a petrified garden, it is also a monument to desire, a sepulchre built out of the fossil-segments of Magda's speech, as she suggests when she says:

> . . . what I am going to do with the painted stones when the machines stop flying I do not know, that is one anxiety I cannot dismiss, I may be driven to building a sepulchre outside the kitchen door, all ready to be crawled into when the great day comes, for I have not the heart to wheel them back into their native veld and disperse them, not after they have been brothers and sisters to each other so long, and participated in my messages. (*HC*, pp. 132–3)

(This would also appear to be an allusion to the fact that Schreiner is buried in a stone cairn on the summit of a small hill near Cradock in the Cape.) And so, recalling Lacan's observation that 'The first symbol in which we recognize humanity in its vestigial traces is the sepulture, and the intermediary of death can be recognized in every relation in which man comes to the life of his history' (*Ecrits*, p. 104), we come to see that Magda's repeated gestures of destruction, along with her terminal gesture of negation, like Lacan's example of Empedocles throwing himself into Mount Etna, are aimed at leaving present in our memory 'this symbolic act of [her] being-for-death' (*Ecrits*, p. 104).

NOTES

1. Not only to Schreiner, but to other woman writers like Pauline Smith, whose pastoral novel, *The Beadle*, has come to be regarded as a milestone in the tradition of white South African writing in English.
2. Accordingly, I will use the terms speech or discourse, rather than narrative, when referring to this novel.
3. Here I become engaged in the somewhat hazardous undertaking of a simultaneous reading of Coetzee's and Schreiner's novels, rendering myself vulnerable to a charge of misreading on two fronts. I must stress, however, that what I am undertaking is primarily a reading of *In the Heart of the Country*, and that without Coetzee's novel I would not have arrived at this reading of *The Story of an African Farm*.
4. Stephen Gray points out that:

   '. . . the logical and coherent tradition of the realist novel in South Africa is a very narrow, but highly organized one. What begins with Schreiner's novel as the liberal tradition in Southern African English fiction does continue in *Turbott Wolfe*, is endemic to *Cry, the Beloved Country*, is reviewed in Lessing's *The Grass is Singing*, and meets its culmination in later novels. But this is not a development in the normal sense of the term; it is not a case of one work influencing the next, for here each work takes *The Story of an African Farm* as a sole common origin without significant regard to intermediate variations'. (p. 136)
5. Having cited a passage from Emerson's 'The American Scholar,' Gray comments as follows:

   'Emerson's declaration of independence from British culture of 1837, made on behalf of the American writer, took four decades to find a sympathetic response in the South African context. When Olive Schreiner opened her 'iron lids' in the 1870's, called herself 'Ralph Iron' and invented a hero called Waldo, and proceeded to celebrate life in the Cape Colony from inside, the South African writer too had taken the vast leap from dependence on 'foreign harvests' to harvesting his own that Emerson's New England romanticism recommended', (p. 133)
6. Règis Durand, 'The Captive King': The Absent Father in Melville's Text', p. 62. Durand is commenting here on Melville's *The Confidence-Man*: it so happens that his entire commentary

on Melville is conducted in terms which might equally well be applied to *In the Heart of the Country*.

7. D.W. Winnicott, 'Mirror-role of Mother and Family in Child Development' in *Playing and Reality* (London: Penguin, 1974) cited by Charles Bernheimer, p. 172.
8. Wilden says:

   'Through the child's accession to language, which for Lacan governs the Symbolic order, and through his advent to the intersubjectivity of rivalry (ideally with the parent of the opposite sex), the boy, by repressing castration, and the girl, by rejecting it (*Verwerfung*), emerge from the Oedipus complex into the subjectivity of normality (again ideally).' (p. 188)
9. Freud says that 'The discovery of her castration is a turning-point in the life of the girl', and that 'Her love has as its object the phallic mother; with the discovery that the mother is castrated it becomes possible to drop her as a love object so that the incentives to hostility, which have been so long accumulating, get the upper hand'. He also says that 'The wish with which the girl turns to her father, is, no doubt, ultimately the wish for the penis, which her mother has refused her and which she now expects from her father'. (Sigmund Freud, 'The Psychology of Women', pp. 162; 163 and 164).
10. Others are: 'I am a child again, an infant, a grub . . .' (*HC*, p. 51; see p. 164, this chapter); 'No one is ancestral to the stone desert, no one but the insects, among whom myself, a thin black beetle with dummy wings who lays no eggs and blinks in the sun, a real puzzle to entomology' (*HC*, p. 18); 'How can I believe this creature was ever a child, how can I believe she was born of humankind? Easier to imagine her crawling from under a stone in her bottlegreen sheath, licking the eggslime off herself before taking her bearings and crawling off to this farmhouse to take up residence behind the wainscot' (*HC*, p. 38).
11. See Jean Laplanche: 'The entire instinct with its own "source", "impetus", "aim", and "object" . . . the instinct, kit and caboodle with its four factors, is in turn the source of a process which mimics, displaces, and denatures ie: the drive' (p. 22).
12. Jameson, 'Imaginary and Symbolic in Lacan,' p. 362, citing Lacan, *Le Seminaire, I* (Paris: Seuil, 1975), p. 178.
13. Lemaire points out that this process is 'realized in the Oedipus through the symbolic castration which legislates the use of the sex through the death of the father by the fact of his accession

to the place of the Other: this is the paternal metaphor. We know that the word is the murder of the thing and that this death is the condition of the symbol' (p. 85).

14. Edmond Ortigues, *Le Discours et le Symbole*, p. 194, cited by Jameson, 'Imaginary and Symbolic in Lacan,' (p. 378).

15. An attitude not in evidence in *The Story of an African Farm*, but strongly expressed in her political articles on South Africa. It is interesting, with respect to the analysis of this attitude which I am embarking on here (via Coetzee), that Dan Jacobson comments upon Schreiner's 'liberalism' as follows:

    'She invariably took upon herself the pain of speaking up for the humiliated and oppressed – Boers, blacks, women, Jews: and what could be more selfless than that? . . . But again and again the effect would be to transcend the torments of the present by a feat of moral and rhetorical levitation which ultimately strikes the reader as having an inner meaning or impulsion quite opposite to that intended. It begins to strike him as strangely selfish, uncaring, preoccupied far more with reassuring the speaker than ministering to the needs of those to whom, or of whom, she is speaking'. (pp. 16–17)

16. These are Coetzee's own translations in the English edition of *In the Heart of the Country* (London: Secker & Warburg, 1977). The page numbers correspond with the South African edition.

17. H.S. Harris, Introduction to the *Difference* Essay, *The Difference Between Fichte's and Schelling's System of Philosophy*, by Hegel. Harris goes on to point out that 'in Fichte's science of knowledge [the absolutely unconditioned first principle] is not a dogmatic *conclusion* from thinking being to substantial being as in Descartes; nor yet is it a necessary 'form,' critically cleansed of all ontic commitment, such as we see in Kant's Ich denke. Fichte's 'Ego' is a primordial *Act*, a *Tathandlung*, a self-establishing, the self-positing of Reason' (p. 11).

18. Schleifer makes the point that 'identification [with the Symbolic father] creates the difference between desire and the law in which temporality itself, as well as narrative 'emerges' (p. 876); and Ricoeur says: ' . . . I take temporality to be that structure of existence that reaches language in narrativity and narrativity to be the language structure that has temporality as its ultimate referent. Their relationship is therefore reciprocal' (p. 169).

19. Lacan says:

    'The linearity that Saussure holds to be constitutive of the chain of discourse, in conformity with its emission by a single voice and with its horizontal position in our writing – if this linearity is necessary, in fact, it is not sufficient. It applies to the chain of discourse only in the direction in which it is orientated in time . . . .

There is in effect no signifying chain that does not have, as if attached to the punctuation of each of its units, a whole articulation of relevant contexts suspended 'vertically', as it were, from that point.' (*Ecrits*, p. 154).

Describing the signifying process of metaphor, he says:

'The creative spark of the metaphor does not spring from the presentation of two images, that is, of two signifiers, equally actualized. It flashes between two signifiers one of which has taken the place of the other in the signifying chain, the occulted signifier remaining present through its (metonymic) connexion with the rest of the chain' (*Ecrits*, p. 157);

that, 'metaphor occurs at the precise point at which sense emerges from non-sense' (*Ecrits*, p. 158); and that in the metaphoric structure 'it is in the substitution of signifier for signifier that an effect of signification is produced that is creative or poetic, in other words, which is the advent of the signification in question' (*Ecrits*, p. 164).

20. Sigmund Freud, 'Negation' (1925), *Standard Edition*, XIX, 239, cited by Wilden, p. 286.

21. Coetzee had made the point that:

'The Afrikaans novel stands in a peculiarly compromised relation to the soil (*bodem*) of South Africa. It is haunted . . . into our day, by the idea of the *plaas* (farm), the plaas that stands somewhere in the not too distant past of every Afrikaner. The natural world of the classic Afrikaans novel is, in fact, coextensive with the *plaas*: there is no sense of nature and the *plaas* being fundamentally different.

From this deeply embedded attitude – that the South African earth *belongs* to certain people and not to others – an attitude embedded not only in ethnic Afrikaans thinking but in the concept of the ancestral farm is the heartland of the Afrikaner – it follows that the classic Afrikaans tradition will never throw up that kind of Great Novel in which all classes and groups of people are seen as having a common birth from a common natal earth – a great National Novel, in fact'. ('The Great South African Novel', p. 81)

4 Waiting for the Barbarians

Of all Coetzee's novels to date, *Waiting for the Barbarians* is the one in which the theme of the Lacanian subject is the least explicit. In the course of my discussion of the novel however, I intend to show how the fundamental premises according to which Coetzee conducts his reading and re-writing of this genre – the liberal humanist novel – *are* Lacanian, and that it is possible to detect in this novel a re-emergance, or repetition, of themes and issues common to the other novels. Because of the implicit level at which these themes are operative, they are far more diffuse, far less readily definable than in the other novels, and function at the level of a network of enigmatic relationships. Undertaking to resolve the enigma of these relationships, particularly the Magistrate's relationship with the barbarian girl, one finds that one's interpretive activity inevitably repeats the structures of these relationships, making it politic to admit from the outset that one is faced, finally, with the residual enigma of one's own relationship to the text, one's own status as reader.

The narrator of *Waiting for the Barbarians* is a magistrate approaching old age, chief official of a remote border post of an unnamed Empire. Desiring nothing more than to see out his life in the peace of the frontier settlement, he becomes caught up in and rendered impotent by a new phase of aggressive imperialism. The Magistrate takes in a barbarian girl, a victim of the most recent round of brutal interrogations, and imposes his fetishistic attentions upon her, before undertaking a long and dangerous journey to return her to her people. Clearly we have here another frontier situation, another encounter between colonizer and colonized. The allusion to Cavafy's poem of the same title, in which the imminent arrival of the Barbarians is 'some sort of a solution',[1] indicates that what is at stake, once again, is the issue of identity: the identity of a group which defines itself in contradistinction to another group; which, indeed, finds its *raison d'être* in the threat, real or imagined, posed by this other group. Although geographically this remote outpost does not correspond to any actual setting in South Africa, it clearly represents a particular phase of South African colonial history: the phase of bureaucratized control which succeeds the phases of exploration and agrarian settlement (represented in *Dusklands* and *In the Heart of the Country* respectively), and which, in the South African context, heralds the phase of militarized totalitarian control (represented in *Life & Times of Michael K*). Equally clearly, the sentiments the Magistrate expresses and the attitudes he manifests in his behaviour replicate those of the liberal protagonists in novels by writers such as William Plomer, Alan Paton, Dan Jacobson, Laurens van der Post (in a novel like *In a Province*), and the early Gordimer (up to *Occasion for Loving*, 1963). These sentiments and attitudes may be summarized as: belief in the power and efficacy of the judiciary system; belief in 'civilization' and the continual progress of humankind; an abhorrence of violence, accompanied by an attitude of tolerance and rationality; a capacity for fairly ruthless self-scrutiny and a sense of guilt which can be incapacitating; and, more significant than all of these, a belief in individual autonomy and in the freedom of choice.[2]

Existing commentaries on the novel recognize the liberal stance of the narrator, but, as is evident in the following passages from various critical texts, the Magistrate's sentiments have been read as reflecting those of Coetzee, or as Coetzee's negative 'diagnostic proposition' concerning the liberal humanist position *per se*:

> In terms of formal organisation, *Waiting for the Barbarians* has much less to discomfort the liberal reader than the earlier novels. The protagonist too, appears to be much closer to the protagonists of liberal fiction, although he is certainly not identical to them. Is Coetzee moving towards a greater sympathy with liberal perspectives? (Vaughan, pp. 125–6)

> The magistrate is, I suppose, both liberal and radical . . . . *Waiting for the Barbarians* is a hopeful book. Because it succeeds in a necessary blurring of what is supposedly civilized and what is not, and because it presents the indecency of Colonel Joll and his men as the grossest barbarity, the reader is left with some measure of comfort in the knowledge that the ordinary, essential rhythms of life can be maintained if only we rid ourselves of the Colonel Jolls. (Roberts, pp. 48–49)

> What distinguishes *Waiting for the Barbarians* from its predecessors [Coetzee's previous two novels] is that it takes the liberal humanist position into account, for this is what the old Magistrate can be seen to represent. Coetzee presents the Magistrate's predicament in such a way as to make it profoundly moving and disturbing, especially to anyone with liberal humanist proclivities. Yet, cogent as the insights are into the consciousness of this master who serves Empire, I feel bound to question the central diagnostic proposition Coetzee offers us concerning him [that is, that the Magistrate and Colonel Joll constitute two sides of imperial rule]. (Wood, p. 129)

The sense of confusion evident in these commentaries concerning the position adopted by Coetzee in *Waiting for the Barbarians* makes it necessary to emphasize that, in giving us a narrator like the Magistrate, Coetzee does not engage in either a critique or an endorsement of the liberal humanist position itself, but in a deconstructive reading of the liberal humanist *novelistic discourse*. The *source* of confusion would appear to be, chiefly, the mode of narration, whether the critic takes it into account at an explicit level or not. The fact that the Magistrate is an autodiegetic narrator, whose narrative is given in the present definite or indefinite virtually throughout, means that we have access only to this single source of information, with no mediating commentary, either from the perspective of a heterodiegetic narrator,[3] or from the perspective of a narrator who is able to comment from a position in the present upon a past self. Unlike Coetzee's previous autodiegetic narrators, Eugene Dawn and Magda, the Magistrate does not provide any explicit self-reflexive commentary which would undermine the mimetic pretensions of the fiction,[4] and alert the reader to the fact that a different convention of representation is operative here; that is, that the narrator's speech represents the *act* of speech itself, and is not a transparent medium for representing physical or psychological reality, as in the traditional realist novel. The tendency, therefore, has been to read the Magistrate's discourse in the conventional manner, as 'representing' a particular reality, and the mode of narration, where it is remarked upon, is seen as supporting rather than subverting the conventions of realism. We find, for example, the following commentary:

> There is never a wasted word nor a misplaced phrase and Mr Coetzee uses a brilliantly successful narrative technique, deceptively simple yet highly unusual. His first-person narrator does not in the usual manner use the past tense with periodic switches to the historic present, nor is there any scaffolding or 'excuse' for the narrative in the form of a diary or letter or even just reminiscence. The whole novel is narrated in the present tense as though, like a film, it is taking place in front of us: 'I carry my sleeping bag out onto the ramparts . . . ' The manoeuvre is so successful that it is totally unobtrusive and can be maintained even when the narrator is most desperately involved in the action and close to being annihilated. We should hardly protest if we read: 'My lifeless body is trampled into the dust.' (Harvey, p. 3)

When this critic says 'We should hardly protest . . . ' what he means is that his sense of *vraisemblance* is not jarred, that he is still able to look through the *narration* of the event to the event itself, in the manner in which the mode of realism has accustomed him.

In contrast, the point I wish to make is that it is necessary to distinguish between speech as 'representing' (in the conventional manner), and speech as 'represented', a distinction which is made by Mikhail Bakhtin in an essay titled 'The Word in the Novel'. Discussing the images of language given by Pushkin in *Eugene Onegin*, Bakhtin says:

> The author sees the limitation and incompleteness of Onegin's language and outlook, at that time still fashionable, he sees its ridiculous, abstracted and artificial aspect . . . but at the same time there is a whole series of important thoughts and observations that he can express only with the help of this 'language', in spite of the fact that, historically, this language as a totality was already doomed. This kind of image of another person's language and outlook, being at the same time both represented and representing, is extremely typical of the novel; it is to this type that the greatest of the novel's images belong (for instance, the image of Don Quixote). The direct poetic (in the narrow sense) means of expression and representation, when they become part of such an image, preserve their own direct meaning, but at the same time they have 'reservations' put on them, they are 'externalized', shown to be historically relative, limited, incomplete – in the novel they become, so to speak, self-critical. (pp. 215–16)

The magistrate's narrative does serve to express 'a whole series of important thoughts and observations', in that it provides a description of a particular phase of colonial history, and gives an account of the atrocities committed by the new guardians of the police state, and of the nature of a particular attempt to resist these atrocities. Thus far the Magistrate's language performs the function of representing a historical situation, and a state of consciousness which is a response to this situation. At the same time, however, this language has 'reservations' put on it, it is represented as 'historically relative, limited, incomplete'. In Bakhtin's analysis, this is a feature of the novel in general, containing, as it does, passages of reported speech, which constitute images of language. However, the Magistrate's autodiegetic narrative can be considered in its entirety as reported speech, as it were, enclosed in quotation marks from beginning to end, so that the novel as a whole constitutes a single image of language, which is undermined from within.

To return to my original point, what we have represented in the figure of the Magistrate is not the liberal humanist position as such, but a particular form of novelistic discourse, a speech act which is constitutive of the liberal humanist writer. This means that the Magistrate's actions and relationships should be read as allegories of the attempts, the limitations and the failures of this discourse itself. And once we are alerted to the allegorical nature of this narrative, we find that the mode of narration functions to direct us to Coetzee's diagnosis of the nature of this attempt and of the sources of its failure. As Harvey points out, Coetzee's 'narrative technique' in this novel is 'highly unusual': as such it must, likewise, be regarded as highly significant, that is to say, relevant to Coetzee's meaning here. It is a mode of narration which has come to be accepted as a convention in the interior monologue, in which the combination of an autodiegetic narrator and present verb forms indicate that the reader is being granted apparently unmediated access to thoughts and states of consciousness; and in the performative mode of contemporary self-reflexive fiction, in which the reader is referred to the discursive performance in progress. It is seldom, if ever, encountered outside these conventions. While narration always takes place in the present and in the first person,[5] in *Waiting for the Barbarians* the use of an autodiegetic narrator and present verb forms means that narrative time and narrated time[6] are conflated to make speech and action coincide in a way which is untenable when one is operating according to the conventions of realism, as is evident from an observation like the following (from a text titled *Time and the Novel* not related in any way to Coetzee's novel):

A narrative in the first person and written

throughout in the present would, if it were possible at all, appear so artificial as to make any identification impossible. It would obviously be limited to sensations and thoughts and exclude all action. It would also obtrude the act of writing itself, and by specifying itself so closely in time would appear even more remote to the reader, for it would impress on him constantly the fact and the act of communication.
(Mendilow, p. 107)

Contrary to Harvey's claim that Coetzee's 'narrative technique' is 'totally unobtrusive', in *Waiting for the Barbarians* we have a mode of narration that does 'obtrude the act of writing itself' (albeit in a subtle way), and does impress on one 'the fact and the act of communication', particularly if one takes into account the fact that:

> *I* refers to the act of individual discourse in which it is pronounced, and by this it designates the speaker. It is a term that cannot be identified except in what we have called elsewhere an instance of discourse and that has only a momentary reference. The reality to which it refers is the reality of discourse.
>
> Now this 'present' in its turn has only a linguistic fact as temporal reference: the coincidence of the event described with the instance of discourse that describes it. The temporal referent of the present can only be internal to the discourse. The *Dictionnaire générale* defines the 'present' as *'le temps du verbe qui exprime le temps où l'on est'*. But let us beware of this; there is no other criterion and no other expression by which to indicate 'the time at which one *is*' except to take it as 'the time at which one is *speaking*'. This is the eternally 'present' moment, although it never relates to the same events of an objective chronology because it is determined for each speaker by each of the instances of discourse related to it. (Benveniste, pp. 226 and 227)

It is a mode of narration which insists upon the discourse *as discourse*, flouting the conventions of *vraisemblance* not only by having the Magistrate narrate actions in the present tense, but also by having him narrate situations of speechlessness which are essentially the equivalent of Harvey's hypothetical phrase, 'My lifeless body is trampled into the dust'. Thus we find the Magistrate saying, 'Words fail me'. 'I guard my silence' and 'I try to call out something, a word of blind fear, a shriek, but the rope is now so tight that I am strangled, speechless' (*Barbarians*, pp. 107, 113, 120), all of which is the equivalent of saying 'I am not speaking'. And we find passages like the following, in which the Magistrate narrates periods of blankness or oblivion:

> I lose myself in the rhythm of what I am doing. I lose awareness of the girl herself. There is a space of time which is blank to me: perhaps I am not even present . . . . My eyes close. It becomes an intense pleasure to keep them closed, to savour the blissful giddiness. I stretch out on the carpet. In an instant I am asleep. (*WB*, pp. 28–29)

In addition to this we find an aberrant use of deictics, the 'indicators of deixis' being

> the demonstratives, adverbs, and adjectives, which organize the spatial and temporal relationships around the 'subject' taken as referent: 'this, here, now', and their numerous correlatives, 'that, yesterday, last year, tomorrow', etc. They have in common the feature of being defined only with respect to the instance of discourse in which they occur, that is, in dependence upon the *I* which is proclaimed in the discourse. (Benveniste, p. 226)

The appropriate deictics for autodiegetic narration and present verb forms are, for example, now, today, this morning, yesterday, tomorrow; the corresponding deictics for the narration of past events are, then, that day or one day, that morning, the previous day, the next day. For the most part the Magistrate's speech adheres to the correct usage as listed here, but there are numerous instances in which one finds deictics which do not locate events accurately in time with respect to the *I* in the present. We find, for example:

> All the next day the Colonel spends sleeping in his room at the inn (p. 21); the next day the Colonel begins his interrogations (p. 22); Early next morning he departs (p. 24); The next day she is not there (p. 25); One evening, rubbing her scalp with oil . . . (p. 31); In this moody state I pay a visit one evening . . . (p. 42); All that day I sit in a trance at my desk (p. 58); Then in mid-afternoon the key scrapes in the lock and the door opens (p. 86); Then one day they throw open the door and I step out to face not two men but a squad standing to attention (p. 117).

With some writers this deviation from accepted usage could be accounted for in terms of an unintentional error. Coetzee, however, has repeatedly demonstrated his concern with the issue of narrative time, and so this must be read as a deliberate deviation, which performs a specific function in this novel. It would seem that, within a narrative which conflates narrative time and narrated time, these deictics function to indicate the *non*-proximity of the speaker to the events described.[7] As in the case of narration (in the present) of moments of speechlessness, this serves as a reminder that narrated time is merely a function of a particular convention, and that in fact all we have is narrative time, all we have is speech, and the events are simply a pre-text for this speech.

Taken together, these features of the mode of narration in this novel allow us to read the Magistrate's narrative as a speech act, without having the Magistrate, as representative of the liberal humanist writer, pronounce upon his discourse *as* discourse, in the manner of Coetzee's self-reflexive narrators. This is essential here, because the liberal humanist discourse is characterized precisely by its refusal to acknowledge its status as discourse, by its insistence upon individual autonomy, and therefore by its refusal to recognize the necessary passage of the self through the Other in speech. Accordingly, the Magistrate does not take into account the fact that writing is going on. Indeed, he is shown going to some lengths to demonstrate that he is *not* writing a diary or a journal, which, in so far as these are written records, are devices which do acknowledge, even if implicitly, their status as linguistic objects. About to set out on a journey to the barbarians, he considers compiling some kind of document, but is unable to do so:

> What the second document is to be I do not yet know. A testament? A memoir? A confession? A history of thirty years on the frontier? All that day I sit in a trance at my desk staring at the empty white paper, waiting for words to come. A second day passes in the same way. On the third day I surrender, put the paper back in the drawer, and make preparations to leave. It seems appropriate that a man who does not know what to do with the woman in his bed should not know what to write. (*WB*, pp. 57–58)

Toward the close of the novel he attempts to write a history of the settlement, but again abandons the project. On only one occasion is he allowed to express a glimmer of insight into the discursive process which translates the self into Otherness:

> In the clear silence of the morning I find an obscure sentiment lurking at the edge of my consciousness. With the buck before me suspended in immobility, there seems to be time for all things, time even to turn my gaze inward and see what it is that has robbed the hunt of its savour: the sense that this has become no longer a morning's hunting but an occasion on which either the proud ram bleeds to death on the ice or the old hunter misses his aim; that for the duration of this frozen moment the stars

> are locked in a configuration in which events are not themselves but stand for other things.
>
> ....
>
> 'Never before have I had the feeling of not living my own life on my own terms', I tell the girl, struggling to explain what happened. (*WB*. pp. 39–40)

Clearly, in the novel 'events are not themselves but stand for other things': referring to the mode of Naturalism in terms which one can apply to the mode of Realism in the liberal novel, Coetzee has said that

> people in Naturalist novels refuse to act as though they are living inside verbal artefacts. But being in a novel is not the same as being in the real world (for example, everything you see inside a novel is likely to have a meaning); and if you refuse to recognize that you are inside a novel you are never going to have anything to say about your situation. Because making sense of life inside a book is different from making sense of real life – not more difficult or less difficult, just different. (Thorold and Wicksteed Interview, p. 3)

Events are not themselves because in the novel they *mean* something; likewise, the self cannot live its own life on its own terms because, in coming to have meaning in the novel, it becomes inscribed in the locus of a code, and so becomes circumscribed by the discourse of the Other.[8]

It is the Magistrate's failure to recognize that he is 'inside a novel' that in *Waiting for the Barbarians* is presented as the source of the failure of the liberal humanist discourse: it is not the performance of the Magistrate as protagonist, but the performative speech act of the liberal writer that Coetzee deconstructs here. Coetzee points out, in an interview, that the Magistrate is 'fundamentally a sympathetic person', and that 'It is perhaps only a minority of people that stand for that rather muddled and perhaps even doomed position that the magistrate takes up. Because it's riddled with contradictions' (Folke Rhedin Interview, p. 6). Referring to Magda's attempt to escape the structure of the Master/Slave relationship imposed by 'centuries of cultural and spiritual deformation', Coetzee says:

> She is the one who makes the massive effort to escape, but there's no saying whether she escapes, much in the same way as we can say that the magistrate in the third book makes an effort, but who is to say that the effort goes far enough. So in one way these people are not trapped in their situation. Or let me put it another way, perhaps they are trapped in their situation but they don't resign themselves to being trapped in their situation. But whether they get out of it in their lifetime, that is another question. (pp. 7–8)

Coetzee's deconstructive reading of this genre is achieved by pointing to the contradictions which do not allow the attempt to escape a particular discursive situation go far enough, which do not allow the liberal writer, in the 'lifetime' of the discourse, to escape the trap inherent in the act of writing. Thus he juxtaposes the function that the liberal writer assumes for him/herself in writing a novel, and the function that the writing and the reading of the novel, as speech act, in fact performs in relation to the writer and the reader. This juxtaposition is organized around the metaphor of sight and blindness (articulated alternately as telling the truth and lying), and here again we find that the mode of narration performs a specific function: it allows Coetzee to reverse the orientation of the traditional liberal novel, and to present us with a narrator who progresses from a position of 'sight', or superior vision, to a position of 'blindness'. This would not be possible with an autodiegetic narrator whose narrative is given in the past historic, for the self narrating the past activities and states of consciousness of a previous self always possesses the advantage of hindsight.

The Magistrate's narrative opens with a comment upon the sunglasses of the Colonel, who has recently arrived 'under the emergency powers' (*WB*, p. 1): 'I have never seen anything like it: two little disks of glass suspended in front of his eyes in loops of wire. Is he blind? I could understand it if he wanted to hide blind eyes. But he is not blind' (*WB*. p. 1). This initiates the theme of the Magistrate's superior capacity for sight in contrast to the willful blindness of the new military dictators, and refers to the stance of the liberal writer, who takes upon him/herself the task of acting as the 'eyes' or the conscience of the society, hoping to effect a change in individual attitudes by unveiling the horrors to which others are blind. This stance reaches a crescendo when the Magistrate, protesting against the Colonel's brutal treatment of barbarian prisoners, cries out to stop him:

> 'Look!' I shout. I point to the four prisoners who lie docilely on the earth . . . . I raise my broken hand to the sky. 'Look!' I shout. 'We are the great miracle of creation! But from some blows this miraculous body cannot repair itself! How—!' Words fail me. 'Look at these men!' I recommence. '*Men*!' (*WB*, p. 107)

The attempt to place before the reader a testament of the injustices of the society approximates the stance to which Coetzee refers in a different context:

> . . . the writer must cultivate stoicism and a literature of witness, seeing himself minimally – as the man who acts, in Sartre's words, 'in such a way that nobody can be ignorant of the world and nobody may say that he is innocent of what it's all about'; with, all the while, an eye on his moral relation to his obsessive story; is he merely fondling his wound?[9]

Coetzee's comment here serves to introduce the issue of the Magistrate's relationship to the barbarian girl, for it seems reasonable to read the Magistrate's repetitive and obsessive act of fondling the girl's feet as a metaphor for the liberal writer's fondling of his/her own wound, that is to say, as an indication of his/her 'moral relation' to his/her 'obsessive story'.

To spell out the terms of this allegory of the act of writing, the barbarian girl, as 'the form to which, it seems [the Magistrate is] in a measure enslaved' (*WB*, p. 42), represents the figure of the suffering victim around which the liberal humanist novel is articulated. When the Magistrate asks the girl 'And why do I want you here?' her answer is 'You want to talk all the time' (*WB*, p. 40): the victim is the source of the liberal discourse, and the liberal writer, in turn, is in a state of 'bondage' (The Magistrate says: 'There are other times when I suffer fits of resentment against my bondage to the ritual of the oiling and the rubbing, the drowsiness, the slump into oblivion,' *WB*, p. 41) enslaved by his/her obsessive guilt in relation to the figure of the victim. The Magistrate cannot make love to the girl, and instead washes, oils and massages the scarred and damaged feet which are the result of Colonel Joll's acts of torture. This ritual produces a climactic state of blankness, or oblivion:

> . . . often in the very act of caressing her I am overcome with sleep as if poleaxed, fall into oblivion sprawled upon her body, and wake an hour or two later dizzy, confused, thirsty. These dreamless spells are like death to me, or enchantment, blank, outside time. (*WB*, p.31)

This blank space, outside time, is a release from the 'life' of the discourse, and describes the effect achieved by the act of writing itself, an act which, like the Magistrate's ministrations to the girl, must be seen as a ritual expiation of guilt. This, then, is the covert function of the liberal 'literature of witness': it is the equivalent of the ritual to which the Magistrate refers when reflecting on Joll's and Mandel's acts of torture:

> Looking at him I wonder how he felt the very first time: did he, invited as an apprentice to twist the pincers or turn the screw or whatever it is they do,

> shudder even a little to know that at that instant he was trespassing into the forbidden? I find myself wondering too whether he has a private ritual of purification, carried out behind closed doors, to enable him to return and break bread with other men. Does he wash his hands very carefully, perhaps, or change all his clothes; or has the Bureau created new men who can pass without disquiet between the unclean and the clean? (*WB*, p. 12)

> 'Forgive me if the question seems impudent, but I would like to ask: How do you find it possible to eat afterwards, after you have been . . . working with people? . . . Do you find it easy to take food afterwards? I have imagined that one would want to wash one's hands. But no ordinary washing would be enough, one would require priestly intervention, a ceremonial of cleansing, don't you think? Some kind of purging of one's soul too – that is how I have imagined it. Otherwise how would it be possible to return to everyday life – to sit down at table, for instance, and break bread with one's family or one's comrades?' (*WB*, p. 126)

In this projection of his own sense of guilt upon the torturers, the Magistrate reveals the source of his attraction to the barbarian girl, and, by extension, the source of the liberal writer's need to engage in the act of writing.

The repeated reference to the breaking of bread is significant, for, along with the ritual of washing the girl's feet, it refers to the quasi-religious dimensions of the liberal novel in the South African context. In addition to this, its association with the Christian ritual of communion, which signifies the absolution from sin and the release from guilt through the sharing of Christ's suffering, and the further association which bread has with suffering via the French translation, pain, direct us to the nature of the liberal writer's relationship to the protagonist as victim: bearing witness to suffering, the liberal writer takes this suffering upon him/herself, and thereby expiates his/her guilt. Reflecting upon an injust sentence which, in the name of justice, he once passed upon a boy, the Magistrate says:

> I remember the uneasy shame I felt on days like that. I would leave the courtroom and return to my apartment and sit in the rocking-chair in the dark all evening, without appetite, until it was time to go to bed. 'When some men suffer unjustly,' I said to myself, 'it is the fate of those who witness their suffering to suffer the shame of it.' (*WB*, p. 139)

The suffering victim becomes a means of establishing an identity for the liberal writer as, in bearing witness to the other's suffering, and in claiming an equivalent suffering for him/herself, the writer casts him/herself in the role of the seer, truth-teller, of blameless one.

It is here, in the barbarian girl's function as a source of identity to the Magistrate, that the theme of the Lacanian subject becomes relevant to a consideration of the Magistrate's discourse. The theme is manifest in the implicit correlation between the Magistrate's dreams, as evidence of unconscious desire, and the figure of the girl; a correlation which becomes apparent when one compares the following passages, the first a description of the dream image, the second giving the Magistrate's perception of the barbarian girl:

> The face I see is blank, featureless; it is the face of an embryo or a tiny whale; it is not a face at all but another part of the human body that bulges under the skin; it is white; it is the snow itself (*WB*, p. 37);

> 'She is incomplete!' I say to myself. Though the thought begins to float away at once, I cling to it. I have a vision of her closed eyes and closed face filming over with skin. Blank, like a fist beneath a black wig, the face grows out of the throat and out of the blank body beneath it,

> without aperture, without entry. (*WB*, p. 42)

The girl becomes the figural embodiment of the Magistrate's desire, and the activities centred around her represent the liberal writer's attempt to give expression to the desiring self via the act of writing. This embryonic, faceless figure is the pre-linguistic self, the equivalent of the infant's experience of the self in and prior to the Mirror Stage. According to Lacan, there is 'a real *specific prematurity of birth in man* . . . a fact recognized as such by embryologists, by the term *foetalization*' (*Ecrits*, p. 4). The Mirror Stage functions to overcome this 'organic insufficiency' by establishing 'a relation between the organism and its reality':

> This development is experienced as a temporal dialectic that decisively projects the formation of the individual into history. The *mirror stage* is a drama whose internal thrust is precipitated from insufficiency to anticipation – and which manufactures for the subject, caught up in the lure of spatial identification, the succession of phantasies that extends from a fragmented body-image to a form of its totality that I shall call orthopaedic – and, lastly, to the assumption of the armour of an alienating identity, which will mark with its rigid structure the subject's entire mental development. Thus, to break out of the circle of the *Innenwelt* into the *Umwelt* generates the inexhaustible quadrature of the ego's verifications.
>
> This fragmented body . . . usually manifests itself in dreams when the movement of the analysis encounters a certain level of aggressive disintegration in the individual. It then appears in the form of disjointed limbs, or of those organs represented in exoscopy, growing wings and taking up arms for intestinal persecutions . . . .
>
> Correlatively, the formation of the *I* is symbolized in dreams by a fortress, or a stadium – its inner arena and enclosure, surrounded by marshes and rubbish-tips, dividing it into two opposed fields of contest where

> the subject flounders in quest of the lofty, remote inner castle whose form (sometimes juxtaposed in the same scenario) symbolizes the id in a quite startling way. (*Ecrits*, pp. 4–5)

The Magistrate's recurrent dream provides us with a juxtaposition of precisely these images: the fortess, the form with a face that 'is not a face at all but another part of the human body that bulges under the skin', and the snow castle on which this form is working. The dream may thus be seen as referring to the deepest sources of this speech act which is the novel itself: the attempt on the part of the fragmented, foetal self of the Imaginary to erect an identity in the Symbolic.[10] The act of writing is one of the ego's attempts at 'verification', one of it's attempts 'to break out of the circle of the *Innenwelt* into the *Umwelt*', and, as I have indicated in the preceding chapters, it takes the form of a 'temporal dialectic that . . . projects the formation of the individual into history'.

The sequence of the dreams, alternating with the Magistrate's actions in relation to the barbarian girl, provides evidence of a fairly definite progression, which traces the pattern of a rising and falling curve, and which marks the stages of the writer's quest for identity and self-transcendence. In the first dream, which precedes the Magistrate's meeting with the girl, the face of the girl working at the castle of snow is not visible: 'She does not turn. I try to imagine the face between the petals of her peaked hood but cannot' (*WB*, p. 10). In the second dream of the girl the face is 'blank, featureless; it is the face of an embryo or a tiny whale' (*WB*, p. 37), and at the peak of the curve is the dream in which the Magistrate sees the girl as 'herself':

> Now I begin to see what the girl is doing. She is building a fort of snow, a walled town which I recognize in every detail . . . . And here is the very spot where I stand! But the square is empty, the whole town is white and mute and empty. I point to the middle of the square. 'You must put people

> there!' I want to say. No sound comes from my mouth, in which my tongue lies frozen like a fish. Yet she responds. She sits up on her knees and turns her hooded face towards me. I fear, at this last instant, that she will be a disappointment, that the face she will present to me will be obtuse, slick, like an internal organ not meant to live in the light. But no, she is herself, herself as I have never seen her, a smiling child, the light sparkling on her teeth and glancing from her jet-black eyes. 'So this is what it is to see!' I say to myself. (*WB*, p. 53)

This creates a *mise-en-abyme* effect, as we find a snow fort within a dream fort within a narrated fort. As the Magistrate walks into the snow fort, the various levels of the narrative structure are conflated in such a way as to show that his identity is less contingent upon this structuring activity than is the fort of snow. If 'this is what it is to see', it is because the dream-image of the girl, perfect and beautiful, is a vision of the integration of self and desire in a living form; it is a vision of the union of the self and its object in complete fullness of being, as opposed to the alienating structure of identity realized in the fort (the equivalent of the *I* of the narrative) which is empty of life. Exclaiming, 'So this is what it is to see!' the Magistrate gives the lie to the stance of witness, as seeing is redefined here as the capacity to look inward to the source of the narrative, to the unconscious desire which emerges in the dream.

The Magistrate tells us that 'The dream has taken root' (*WB*, p. 53), and at this point he conceives the plan of taking the girl back to her people; 'I ask the girl about her sisters. . . . 'Would you not like to see your sisters again?' I ask, (*WB*, p. 53). The journey away from the fort, to return the girl to her people, functions in more than one way to establish an identity for the Magistrate (and thus to imply the forms of identity the liberal writer seeks via the novel). The girl's partial blindness is a sign of her state of incompleteness, in Hegelian terms, of her 'inessential consciousness' in relation to the Magistrate's position of mastery. She cannot reciprocate the Magistrate's desire, cannot provide proof of his identity, because she cannot return the look of recognition he seeks. Looking into her eyes, he finds no answering desire there, but only the image of his own desire given back to him: 'I take her face between my hands and stare into the dead centres of her eyes, from which twin reflections of myself stare solemnly back' (*WB*, p. 41). The act of returning the girl to her people is an attempt to restore her to 'herself', to a state of wholeness, so that she *would* be able to provide this kind of reciprocal recognition. On the journey out, the Magistrate asks himself:

> Is it then the case that it is the whole woman I want, that my pleasure in her is spoiled until these marks on her are erased and she is restored to herself; or is it the case (I am not stupid, let me say these things) that it is the marks on her which drew me to her but which, to my disappointment, I find, do not go deep enough. Too much or too little: is it she I want or the traces of a history her body bears? (*WB*, p. 64)

He refers here to the dual aspects of his need, as liberal writer, for the form or figure of the girl as one of the oppressed. On the one hand, the writing expresses a genuine desire to change the relationship between oppressor and oppressed, as in the case of Magda's gestures toward Hendrik and Klein-Anna, to replace the Master/Slave relationship with a relationship of equality; on the other hand, she is able to provide him with a history, or simply a story, of suffering, with which he can identify, in the full sense of the term.

The act of returning the girl to her people allows the Magistrate to cast himself in the role of the one who suffers, and the hardships of the journey (which take him away from the fort that stands for the fixation of his identity in the Symbolic) are the self-imposed suffering, or penance, which, it seems, frees him to consummate his relationship with the girl. This consummation is, significantly, preceded by the baking and sharing of bread (*pain*). Handing the girl over to the barbarian horsemen, the Magistrate says: 'Tell them why we are here. Tell them your story. Tell them the truth' (*WB*, p. 71). She is to be an emissary; the liberal novel carries a message of goodwill, but is also a testament of liberal innocence destined not only for the eyes of the oppressor, but also for the eyes of the oppressed. When the girl says 'You really want me to tell them the truth?' he continues: 'Tell them what you like. Only, now that I have brought you back, as far as I can, I wish to ask you very clearly to return to the town with me. Of your own choice' (*WB*, p. 71). In asking her to return with him, he is asking for her recognition as a free and independent being, and thereby reveals his liberal, and existentialist, belief in freedom as the capacity to exercise free choice.

However, saying goodbye to the girl, the Magistrate describes himself as 'returning, with apologies, a body we have sucked dry' (*WB*, p. 72). Having served the purpose of embodying his desire, of providing a vehicle for his discourse, and thus the means of creating an identity for himself, she has no further use for the Magistrate, who finds only blankness at what was once the source of her attraction for him. As opposed to the ecstatic visionary quality of the dream in which she appears perfect, whole, he now says:

> There is only blankness, and desolation that there has to be such blankness. When I tighten my grip on her hand there is no answer. I see only too clearly what I see: a stocky girl with a broad mouth and hair cut in a fringe across her forehead staring over my shoulder into the sky; a stranger, a visitor from strange parts now on her way home after a less than happy visit. (*WB*, p. 71)

Up to this point the narrative implies the possibility of desire fulfilled, reparation made, guilt expiated; beyond this point it constitutes the refutation of these possibilities, the downward curve in the 'cycles of desire and apathy in a body that is slowly cooling and dying' (*WB*, p. 46). Leaving the girl behind, the Magistrate takes her place as victim, and from this point on plays the role of both tragedian and tragic hero.

On his return to the fort it becomes evident that the journey to the barbarians has functioned as the means whereby he is able to dissociate himself from the guardians of Empire, and set himself in opposition to the state, and as such constitutes the equivalent of the liberal writer's gesture of defiance toward the government.

Placed in confinement on his return, he says:

> I am aware of the source of my elation: my alliance with the guardians of the Empire is over, I have set myself in opposition, the bond is broken, I am a free man. Who would not smile? But what a dangerous joy! It should not be so easy to attain salvation. And is there any principle behind my oppositon? Have I not simply been provoked into a reaction by the sight of one of the new barbarians usurping my desk and pawing my papers? As for this liberty which I am in the process of throwing away, what value does it have to me? Have I truly enjoyed the unbounded freedom of this past year in which more than ever before my life has been mine to make up as I go along? For example: my freedom to make of the girl whatever I felt like, wife or concubine or daughter or slave or all at once or none, at whim, because I had no duty to her save what it occurred to me to feel from moment to moment: from the oppression of such freedom who would not welcome the liberation of confinement? In my opposition there is nothing heroic – let me not for an instant forget that. (*WB*, p. 78)

The Magistrate alludes here to the paradoxical nature of the liberal and existentialist notion of freedom,[11] according to which freedom of choice amounts to nothing more than a choice between two alternatives: alliance with or opposition to those in power.[12] It has been demonstrated that his proclaimed freedom with respect to the girl has in fact been no freedom at all: her form has been imposed on him from without (as the discussion which follows will show), and the obsessive nature of his attentions to her indicates that the form of the relationship, too, has been severely circumscribed. Although hypothetically the nature of narrative means that the narrator's life is his/her's to make up as he/she goes along, the liberal writer is unable to put this freedom into practice, to tell a different kind of story, to envisage a different kind of relationship with one of the oppressed. The burden and responsibility of this freedom are exchanged for the proclaimed freedom from an identity as oppressor, but, setting himself in opposition to those in control, the Magistrate (as writer) voluntarily accepts the restrictions of a stance from which he can do no more than utter an impotent protest. And so we see that, via the figure of the Magistrate, Coetzee presents a critique of the existentialist nature of the liberal novelistic discourse; a critique which approximates Lacan's denouncement of 'the illusion of autonomy to which [the existentialist philosophy] entrusts itself' (*Ecrits*, p. 6). Lacan claims that

> . . . existentialism must be judged by the explanations it gives of the subjective impasses that have indeed resulted from it; a freedom that is never more authentic than when it is within the walls of a prison; a demand for commitment, expressing the impotence of a pure consciousness to master any situation; a voyeuristic-sadistic idealization of the sexual relation; a personality that realizes itself only in suicide; a consciousness of the other that can be satisfied only by Hegelian murder. (*Ecrits*, p. 6)

In prison, having assumed this new identity of victim, the Magistrate is at first dismayed by the pettiness of his suffering:

> No one beats me, no one starves me, no one spits on me. How can I regard myself as a victim of persecution when my sufferings are so petty? Yet they are all the more degrading for their pettiness. I remember smiling when the door first closed behind me and the key turned in the lock. It seemed no great infliction to

move from the solitariness of everyday existence to the solitude of a cell where I could bring with me a world of thoughts and memories. But now I begin to comprehend how rudimentary freedom is. What freedom has been left to me? The freedom to eat or go hungry; to keep my silence or gabble to myself or beat on the door or scream. If I was the object of an injustice, a minor injustice, when they locked me in here, I am now no more than a pile of blood, bone and meat that is unhappy. (*WB*, p. 85)

And when he dreams of the girl she is no longer whole, but broken, in pieces:

She brings her legs forward awkwardly and touches her ankles. She is so small that she is almost lost in the man's coat she wears. I kneel, unlace the capacious woollen socks, unwrap the bandages. The feet lie before me in the dust, disembodied, monstrous, two stranded fish, two huge potatoes . . . .

I enter the barracks gateway and face a yard as endless as the desert. There is no hope of reaching the other side, but I plod on, carrying the girl, the only key I have to the labyrinth, her head nodding against my shoulder, her dead feet drooping on the other side. (*WB*, p. 87)

The girl is the key to the labyrinth because, as the source of an alternate identity, she offers the means of finding a way out of the labyrinth of the self, a means of self-transcendence. However, there are other dreams in which the figure of the girl threatens to engulf the Magistrate, dreams which may be read as expressing a fear that the self that is brought into being by the narrative is going to be *trapped* in this identity of suffering victim, and that the pettiness of the suffering is *not* going to allow for self-transcendence through the expiation of guilt:

There are other dreams in which the figure that I

> call *the girl* changes shape, sex, size. In one dream there are two shapes that arouse horror in me: massive and blank, they grow and grow till they fill all the space in which I sleep. I wake up choked, shouting, my throat full. (*WB*, p. 87)

Colonel Joll's return from an expedition with a group of prisoners provides the Magistrate with an opportunity for 'saving' himself. He says:

> I cannot save the prisoners, therefore let me save myself. Let it at the very least be said, if it ever comes to be said, if there is ever anyone in some remote future interested to know the way we lived, that in this farthest outpost of the Empire of light there existed one man who in his heart was not a barbarian. (*WB*, p. 10)

Echoing Magda's lament. 'How shall I be saved?' (*In the Heart of the Country*, p.16), this suggests that what is at stake here is, likewise, the achievement of self-transcendence. Again taking on the role of official agent of sight, he urges the crowd to 'Look! . . . Look at these men!' (*WB*, p. 107), and receives a blow across the face which almost blinds him. This outburst of self-righteous rage and the blow which it earns him, although it does not blind him, does mean that the suffering he experiences is no longer petty. During his night of pain he dreams of the girl, again whole and perfect, bringing him a gift of broken bread, 'a loaf of bread, still hot, with a coarse steaming broken crust' (*WB*, p. 109), and later he tells Mai, the cook, 'When I dreamed of a woman I dreamed of someone who would come in the night and take the pain away' (*WB*, p. 128). The gift of broken bread is a symbol of forgiveness: if, in bringing bread (*pain*), the girl takes the pain away, it is because the dream offers the solace of guilt expiated through suffering, and the girl, again whole and perfect, is a symbol of self-transcendence achieved through this expiation.

However, subjected to torture following this, he finds his notions of suffering brutally reversed, as he discovers that pain does not grant self-transcendence, and, reducing him to a state of bestiality, does not even provide proof of an essential humanity.[13] Thus he says: 'In my suffering there is nothing ennobling. Little of what I call suffering is even pain' (*WB*, p. 115), and complains: 'There is no consoling grandeur in any of this. When I wake up groaning in the night it is because I am reliving in dreams the pettiest degradations. There is no way of dying allowed me, it seems, except like a dog in a corner' (*WB*, p. 117).[14] Mandel tells him to 'behave like a man' (*WB*, p. 117), and then proceeds to turn him into something else altogether, dressing him in a woman's smock and making him fly at the end of a rope, like a bird or a moth with its wings pinned together. About to be hanged in front of the crowd, the Magistrate says:

> This is not a contest of patience, then: if the crowd is not satisfied the rules are changed. But of what use is it to blame the crowd? A scapegoat is named, a festival is declared, the laws are suspended: who would not flock to see the entertainment? (*WB*, p. 120)

This introduces the function that the liberal novel performs in relation not only to the writer, but also in relation to the reader, a function which is, as Coetzee points out in the paper on la Guma, essentially that of the religious tragedy:

> A favoured mode among White South African writers has been tragedy . . . . Tragedy is typically the tragedy of inter-racial love: a White man and a Black woman, or vice versa, fall foul of the laws against miscegenation, or simply of White prejudice, and are destroyed or driven into exile. The overt content of the fable here is that love conquers evil through tragic suffering when such suffering is born witness to in art; its covert content is the apolitical doctrine that defeat can turn itself, by the twist of tragedy, into victory. The tragic hero is a scapegoat who takes our punishment. By his suffering he performs a ritual of expiation,

> and as we watch in sympathy our emotions are purged, as Aristotle noted, through the operations of pity and terror. We leave the theatre or close the book
>
> with new acquist
> Of true experience from this great event,
> With peace and consolation . . .
> And calm of mind, all passion spent.
>
> Religious tragedy reconciles us to the inscrutable dispensation by giving a meaning to suffering and defeat. As tragic art it also confers immortality: Oedipus and Lear may be destroyed by the gods, but we resurrect them ritually on our stage. An annual Shakespeare festival is as ritually appropriate as Easter.
>
> What is unique to religious tragedy is ritual catharsis . . . . religious tragedy is apolitical or quietistic. The predominant example of religious tragedy in South Africa is Alan Paton's *Cry, the Beloved Country*. ('Man's Fate in the Novels of Alex la Guma,' p. 17)

If, in relation to white readers, this mode performs a cathartic ritual of expiation, in relation to black readers it performs a gesture of reparation on behalf of Empire, that is to say, on behalf of the oppressor. About to set out on the journey to the barbarians, the Magistrate addresses a letter to the provincial governor, saying: 'To repair some of the damage wrought by the forays of the Third Bureau . . . and to restore some of the goodwill that previously existed, I am undertaking a brief visit to the barbarians' (*WB*, p. 57). And, handing the girl over to her people, he describes himself as 'a go-between, a jackal of Empire in sheep's clothing' (*WB*, p. 72).

I cite at such length from Coetzee's commentary on the mode of religious tragedy because I believe it provides certain fundamental insights into the nature of his own project in *Waiting for the Barbarians*. He deconstructs this particular mode – the liberal novel as religious tragedy – by reversing the conventional orientation whereby the hero, and in his/her wake the reader, is lead to comprehend and accept the meaning of suffering and defeat. That this is indeed one of the expectations inherent in the mode is evident from an observation like the following:

> Every yard of this barren ground and everything that happens to the people who inhabit it seems charged with significance . . . . Yet, as we read, we wait, enthralled, for the revelation that we feel must be imminent; the moment when all this significance will fall into place in a moment of Aristotelian 'recognition'; when we shall be able to say: 'Ah, yes! That is what life is! How illuminating! How profound!' or '*That* is what is wrong with our society' or even, more humbly, 'That is what he wanted us to see.' But that moment never comes. (Harvey, p. 4)

The Magistrate's narrative provides no such moment of recognition: suffering and defeat have no *meaning* here,[15] provide no aura of transcendence, and, as I have indicated, the Magistrate moves from a position of 'sight' to a position of 'blindness'.

There are allusions throughout Coetzee's novel to that archetypal tragedy, the tragedy of Oedipus, which is, likewise, articulated around the notion of blindness and sight. These allusions function mainly at the level of the structure of opposition between the Magistrate and Colonel Joll (or Mandel, who, within this structure, is interchangeable with Joll), which replicates the structure of opposition between Oedipus and Tiresias. René Girard describes this opposition as that of 'enemy brothers', or rivals, each of whom is a double of the other (*Violence and the Sacred*, pp. 71 and 79). Girard claims that the act of establishing the 'guilt' of the one or the other is merely an arbitrary means of turning *either* one of the rivals into a surrogate victim, or scapegoat, whose ritual killing or banishment will serve to exorcise the violence *within* the community, and restore it to a condition of unanimity; and that this is a function performed alike by religious ritual and the judicial system (*Violence and the Sacred*, pp. 78–79 and p. 23). His analysis of tragedy thus endorses Coetzee's exposition of religious tragedy as politically quietistic. Arguing that 'the characters in tragedy are ultimately indistinguishable', Girard says:

> Tyranny, too, is essentially unstable. A newcomer can ascend unexpectedly to the very summit of power, only to plummet, while one of his opponents assumes his lost position. In short, there is always a tyrant and always an oppressed, but the roles alternate. There is always one character who is angry; but while one of the enemy brothers rants and rages, the other may temporarily regain his composure. (*Violence and the Sacred*, p. 149)

The Magistrate, like Oedipus, assuming himself to be in possession of the truth and to be free of guilt, rails against both Joll and Mandel:

> When I turn to Colonel Joll he is standing not five paces from me, his arms folded. I point a finger at him. '*You*!' I shout. Let it all be said. Let him be the one on whom the anger breaks. 'You are depraving these people!'
>
> He does not flinch, he does not reply.
>
> '*You*!' My arm points at him like a gun. My voice fills the square. There is utter silence; or perhaps I am too intoxicated to hear. (*WB*, p. 106)

Joll and Mandel, for the most part, retain their composure, but in a passage like the following Joll returns the abuse:

> 'Those pitiable prisoners you brought in – are *they* the enemy I must fear? Is that what you say? *You* are the enemy, Colonel!' I can restrain myself no longer. I pound the desk with my fist. '*You* are the enemy,

> *you* have made the war, and *you* have given them all the martyrs they need – starting not now but a year ago when you committed your first filthy barbarities here! History will bear me out!'
>
> 'Nonsense. There will be no history, the affair is too trivial.' He seems impassive, but I am sure I have shaken him.
>
> 'You are an obscene torturer! You deserve to hang!'
>
> 'Thus speaks the judge, the One Just Man,' he murmurs.
>
> We stare into each other's eyes. (*WB*, p. 114)

The barbarian girl, as the object of the Magistrate's desire, introduces a third element into this dual structure, and here Coetzee seems to appropriate Girard's model of the triangular structure of desire, with which he demonstrates his familiarity in the paper 'Triangular Structures of Desire in Advertising'. Coetzee summarizes and comments upon Girard's thesis as follows:

> . . . it is clear that triangular desire is in essence vicarious. In literature, Emma Bovary and Don Quixote are the major exemplars of vicarious desiring. Not only do they imitate the outward behaviour of models they find in books, but they freely allow their desires to be defined for them by these models. Thus in their cases there is not simply the desiring subject and the desired object, but also the characteristic third point of the triangle, the model through whom desires are mediated. Girard's general thesis is that Flaubert and Cervantes, as well as the authors of certain other *romanesque* (as opposed to *romantique*) novels, 'apprehend intuitively and concretely, through the medium of their art, if not formally, the system (of triangular desire) in which they were first imprisoned together with their contemporaries.' The aims of *romanesque* art are thus critical and liberatory.
>
> The greater part of Girard's study is taken up with the

> analysis of more complex forms of mediated desire than Emma Bovary's or Don Quixote's forms in which the mediator is not a remote or fictional character but someone whose sphere of possible action impinges on the subject's and who is therefore in some degree a rival as well as a model (from this point Girard's thought on mimetic rivalry in *Violence and the Sacred* develops naturally) . . .

> Girard writes in a philosophical tradition stretching from Hegel to Sartre which attaches crucial importance to the ability of the subject to choose his own desires. In fact, in Hegel the stage of self-consciousness does not arrive, the 'I' does not come into being, until the subject becomes aware of itself as the locus of a lack, a desire. Thus the being of the 'I' is wholly implicated in its desire; and for the 'I' to yield its autonomy as a desiring subject is to yield its being. This yielding is what Girard calls an 'ontological sickness' (1961, p. 96): in turning his desire toward the desiring mediator, the subject yields his ontological autonomy:
>
>> The subject is unable to desire on his own; he has no confidence whatever in a choice that would be solely his own. The rival (and model) is needed because his desire alone can confirm . . . value (1978, p. 66).[16]

In *Waiting for the Barbarians* the apices of the triangular structure are occupied by the Magistrate, as desiring subject, Colonel Joll (or Mandel, both standing merely for the oppressor), as the mediator of the desire, and the barbarian girl, as object of desire. The Magistrate's desire, prefigured in the vague, undefined form of the hooded child in his first dream, is usurped, as it were, by the form of the barbarian girl as victim of Joll's acts of torture. It is *as* victim of Joll's cruelty, *as* object of his perverse desire, that the girl becomes the object of the Magistrate's (mediated) desire, and for this reason the Magistrate is unable to recall an image of the girl prior to her subjection to torture:

> I cast my mind back, trying to recover an image of her as she was before. I must believe that I saw her on the day she was brought in by the soldiers roped neck to neck with the other barbarian prisoners . . . . On that day she was still unmarked; but I believe she was unmarked as I must believe she was once a child . . . . Strain as I will, my first image remains of the kneeling beggar-girl. (*WB*, p. 33)

And it is for this reason, too, that the Magistrate wishes to know the girl as she was, whole and perfect; for only in knowing her thus can he free himself from bondage to her form as victim, and free himself to establish a different kind of relationship with her, unmediated by the oppressor.

Clearly, the Girardian view of mediated desire is a means of undermining the Magistrate's claim concerning his 'freedom to make of the girl whatever [he] felt like' (*WB*, p. 78); a means of deconstructing the liberal (and existentialist) insistence upon individual autonomy. Reading the Magistrate's ministrations to the barbarian girl as an allegory of the act of writing, it becomes apparent that the text itself is an object of desire, the form of which is mediated by the presence of the very oppressor against whom the liberal writer sets him/herself in opposition. The Magistrate is made to articulate his awareness of the nature of this triangular relationship in passages like the following:

> I am disquieted. 'What do I have to do to move you?' . . . 'Does no one move you?'; and with a shift of horror I behold the answer that has been waiting all the time offer itself to me in the image of a face masked by two glassy insect eyes from which there comes no reciprocal gaze but only my doubled image cast back at me.
>
> I shake my head in a fury of disbelief. *No! No! No!* I cry to myself. It is I who am seducing myself,

> out of vanity, into these meanings and correspondences . . . . There is nothing to link me with torturers, people who sit waiting like beetles in dark cellars. How can I believe that a bed is anything but a bed, a woman's body anything but a site of joy? I must assert my distance from Colonel Joll! I will not suffer for his crimes! (*WB*, p. 44)

Moving from this denial (which *implies* recognition) to an *explicit* recognition of the way in which he has allowed his desire to be mediated by Joll. the Magistrate says towards the close:

> From the moment my steps paused and I stood before her at the barracks gate she must have felt a miasma of deceit closing about her: envy, pity, cruelty, all masquerading as desire. And in my lovemaking not impulse but the laborious denial of impulse! . . . If only she had found the words to tell me! 'That is not how you do it,' she should have said, stopping me in the act. 'If you want to learn how to do it, ask your friend with the black eyes.' Then she should have continued, so as not to leave me without hope' 'But if you want to love me you will have to turn your back on him and learn your lesson elsewhere.' If she had told me then . . . I might have saved myself from a year of confused and futile gestures of expiation. (*WB*, p. 135)

Wilden points out that

> René Girard's pioneering work on identification, rivalry, and mediated desire in the novel, from Cervantes to Proust, was once thought by some to have been influenced by Lacan, at a time when Lacan was generally unknown in the United States. But it was the Hegelian, Freudian, and existentialist sources which were similar in the two writers, whereas the approach and conclusions remain fundamentally different. (p. 287)

The Hegelian figure on which Girard's critique of the Romantic solipsist is founded is the *belle âme*, a figure which, as Wilden points out, Hegel developed in 'dealing with a whole tradition of the Romantic 'literature of the self' (p. 287). The *belle âme* operates according to what Hegel calls 'The Law of the Heart':

> The individual, then, fulfils, carries out the law of his heart. This law becomes a universal ordinance, and pleasure becomes a reality which, as it stands, conforms to law. But in this realisation, the law has, in point of face, escaped the individual . . . . The law of the heart ceases through its very realisation to be a law of the heart. For it thereby takes on the form of actually 'being', and is now universal power, which holds this particular 'heart' to be a matter of indifference; so that the individual, in establishing his own ordinance, no longer finds it to be his own. By realising his law he consequently brings about, not *his* law, but – since the realisation is inherently and implicitly his own, but explicity alien and external – merely this: he gets involved and entangled in the actual ordinance, and, indeed, entangled in it, not merely as something alien to himself but as a hostile, overpowering dominion.
>
> . . . .
>
> This consciousness is unaware that effective realisation involves objective existence, and is in truth the inherently universal in which the particular life of consciousness, which commits itself to it in order to have being in the sense of an immediate individual life, is really submerged. Instead of obtaining this particular life of its own in that objective existence, it thus becomes estranged from itself. (*The Phenomenology of Mind*, pp. 359–60 and pp. 361–62)

The *belle âme* wishes to preserve a sense of subjectivity distinct and, as it were, uncontaminated by what Hegel calls the 'universal', or what we might call, in Lacanian terms, the Other.[17] The *belle âme* denies objective existence and, in Wilden's words, 'refuses necessary alienation and becomes more or less estranged from others and from the world as a result' (p. 291). The failure to impress on others the individual 'law of the heart', along with the frustration of finding the individuality, or subjectivity, of this law subverted by the universal or the objective, means that:

> The heart throb for the welfare of mankind passes . . . therefore into the rage of frantic self-conceit, into the fury of consciousness to preserve itself from destruction; and to do so by casting out of its life the perversion which it really is, and by straining to regard and to express that perversion as something else. (*The Phenomenology of Mind*, p. 364)

Now, I believe it is possible to approach the figure of the Magistrate, as representing the liberal writer, via the figure of the *belle âme*.[18] He refuses this 'necessary alienation' and, like the typical protagonist of the liberal novel, becomes progressively isolated from the community as a result.[19] He attempts to take up a stance *outside* the system in order to oppose this system, failing to see how the self is constituted in and by the *utterance* of this opposition, and how the nature of this utterance is mediated by the very system he would condemn. We see the 'heart throb for the welfare of mankind [pass] into the rage of frantic self-conceit' as, representing the liberal writer's gesture of impotent and self-righteous rage, he says: 'I cannot save the prisoners, therefore let me save myself' (*WB*, p. 104). And, in a passage like the following, we find him blaming Empire for a disruption of time and a subversion of self-present being which is, in fact, an effect of the discourse itself:

> What has made it impossible for us to live in time
> like fish in water, like birds in air, like children?
> It is the fault of Empire! Empire has created the

> time of history. Empire has located its existence not in the smooth recurrent spinning time of the cycle of the seasons but in the jagged time of rise and fall, of beginning and end, of catastrophe. Empire dooms itself to live in history and plot against history. One thought alone preoccupies the submerged mind of Empire: how not to end, how not to die, how to prolong its era. (*WB*, p. 133)

He echoes Magda's lament, 'Once I lived in time as a fish in water, breathing it, drinking it, sustained by it' (*In the Heart of the Country*, p. 80), but, unlike Magda, does not recognize that it is speech, or the narrative, itself which has drawn him out of the lived experience of organic time into the time of rise and fall, of beginning and end. Although he is allowed to hint at this when he says, at a later stage:

> I lie on the bare mattress and concentrate on bringing into life the image of myself as a swimmer swimming with even, untiring strokes through the medium of time, a medium more inert than water, without ripples, pervasive, colourless, odourless, dry as paper. (*WB*, p. 143)

Beginning with 'Summer . . . wheeling slowly towards its end,' (*WB*, p. 2), the Magistrate's entire narrative is articulated around the cycle of the seasons: as a neo-Romantic, he attempts to appropriate the cyclical time of the natural world to compensate for human mutability and death. Coetzee's presentation of the Magistrate sets against this Romantic view of time the Hegelian dialectic, whereby 'Self-formation is not to develop harmoniously as if by organic growth, but rather to become opposed to oneself and to rediscover oneself through a splitting [*déchirement*] and a separation.'[20] There is of course no 'submerged mind of Empire', and it is the metonymic process of the death instinct which, in the narrative, is preoccuped with 'how not to end, how not to die, how to prolong its era'.

Judging others, and refusing to see itself as constituted by this discourse in which it judges others, the *belle âme*, as Lacan points out, 'does not recognize his very own *raison d'être* in the disorder that he denounces in the world' (*Ecrits*, p. 70). The liberal writer, likewise, does not recognize the *raison d'être* of his/her discourse in the disorder which it denounces, as the Magistrate indicates in his continuing diatribe against Empire:

> By day it pursues its enemies. It is cunning and ruthless, it sends its bloodhounds everywhere. By night it feeds on images of disaster: the sack of cities, the rape of populations, pyramids of bones, acres of desolation. A mad vision yet a virulent one: I, wading in the ooze, am no less infected with it than the faithful Colonel Joll as he tracks the enemies of Empire through the boundless desert . . . . (*WB*, p. 133)

The liberal novel grows out of the need to condemn the enemy, that is to say, the oppressor, and feeds on images of disaster, as the Magistrate implies by his admission that he is 'infected', no less than Joll, by the horrors which he denounces. The self 'wading in the ooze' is the equivalent of the 'organism [which] represses its entropic yearning for the mud' (*Dusklands*, p. 29): the extra-linguistic self which erects itself into being and prolongs its existence in the narrative.

The Magistrate says: 'I wanted to live outside history. I wanted to live outside the history that Empire imposes on its subjects, even its lost subjects' (*WB*, p. 154), expressing the desire to withhold his subjectivity from the object in which it is constituted, that is, from the discourse which inevitably locates the subject of utterance in history. If he is allowed to express an awareness of his complicity with Joll, of the way in which his desire has been mediated by the oppressor, he is not allowed, as narrator, to make explicit the fact that he is a figure in a novel, a subject of utterance, and is not allowed, as representative of the liberal writer, to make explicit the nature of the discourse as speech act. And so, finally, he is not allowed to arrive at an awareness of the real nature of the guilt of the liberal writer, the guilt which inevitably falls upon all subjects of utterance within a particular discursive context, and to which he alludes, ironically, when he has to enforce an unjust sentence on a boy:

> 'We cannot just do as we wish,' I lectured him. 'We are all subject to the law, which is greater than any of us. The magistrate who sent you here, I myself, you – we are all subject to the law.' . . . 'You feel that it is unjust, I know, that you should be punished for having the feelings of a good son. You think you know what is just and what is not. I understand. We all think we know.' . . . 'But we live in a world of laws,' I said to my poor prisoner, 'a world of the second-best. There is nothing we can do about that. We are fallen creatures.' (*WB*, pp. 138–139)

Familiarity with Coetzee's ongoing theme of the Lacanian subject allows us to read this as referring to the law of language, and to the fall into language which, in its institution of repression in relation to every son and every daughter, makes this a world of 'second-best', a world of mediated desire.

The guilt which inheres in speech is not the same as the guilt which, in some cases, appears to arise out of the fact that the protest is being registered in the form of a novel rather than by means of action;[21] guilt which, arising out of the act of writing, cannot be expiated in and by this same act of writing. Thus, while liberal writing attempts to expiate guilt, in part by the writer's excoriation of him/herself, and possibly by the confession of a tacit collaboration with the system, it does not finally arrive at a realization that the 'guilt' of collaboration inheres in speech itself, and that as such it is a form of guilt that is common to everyone within a particular realm of discourse, within a particular Empire of signifiers. Oedipus begins proclaiming his own innocence and his own superior vision, and ends by blinding himself at the moment of recognition of his guilt (in Freudian terms, the shared guilt of the desire for incest and patricide). The Magistrate, likewise, sets out from a position of 'sight', but is not blinded, that is to say, he does not achieve the psychological recognition or 'insight' implied in the condition of physical blindness. Instead he ends by saying: 'There has been something staring me in the face, and still I do not see it: (*WB*, p. 155).

Girard claims that

> Novelistic genius begins with the collapse of the 'autonomous' self . . . . Romantic pride willingly denounces the presence of the mediator in Others in order to found its own autonomy on the ruins of rival pretensions. There is novelistic genius when what is true about Others becomes true about the hero, in fact true about the novelist himself. After cursing Others, the Oedipus-novelist realizes he himself is guilty. (*Deceit, Desire and the Novel*, p. 38)

Denouncing the presence of the mediator in liberal writing, Coetzee avoids making the error of claiming autonomy for his own writing: he does this, as I have indicated repeatedly, by means of the allegorical relationship of his novels to prior texts, which, it is implied, act as mediators of his desire. In *Waiting for the Barbarians* it becomes apparent that the mode of narration, too, is motivated by the need to avoid the stance of an illusory autonomy, which the use of a heterodiegetic narrator would imply. While Coetzee's mode of writing, in general, is motivated by the attempt to *avoid* the mediation of desire and the interception of the message in and by the Other, at the same time it always implies the recognition that the very existence of a message, that is to say, of meaning, depends upon the passage of the self through the Other. Conducting his reading of the genre from within the genre, Coetzee avoids the stance of the *belle âme*, and erects the subject of utterance into being *via* this reading rather than claiming a position of autonomy outside the reading or outside the discourse.

Coetzee's novels confess their complicity with the texts of which they constitute a reading in a way which, as I indicated in my first chapter, is not possible for the conventional critical text. As I indicated at the outset of *this* chapter, the attempt to resolve the enigma of the Magistrate's relationship with the girl and with Joll involves the reader in a repetition of these forms of relationship. It does this because our own desire is, likewise, mediated by the context of relationships in which the reading occurs, is directed towards the object which is the text, and is displaced in a voyeuristic and fetishistic ritual which is essentially the equivalent of the Magistrate's displacement of desire onto the barbarian girl's broken feet. Lacanian desire is by definition displaced, or alienated, in the signifier, but in the case of the fetish, desire is, as it were, doubly displaced, onto the signifier of a signifier:

> Since the phallus is not real, but Imaginary – though not necessarily hallucinated – Lacan relates it to (unconscious) desire and to (conscious) demand. The fetishist, for instance, is in fact demanding that there be something where there is nothing. His demand is a disavowal of reality (Freud). But the fetish (the shoe, the bound foot) is not simply a symbol for the phallus, since the phallus is already an Imaginary symbol. The fetish is a metonymic displacement – and displacement of any kind is always onto 'something insignificant' (that is, onto something highly meaningful) – and it is this displacement, not the symbolic substitution of the phallus for the organ itself, which maintains the lack of being (the lack of object) in the subject's relation to objects, by directing the subject's conscious demand onto something he does not want. (Wilden, p. 187)

As I have suggested, the ritual of unbinding and washing the girl's damaged feet is an allegory of the liberal writer's act of writing, an act in which desire is mediated by the oppressor, and thus becomes displaced in the writer's conscious demand for 'something he does not want'. That is to say, desire is displaced onto the victim's signs of suffering at the hands of the oppressor, rather than in a demand for a relationship *different* from that defined by the oppressor.

If this ritual refers to the impotence of the liberal writer, it also refers to the impotence of the (in most instances liberal) reader, for, as André Green points out, 'The written word has become an invisible fetish, as indispensable to pleasure as the fetish is to the fetishist' (p. 26). According to Green, the pleasure of reading is voyeuristic: in other words, it is an activity which attempts to gratify desire by looking without being seen (which the girl's blindness appears to offer the Magistrate the opportunity of doing). Green says:

> Reading and writing are sublimations, which means that the underlying partial drives are inhibited from attaining their goals, displaced and desexualized. Once broken down into their constituent parts, those partial drives have to do with scopophilia [voyeurism]. The desire to see is patent in the act of reading . . . . What is it then that draws us toward reading? The drive toward pleasure through a visual introjection which satisfies a certain type of curiosity. (pp. 22–23)

However, because this pleasure is experienced 'through the mediation of the written word', which 'presupposes the absence of any representation' (p. 23), the reader-as-voyeur, looking without being seen, finds in fact that the act of reading, of deciphering the symbols, exposes him/her to sight:

> To read a text is to translate a systematic set of symbols which represent nothing by themselves. In other words, writing does not show anything beyond the combination of symbols: that's the experience we go through when confronted with a book written in a totally foreign language: if the reader is a voyeur, what he sees in a book are signs that represent no object directly. In order to see, it will be necessary to read, that is to say, bind symbols together, respect the intervals between words, recognize punctuation, and finally set the tone which indicates that the recognition has moved away from the elements into the configuration of meaning. The articulation of

> words, syntagms, and text is dependent on an intense consumption of visual and intellectual energy. Yet as the reading goes on, the reader 'sees', that is to say, he works out a representation of what the text is about. So that it is the text which now 'regards' the reader – in both senses of the term – since what he sees in this *secondary vision*, he sees within himself, not in the text. He has switched, in his voyeurism, from an active position to a passive one. (Green, p. 24)

Via the device of the poplar slips, bearing an archaic script, which the Magistrate finds in the desert, *Waiting for the Barbarians* provides us with two models of reading. In the first model, the Magistrate, as voyeur, fails in his attempt to decipher the archaic script, which is the equivalent of 'a book written in a totally foreign language':

> I sat watching the moon rise, opening my senses to the night, waiting for a sign that what lay around me, what lay beneath my feet, was not only sand, the dust of bones, flakes of rust, shards, ash. The sign did not come . . . . Ridiculous, I thought: a greybeard sitting in the dark waiting for spirits from the byways of history to speak to him before he goes home to his military stew and his comfortable bed. (*WB*, p. 16)

This is an appeal to the symbols to 'reveal' their meaning; it is reading as a search for self-present meaning, the illusory nature of which Christopher Norris refers to when he says:

> Language can fulfil the condition of self-present meaning only if it offers a *total and immediate* access to the thoughts that occasioned its utterance. But this is an impossible requirement. We simply cannot have what Derrida calls 'a primordial intuition of the other's lived experience.' (p. 46)

The correlative to this is the Magistrate's attempt to decipher the scars and marks which are the signs of suffering on the barbarian girl's tortured body. He says: 'It has been growing more and more clear to me that until the marks on this girl's body are deciphered and understood I cannot let go of her' (*WB*, p. 31). He reveals his desire to see without being seen when he says, 'As for me, under her blind gaze, in the close warmth of the room, I can undress without embarrassment' (*WB*, p. 30), and when he examines her eyes, believing that she cannot see him:

> I look into the eye. Am I to believe that gazing back at me she sees nothing – my feet perhaps, parts of the room, a hazy circle of light, but at the centre, where I am, only a blur, a blank? I pass my hand slowly in front of her face, watching her pupils. I cannot discern any movement. She does not blink. But she smiles: 'Why do you do that? Do you think I cannot see?' (*WB*, p. 31)

This need to see, to know, to decipher, to understand, is the equivalent of the attempt on the part of both the liberal writer and the liberal reader to situate the suffering of the victim, and the sense of guilt and impotence which this suffering arouses in the writer/reader, in a narrative context which will give it 'meaning', or explain it. As Magda says, 'To explain is to forgive, to be explained is to be forgiven' (*In the Heart of the Country*, p. 5): the act of interpretation, or explanation, is a form of forgiveness – really self-forgiveness[22] – on the part of the writer and the reader. Returning the Harvey's commentary on the novel:

> Yet, as we read, we wait, enthralled, for the *revelation* that we feel must be imminent; the moment when all this significance will fall into place in a moment of Aristotelian 'recognition'; when we shall be able to say: 'Ah, yes! That is what life is! How illuminating! How profound!' or '*That* is what is wrong with our society' or even

> more humbly, '*That is what he wanted us to see*' (p. 4; see p. 235, this chapter. My emphasis, except for '*that*'),

it becomes apparent how the realization of 'meaning' produces a sense of release; the sublimation of the desire at the source of this voyeuristic curiosity, this wish to 'see'. As a mode of reading or writing, this desire to explain is politically quietistic, as Coetzee points out, because it allows the reader to leave the text with curiosity sated and with 'calm of mind, all passion spent' ('Man's Fate in the Novels of Alex la Guma', p. 17; see p. 233, this chapter).

The alternative to this model of reading is to be found in the Magistrate's act of deciphering the archaic script on the poplar slips under surveillance by Colonel Joll. He gives a reading, or a translation, which is a testimony of barbarian suffering, a reading that is intended as a gesture of defiance and provocation, and as a reminder of the other's guilt. Thus, terminating the translation, the Magistrate says:

> I have not failed to keep an eye on Joll through all this. He has not stirred again, save to lay a hand on his subordinate's sleeve at the moment when I referred to the Empire and he rose, ready to strike me.
>
> If he comes near me I will hit him with all the strength in my body. I will not disappear into the earth without leaving my mark on them. (*WB*, p. 112)

Fabricating a story of barbarian suffering around this 'set of symbols which represent nothing by themselves', the Magistrate produces a reading which 'reads', or in Green's terms, 'regards' *him*. It is a reading which is produced within the context of a relationship, and which has to do with the *identity* of the reader, as, via this reading, the Magistrate erects for himself an identity as truthteller, and claims for himself a position of innocence in relation to the other's guilt. It is a reading whose function in relation to the Magistrate's identity is the equivalent of the novel's or the critical text's function in relation to the identity of the liberal writer or reader.

The liberal writer, acting as an *agent* of sight, or witness, fails to take into account the way in which the narrative exposes the *self* to sight (just as the act of interpretation exposes the self of the critic to sight). At the same time, s/he fails to take into account the 'absence of representation' of writing, which means that his/her text, like the archaic script, will cease to signify with the shifting of the historically defined parameters for making meaning. The only constant is the act of communication, the speech act which takes place in the transferential relationship between desiring writer and desiring reader, so that, in one sense, the text is always an allegory in which, as the Magistrate tells Joll, 'There is no knowing which sense is intended' (*WB*, p. 112). And so, attempting finally to write a history of the imperial outpost, the Magistrate finds, instead, a message of desire coming off his pen:

> 'No one who paid a visit to this oasis,' I write, 'failed to be struck by the charm of life here. We lived in the time of the seasons, of the harvests, of the migrations of the waterbirds. We lived with nothing between us and the stars. We would have made any concession, had we only known what, to go on living here. This was paradise on earth.'
>
> For a long time I stare at the plea I have written. It would be disappointing to know that the poplar slips I have spent so much time on contain a message as devious, as equivocal, as reprehensible as this. (*WB*, p. 154)

At this point it should be mentioned that Coetzee's novel prefigures a third model of reading: a model of penetration, as opposed to the Magistrate's attempts to decipher the surface marks left on the girl's body by another. Comparing his attraction to the girl at the inn, who satisfies his desire in a purely sexual way, with his attraction to the barbarian girl, of whom he says, 'There is no link I can define between her womanhood and my desire. I cannot even say for sure that I desire her', the Magistrate alludes to these different attitudes toward the text:

> But with this woman it is as if there is no interior, only a surface across which I hunt back and forth seeking entry. Is this how her torturers felt hunting their secret, whatever they thought it was? For the first time I feel a dry pity for them: how natural a mistake to believe that you can burn or tear or hack your way into the secret body of the other! (*WB*, p. 43)

Questioned by the Magistrate concerning his capacity to pick up 'the tone of truth', Joll says:

> 'No, you misunderstand me. I am speaking only of a special situation now, I am speaking of a situation in which I am probing for the truth, in which I have to exert pressure to find it. First I get lies, you see – this is what happens – first lies, then pressure, then more lies, then more pressure, then the break, then more pressure, then the truth. That is how you get the truth.' (*WB*, p. 5)

Together, Joll's and the Magistrate's reflections on the act of torture evoke the Barthesian image of the critical commentary, whereby the text is ceaselessly 'broken', and which 'consists precisely in *manhandling* the text, *interrupting* it' (*S/Z*, p. 15). They evoke, likewise, Coetzee's description of certain models of psychoanalysis (or, one might add, of psychoanalytic criticism):

> In some models of psychoanalysis, we might note, the analyst, listening for the truth of the patient, listens not for the patient's truths, the truths the patient finds or tells, but for the patient's lies and silences and evasions, believing that there lie the clues to the 'real' truth. The patient's lie becomes

the analyst's truth. ('Truth in Autobiography', p. 4)

This approximates, in some measure, the kind of psychoanalytic reading which Coetzee produces in relation to the texts he writes: re-writing the liberal humanist novel, we see him deconstructing the liberal writer's stance as truth-teller, along with the belief that the truth is accessible and can be told; we see him listening for the 'lies' which reveal the 'truth' concerning the function of this writing, a 'truth' which he has the Magistrate finally confess:

> For I was not, as I liked to think, the indulgent pleasure-loving opposite of the cold rigid Colonel. I was the lie that Empire tells itself when times are easy, he the truth that Empire tells when harsh winds blow. Two sides of imperial rule, no more, no less. (*WB*, p. 135)

If the 'lie' was that he was able to tell the truth, the 'truth' is that he was a lie.

These images in which the act of torture is conflated with the critical activity constitute the 'confession' of Coetzee's writing; the confession of a text which does not attempt to exculpate itself by withdrawing from the historical context in which it is produced. Instead, it implicates itself, and the ruthless deconstructive activity of contemporary critical practice, within the discursive context of what Wilden describes as 'a social and political morality still structured on our sadomasochistic desire to dominate the others we have chosen for our personal and societal scapegoats' (p. 293). However, the fact that Coetzee not only reads, but re-writes the texts he deconstructs in the form of the novel means that his texts do not claim criticism's privilege to tell the 'truth' of literature, while assuming that it has no secrets of its own. In the lecture, 'Truth in Autobiography', Coetzee asks:

> If the desire of literary criticism is to tell every truth, to unveil whatever is veiled, to expose very [sic] secret to sight, why does it not tell its own

> secrets? Or does it claim to have none? (p. 5)

It is possible to say that, in contrast, his own criticism-as-fiction admits to the way in which the truths it exposes as criticism at the same time constitute the untruths of the fiction, and conceal the secrets of the self of enunciation.

Returning, now, to the device of the archaic script, we find that it functions, not only to refer to different models of reading. but also as a means of conflating the liberal writer's blindness, or repression, in relation to the nature of his/her discourse, with the repressions of the liberal text in relation to history. The Magistrate's various attempts to account for the provenance of the archaic script are contradictory: when he talks about the ruins in the desert, it is not clear whether by 'barbarians' he means the current barbarians, or the 'other' against which the previous Empire had to defend itself; translating the symbols in Joll's presence, he accords them meanings appropriate to the situation of the current barbarians, but then goes on to say, 'There is no agreement among scholars about how to interpret these relics of the ancient barbarians' (*WB*, p. 112), and later refers to the current barbarians as 'men with bows and arrows and rusty old guns who live in tents and never wash and *cannot read or write*' (*WB*, p. 143; my emphasis). This involves the repression of the fact that the current Empire has replaced a previous civilization, a fact that would negate Empire's *raison d'être* as the upholder of 'civilized' values in the face of the 'barbarian' onslaught. The fear of this onslaught is evident in the Magistrate's self questioning:

> And do I really after all believe what I have been saying? Do I really look forward to the triumph of the barbarian way: intellectual torpor, slovenliness, tolerance of disease and death? If we were to disappear would the barbarians spend their afternoons excavating our ruins? Would they preserve our census rolls and our grain-merchants' ledgers in glass cases, or devote themselves to deciphering the script of our love-letters? (*WB*, p. 52)

However, failing, at the end, to write a history of the outpost, he decides instead to bury the poplar slips bearing the archaic writing in the desert where he found them:

> I think: 'When one day people come scratching around in the ruins, they will be more interested in the relics from the desert than in anything I may leave behind. And rightly so.' (Thus I spend an evening coating the slips one by one in linseed oil and wrapping them in an oilcloth. When the wind lets up, I promise myself, I will got out and bury them where I found them.)
>
> I think: 'There has been something staring me in the face, and still I do not see it.' (*WB*, p. 155)

Burying the slips in the desert, he is merely preserving the past for a future in which he perceives he has no part, instead of actively engaging in the present moment of history by means of a creative reconstitution of the past in anticipation of the future. The 'something' which has been staring him in the face is the *fact* of the discourse, the fact that it *is* the history which the Magistrate believes he has failed to write, and the fact that it *will be* a relic from the desert, as 'meaningless' to the future inhabitants of Empire as the archaic script is to him.

In one of the final scenes, following the routing of the imperial forces by the barbarians, and the abandoning of the outpost by the remaining soldiers, the remains of a burial site are discovered within the walls of the fort, providing a sequel to the Magistrate's earlier claim, 'There are no human remains among the ruins. If there is a cemetery we have not found it' (*WB*, p. 15). And the Magistrate has a final dream, in which the beginnings of Empire in these human remains on which the fort is built, and the beginnings of the self in the narrative are conflated: the Magistrate stands in the ancient grave, out of which he pulls a bent and tarnished fork, and a dead parrot with empty eye sockets; the former a reference to the liberal writer's previous 'incarnation' as Magda, who uses a fork in self-defence against the servant, Hendrik,[23] the latter a reference to the Magistrate as writer, and to the blind and repetitive nature of his discourse. The dream invokes the repetition of individual and shared history as a return of the repressed; not in the sense of an animistic view of a history which 'repeats itself', but in the sense of a past which, while it is seemingly obliterated, nevertheless persists in and impinges upon the present.

The final image is of a group of children in the middle of the square building a snowman without arms: in place of the snow castle and fort of the Magistrate's dreams, we have a snowman, standing for the self which is objectified in the narrative, for the identity which is as transient as that of a snowman. The narrative provides an identity which can never be the measure of the unconscious desiring self projected in the dreams of the girl, and the Magistrate concludes:

> It is not a bad snowman.
> This is not the scene I dreamed of. Like much else nowadays I leave it feeling stupid, like a man who lost his way long ago but presses on along a road that may lead nowhere. (*WB*, p. 156)

The road that leads nowhere is both the impasse with which the liberal novel so frequently terminates,[24] and the *aporia*, or 'unpassable path', which Coetzee's reading of the genre has revealed, an *aporia* which is a feature of the liberal discourse itself. According to Christopher Norris,

> *Aporia* derives from the Greek word meaning 'unpassable path,' a sense that fully lives up to its later paradoxical development. In Derrida's hands it represents the nearest one can get to a label or conceptual cover-term for the effects of differance and the 'logic' of deviant figuration. What deconstruction persistently reveals is an ultimate impasse of thought engendered by a rhetoric that always insinuates its own textual workings into the truth claims of philosophy. (p. 49)

We have in this final scene an image of a man dispossessed: the figure of Oedipus, stripped of the trappings of transcendent suffering, and denied even the consolation of a moment of insight or 'recognition'. Shoshana Felman makes the point that:

> In dramatizing language as the scene (the acting out) of the unconscious (in both its clinical and literary implications), the Oedipus is achetypal [sic] of the psychoanalytic myth in that it is the story of the narrative expropriation of the story by itself, the story of, precisely, the *acknowledgement* of the misrecognition of the story by itself. Misleadingly, the Oedipus appears, at first, to be the myth of a possession (of a kingdom, of a woman, of the solution to a riddle, of one's own story). But as it turns out, the Oedipus is not the myth of the possession of a story, but the myth, precisely, of the dispossession by the story – the dispossession of the possessor of the story. ('Beyond Oedipus', p. 1046)

The liberal writer fails to recognize, or acknowledge, this dispossession, and so does not achieve what Felman, citing Lacan, refers to as

> 'the *assumption* of one's history,' that is, the ultimate acceptance – and endorsement – of one's destiny, the acknowledgement of responsibility for the discourse of the Other in oneself, but also the forgiving of this discourse. ('Beyond Oedipus', p. 1027)

From this it would seem, paradoxically, that it is the Otherness of the discourse which, while it inculpates the subject of the utterance, makes it possible for the self to retain its innocence, however circumscribed, and which, in the 'forgiving of this discourse', makes some kind of self-forgiveness possible.

The Magistrate is dispossessed of an Empire, of a woman,

of his own story, of the 'truth'. He is dispossessed of his desire, as we see in the final scenes, in which he has erections which 'have nothing to do with desire' (*WB*, p. 150), and sleeps with a woman who is preoccupied with nurturing the children she has borne from other men. This dispossession is, however, not finally devoid of hope, for the presence of children in the closing scenes of the narrative[25] implies a projection into a future in which the text will be 're-possessed', a future in which different forms of possession will be possible.

NOTES

1. See Appendix for a complete transcription of the poem.
2. Michael Vaughan, engaging in a critique of liberal hegemony in South African English fiction in his paper, 'Literature and Politics: Currents in South African Writing in the Seventies', makes the point that 'Twentieth century South African fiction in English has been dominated by an aesthetics of liberalism', and goes on to say: 'This aesthetics is grounded in an ontology of the individual person . . . . An important aesthetic implication of this ontology of the individual is that literature should be concerned with forms of interaction between people as interactions between individual persons' (p. 119). And Stephen Watson, in his M.A. Dissertation, 'The Liberal Ideology and Some English South African Novelists,' points out that:

   > '. . . the political doctrines and practises . . . which liberalism considers valuable and desirable, are an extension of the historically unprecedented value which it places on the individual; the political content of liberalism is a logical consequence of what it regards as desirable for the individual. And it is the emphasis on the latter which is, perhaps, the most remarkable feature of liberalism as a whole.' (p. 67)

   He goes on to say that

   > '. . . not only is the 'liberal' novel in general concerned above all with the development of 'aesthetic individualism' (originality, spontaneity, integrity) in its particular characters, but also the endeavour to achieve 'self-realization' (along with the elitism and other contradictions that go with it) is absolutely

central to a novel like Olive Schreiner's *The Story of an African Farm* as well as to many others which follow it in time; and this centrality of a primary focus on 'self-realization' is a major index to the fact that the liberal ideology is the informing one in a particular work.' (p. 68)

3. In Gerard Genette's terminology, a heterodiegetic narrator is a narrator who is absent from the tale s/he tells (*Narrative Discourse*, p. 245).
4. Eugene Dawn, for example, makes comments like, 'One, two cars are pulling up, in the present definite this time' (*Dusklands*, p. 40 40), and 'A convention allows me to record these details' (*Dusklands*, p. 44). As I indicated in the previous chapter, Magda constantly refers to the fact that she is constituted by her discourse.
5. Genette points out that the common locutions, of first and third person, are inadequate, 'in that they stress variation in the element of the narrative situation that is in fact invariant – to wit, the presence (explicit or implicit) of the 'person' of the narrator. This presence is invariant because the narrator can be in his narrative (like every subject of an enunciating in his enunciated statement) only in the 'first person' (pp. 243–44).
6. Narrative time is the time of the discourse, and so is always in the present, while narrated time is the time of the story, the events of which may be located in the past, present or future in relation to the time of the discourse. In his paper, 'Time, Tense and Aspect in Kafka's 'The Burrow', Coetzee points out the necessity of distinguishing between 'narrative time (which tracks the process of feeding),' and 'narrated time (that which is fed upon)' (p. 573).
7. See John Lyons:

   'The conditions which govern the selection of 'this' and 'that' with reference to events immediately preceding and immediately following the utterance, or the part of the utterance in which 'this' and 'that' occur, are quite complex. They include a number of subjective factors (such as the speaker's dissociation of himself from the event he is referring to), which are intuitively relatable to the deictic notion of proximity/non-proximity, but are difficult to specify precisely.' (p. 668)
8. See Wilden:

   ' .... the *meaning* of the sentence is *retroactively* revealed by a sort of reading backwards from the end .... In other words, for the complete message of the conscious subject to be understood (by the emitter or by the receiver) at any level at all, there must be an unconscious reading in reverse at the *end* of the message, a reference to the locus of the code *after the* complete message has been received . . . ' (pp. 274–75)

9. 'Man's Fate in the Novels of Alex la Guma,' p. 16. Coetzee is talking, here, about the problems facing black South African writers in exile.
10. Jane Gallop points out that

    'The specific difficulty in thinking the temporality of the mirror stage is its intricacy of anticipation and retroaction. The retroaction is based on the anticipation. In other words, the self is constituted through anticipating what it will become, and then this anticipatory model is used for gauging what was before. For example, the anticipatory totalized body image produces the retroactive phantasy of the body in bits and pieces.' (p. 121)
11. Stephen Watson points out that with 'the relegation of the English as a group to a politically powerless minority in South Africa . . . the English liberal ideology has become more and more existential in character', and that 'over the last three decades an increasingly existential element has emerged and become apparent in white South African literature. More and more this literature, whether poetry, fiction, or drama, has become one of anomie, alienation, angst, and of bewilderments about identity' ('The Liberal Ideology and Some English South African Novelists', p. 58).
12. Asked in an interview whether the Magistrate has a choice, Coetzee replies:

    'Well – yes – there is a choice I think, though for someone in his situation it's not easy. It's not difficult for someone in his situation to learn perhaps to turn a blind eye to what's going on. That's the temptation that is the choice. He could turn a blind eye and live out his days in comfort'.

    In response to the interviewer's further remark: 'But when I say choice, I mean a sort of transcendent choice where you as it were go over the edge to something new', Coetzee says:

    'No, there is no choice for people like that . . . You know, hypothetically the choice would be in fact between the police and the empire and what they stand for, and the barbarian way of life. He cannot choose the barbarian way of life although he makes vague gestures in that direction, in the direction of the barbarian girl.' (Rhedin Interview, p. 7)

13. Reviewing *The Guest*, a film on Eugene Marais, Coetzee says:

> 'What conditions of life in the Transvaal of the 1920s does Eugene Marais find insupportable enough to drive him to drugs and death? The answer: being a white man in Africa is what is insupportable. Not because of the burden of guilt (this is the theme of a later literature) but because of the burden of consciousness. The theme of *The Soul of the Ape*, on which *The Guest* relies heavily, is that consciousness is a form of pain, that the highest consciousness is the most exquisite pain.' ('The Burden of Consciousness in Africa', p. 96)

Clearly, what is represented in the Magistrate's discourse is this later literature articulated around the burden of guilt, but his notion of pain is made to reveal remnants of this earlier theme of pain as ennobling.

14. The image of the dog dying in a corner is repeated in *Life & Times of Michael K* in which the medical officer/narrator says: 'For God's sake close the story of Michaels here and now. . . The poor simpleton has gone off like a sick dog to die in a corner' (p. 212). The image carries an allusion to the death of Josef K. in Kafka's *The Trial*, and I will elaborate upon its significance in the chapter which follows. Suffice it to say at this point that it refers to the liberal writer's sense of despair at not being able to terminate the narrative in a way which will be liberating in its transcendence of a situation of suffering and defeat.

15. Harvey nevertheless *makes* all this significance fall into place in a typically liberal resolution of ambiguities:

> 'It is, in a very real sense, *about*: war and peace, life and death, justice, torture and cruelty, conscience, political policy, history and time, 'Empire', civilization and barbarism, 'subject races', survival, sex, love and human loneliness. All this in 156 pages!
>
> And yet it is, truly, *about* all these things (and more); they are not merely mentioned in passing. Almost any one of them traced carefully through the book might be seen as an important, even dominant motif. Which means, of course, that Mr Coetzee has seen, and can make us see, how all these themes are of one, bewildering piece. If the book has a 'message' then this is it'. (pp. 4–5)

16. J.M. Coetzee, 'Triangular Structures of Desire in Advertising,' p. 36, citing René Girard, *Deceit, Desire and the Novel* (1961; trans. 1965) and *Violence and the Sacred* (1972; trans. 1977). See my

Chapter Two, p. 98.

17. Wilden points out that 'Lacan equates the *belle âme* with the subject in analysis', and that 'This is to condemn the subject of the *parole vide* or, in Girard's view, the subject who has not discovered himself through the *expérience romanesque* in the others he condemns.' (p. 288).

18. In her commentary on *Waiting for the Barbarians*, Menan du Plessis cites Wilden on the dialectic of the *belle âme*, but is not clear concerning the possible connection between the figure of the *belle âme* and the Magistrate, saying: ' . . . in *Waiting for the Barbarians* I think one detects some forms of the self-other dialectic in external manifestation'; and saying also that 'while the nature of his [the Magistrate's] discourse may preserve him from the tedious soul-searching and complaint of the Hegelian 'beautiful soul', it also has the effect of screening him from some of the truths about himself'. She identifies these truths as 'truths of the unconscious', but does not recognize *the* truth which he screens himself from as the knowledge of the objective existence of the discourse itself. (pp. 82 and 81)

19. Stephen Watson points out that in the liberal novel 'An irreconcilable conflict is . . . established between the dreams of an individual character and the many forms of determinism which circumscribe the individual life in South Africa. This conflict is then artistically 'dissolved' by death (tragedy), by renunciation (escapism), or culminates in a sterile impasse'.

    He goes on to say that

    'In this geographical context, the liberal novel is a novel of isolation, anomie, and loneliness, of solitary heroes and heroines (or anti-heroes) alienated from any authentic community and engaged in a hopeless endeavour to realize themselves in situations in which their very isolation renders them impotent in the struggle to do that'. ('The Liberal Ideology and Some English South African Novelists', pp. 54 and 87)

20. Jean Hyppolite, *Genèse et structure de la Phénoménologie de l'Esprit* (Paris: Aubier, 1946), II, 372, cited by Wilden (p. 285).

21. One finds, for example, Nadine Gordimer's 'The Essential Gesture: Writers and Responsibility', the covert function of which is the defence of her own position as a white writer in South Africa. Citing Camus' 'It is from the moment when I shall no longer be more than a writer that I shall cease to write', she tries to make a case for certain writing as being 'more than writing' (something which Coetzee's writing demonstrates, but in quite a different

way). Thus she refers to 'the white writer's task as cultural worker . . . to raise the consciousness of white people, who, unlike himself, have not woken up', and to 'describe a situation so truthfully that the reader can no longer evade it.' (pp. 13, 14 and 15.)

22. In the lecture, 'Truth in Autobiography', Coetzee, discussing the mode of the confession, points out that 'To Dostoevsky, confession, penance, and forgiveness (essentially self-forgiveness) go together . . .' (p. 4). While in *Waiting for the Barbarians* the reading which Coetzee gives us of the liberal humanist novel is articulated around the mode of tragedy, and not around the mode of confession, which is overtly concerned to explore the self in a way that the liberal humanist novel is not, there are aspects of the mode of confession which serve to define certain elements of the liberal humanist novel. There is, for example, the capacity for ruthless self-scrutiny, to which Coetzee refers as he continues his commentary on the confessional mode, pointing out how the writer might make him/her self out to be worse than s/he really is, in order to feel good about his/her ruthless honesty. It is to this that the Magistrate alludes when, perceiving himself to be Joll's double, he says '*No! No! No!* . . . It is I who am seducing myself, out of vanity, into these meanings and correspondences' (*WB*, p. 44)

23. 'I struggle against him. I pick up the first thing I see, a fork, and lunge with it, scraping his shoulder. The skin is not even pierced, but he sucks in his breath with surprise and hurls me against the wall, his whole weight upon me. The fork falls' (*Heart of the Country*, p. 104).

24. See note 19 this chapter, in which I cite Stephen Watson: 'This conflict (between the individual and society) is then artistically 'dissolved' by death (tragedy), by renunciation (escapism), or culminates in a sterile impasse' (p. 54).

25. In the interview with Folke Rhedin, Coetzee says:

    ' . . . I'm sure you remember that there is a very strong presence of children in that book and there is no saying – although the book doesn't deal directly with it – what those children might do and what sort of life they might lead. They might be able to make choices that he [the Magistrate] finds impossible.' (p. 7)

5 Life & Times of Michael K

No papers, no money; no family, no friends, no sense of who you are. The obscurest of the obscure, so obscure as to be a prodigy.

Life & Times of Michael K, p. 195

This is Michael K, who has no friends and no family, but whose obscurity and whose name grant him the distinction of being the literary descendant of Kafka's K., who, 'By his mute presence, if by nothing else . . . constitutes an invitation to penetrate into his poor life, to look around there as in one's own property and there to suffer with him under the weight of his futile demands' (*The Castle*, p. 252). It is their obscurity, their mute presence, which makes these figures, K. and Michael K, and also Josef K, ideal 'subjects'. They are the dispossessed ones, subjects of the utterance who, in Coetzee's and Kafka's texts, are presented as victims of the process (*The Trial*) or the 'life sentence'[1] which is the narrative itself.

At the same time, Michael K is the descendant of those figures who, in the context of white South African writing, represent the oppressed, handicapped, illiterate, if not inarticulate, victims of the system; the type of figure that appears to offer the writer the opportunity for telling a story, for articulating an experience which, by virtue of the illiterate or inarticulate condition of the victim, would otherwise remain untold. The most notable example of this genre in the South African context[2] is Elsa Joubert's *Die Swerfjare van Poppie Nongena* (1978), translated as *The Long Journey of Poppie Nongena*, concerning the genesis of which a group of Dutch commentators (referring to a statement by Joubert) have the following to say:

> Hierin vertelt zij dat ze reeds lang bezig was een
> boek te schrijven dat een inzicht kunnen geven in
> de belevingswereld van de zwarten, zowel voor zichzelf

> als voor de blanken in het algemeen. Dit vooral, omdat, volgens Elsa Joubert, men bestrijdt waar men bang voor is, en men is bang voor dat wat men niet kent. Door de belevingswereld van de zwarte te leren kennen wordt er angst weggenomen – dus ook strijd. Elsa Joubert probeerde al jaren een dergelijk boek te schrijven. Zij nam hiertoe kennis van de zwarte afrikaanse literatuur, bezocht veel zwarte woonwijken, ging naar zwarte kerken en bezocht zelfs toordokters'. Toen de onlusten in Soweto uitbraken, werd het haar echter duidelijk dat een door haar geschreven doek altijd de visie van een blanke zou blijven. In diezelfde tijd kreeg zij bezoek van Poppie, en zij besefte dat hier haar kans lag, om nu ook de visie een zwarte in een boek te integreren. (Janssen, Lijphart, van Ijzeren, p. 59)

> In this article she [Elsa Joubert] tells that she had been occupied for some time with writing a book which would give insight into the life world of the blacks, both for herself and for whites in general. This, chiefly, because, according to Elsa Joubert, one opposes what one fears, and one fears what one does not know. Through coming to know the life experience of blacks, anxiety, and thus also conflict, is removed. Elsa Joubert had tried for years to write such a book. For this purpose she had familiarized herself with black Afrikaans writing, had visited many black townships, had been to black churches, and even visited 'witchdoctors'. With the outbreak of uprisings in Soweto, it became clear to her that such a book written by her would always remain the vision of a white person. At the same time she received a visit from Poppie, and she realized that here was the chance to integrate the vision of a black person in a book. (My own translation from the Dutch.)

In *Life & Times of Michael K* Coetzee engages in a psychoanalytic reading and re-writing of *this* genre; a genre which may be defined by the desire to articulate the experiences and sufferings of a (usually) black or so-called coloured victim of the system. That, on a superficial reading, it appears to be no more than another novel of this type is evident from Nadine Gordimer's comment:

> You can shake your head decently over yet another evocation of commonplace misery; the only particular reaction, this time, a slight sense of impatience – did it all have to be laid on so thick? Does the man have to be harelipped, etc., on top of everything else? ('The Idea of Gardening', p. 3)

Gordimer dismisses the possibility of an allusion to Kafka in the name, Michael K, saying, 'the initial probably stands for Kotze or Koekemoer, and has no reference, nor need it have, to Kafka' (p. 3). However, it is precisely the allusion to Kafka, via the name of the protagonist and also in other aspects of Coetzee's novel, that alerts us to the fact that what we have in *Life & Times of Michael K* is not simply 'another evocation of commonplace misery', written in the mode of realism; it alerts us to the fact that the codes of this genre are being subverted by means of a different generic model, that is to say, by means of writing in the mode of text construction. In making this claim I am aware that my reading of *Life & Times of Michael K* is generated out of a particular reading of Kafka's texts, but as it is beyond the scope and purposes of this study to establish the grounds for such a reading, I will do no more than refer the reader to readings of Kafka's texts by Coetzee, Sussman, Cohn, and Bernheimer.[3] If, in the mode of realism, Michael K is the victim of an oppressive and exploitative system, in the mode of text construction he is the victim of a hierarchy of authorities, which range from the structural needs of the narrative and the prescribed codes of the genre, to the desire of both writer and reader, and to the ultimate *author*-ity of the discursive context, of language as Other. And if, in the mode of realism, the obscurity and mute presence of this type of protagonist offer the possibility of a story, of exposing to view what has up until now remained concealed, in the mode of text construction this same obscurity allows the writer to construct a figure of so little substance that s/he is able, in some measure at least, to elude this hierarchy of authorities, and to maintain the necessary concealment of the self. A figure like Michael K makes it possible to say something by saying nothing', or very little; he makes it possible to provide evidence of the self's presence by means of an absence, to manifest the self in that movement of disappearance, or fading, that Lacan calls *aphanisis*.

This is the first of Coetzee's novels in which we find a heterodiegetic narrator (in Sections I and II); that is to say, an 'absent' narrator, who makes no reference to the discursive situation. As in the case of *Waiting for the Barbarians*, it is possible to say that this mode of narration is dictated by the genre, in which the self-effacing narratorial stance is motivated in the desire to create the impression that a life is unfolding itself before the reader with no intervention by the writer. Hovering between the factual pole of the biography and the fictional pole of the novel,[4] this genre claims to give a voice to the voiceless victim. The correlative to this is the implication that the protagonist is a free agent: free from the shaping and controlling presence of the writer, and, by extension, able to maintain his/her freedom and autonomy despite the oppressive structures of the system. Accordingly, one of the reader expectations inherent in this genre is that the illusion of unmediated access to another's life and thoughts should not be disturbed by narratorial intrusion; an expectation which is implicit in the following complaint concerning a certain unevenness in the mode of narration of *The Long Journey of Poppie Nongena*:

> Dit bly vir my egter 'n slordigheid dat die verteller Poppie soms loslaat, of mededelings maak oor wat in die gedagtewêreld van ander figure plaasvind . . . Wanneer die ongeskrewe reël verbreek word, praat ek van 'n breuk in die perspektief, want dan staan Poppe nie meer sentraal nie.
>
> For me it remains a form of untidiness when the narrator abandons Poppie, or offers an interpretation

> of what is taking place in the mind of other figures. When the unwritten rule is broken, I am talking about a break in the perspective, because then Poppie no longer occupies a central position. (Gerrit Olivier, *Standpunte* May 1980, cited by Janssen, Lijphart and van Ijzeren, p. 60. My translation from the Afrikaans.)

On the other hand, if the narrative is based on factual data observed in the empirical world, as in the case of *The Long Journey of Poppie Nongena*, which is based on tape-recorded interviews with a woman who came to Joubert for help, the material must be organised in the form of a story. It cannot be left in its raw state because it lacks interest, and, one might add, it lacks persuasive power:

> Ek wou eers die bande wat ek oorgetik het, net so gebruik, maar het na 'n probeerslag besef dit sal nie werk nie. Dit was vervelig en daar was geen verband of ontwikkeling in die gebeure nie. Die boek moes nie net 'n feitelike verslag wees nie.
>
> Daarna het ek die verhaal laat vertel deur 'n alsiende derdepersoonsverteller, maar ook dit het nie gewerk nie. Dit was weer 'n witmens wat van buite die storie vertel het. Dit het nie oortuig as outentiek nie. Ek het geprobeer om eers vir Poppie te laat vertel en dan weer vir my, maar ons vertelstyle was te verskillend.
>
> Uiteindelik het ek dit toe reggekry on die hele verhaal in haar verteltrant, haar 'sleutel' te vertel. In die boek verskuif die perspektief van Poppie na 'n verteller na dramatisering van gebeure om verveling en gelykmatigheid te voorkom.

> Initially, I wanted to use the tapes which I had transcribed just as they were, but after a trial realized that this would not work. It was boring, and there was no connection or development in the events. I didn't want the book to be just a factual report.

> After this, I tried having the story told by an omniscient third-person narrator, but this didn't work either. Again it was a white person telling the story from outside. It wasn't convincingly authentic. I tried alternating the narration between Poppie and myself, but our styles of narrating were too different.
>
> Eventually I got it right by narrating the whole story in her tone or 'key'. In the book the perspective shifts from Poppie to a narrator to dramatization of events in order to prevent boredom and monotony. (Elsa Joubert, *Volksblad*, 11 April 1979, cited by Janssen, Lijphart and van Ijzeren, p. 59. This is my own translation of the Afrikaans of the Joubert article.)

What is at work here is what Hayden White calls 'narrativizing discourse' (see my Chapter Two, p. 78); the imposition of the form of a story, while the intervention of the narrator is concealed in order to create the impression that people and events tell themselves; White says:

> Narrative becomes a *problem* only when we wish to give *real* events the *form* of story. It is because real events do not offer themselves as stories that their narrativization is so difficult.
>
> What is involved, then, in that finding of the 'true story', that discovery of the 'real story' within or behind the events that come to us in the chaotic form of 'historical records'? What wish is enacted, what desire is gratified, by the fantasy that *real* events are properly represented when they can be shown to display the formal coherency of a story? In the enigma of this wish, this desire, we catch a glimpse of the cultural function of narrativizing discourse in general, an intimation of the psychological impulse behind the apparently universal need not only to narrate but to give events an aspect of narrativity. (p. 8)

Scaling down the perspective, apparently reducing the narrative tone to that of the protagonist, but at the same time organizing what is told in the sequential form of a story, which has a beginning, a middle, and an end, this mode of narration simultaneously appropriates for itself the authenticity and authority of the Real, and the effects of the Imaginary, which 'makes the real desirable, makes the real into an object of desire' (White, p. 24).

In *Life & Times of Michael K* there are repeated references to this need to translate the random and chaotic quality of the lived experience of the victim into the form of a story. For example, Michael K is made to reflect:

> They want me to open my heart and tell them the story of a life lived in cages. They want to hear about all the cages I have lived in, as if I were a budgie or a white mouse or a monkey. And if I had learned story-telling at Huis Norenius instead of potato-peeling and sums, if they had made me practise the story of my life every day, standing over me with a cane till I could perform without stumbling, I might have known how to please them. I would have told the story of a life passed in prisons where I stood day after day, year after year with my forehead pressed to the wire, gazing into the distance, dreaming of experiences I would never have, and where the guards called me names and kicked my backside and sent me off to scrub the floor. When my story was finished, people would have shaken their heads and been sorry and angry and plied me with food and drink; women would have taken me into their beds and mothered me in the dark. (L&T, p. 247)

He refers to the covert function of this genre in relation to both writer and reader, a function which may be assimilated with that of liberal writing in general. 'People would have shaken their heads and been sorry and angry and plied me with food and drink', says Michael K, indicating that this type of 'story', like the mode of religious tragedy, produces in the reader a form of cathartic pity and terror, and arouses a response that is merely another form of charity. Immediately preceding the passage I have cited here, Michael K reflects: 'I have become an object of charity . . . . Everywhere I go there are people waiting to exercise their forms of charity on me' (*L&T*, p. 246). Set against this essentially negative view of the function of storytelling is the kind of storytelling to which Michael K refers when contemplating joining the band of guerilla fighters. Of these men he says:

> The stories they tell will be different from the stories I heard in the camp, because the camp was for those left behind, the women and children, the old men, the blind, the crippled, the idiots, people who have nothing to tell but stories of how they have endured. Whereas these young men have had adventures, victories and defeats and escapes. They will have stories to tell long after the war is over, stories for a life-time, stories for their grand-children to listen to open-mouthed. (*L&T*, p. 150)

This provides a description of the very sources of narrative in the oral transmission of stories *within* a community whose traditions they affirm and strengthen. These are 'stories for a lifetime', stories which recuperate the past for meaningful living in the future. In contrast, the genre we are dealing with here tells stories of those who have been left behind, who have merely endured, and has its genesis in the whites' need to assuage both their cuiosity and their guilt.

The title of Coetzee's novel suggests that we are going to be given a 'life', situated in and explained by the context of his 'times'. In the novel, the correlative to the production of the story, which is achieved by the sequential structuring of segments of narrated time, is the construction of character. The character is constructed by organizing various elements into the coherent and meaningful structure of a 'life', which, like the story, demonstrates a significant progression, usually toward the achievement of some kind of wisdom or insight. In the novel in general, but in this genre in particular, the production of the story is largely achieved via the construction of the character. Hélène Cixous makes the point that

> 'Character occupies a privileged position in the novel or the play: without 'character,' passive or active, no text. He is the major agent of the work, at the center of a stage that is commanded by his presence, his story, his interest. Upon his 'life' depends the life of the text – so they say. (p. 386)

Or, as Barthes puts it,

> . . . *the character and the discourse are each other's accomplices:* the discourse creates in the character its own accomplice: a form of theurgical detachment by which, mythically, God has given himself a subject, man a helpmate, etc., whose relative independence, once they have been created, allows for *playing*. Such is discourse: if it creates characters, it is not to make them play among themselves before us but to play with them, to obtain from them a complicity which assures the uninterrupted exchange of the codes: the characters are types of discourse and, conversely, the discourse is a character like the others. (*S/Z*, pp. 178–79)

In recent theoretical writing, the notion of character has come in for a good deal of criticism for its role in endorsing cultural codes and fixing the subject in the Symbolic. Thus Cixous complains that

> . . . through 'character' is established the identification circuit with the reader: the more 'character' fulfills the norms, the better the reader recognizes it and recognizes himself. The commerce established between book and reader is thus facilitated. . . . *Porte-parole* of sense, it is bound up with the authority of the author and expresses his messages.
>
> . . . .
>
> The ideology underlying this fetishization of 'character' is that of an 'I' who is a *whole* subject (that of the 'character' as well as that of the

> author), conscious, knowable; and the enunciatory 'I' expresses himself in the text, just as the world is represented complementarily in the text in a form equivalent to pictorial representation, as a simulacrum. (p. 385)

A character thus becomes an item of exchange that has to do with the economy of the text: it ensures the life of the discourse, and ensures the commerce between reader and writer as it constitutes the identity of each in a way that reinforces, rather than disturbs, the identity already granted to them in the Symbolic.

Robbe-Grillet refers to the necessary elements of conventional character construction when he says:

> A character must have a proper name, two if possible: a surname and a given name. He must have parents, a heredity. He must have a profession. If he has possessions as well, so much the better. Finally, he must possess a 'character,' a face which reflects it, a past which has molded that face and that character. His character dictates his actions, makes him react to each event in a determined fashion. His character permits the reader to judge him, to love him, to hate him. It is thanks to his character that he will one day bequeath his name to a human type, which was waiting, it would seem, for the consecration of this baptism. (p. 27)

Clearly, Michael K has none of these attributes: no family, no heredity, no possessions. His profession is gardening, the significance of which I will come to at a later stage in this discussion. His face, with 'the mouth that would not close and the living pink flesh it bared' (*L&T*, p. 3), is a sign of the handicapped being, a visible sign of the inarticulate condition. Michael K does not have a 'character' which 'makes him react to each event in a determined fashion': on the contrary, when another figure says 'People must help each other, that's what I believe', Michael K's response is: 'Do I believe in helping people? . . . He might help people, he might not help them, he did not know beforehand, anything was possible. He did not seem to have a belief regarding help' (*L&T*, p. 65). And he has only half a name, like Josef K and K, of whom Robbe-Grillet says: 'he is content with an initial, he possesses nothing, has no family, no face; he is probably not even a land surveyor at all' (p. 28).

This introduces the issue of the name, which forms part of the title of Coetzee's novel. Ann Jefferson makes the point that 'The use of a proper name in a title frequently acts as a sign that the character referred to will serve as the *telos* of the novel in question', and she goes on to say: 'One of the most powerful effects of literature (in general) is its transformation of the normal use of names through its ability to make them speak, so that they not only refer but also signify' (pp. 63 and 74). She refers to Barthes' execration of the proper name in *S/Z*, in which he says:

> By restoring to the discourse its hero's proper name, we are merely acting in accordance with the economic nature of the Name: in the novelistic regime (and elsewhere?), it is an instrument of exchange: it allows the substitution of a nominal unit for a collection of characteristics by establishing an equivalent relationship between sign and sum (p. 95),

And

> What gives the illusion that the sum is supplemented by a precious remainder (something like *individuality*, in that, qualitative and ineffable, it may escape the vulgar bookkeeping of compositional characters) is the Proper Name, the difference completed by what is *proper* to it. The proper name enables the person to exist outside the semes, whose sum nonetheless constitutes it entirely (p. 191).

In the mode of realism, the name creates the illusion of a

being with a life of his/her own outside the text, the illusion that the features mentioned constitute a partial delineation of an actual whole, while what we have, in fact, is a signifying process, filling up the name with a meaning that is ultimately closed off as this name comes to function as a token of exchange between writer and reader and reader and reader, comes to stand for a type which is assimilated into the liberal discourse and so loses its power to disturb.[5] We shall see that in *Life & Times of Michael K* Coetzee is concerned, precisely, to demonstrate that 'the sum *is* supplemented by a precious remainder', not in the manner of realist texts, which posit this remainder as a 'real' point of reference outside the text, but from the perspective of writing as a speech act which simultaneously excludes and reveals the unconscious of both writer and reader.

And so it becomes apparent that the choice of a type, and of a name appropriate to this type, does not occur outside the processes which determine character construction, but, on the contrary, initiates the process. The initial K could stand for Kotze or Koekemoer, as Gordimer would have it, but on the other hand it could also stand for Khamieskroon killer, that mysterious figure whose photograph Michael K cuts out of the newspaper and sticks on the refrigerator door:

> Though the handcuffs brought his shoulders forward and down, the Khamieskroon killer looked at the camera with what seemed to K a smile of quiet achievement. Below was a second picture: a rifle with a sling photographed against a blank background and captioned 'Killer's weapon.' (*L&T*, p. 22)

The Kamieskroon killer functions to suggest an alternate type which might be used as a model in the process of character construction; but Michael K is *not* a criminal or an insurgent, and this is so because a primary requirement of this generic character type is *innocence*. It is this quality of innocence which allows for the consensus of cathartic feelings of pity and guilt between writer and reader, and which allows both writer and reader to 'identify' with the figure of the victim in a way that Gordimer's comment on this novel exemplifies. She says:

> As the reader is drawn into the novel there comes the extraordinarily rare occurrence of one's response to its events opening up along with that of the central character himself. This is the reverse of facile identification: a prehensile comprehension stirs to take hold where the grasp of familiarity doesn't reach. A fellow inmate of the labour camp says to Michael K, 'You've been asleep all your life. It's time to wake up.' For the reader too . . . . Coetzee has won (or lost?) his inner struggle and now writes, from among the smell of weary flesh, a work of the closest and deepest engagement with the victimized people of Michael K's life and times. ('The Idea of Gardening,' p. 3)[6]

Several instances of misnaming are narrated in Coetzee's novel – Michael K is referred to as Michael Visagie, and both the captain of police and the medical officer call him Michaels – and in a sense one can say that all fictional naming is only approximate, that the name is always a misnomer, in that all characters function only to *re*-present the unconscious self. By the same token, one can say that a story is always the 'wrong' story, as Michael K is made to reflect:

> Always, when he tried to explain himself to himself, there remained a gap, a hole, a darkness before which his understanding baulked, into which it was useless to pour words. The words were eaten up, the gap remained. His was always a story with a hole in it: a wrong story, always wrong. (*L&T*, pp. 150–51)

Similarly, the use of the initial in the names K, Josef K and Michael K suggests that what we have in these figures is an incomplete, or partial, representation, not in the sense that Barthes criticizes in the realist text, but in the sense that the figure is a stand-in for the self of enunciation, whom he can do no more than partially represent. Michael K's function in relation to the self of enunciation is equivalent to that of Kafka's K., as this is described by Charles Bernheimer:

> At issue here is the function of the subject in structuring the text. From the point of view of the unconscious, the subject is nothing more than a provisional illusion sustained at the sufferance of the unconscious itself. Indeed, it could be said that the unconscious calls the subject into being – much as K is called to the Castle – so that this subjective agency will testify to the power of that which undermines it. If their operation is to be experienced and described, the mechanisms of displacement and condensation require a conscious witness. Thus the subject acts as an agent of representation through whose mimetic procedures the erosive effects of the unconscious are imaged. (p. 229)[7]

And so, in *Life & Times of Michael K*, Coetzee gives us a protagonist who has none of the usual attributes one expects in a character, and whose story is articulated around his attempt to escape the temporality which the structuring process of the narrative would impose on him. As such, his story constitutes an allegory of Coetzee's act of writing; an allegory of the attempt on the part of the self of enunciation to escape the 'meaning' which attaches itself to the subject of utterance. We shall see that the story of Michael K becomes the means by which 'the erosive effects of the unconscious are imaged', and that the allegorical structure of the novel is the means by which Coetzee confesses, rather than denies, the way in which the figure of Michael K conveys his 'meaning', and thus serves his needs as writer.

In this context, the 'Life & Times' of the title refers to the structuring activity of the narrative; to the 'life' which is constructed via the articulation of segments of narrated 'time'. In the first section of the novel, Coetzee adopts the structuring devices, or codes, of the genre, only to undermine them in various ways. It is possible to say that all of these devices arise out of the genre's fundamental need, which is the effacing of the narratorial voice in order to grant a voice, and freedom, to the victim. While the mode of narration here is too 'personalized' (in the sense that it is given in the key of the protagonist) to approximate the French preterite,[8] Barthes' commentary on this verb form is nevertheless useful in indicating how, in the apparent absence of a narrator, temporality takes on the function of causality:

> Through the preterite, the verb implicitly belongs with a causal chain, it partakes of a set of related and orientated actions, it functions as the algebraic sign of an intention. Allowing as it does an ambiguity between temporality and causality, it calls for a sequence of events, that is, for an intelligible Narrative. This is why it is the ideal instrument for every construction of a world; it is the unreal time of cosmogonies, myths, History and Novels. It presupposes a world which is constructed, elaborated, self-sufficient, reduced to significant lines, and not one which has been sent sprawling before us, for us to take or leave. Behind the preterite there always lurks a demiurge, a God or a reciter. The world is not unexplained since it is told like a story; each one of its accidents is but a circumstance, and the preterite is precisely this operative sign whereby the narrator reduces the exploded reality to a slim and pure logos, without density, without volume, without spread, and whose sole function is to unite as rapidly as possible a cause and an end. (*Writing Degree Zero*, pp. 30–31)[9]

Barthes' criticism of the preterite, like White's criticism of 'narrativizing discourse', is oriented around the fact that the narrator lurks behind the narrative, not owning his/her intentions or meaning. The apparent absence of the narrator means that s/he cannot make explicit the causal structure which links events without obtruding his/her presence, and so causality has to be implied by the sequential ordering of events.

And because the narrator cannot refer to the discursive situation, to the time of narration, this is a mode of narration which, like the preterite, 'does not itself refer to the past time-sphere or, indeed, to any time-sphere at all' (Bronzwaer, p. 45) As Käte Hamburger says, concerning the use of the preterite in the novel:

> [it] loses its function to refer to the past, which is caused by the fact that the time of the action, and therefore the action itself, is not related to a real I-*origio*, a real subject of utterance, but to the fictive I-*origines* of the characters.[10]

In Coetzee's novel, we find the function of indicating a specific time-sphere, and also the passage of time, is achieved by temporal markers, which, in turn, imply a causal connection between the segments of narrative. Thus, in the opening sections of the narrative, we find the repeated use of the conjunction 'because': 'Because their smiles and whispers hurt her, she kept it away from other children' (p. 4); 'Because of his disfigurement and because his mind was not quick, Michael was taken out of school after a short trial' (p. 4); 'Because of his face K did not have women friends' (p. 5). It is as though, by means of this very explicit indication of causality, Coetzee draws attention to the way in which the temporal markers, which replace the causal conjunctions from this point on, perform essentially the same function. Beginning with the next paragraph, we find that paragraph after paragraph opens with this kind of reference to time:

> Late one morning in June, in the thirty-first year of his life . . . . (p. 5); for months Anna K had been suffering from gross swelling of the legs and arms . . . . (pp. 5–6); For eight years Anna K had been employed as a domestic servant . . . . (p. 7); Early one Sunday morning he visited De Waal Park . . . . (p. 13); Then late one afternoon in the last week of June . . . . (p. 14); Then one morning Michael K started up at the scrape of the front-door lock . . . . (p. 23); and so on.

In addition to this very deliberate articulation of segments of narrated time, Michael K is made to reflect upon his life in terms which refer to his dependence upon the narrative structuring of time:

> It appeared that he had to stay in Stellenbosch for a certain length of time. There was no way of shortening the time. He stumbled through the days, losing his way often (*L&T*, p. 47);
>
> He did not know what was going to happen. The story of his life had never been an interesting one; there had usually been someone to tell him what to do next; now there was no one, and the best thing seemed to be to wait (*L&T*, p. 92)

Coetzee thus foregrounds this structuring activity which creates the illusion of sequence and which explains the world without appearing to do so; at the same time he undermines it by means of the allegory of the narrating self, in which, as we shall see, Michael K refuses the temporality of narrative, and so refuses the structure of causality which it implies: he refuses to be explained, to be reduced to a coherent and easily assimilated unit of meaning.

One of the conventions whereby the absent narrator conveys the voice and the point of view of the protagonist is free indirect speech, which we find used fairly extensively in the first section of the novel, as, for example, in the following passage:

> Now was the time. No sooner had they returned to the room than he came out with the plan he had been pondering ever since building the first barrow. They were wasting their time waiting for permits, he said. The permits would never come. And without permits they could not leave by train. Any day now they would be expelled from the room. Would she therefore not allow him to take her to Prince Albert

> in the cart? She had seen for herself how comfortable it was. The damp weather was not good for her, nor was the unending worry about the future. (*L&T*, p. 24)

As is evident from this example, free indirect speech disrupts the categories of tense and person. Much has been written about the linguistic features of free indirect speech, but there seems to be some degree of consensus concerning the 'ambiguity or indeterminacy of its vocal origin' (Jefferson, p. 145). The apparent duality of free indirect speech, which combines the voice of narrator and character, 'prevents free indirect speech from being read as the record of an actual voice.'[11] However, free indirect speech proves problematic in this respect only if one attempts to read the narrator's speech as a real voice issueing from a determinate source: if, on the contrary, one accepts that the status of the narrator is equally as figural as that of the character, it becomes evident that the voices of *both* are disembodied, even when not fused in free indirect speech.[12] The speech of neither the character nor the narrator is that of a real 'person', and ultimately only '*re*-presents' an inaccessible self of enunciation, in that the text as a whole gives this self a place from which to speak. In a text which would *conceal* the act of narration, free indirect speech, by problematizing the provenance of the utterance, raises questions concerning not only the narrator's voice, but also the act of enunciation. The disembodied nature of all narrative voices makes the incongruity of deictic and verb form in an utterance like 'Now was the time' not only possible but significant: one can say that 'now was the time' reflects the relationship of the narrative 'now' to the 'now' of the narrating instant, in that the 'now' of narrative time is always located in the past, relative to the always immanent 'now' of the self which is yet to be realized in the narrative to come.

The narrative voice is, furthermore, divided up or parcelled out in the form of figures introduced to provide expository commentary, figures of the type that Sussman calls textual mediators or information givers.[13] Robert, the man whom Michael K meets in the Jakkalsdrif camp, is the most significant of these figures, and there is a passage in which K is made to reflect upon the relationship between himself and Robert in terms which might be applied to the relationship between writer and protagonist:

> It seemed more like Robert than like him, as he knew himself, to think like that. Would he have to say that the thought was Robert's and had merely found a home in him, or could he say that though the seed had come from Robert, the thought, having grown up inside him, was now his own? He did not know. (*L&T*, p. 130)

We find in this passage the theme of organicism, of insemination, birth, and growth, on which the allegory of the novel as a whole is founded. This theme is present from the first sentence, which describes K's birth, setting up the triangular structure of K, mother, and midwife, a structure in which, as we shall see, the father is conspicuous by his absence. This first sentence, 'The first thing the midwife noticed about Michael K when she helped him out of his mother into the world was that he had a hare lip' (*L&T*, p. 3), is an example of the formulaic opening, which is another of the codes which Coetzee subverts in order to make it refer to the act of narration. In his paper, 'The First Sentence of Yvonne Burgess's *The Strike* ', Coetzee analyzes Burgess's opening sentence, which is, 'Finlay closed the book and considered the title appreciatively', as follows:

> (1) *The* book, *the* title: why this deviant use of *the*, and emphasized by repetition too?[14]
> (2) *Finlay*. What is *Finlay*? 'Finlay' denotes a person whose name is Finlay. Does it have any meaning?
> (3) Considered *appreciatively*. Somewhere in the deep structure of this phrase 'Finlay' appreciates a book. Does Finlay give signs that denote appreciation, and does whoever decodes his signs do so without qualm? Or is it that 'Finlay' is aware of himself appreciating a book? And if the latter, is

> 'Finlay' not in fact *I*?
>
> So this first sentence is truly a labyrinth. What 'Finlay' closes is not a book but the book; and it is the book because it is the book that 'Finlay' closes. 'Finlay' is Finlay, the one who closes the book. And he gives signs that can only be seen by an eye that cannot be seen.

The same kind of analysis could be applied to the first sentence of Coetzee's novel: one might ask 'Who is the midwife, who is this Michael K that is helped out of his mother, and who is it that records that the first thing the midwife notices about Michael K is that he has a hare lip?' However, in this case the tripartite structure appears to be deliberately labyrinthine, with mother, midwife, and child as the three mutually defining elements of a structure that refers back to the eye/I that cannot be seen, and ultimately to the self that cannot be spoken. They may be regarded as the three components of the utterance which represents this self: the midwife is the 'silent' narrator, and Michael K is the character, the one delivered by the midwife/narrator, split off from the mother, who is the source of desire, and therefore also the source of the narrative. The fact that the hare lip is *the* first thing that the midwife notices serves to specify the primacy of impaired speech, or inarticulacy, in a genre which makes the innocent victim the object of narration.

The self-effacing stance of the midwife/narrator is, furthermore, implied in the absence of conventional predicates. However, while the narrator refrains from qualifying K by means of adjectives such as 'resourceful', 'hardworking', 'tenacious', or others that might be appropriate to a figure such as this, K *is* qualified by means of similes (including the simile implied in his 'hare' lip) which liken him to animals or insects;

> He stole his mother's tea and that of the old woman in the next bed, gulping it down like a guilty dog (p. 41); He climbed into a great wire cage containing

> soiled linen and slept there, curled up like a cat (p. 43); he stood and ate, taking bites of good flesh here and there, chewing as quickly as a rabbit (p. 53); he baulked, like a beast at the shambles (p. 55); Like a worm he began to slither toward his hole (p. 147); He thought of himself as a termite boring its way through rock (p. 91); He crouched in the lee of the dam wall, sodden, feeling like a snail without its shell (p. 154); Like a parasite dozing in the gut, he thought; like a lizard under a stone (p. 159); I am more like an earthworm, he thought. Which is also a kind of gardener. Or a mole, also a gardener, that does not tell stories because it lives in silence (p. 248).

In addition to betraying an attitude of denigration on the part of the writer toward the victim-as-protagonist, these similes work together to convey the way in which this genre functions as a fable does, with a lesson or a moral embedded in events. If in this genre, the victim is the source of a story, s/he is also the vehicle for a religious, or quasi-religious, form of moral instruction, as is evident in the medical officer's allusion to the parable of the sparrows:

> 'You ask why you are important, Michaels. The answer is that you are not important. But that does not mean you are forgotten. No one is forgotten. Remember the sparrows. Five sparrows are sold for a farthing, and even they are not forgotten.' (*L&T*, p. 186)

On more than one occasion K is made to reflect upon the fact that there is a lesson to be learned:

> The lesson, if there was a lesson, if there were lessons embedded in events, seemed to be not to kill such large animals (p. 78); Is this my education? he wondered. Am I at last learning about life here in a camp? It seemed to him that scene after scene of life was playing itself out before him and that the

> scenes all cohered. He had a presentiment of a single meaning upon which they were converging or threatening to converge, though he did not know yet what that might be (p. 122); (Is that the moral of it all, he thought, the moral of the whole story . . . .) (p. 249).

Here Hayden White's critique of 'narrativizing discourse' again proves relevant to the structures of meaning which we encounter in this genre. He says:

> If every fully realized story, however we define that familiar but conceptually elusive entity, is a kind of allegory, points to a moral, or endows events, whether real or imaginary, with a significance that they do not possess as a mere sequence, then it seems possible to conclude that every historical narrative has as its latent or manifest purpose the desire to *moralize* the events of which it treats. Where there is ambiguity or ambivalence regarding the status of the legal system, which is the form in which the subject encounters most immediately the social system in which he is enjoined to achieve a full humanity, the ground on which any closure of a story one might wish to tell about a past, whether it be a public or a private past, is lacking. And this suggests that narrativity, certainly in factual storytelling and probably in fictional storytelling as well, is intimately related to, if not a function of, the impulse to moralize reality, that is, to identify it with the social system that is the source of any morality that we can imagine. (pp. 17–18)

In the context of the South African social system, the genre we are dealing with here attempts to cope with ambiguity or ambivalence concerning the status of the legal system by means of a protagonist whose projected freedom denies the power of the corrupt system currently operative. However, in its insistence upon the innocence of the victim, and in its concomitant tendency to moralize events, its effect is to implicitly endorse this system. While Coetzee's novel conforms to the codes of the genre in conveying a lesson, we shall see that this is a lesson whose application, like that of Kafka's fables and parables remains restricted to the act of reading and of writing, and to the process of subject constitution this involves.

Turning now, to the allegory which conveys the 'lesson' of Coetzee's novel, we find that in the first section of the novel it is articulated around the activities of cultivation and escape, both of which refer to the unconscious desire, which, while it is the source of the life and growth of the text, nevertheless escapes the conscious processes of reading and writing, manifesting itself only in the gaps and slips and lapses. Michael K slips out of Cape Town, away from the Visagie grandson, out of the Jakkalsdrif camp. He conceals himself in the mountains and on a deserted farm. On the farm he constructs a burrow for his dwelling place, which, as a *structure* involving no *construction*, merely the hollowing out of a pre-existent form, is, like Kafka's burrow, 'a metaphor for the linguistic construct' (Coetzee, 'Time, Tense and Aspect in Kafka's 'The Burrow', p. 577). K is made to reflect upon the nature of his dwelling in the following terms:

> What a pity that to live in times like these a man must be ready to live like a beast. A man who wants to live cannot live in a house with lights in the windows. He must live in a hole and hide by day. A man must live so that he leaves no trace of his living (*L&T*, p. 135);
>
> I am not building a house out here by the dam to pass on to other generations. What I make ought to be careless, makeshift, a shelter to be abandoned without a tugging at the heartstrings (*L&T*, p. 138).

We are referred, here, to the strategies of Coetzee's texts, to the way in which they inhabit the borrowed form, the makeshift shelter, in an attempt to avoid constructing another, alternative myth: 'The worst mistake, he told himself, would be to try to found a new house, a rival line, on his small beginnings out at the dam' (*L&T*, p. 142–43). This text in particular must not be too closely bound to Coetzee's own meanings; he must be able to abandon it, without a tugging at the heartstrings, to the successive meanings which each new reading will generate.

The moments at which K feels he has escaped pursuit and detection for a while are described as 'pocket[s] outside time' (*L&T*, p. 82), 'islands without an owner' (*L&T*, p. 84). As opposed to the ongoing movement of his almost continuous flight, these are moments of stasis, where nothing happens and nothing needs to be said:

> I could live here forever, he thought, or till I die. Nothing would happen, every day would be the same as the day before, there would be nothing to say. The anxiety that belonged to the time on the road began to leave him (*L&T*, pp. 63–64);
>
> In his first days in the mountains he went for walks, turned over stones, nibbled at roots and bulbs . . . But now he ceased to make an adventure of eating and drinking. He did not explore his new world. He did not turn his cave into a home or keep a record of the passage of days . . . . He wondered if he were living in what was known as bliss. (*L&T*, p. 93)

Whereas in the camps he is 'devoured by time' (*L&T*, p. 134), in the state of freedom time is 'poured out upon him in . . . an unending stream' (*L&T*, p. 139), and he experiences idleness as a 'yielding up of himself to time, to a time flowing slowly like oil from horizon to horizon over the face of the world' (*L&T*, p. 158). If K is 'outside time', it is because these are projected moments outside the temporality of the narrative, in Schleifer's words, outside 'temporality . . . as a concept, which emerges and is recognized simultaneously with the emergence of the subject' (p. 876). And, instead of being 'devoured' by the articulation of segments of narrated time, which translate the present moments of lived time into non-present moments of the 'dead past' (see my Chapter One, p. 39), he experiences an abundance of *lived* time, which does not have to be recorded or accounted for in the manner of narrated time: 'He had kept no tally of the days nor recorded the changes of the moon. He was not a prisoner or a castaway, his life by the dam was not a sentence that he had to serve out' (*L&T*, pp. 157–58).

These moments outside time and space are not the projected moments of self-presence which Derrida describes as *utopia*:

> The neume, the spell of self-presence, inarticulate experience of time, tantamount to saying: *utopia*. Such a language – since a language must be involved – does not, properly speaking, take place. It does not know articulation, which cannot take place without spacing and without organization of spaces. There is no language before differences of locale. (*Of Grammatology*, p. 251)[16]

These moments are more accurately described by means of Barthes' term, *atopia*:

> *Pigeonholed*: I am pigeonholed, assigned to an (intellectual) site, to residence in a caste (if not in a class). Against which there is only one internal doctrine: that of *atopia* (of a drifting habitation). Atopia is superior to utopia (utopia is reactive, tactical, literary, it proceeds from meaning and governs it). (*Roland Barthes*, p. 49; see my Chapter One, pp. 52–53)

What is projected in K's escape to these moments outside time, where time is poured out upon him in an 'unending stream', is not a situation of self-present meaning, free from intervention by the Other, but a 'drifting habitation', a writing which has no fixed abode, in that it escapes the conscious processes of meaning. At this point it is important to distinguish between Magda's lament concerning her situation on an 'island out of space, out of time' (*HC*, p. 122) where all things are possible, and the positive presentation of Michael K's escape to these hiding places outside time and space. The difference lies in the fact that, via the figure of Magda, Coetzee represents a form of writing that aims at *self*-realization and *self*-transcendence on the part of the writer, and at the same time he represents the sense of frustration that arises out of the failure of the writing to achieve this. Magda laments the failure of the self of enunciation to bring itself into being in the text; she laments the impossibility of realizing the present moment of narration in narrative time, of pronouncing a narrative 'now' which is equal to the 'now' of narration. Via the figure of Michael K, on the contrary, Coetzee represents a mode of writing ostensibly *not* motivated by the need to bring the self into being, but by the wish to give speech, and thereby life, to *another*, to an inarticulate and oppressed victim, and in so doing to project the potential freedom of this other being. In this instance, then, the capacity of the protagonist to *escape* the temporal structures of the narrative implies an escape from causality, from explanation. Evading the 'single meaning' on which the scenes of his life threaten to converge (*L&T*, p. 122), K evades the intentions of the writer, who would erect him/herself into being via the figure of the victim.

Gordimer complains that Coetzee 'does not recognize what the victims, seeing themselves as victims no longer, have done, are doing, and believe they must do for themselves' ('The Idea of Gardening', p. 6). However, if, as she claims, 'Freedom is defined negatively' in this novel, this is because freedom is presented, here, from a perspective interior to the act of writing and reading, and Michael K's determination to be 'out of all the camps at the same time' represents the possibilities for freedom inherent in the process of textuality itself. These possibilities for freedom inhere in the fact that the text itself may be regarded as an atopic site, a drifting habitation taken up and abandoned with each successive reading. In Green's analysis of the act of writing and reading, the text is

> A metaphorical locus, a *potential space*, to use

> Winnicott's expression, [that] has come to exist between writer and reader, within which the field of illusion is constituted as the celebration of a trans-narcissistic object. This metaphorical locus is one of the loci inhabitated by the non-represented and non-representable unconscious fantasy. This non-representability of the unconscious fantasy has its counterpart in the non-representability of the writing process. (p. 26; see my Chapter One, p. 52)

This locus exists at the intersection between the acts of reading and writing. In the case of the act of writing, the non-representability of the unconscious ensures that the meaning that *is* represented in the text is never equal to the inexpressible and inaccessible meanings which persist while they are repressed by the conscious processes of writing. In turn, the non-representability of the writing process, in which the text is a 'set of symbols which represent nothing by themselves', and in which 'the deciphering process alone will open the way to representation' (Green, p. 24), means that each new act of narration that arises out of each new reading is a product of the unconscious of the reader, which again eludes the conscious meanings s/he finds in the text.

Like Magda, who says: 'The host is dying, the parasite scuttles anxiously about the cooling entrails wondering whose tissues it will live off next' (*HC*, p. 119), Michael K thinks of himself as 'a parasite dozing in the gut' (*L&T*, p. 159). However, while Magda's parasitic status refers only to the way in which, as stand-in for the self of enunciation, she inhabits the borrowed form of a pre-existing genre, K goes on to reflect upon the *reciprocity* between host and parasite:

> Parasite was the word the police captain had used: the camp at Jakkalsdrif, a nest of parasites hanging from the neat sunlit town, eating its substance, giving no nourishment back. Yet to K lying idle in his bed . . . it was no longer obvious which

> was host and which parasite, camp or town . . . . Parasites too had flesh and substance; parasites too could be preyed upon. Perhaps in truth whether the camp was declared a parasite on the town or the town a parasite on the camp depended on no more than on who made his voice heard loudest. (*L&T*, pp. 159–60)

This recalls J. Hillis Miller's argument, in 'The Critic as Host', that the text which 'hosts' the criticism is equally as parasitic as the criticism which 'feeds' on the text. Thus the term 'para-site' comes to signify as a locus of substitution, and refers to the way in which Coetzee's novel, which is parasitic in relation to the previous texts which it deconstructs, will in turn become the host to successive parasitic readings (or, in Hillis Miller's terms, will become parasitic in relation to the readings in which it survives).

Michael K's capacity to escape the camps, then represents what Bernheimer refers to as 'the *erosive* effects of the unconscious' (my emphasis; see p. 278, this chapter). We come not to his work as a gardener, a cultivator of pumpkins and melons, in which is represented the *procreative* effects of the unconscious as the source of both writing and reading. In growing his own food out on the abandoned farm, as in everything else, K is motivated by a single purpose, by the belief that 'he had been brought into the world to look after his mother' (*L&T*, p. 9). This belief moves him in his attempt to realize his mother's wish to return to the farm where she was born, and, when she has died, to return her ashes to what he can only assume is her birthplace. The act of returning his mother to the earth is 'the beginning of his life as a cultivator' (*L&T*, p. 81), and 'after her season in the earth' the mother is 'washed clean, blown about, and drawn up into leaves of grass' (*L&T*, p. 171). (The allusion to Whitman's title here suggests that the leaves of grass are, equally, the leaves of the text.) Lying in his burrow, K thinks of his mother: 'She had asked him to bring her back to her birthplace and he had done so, though perhaps only by a trick of words' (*L&T*, p. 160). K's activity as cultivator has its genesis in desire; in the desire which is the desire of the Other's desire and, more specifically here, the desire of the mother's desire.[17] It stands for the act of writing, which, like K's act of producing pumpkins from the earth which contains his mother's remains, is an attempt to give expression to desire, and is, likewise, no more than 'a trick of words', because desire is beyond articulation.

The mother, then, is the source of growth and the source of the text: when the medical officer asks K where his mother is, K replies, 'She makes the plants grow' (*L&T*, p. 178). The activity of cultivation is described in terms which make it the equivalent of the act of procreation: K makes his burrow in a place where 'two low hills, like plump breasts, curved toward each other' (*L&T*, p. 137), and the motion of the pump, bringing water up from the earth, enacts a form of penetration and climax:

> He stood leaning against the frame of the pump, feeling the tremor that passed through it each time the piston reached the bottom of its stroke, hearing the great wheel above his head cut through the dark on its greased bearings. (*L&T*, p. 143)

That this is meant to be read as a metaphor of the act of copulation is evident as the passage continues: 'How fortunate that I have no children, he thought: how fortunate that I have no desire to father' (*L&T*, p. 143). If he is father to his pumpkins and melons, which he thinks of as 'these poor second children of his' (*L&T*, p. 139), he is also mother to them, bound to them by an umbilical cord:

> There was a cord of tenderness that stretched from him to the patch of earth beside the dam and must be cut. It seemed to him that one could cut a cord like that only so many times before it would not grow again (*L&T*, p. 90);

> . . . there must be men to stay behind and keep gardening alive, or at least the idea of gardening;

> because once that cord was broken, the earth would grow hard and forget her children (*L&T*, p. 150)

This feeling of parental attachment to the products of his cultivation describes the writer's relationship to the text as offspring. Referring to the acts of reading and of writing as reciprocal acts of voyeurism and exhibitionism, as the desire to both see and be seen, Green says:

> . . . the object shown by the writer is not present on his body – it is a created object. A new transformation must be taken into account at this point. What the writer shows is the result of a creative process, somewhat like the royal child shown to the people as proof that birth has really occurred.
>
> It has thus become clearer why it is not only the penis that is involved here, but the series penis-feces-child – a child that the writer has brought into the world by himself, without anybody's help, for even though he may be indebted to his precursors, he is its sole creator, the only father – both the father and the mother, for that matter. It becomes apparent that both aspects of sexual curiosity are fused into one, the desire to show-see a penis and the desire to find an explanation for the mystery of birth. The writer bypasses any sexual theory involving the parents, since he is at the same time both parents joined for the procreation of the child he has produced. (p. 26)

This curiosity concerning the mystery of birth is evident in a passage like the following:

> He tried to imagine a figure standing alone at the head of the line, a woman in a shapeless grey dress who came from no mother; but when he had to think of the silence in which she lived, the silence of time before the beginning, his mind baulked. (*L&T*, pp. 160–161)

In this vision child descends from child as meaning is substituted for meaning in a way that 'bypasses any sexual theory involving the parents', and that does not allow for growth into maturity in the form of an established 'paternal' meaning. This vision does not allow for the positing of textual origins, except in the form of 'the silence of time before the beginning', which is the silence of time before speech itself. K's activity as cultivator involves the planting of seeds and the growing of fruit which provides more seed – 'It was no longer a matter of growing a fat crop, only of growing enough for the seed not to die out' (*L&T*, p. 154) – and is closer to the process of dissemination than insemination. It is dissemination in the Derridean sense:

> A sowing that does not produce plants, but is simply infinitely repeated. A semination that is not *in*semination but *dis*semination, seed spilled in vain, an emission that cannot return to its origin in the father. Not an exact and controlled polysemy, but a proliferation of always different, always postponed meanings. (Spivak, Translator's Preface to *Of Grammatology*, p. lxv)

With respect to the future, dissemination describes a gesture which would forego paternal control, or mastery, over its progeny, and would release the text into the world to achieve itself there in a process without end. As I indicated in the chapter on *Dusklands* (see note 30, p. 144), the description of the picking and eating of the first pumpkin is reminiscent of the scene in which Eugene Dawn stabs his child:

> Then came the evening when the first pumpkin was ripe enough to cut. It had grown earlier and faster than the others, in the very centre of the field. K had marked it out as the first fruit, the firstborn. The shell was soft, the knife sank in without a struggle. The flesh, though still rimmed with green, was a deep orange. On the wire grid he had made he laid

> strips of pumpkin over a bed of coals that glowed brighter and brighter as the dark came on. The fragrance of the burning flesh rose into the sky. Speaking the words he had been taught, directing them no longer upward but to the earth on which he knelt, he prayed: 'For what we are about to receive make us truly thankful'. With two wire skewers he turned the strips, and in mid-act felt his heart suddenly flow over with thankfulness. It was exactly as they had described it, like a gush of warm water. Now it is completed, he said to himself. (*L&T*, pp. 155–56)

In Chapter Two I commented upon Eugene Dawn's act of stabbing the child by means of reference to Derrida's metaphor of dissemination/castration:

> Castration, the lack of superintendence by phallic authority, is what transforms the 'author' or the 'book' into a 'text'. Presence can be articulated only if it is fragmented into discourse; 'castration' and dismemberment being both a menace to and the condition of the possibility of discourse. Somewhat extravagantly, the phallus may itself be seen as the knife that severs itself to perpetuate its dissemination. (Spivak, Translator's Preface to *Of Grammatology*, pp. lxv–lxvi.

While this metaphor seems equally valid in this context, the act of cutting and eating the pumpkin represents a *positive* attitude on the part of the writer toward the process of dissemination, as opposed to the dissemination which achieves itself *in spite of* Eugene Dawn's attempt (as representative of the self-reflexive writer) to maintain his position of mastery in relation to the text's meaning. The cutting and eating of the first fruit is presented as a sacrificial ceremony, in Green's words, 'as the celebration of a transitional trans-narcissistic object', the text.

In so far as he stands for a mode of writing that would relinquish control over meaning, Michael K is necessarily sexless. The medical officer/narrator of Section II says of him:

> With Michaels it always seemed to me that someone had scuffled together a handful of dust, spat on it, and patted it into the shape of a rudimentary man, making one or two mistakes (the mouth, and without a doubt the contents of the head), omitting one or two details (the sex), but coming up nevertheless in the end with a genuine little man of earth . . . . (*L&T*, p. 22)

K does not possess the Phallus which would make him the father, embodiment of paternal authority and apparent master of meaning. The condition of sexlessness functions, furthermore, to imply that K has not been admitted to the Symbolic: he had not undergone the passage, via the Father's recognition, from the stage at which he wishes to be the Phallus, the desire of the mother's desire, to the stage at which he possesses the symbolic Phallus. Like Magda, he has not achieved a sexual identity in the Symbolic, but unlike Magda, he is presented as having no desire for such an identity. K does not have a father, or, as he is made to reflect:

> . . . my father was Huis Norenius. My father was the list of rules on the door of the dormitory, the twenty-one rules of which the first was 'There will be silence in the dormitories at all times' . . . . (*L&T*, p. 143)

Describing the child's accession to the Symbolic, Lemaire says:

> If the child does not accept the Law, or if the mother does not recognize this position in the father [as the embodiment of the law], the subject will remain identified with the phallus and subjected to the mother's desire. (p. 83)

There is no father, so K remains subjected to the mother's

desire, and, in a sense, outside language, relegated to the realm of silence: 'Year after year Michael K sat on a blanket watching his mother polish other people's floors, learning to be quiet' (*L&T*, p. 4). The basic organic need is hunger, and this need has been only partially satisfied in K, for he 'could not suck from the breast and cried with hunger' (*L&T*, p. 3), and had to be fed with a teaspoon. At Huis Norenuis K had been hungry, but 'Whatever the nature of the beast that had howled inside him, it was starved into stillness' (*L&T*, p. 94). In K the organic need is not eroticized via the first object of instinct, the breast: it is thus not transformed into a sexual drive, but persists at the most basic level as the most radical lack.[18]

In Section II, the allegory is organized around the theme of food and fasting, as fasting becomes a form of escape, and defines K's determination to avoid the meaning which the medical officer/narrator (as writer) would impose on him, force feeding him, fleshing him out, rehabilitating him so that he can be reappropriated by the State, complete, coherent, and confirming to the codes of characterization. This section describes K's confinement in the Kenilworth camp, where he has been taken following his arrest, under suspicion of having supplied food to guerilla bands. It functions as a *mise-en-abyme* device,[19] with the camp representing the structure of the narrative as a whole, and the unnamed medical officer, who takes on the task of the 'absent' narrator of Sections I and III, representing the writer. On one level, K's refusal to eat camp food again represents Coetzee's attempt to speak without being spoken, to represent the self of enunciation without this self being usurped by the subject of utterance. On another level, in the medical officer's relation with Michael K, we witness the development of an attempt to envisage a different kind of relationship between writer and victim, and to write about one of the oppressed in a way which is other than that inscribed in the genre.

On the first level, the theme of fasting derives much of its significance from the allusion to Kafka, in whose stories fasting represents the attempt to make the writing self-sufficient that is to say, minimally bound to represent anything other than itself. Derrida describes Kafka's project as follows:

> If there is a literary originality, which is by no means a simple certainty, it must free itself if not from the metaphor, which tradition too has judged reducible, at least from the savage spontaneity of the figure as it appears in nonliterary language. This modern protestation can be triumphant or, in Kafka's manner, denuded of all illusion, despairing, and no doubt more lucid: literature which lives by being outside of itself, within the figures of a language which is primarily not its own, would die as well through a re-entry into itself by way of the non-metaphor. 'From a letter: "During this dreary winter I warm myself by it." ' Metaphors are one among many things which make me despair of writing [*Schreiben*]. Writing's lack of independence of the world, its dependence on the maid who tends the fire, on the cat warming itself by the stove; it is even dependent on the poor old human being warming himself by the stove. All these are independent activities ruled by their own laws; only writing is helpless, cannot live in itself, is a joke and a despair' (Kafka, *Journal*, 6 November 1921).[20]

As I have indicated, K's and Josef K's freedom from psychological and material encumbrances offers a way of writing which is freed from the necessity of representing character, and so can represent its own processes. And in stories such as 'The Fasting Showman' (sometimes translated as 'The Hunger Artist') and 'Investigations of a Dog', writing's determination to live in itself is thematized in the acts of fasting of the showman, in the former, and of the dog narrator in the latter. It is as though Kafka (and Coetzee after him), like these figures, is conducting an experiment concerning the nature of writing, an experiment which involves the representation of a figure so deprived, so starved of all the means of sublimating desire, that the act of constructing a narrative around him is itself a form of fasting.[21] Thus Henry Sussman says of Josef K:

> What the contest of endurance initiated by the trial requires of K may be described literally as the capacity to hold his breath in an atmosphere exhausted by codified writing.
>
> There is much evidence in Kafka's writings to suggest that his own approach to fiction is marked by a concerted exercise in the control of breathing. (p. 45)

This analysis might equally well be applied to Michael K and to Coetzee's novel, substituting 'camp' for 'trial', and fasting for the image of controlled breathing: indeed, the medical officer says of K:

> 'You did not want to die, but you were dying. You were like a bunny-rabbit sewn up in the carcase of an ox, suffocating no doubt, but starving too, amid all those basketfuls of meat, for the true food.' (*L&T*, p. 225)

And when the medical offer says:

> 'It's not a question of dying . . . . It's not that he wants to die. He just doesn't like the food here. Profoundly doesn't like it. He won't even take baby food. Maybe he only eats the bread of freedom' (*L&T*, p. 200),

he echoes the dying words of Kafka's fasting showman:

> 'Forgive me, everybody,' whispered the fasting showman; only the overseer, who had his ear to the bars, understood him. 'Of course,' said the overseer and tapped his forehead with a finger to let the attendants know what state the man was in, 'we forgive you.' 'I always wanted you to admire my fasting,' said the fasting showman. 'We do admire it,' said the overseer, affably. 'But you shouldn't admire it,' said the fast-

> ing showman. 'Well then we don't admire it,' said the overseer, 'but why shouldn't we admire it?' 'Because I have to fast, I can't do anything else,' said the fasting showman. 'What a fellow you are,' said the overseer, 'and why don't you do anything else?' 'Because,' said the fasting showman . . . 'because I couldn't find any food I liked . . . . ('A Fasting Showman', pp. 173–74)

Thus, via the figure of K and the theme of fasting, as via the theme of escape, Coetzee refers to the capacity of the unconscious to elude the conscious processes and meanings of writing, to refuse 'incarnation' in the Word. Here the significance of the tripartite structure, Major van Rensburg, commander of the Kenilworth camp/medical officer narrator/Michael K, becomes apparent: this is a 'holy' trinity, which functions as a metaphor of the hierarchical structure, author/writer/unconscious. Within this trinity, K is, if not the *holy* ghost, then a figure so insubstantial as to be a spirit, 'not of our world' (*L&T*, pp. 179 and 184). He is a 'spirit invisible, a visitor on our planet, a creature beyond the laws of nations', one of the 'universal souls' (*L&T*, p. 207), and as such represents that which *eludes* representation, that which refuses to be 'embodied' in the meaning of the text. The narrator, representing the writer, is the saviour who intercedes on behalf of K. He says:

> The laws are made of iron, Michaels, I hope you are learning that. No matter how thin you make yourself, they will not relax. There is no home left for universal souls, except perhaps in Antartica or on the high seas . . . . You are going to die, and your story is going to die too, for ever and ever, unless you come to your senses and listen to me. Listen to me, Michaels. I am the only one who can save you. I am the only one who sees you for the original soul you are. I am the only one who cares for you. (*L&T*, p. 207)

Perceiving his role as that of intercession between a corrupt system and the oppressed victim, at this point the narrator does not acknowledge the way in which his own needs are being served via the figure of K, and appeals to K to yield his story for his own sake. This refers to the covert function of this genre, to the desire to 'save' an oppressed person; near the beginning of this section we find an allusion to a less commendable function, which is the parallel need to 'save' the writer: the commander of the camp says:

> 'perhaps we are soft . . . . Perhaps we are even scheming a bit, at the back of our minds. Perhaps we think that if one day they come and put everyone on trial, someone will step forward and say, 'Let those two off, they were soft.' Who knows? . . . ' (*L&T*, p. 181)

Immediately following K's escape from the Kenilworth camp, the narrator is shown in the act of assuming that K's story can be neatly tied up by means of the collaboration of all those in control of the camp. He says:

> 'Now at least let him go in peace. I'll write out a death certificate, you countersign it, some clerk in the Castle will file it away without giving it a glance, and that will be the end of the story of Michaels.' (*L&T*, p. 212)

The Castle here refers to the actual military headquarters situated in the castle built at the time of the early Dutch settlement at the Cape, but it also provides a convenient allusion to Kafka's *The Castle*, and so to the ultimate, inscrutable system of language which circumscribes all attempts at making meaning. Working in collaboration with this system is the commander of the camp, the Author as God. The medical officer says to him: 'For God's sake close the story of Michaels here and now' (*L&T*, p. 212), and describes him 'labouring at his desk to balance the bodies out against the bodies in' (*L&T*, p. 214). Captain van Rensburg's name is Noël, and he plays cricket 'in a white tracksuit with red piping that made him look like Father Christmas in thermal underwear' (*L&T*, p. 210), which suggests that if he is not

God, then he is a parodic substitute for him in the person of Father Christmas. As Author, the commander is concerned with 'flow' (*L&T*, p. 181), with the movement of bodies, or characters, in and out of the narrative. He is bound to uphold, to a certain degree at least, the rules which he receives from above, from a language, or a system, which for the most part dictates what meanings are possible. Elizabeth Bruss (citing Edward Said, who is citing Michel Foucault – proof of the difficulty of establishing 'authorship') says:

> 'The author is he who implants, into the troublesome language of fiction, its unities, its coherences, its links with realities . . . . The author principle limits this same chance element the hazards of discourse through the action of an identity whose form is that of *individuality* and the *I.*' In Foucault's treatment, authorship is at once an artifact of history, a rule of formation (which controls and distributes access to discourse and keeps the construal process within a certain, arbitrary limit), and a carefully preserved delusion. The fact is that discursive practices precede and exceed individual writers, who are born and educated into possibilities and procedures that they may exploit in different ways but that they neither originate nor control. Thus, *author* turns out to be a misnomer: not a divine creator, not even a divine creation, but a secular invention and an economic convenience.[22]

Not a divine creator, not even a divine creation, but a secular invention and an economic convenience: in other words, not God but Father Christmas.

The correlative to Michael K's capacity to escape the temporality of the narrative is his capacity to remain outside history. The medical officer says of him:

> We have all tumbled over the lip into the cauldron of history: only you, following your idiot light, biding your time in an orphanage (who would have thought of

> *that* as a hiding-place?), evading the peace and the war, skulking in the open where no one dreamed of looking, have managed to live in the old way, drifting through time, observing the seasons, no more trying to change the course of history than a grain of sand does. (*L&T*, pp. 207–08)

While this is reminiscent of the Magistrate's lament (in *Waiting for the Barbarians*, p. 133) concerning his unwilling involvement in the time of Empire, and of his desire to live in the time of the seasons, 'like fish in water, like birds in air, like children', K's capacity to elude history is presented *positively*, as opposed to the negative presentation of the Magistrate's desire to live outside history. Whereas with the Magistrate this desire refers to the liberal writer's assumption that it is possible to remain outside the discursive context, to maintain one's 'self-possession' while delivering a critique of the system, K's status as one of the dispossessed and his position outside history refer to the way in which unconscious meaning always *escapes* the conscious processes of the discourse, and so escapes subjection to history. The medical officer's demand that K should yield his story, and his claim that he can 'save' K from obscurity, refer to the desire of the writer of this particular genre to insert the victim in history by recording his/her life. Thus the medical officer says:

> We ought to value you and celebrate you, we ought to put your clothes on a maquette in a museum, your clothes and your packet of pumpkin seeds too, with a label; there ought to be a plaque nailed to the racetrack wall commemorating your stay here. (*L&T*, p. 208)

This is an ironic exposition of the writer's belief that the life of *another* can be rendered, complete and independent, in the discourse. Talking about texts that are de-mystified and ironical, de Man points out that

> the target of their irony is very often the claim to

> speak about human matters as if they were facts of history. It is a historical fact that irony becomes increasingly conscious of itself in the course of demonstrating the impossibility of our being historical. (p. 194)

It is possible to say that, via the figure of Michael K, Coetzee, likewise, demonstrates the impossibility of the unconscious, extra-linguistic self being historical, that is to say, of being inserted in history via the discourse.

The medical officer, as representative of the writer, is not presented as being guilty of the same blindness, or self-deception, as the Magistrate, for he does refer to his own insertion in time and in history. Unlike K, who escapes to pockets *outside* time, he thinks of himself as 'a castaway marooned *in* a pocket of time, the time of waiting, camp time, war-time' (*L&T*, pp. 216–17; my emphasis). And he indicates his own dependence upon the life of the discourse, which, in Lacanian terms, is a life that brings death,[23] when he talks about 'living in suspension, alive but not alive' (*L&T*, p. 216), and when he says: 'Even the concussion case, turned wholly inward, wrapped up in the processes of his own slow extinction, lives in dying more intensely than I in living' (*L&T*, p. 217). This is in contrast to Michael K, whose fasting implies a retreat out of the life of the discourse, into the death, or silence, which brings life.

The medical officer's attempts to make K eat, to keep him alive, are the equivalent of the writer's endeavours to keep the character 'alive' in the narrative, which is a 'life sentence' in that it controls this 'life', its entries and exits, via its syntagmatic structures. Following K's escape from the camp, the medical officer pleads with the commander not to have him brought back:

> 'For God's sake close the story of Michaels here and now,' I told him. 'The poor simpleton has gone off like a sick dog to die in a corner. Let him be, don't haul him back and force him to die here under a spotlight with strangers looking on.' (*L&T*, p. 212)

This is an allusion to the closing scene of *The Trial*, in which Josef K. dies 'like a dog',[24] and amounts to a plea not to have the protagonist, as vehicle of the utterance, subjected to the ending dictated by the form of the text. It is a gesture which would grant the protagonist a measure of freedom with respect to the choice of an end, a freedom not available to the subject of utterance, who must submit to the end imposed by the termination of the discourse. As Peter Brooks points out, 'repetition, taking us back over the same ground, could have to do with the choice of ends' (p. 286). Accordingly, in the final section of the novel K returns to the starting point, to his mother's room under the stairs, and the narrative leaves him about to repeat his journey away from Cape Town, this time with another passenger, in search of a place where he can again grow his pumpkins.

We come, now, to the other level on which this allegory functions: to the attempt to envisage a different kind of relationship between writer and victim. In this respect, the change from the heterodiegetic narrator of Section I to the homodiegetic narrator[25] of Section II is significant, for in admitting to the presence of the narrator (as stand-in for the writer), Coetzee is able to demonstrate how the writer's needs are fulfilled via the figure of the victim. The abbreviated syntax and present verb forms suggest that what we have here is a diary or journal, thus a form of writing which refers, implicitly, to its status *as* writing. We find, for example, a passage like the following:

> Have been struggling with the patient Michaels. He insists there is nothing wrong with him, he only wants something for his headache. Says he is not hungry. In fact he cannot hold his food down. Am keeping him on a drip, which he fights against feebly. (*L&T*, p. 178)

The device of the journal allows for the presentation of separate segments of time, and thus for the presentation of a subject in the process of change. In the first journal entries the stance of the medical officer toward K repeats the narratorial stance of Section I: his comments constitute a profound misinterpretation of K, whom he calls by the wrong name, committing the same error as the captain of police in Section I. He rejects the official military 'interpretation' of K, substituting for it his own equally derogatory and inaccurate assessment of the new patient:

> Noël brought out the register. 'According to this,' he said, 'Michaels is an arsonist. He is also an escapee from a labour camp. He was running a flourishing garden on an abandoned farm and feeding the local guerilla population when he was captured. That is the story of Michaels.'
>
> I shook my head. 'They have made a mistake,' I said. 'They have mixed him up with some other Michaels. This Michaels is an idiot. This Michaels doesn't know how to strike a match. If this Michaels was running a flourishing garden, why was he starving to death?' (*L&T*, pp. 180–81)

The identity of the intitial stance of this narrator and the stance implicit in Section I is evident in subtle repetitions, such as the medical officer's statement: 'There is nothing special about you, you can rest easy about that' (*L&T*, p. 186), which echoes the words of the man who sits next to K on the train: 'There's nothing special about you . . . . There's nothing special about any of us' (*L&T*, p. 59). The connection is, furthermore, implied via the medical officer's repeated use of animal and insect similes, of which the following are just a few examples:

> I passed him sitting on the grass holding his face up to the sun like a lizard basking (p. 181); he pulled away with surprising strength, waving an arm like an insect's claw (p. 186); He moistened his lips with his lizard tongue (p. 190); keeping you alive is like keeping the weakest pet duckling alive, or the runt of the cat's litter, or a fledgling expelled from the nest (p. 195); You are like a stick insect, Michaels, whose sole defence against a universe of

> predators is its bizarre shape (p. 204); I thought that putting you through the motions of rehabilitation would have been like trying to teach a rat or a mouse or (dare I say it?) a lizard to bark and beg and catch a ball (p. 223).

The medical officer's interest in K, and the demands he makes of him, refer to the writer's motivation in adopting a figure like this. Thus we find him repeatedly exhorting K to tell his story, asking him, 'Where is your stake in the future? Do you want the story to end with you?' (*L&T*, p. 191), and saying:

> 'It is time to deliver, my friend. You've got a story to tell and we want to hear it.' . . . 'You want to live don't you? Well, then, *talk*, make your voice heard, tell your story! We are listening! Where else in the world are you going to find two polite civilized gentlemen ready to listen to your story all day and all night, if need be, and take notes too?' (*L&T*, pp. 191–92)

He also insists, 'Tell us the truth, tell us the whole truth' (*L&T*, p. 189), demonstrating his affinity to the Magistrate in *Waiting for the Barbarians*, whose narrative is motivated by the belief that the truth can and must be told.

Initially, the medical officer refers to K as *he*, and claims to be doing what he does only for K's benefit. This, too, repeats the stance of the heterodiegetic narrator of Section I, the stance of a mode of writing motivated by the fallacious belief that it can bring another person to life by means of the pronoun of non-person. As Benveniste points out,

> We must bear in mind that the 'third person' is the form of the verbal (or pronominal) paradigm that does *not* refer to a person because it refers to an object located outside direct address. But it exists and is characterized only by its opposition to the person *I* of the speaker who, in uttering it, situates it as

> 'non-person.' Here is its status. The form *he* . . . . takes its value from the fact that it is necessarily part of a discourse uttered by '*I*'. (p. 229)

And, as Jefferson points out, 'behind every utterance there is always an *I* addressing a *you* however much the utterance itself may appear to be concerned with an external *he*' (p.100). Now in Section II it is possible to trace the stages in the development of a relationship with the victim *other* than that inscribed in the generic codes via the progression from the use of the referential pronoun, *he*, to the use of the pronouns of communication, *I* and *you*. Gradually K becomes no longer 'an object located outside direct address', as the narrative is increasingly made up of passages of narrated dialogue and of the medical officer's interior speech addressed to K. The moment at which the medical officer and K confront one another, each of them asking, 'What am I to this man?' (*L&T*, p. 203), appears to represent a turning point, for following this the medical officer undertakes to address K in a letter beginning 'Dear Michaels', and ending, 'A friend'. This letter, however, repeats the demand that K should yield his story, and it is only following K's escape from the camp that the medical officer confesses his own needs in relation to him.

The closing passages of Section II take the form of the medical officer's fantasized pursuit of K, and of a meeting between them: 'And here, in the light of day, you would at last have turned and looked at me . . . . ' (*L&T*, p. 222). The confession which follows is addressed to K, and begins:

> And I would have come before you and spoken. I would have said: 'Michaels, forgive me for the way I treated you, I did not appreciate who you were till the last days. Forgive me too for following you like this.' (*L&T*, p. 222)

He refers to the writer's need to avoid having his meaning circumscribed in and by the Other, to evade the ideologies inscribed in the discourse, as he continues:

> 'My need is a very simple one . . . . I am convinced there are areas that lie between the camps and belong to no camp, not even to the catchment areas of the camps . . . . I am looking for such a place in order to settle there, perhaps only till things improve, perhaps forever. I am not so foolish, however, as to imagine that I can rely on maps and roads to guide me. Therefore I have chosen you to show me the way.' (p. 223).

In his obscurity, his adherence to no code, his allegiance to no system, his commitment to no cause, K offers a model of resistance which the medical officer describes as follows: 'As time passed . . . I slowly began to see the originality of the resistance you offered. You were not a hero and did not pretend to be, not even a hero of fasting. In fact you did not resist at all' (*L&T*, pp. 223–224). It is possible to say of Michael K, as Sussman says of Josef K, that his personality

> is defined by the battles he refrains from fighting, by his refusal to trace out the narrative's implications. K's 'existence' is defined negatively by the novel as that which is played out elsewhere. Existence makes itself most strongly felt in the domain of script, where it is apparent as absence. Hence, the sufficiency of the initial *K*. (p. 53)

Michael K's freedom from any of the conventional attributes of the 'character' offers a way of alluding to the unconscious self which is not fixed in the Symbolic as a subject of utterance, and which is 'apparent as an absence' in the discourse; his life on the run, his status as 'a great escape artist, one of the great escapees' (*L&T*, p. 228), function as a metaphor of that which eludes the conscious meanings of both writer and reader. As Hélène Cixous says:

> A 'character' is always in store for the subject along the chain where everything is coded in advance. 'Character' and I.D. card go together in this restricting

> process of which literary interpretation (by means of the encoding – the laying of the wires for a current – that it effects) becomes the reinforcement and reflection. Now, if 'I' – true subject, subject of the unconscious – am what I can be, 'I' am always on the run.
>
> . . . .
>
> 'I' must become a 'fabulous opera' and not the arena of the known . . . . In texts that evade the standard codes, the 'personage' is, in fact, Nobody – he is that which escapes and leads somewhere else. How could he carry me away otherwise? (pp. 384 and 387–88)

Michael K is this 'Nobody', who can 'lead somewhere else', to the 'areas that lie between the camps and belong to no camp', that is to say, to the nonrepresentable unconscious, which resurfaces and undermines the conscious meanings of each successive reading.

Coetzee's text does not deny, or conceal, its attempt to posit some kind of meaning via the figure of K, but at the close of Section II the medical officer envisages K running to escape the meaning which he would impose on him, the meaning of this text. The medical officer attempts to make this meaning explicit in a passage of discourse which not only pronounces upon, but demonstrates the nature of meaning, as it seeks to define a particular meaning in relation to other terms. There are a number of stages in this expository section, which are best dealt with one by one, although these subdivisions are, of course, arbitrary, being the product of a structuring grid which allows me to convey my own meaning concerning the meaning of this text.

> 'This is not my imagination,' I would say to myself. 'This sense of a gathering meaningfulness is not something like a ray that I project to bathe this or that bed, or a robe in which I wrap this or that patient according to whim.'
> (*L&T*, p. 226)

The reference to a 'sense of a gathering meaningfulness' is an admission of the way in which this text does use the figure of K as a focus of meaning, a point about which it can 'collect its scattered energies into a momentary intensity.'[26] However, it is preceded by a denial that this meaning arises out of the imagination, that is to say, out of what had traditionally been regarded as the independent creative faculty capable of bathing or clothing forms with a transcendent symbolic meaning.

> 'Michaels means something, and the meaning he has is not private to me.' (*L&T*, p. 226)

To say that meaning is not private is tautologous if one accepts that meaning *is* meaning only because it is not private, because it is produced within a system of differences and within a discursive context. K's meaning is produced within the context of several overlapping systems: the systems of the particular genre, of South African literature, of literature in general, and of the literary and psychoanalytic theories on which Coetzee's novels are founded.

> 'If it were, if the origin of this meaning were no more than a lack in myself, a lack, say, of something to believe in, since we all know how difficult it is to satisfy a hunger for belief with the vision of times to come that the war, to say nothing of the camps, presents us with, if it were a mere craving for meaning that sent me to Michaels and his story . . .' (*L&T*, p. 226)

This refers to the Lacanian notion of the process of signification which arises out of a lack and is an attempt to satisfy the hunger, the craving, for the absent source of desire. There is no denial here, as the medical officer says: 'if the origin of this meaning were *no more than* a lack', and 'if it were a *mere* craving', In other words, it *is* this, but it is more than this.

> ' . . . if Michaels himself were no more than what he

> seems to be (what you seem to be), a skin and bones man with a crumpled lip . . .' (*L&T*, p. 226)

That is to say, if the function of this narrative were merely to represent this thin and maimed victim . . .

> ' . . . then I would have every justification for retiring to the toilets behind the jockey's changing-rooms and locking myself into the last cubicle and putting a bullet through my head.' (*L&T*, p. 226)

If any of the foregoing conditions were operative, that is, if meaning were purely private, subjective, or if, on the contrary, the text constituted nothing more than an objective 'reproduction' of a victim from the empirical world, then the act of writing would be superfluous, futile, and the writer might as well put a bullet through his head.

> 'Yet have I ever been more sincere than I am tonight?' And standing in the doorway I would turn my bleakest stare in upon myself, seeking by the last means I knew to detect the germ of dishonesty at the heart of the conviction – the wish, let us say, for example, to be the only one to whom the camp was not just the old Kenilworth racetrack with prefabricated huts dotted across it but a privileged site where meaning erupted into the world. But if such a germ lurked within me it would not raise its head, and if it would not what could I do to compel it? (I am dubious anyhow that one can separate the self that scrutinizes from the self that hides, setting them at odds like hawk and mouse . . .)' (*L&T*, pp. 226–27)

The question concerning sincerity refers to this entire passage of discourse, which constitutes this text's endeavour to unveil its own truths and untruths, and is the counterpart of the truth-telling, or truth-revealing, function traditionally associated with this genre. Here sincerity replaces authenticity, as the truth-telling gesture is made in relation to the writer, who must be sincere, instead of in relation to the life of another, which must be authentically rendered (Thus Elsa Joubert says: 'Again it was a white person telling the story from outside. It wasn't convincingly authentic', (p. 274, this chapter). Talking about the notion of sincerity in relation to Rousseau's confessional autobiography, Coetzee defines sincerity as 'the immediate presence of the moral self to the self', and goes on to say:

> If we look into its genealogy, does sincerity not begin to look more and more like a concept invented, or elevated to a central position, by Romanticism to privilege certain utterances as *not* having been engendered by rhetoric and therefore as belonging to an art above art? Sincerity, in this reading, becomes the master-term of a new anti-rhetorical rhetoric, an invention of devilish ingenuity, in that it claims to stand outside all systems of rhetoric. The questions that we, as post-Dostoevskians, are entitled to ask of the inventors of sincerity is: *cui bono*? Was the absolute of sincerity invented in a spirit of sincerity? Whatever way the question is answered, the concept of sincerity is, to use Rousseau's term, *poisoned* (which is not to say that it dies: we all know how it lives on). ('Truth in Autobiography', pp. 4 and 5)

Now Coetzee's rewriting of the genre, by revealing the rhetorical devices at play, and by thematizing the question *cui bono*? gives us a deconstructive reading of a mode of writing that claims to stand outside all systems of rhetoric in order to reveal the full and immediate presence of another life. Sincerity, in the case of Coetzee's text, may be read as the attempt to provide an answer to the question, *cui bono*, the attempt to reveal rather than conceal its own covert meaning and motivation. However, the medical officer indicates that it is not possible for writing to refer to its own final truth when he says: 'I am dubious anyhow that one can separate the self that scrutinizes from the self that hides, setting them at odds like hawk and mouse'. As this implies, there is always another self on the periphery of the 'ultimate' proclamation of truth, waiting to pronounce upon the truth or untruth of this stated truth. The medical officer's expression of doubt here constitutes a refusal of what Bruss describes as 'the bad faith of pretending to do the impossible, to catch [one]self in the act when in fact the act of scrutiny can never be the same as the act it scrutinizes, leaving an eternal blind spot that no discourse can overcome' (p. 75). It is by virtue of this 'blind spot' that the meaning of the text eludes even the writer's most rigorous and sincere attempts to pronounce upon his/her meaning, a meaning which, in the case of Coetzee's text, the medical officer pronounces upon as follows:

> 'Your stay in the camp was an allegory . . . . It was an allegory – speaking at the highest level – of how scandalously, how outrageously a meaning can take up residence in a system without becoming a term in in.' (L&T, p. 228)

This is a snake which swallows its own tail, for the meaning of this text is that its meaning cannot be reduced to this meaning! That is to say, the meaning which this text conveys via the figure of K cannot be reduced to a term in the system which the novel itself inevitably constitutes. If K's stay in the camp refers to the inadequacy of the discourse to convey and to confine meaning, his garden refers to that which gives rise to, but ultimately eludes, conscious discourse, that which is the source of writing's 'perennial alterity'.[27]

> 'Let me tell you the meaning of the sacred and alluring garden that blooms in the heart of the desert and produces the food of life. The garden for which you are presently heading is nowhere and everywhere except in the camps. It is another name for the only place where you belong, Michaels, where you do not feel homeless. It is off every map, no road leads to it that is merely a road, and only you know the way.' (*L&T*, p. 228)

Section III goes on to prefigure this displacement of meaning from the unconscious of the writer to the unconscious of the reader, a process that is anticipated in the confusion of tenses in the closing passages of Section II. Beginning with the passage:

> Whereas I – if one dark night I were to slip into overalls and tennis shoes and clamber over the wall (cutting the wire, since I am not made of air) – I am the kind who would be snapped up by the first patrol to pass while I yet stood dithering over which way lay salvation. The truth is that the only chance I had is gone, and gone before I knew. The night that Michaels made his break, I should have followed (*L&T*, p. 221),

we encounter the past conditional, the 'would have's' and 'should have's' which denote non-fulfilment of a condition. Then, from the point at which the medical officer projects an encounter between himself and K, with his glittering eye/I holding the *You* as he delivers his discourse concerning K's 'meaning', we find the iterative use of *would*: 'You would lie on your bed . . . . I would stand in the doorway . . . . I would turn my bleakest stare in upon myself . . . . ' (*L&T*, pp. 225–26). In this case, *would* denotes repeated moments of past time, but in another context *would* is able to denote a potential future, as it does in the final paragraph of Section III:

> Would I be imagining it, or would it be true that at this point you would begin to throw your most urgent energies into running, so that it would be clear to the meanest observer that you were running to escape the man shouting at your back, the man in blue who must seem to be persecutor, madman, bloodhound, policeman? (*L&T*, pp. 228–29)

The temporal instability of the *I* is implied by the blurring of past and future time categories, the blurring of the retroactive and anticipatory aspects of the self, whose meaning can, finally, only be phrased in the form of a question: ' "Am

I right?" I would shout. "Have I understood you? If I am right, hold up your right hand, if I am wrong hold up your left" ' (*L&T*, p. 229). We are reminded that, as Lacan says:

> .... the function of language is not to inform but to evoke.
>
> What I seek in speech is the response of the other. What constitutes me as subject is my question. In order to be recognised by the other, I utter what was only in view of what will be. In order to find him, I call him by a name that he must assume or refuse in order to reply to me.
>
> I identify myself in language, but only by losing myself in it like an object. What is realized in my history is not the past definite of what was, since it is no more, nor even the present perfect of what has been in what I am, but the future anterior of what I shall have been for what I am in the process of becoming. (*Ecrits*, p. 86; see my Chapter One, p. 41)

Section III stands in the relation of a supplement to Sections I and II: it enacts a gesture whereby K is released into the world to achieve his meaning there, and is the counter-proof to the medical officer's statement that 'that will be the end of the story of Michaels' (*L&T*, p. 212). Having escaped the camp, K encounters further attempts to impose meaning on him, to make a 'new man' of him (*L&T*, p. 212). If Robert, who, in Section I, tells K that 'It's time to wake up' (*L&T*, p. 121), is a textual mediator representing the writer, then the stranger who picks K up on the beach, and who says: 'Come, let us give this man something to wake him up!' (*L&T*, p. 236), may be read as a textual mediator representing the reader. The stranger, like the medical officer, wants to feed K, wants to make a man out of him, wants to make meaning out of him. Two models of reading are prefigured in K's encounter with the stranger and with the woman who is apparently the stranger's sister, both of these encounters providing images of dissemination, of

> A sowing that does not produce plants, but is simply infinitely repeated, a semination that is not *in*semination but *dis*semination, seed spilled in vain. an emission that cannot return to its origin in the father. (Spivak, Translator's Preface to *Of Grammatology*, p. lxv; see p. 295, this chapter)

The man robs K of his packet of seeds in the night, an act which, as a metaphor of a mode of reading, may be read as a gesture of furtive and frustrated mastery. The seeds are not what the man is looking for, and he spills them on the barren soil of Signal Hill. Recovering as many of the scattered seeds as he can, K thinks: 'What a pity – in the shade of a pine tree nothing will grow' (*L&T*, p. 241).

The woman, too, makes K spill his seed in vain, as she waylays him in a public toilet, and brings him to a climax against his will. The woman is a prostitute, and the encounter with her would appear to be a metaphor of the Barthesian model of reading based on the contract of prostitution:

> . . . the model of the good contract is the contract of Prostitution. For this contract, declared immoral by all societies and by all systems (except the most archaic), liberates in fact from what might be called the *imaginary embarrassments* of the exchange: what am I to count on in the other's desire, in *what I am for him*? The contract eliminates this confusion: it is in fact the only position which the subject can assume without falling into two inverse but equally abhorred images: that of the 'egoist' (who demands without caring that he has nothing to give) and that of the 'saint' (who gives but forbids himself ever to demand): thus the discourse of the contract eludes two plenitudes; it permits observing the golden rule of any *habitation*, discerned in the Shikidai passageway: *no will-to-seize and yet no oblation*. (*Roland Barthes*, p. 59)

Kritzman explicates this passage as follows:

> Just as writing must affirm meaning without specifically articulating it, Barthes adopts the sexual metaphor of prostitution in order to delineate a relationship in which the domination/submission paradigm is abandonned for a gratuitously 'playful' sexuality suspended somewhere between the satiety of pleasure and the complete absence thereof. The ideal to which Barthes subscribes is to escape from the contingency of a priori roles so that the demythologized love relationship would portray a fiction without names, a game in which no one player would have a hold over another . . . . Prostitution, like writing, provokes a special form of gratification through gratuitous play. It is a contract that keeps desire alive, an intransitive relationship which may be regarded as symptomatic of a signifying process publicizing its categorical disembodiment from the limits of interpretation and the problems of classification. (pp. 194–95)

While Kritzman's commentary on the metaphor of prostitution is, in many respects, relevant to the meaning which Coetzee attaches to K in this novel, he underestimates the difficulties of 'affirming meaning without specifically articulating it', and of bypassing the Master/Slave relationship, in a way that Coetzee does not. Barthes appears to choose the metaphor of prostitution, not, primarily, because it presupposes 'a gratuitously "playful" sexuality' (and I have doubts as to whether it does presuppose this, or whether it presupposes this more than various other forms of sexual relationship), but because it provides a model of an erotic relationship in which the existence and the effect of a contract are made entirely explicit. Thus this passage, titled 'Ambiguous praise of the contract', begins:

> His first image of the *contract* (the pact) is more or less objective: sign, language, narrative, society function by contract, but since this contract is generally masked, the critical operation consists in deciphering the confusion of reasons, alibis,

> appearances, in short, the whole of the social *natural*, in order to make manifest the controlled exchange on which the semantic process and collective life are based. (*Roland Barthes*, p. 59)

Talking about Rousseau's autobiography, Coetzee, too, refers to the existence of this pact:

> That story is written within the limits of a pact, the pact of autobiography, one of the many pacts negotiated over the years between writers and readers (and always open to renegotiation) for each of the genres and subgenres, pacts which cover, among other things, what demands may be made of each genre and what may not, what questions may be asked and what may not, what one may see and what one must be blind to. (Another of the clauses is that one shall be blind to the existence of the pact.)
>
> Yet . . . have I not, in unveiling what I seem to be claiming to be the secret of the economy of Rousseau's *Confessions*, broken the very pact I have been talking about? On the one hand I claim that reading autobiography requires a convention of blindness; on the other I read Rousseau with my eyes wide open. By my own definition, can the activity I have been engaged in be called reading autobiography? And if the answer is, No, I have not been reading autobiography, I have been engaged in a different activity called literary criticism, which submits to no rules, then I ask: If the desire of literary criticism is to tell every truth, to unveil whatever is veiled, to expose very [sic] secret to sight, why does it not tell its own secrets? Or does it claim to have none? ('Truth in Autobiography', p. 5)

The answer to Coetzee's question could be that criticism lacks the means to refer to the fact that it *has* a secret, in a way that his own criticism-as-fiction does not. His metaphor of prostitution disrupts the terms of the contract, as here it is the reader, rather than the text, who takes on the role of prostitute, a prostitute who is not paid, and whose act of cunnilingus constitutes a kind of rape with the tongue, a reading which would coerce the text into yielding up its meaning. Thus Coetzee's metaphor undermines the assumption that the relationship of mastery and servitude between reader and text can be overcome in the conventional forms of criticism, even when this criticism does make explicit the terms of the contract which determines the limits of meaning (as Coetzee does in relation to the genres which he reads and re-writes in his novels), or even when it ignores the contract and engages in gratuitous play. Making the limits of the contract explicit is, it would seem preferable to remaining blind to them, but criticism cannot, thereby, deny its position of mastery, for, as Spivak says, criticism 'can do no more than *decide* to deny its desire as master' ('The Letter as Cutting Edge', p. 223; see p. 45, my Chapter One).

The prostitute kisses K 'full on the mouth, her tongue cleaving his lips' (*L&T*, p. 244). Now, in the context of the foregoing reading of Coetzee's novel, K's hare lip, the mouth which will not close and which bares its 'living pink flesh' (*L&T*, p. 3), is a sign of more than just the inarticulate condition of the victim. As the cut which constitutes the erogenous zone,[28] it is a sign of the incision which Coetzee makes in the generic codes, revitalizing or eroticizing the automatized speech forms, performing what Barthes calls the redistribution of language:

> As textual theory has it: the language is redistributed. Now, *such redistribution is always achieved by cutting.* Two edges are created: an obedient, conformist, plagiarizing edge (the language is to be copied in its canonical state, as it has been established by schooling, good usage, literature, culture), and *another edge*, mobile, blank (ready to assume any contours), which is never anything but the site of its effect: the place where the death of language is glimpsed. These two edges, *the compromise they bring about*, are necessary. Neither culture nor its destruction is erotic; it is the seam between them, the fault, the flaw, which becomes

> so. (*The Pleasure of the Text*, pp. 6–7)

The figure of K represents the site of language's effect, this place where 'the death of language is glimpsed'. Resisting all the forms of charity, all the meanings imposed on the text, he returns to his mother's room under the stairs. He traces a circular movement, coming back to the starting point of the narrative, to the womb/room, the source of desire which generated the text as journey, and in which the journey of interpretation, likewise, has its genesis. Resting in the room, K reflects upon the 'truth' of himself, a truth which, belonging to the realm of the unconscious, lies in his silence:

> It excited him, he found, to say, recklessly, *the truth, the truth about me. I am a gardener* . . . . I am more like an earthworm, he thought. Which is also a kind of gardener. Or a mole, also a gardener, that does not tell stories because it lives in silence. (*L&T*, pp. 247–48)

In the room K finds three statues: 'a deer with chocolate-brown eyes, a gnome in a buff jerkin, knee-breeches and a green tasselled cap, and, larger than the other two, a creature with a peg nose whom he recognized as Pinocchio' (*L&T*, p. 246). These are the images of K which are conveyed in the three sections of the novel: a gentle animal in Sections I and II, a being with supernatural powers in Section II, and in Section III a craftsman's creation that comes alive and lives a life of his own beyond the dictates of his paternal creator.

And so we come, finally, to the 'lesson' which K learns, to the moral that Coetzee's novel, true to the generic codes,[29] conveys via the story of K. K says:

> . . . if there was one thing I discovered out in the country, it was that there is time enough for everything.
>
> (Is that the moral of it all, he thought, the moral of the whole story: that there is time enough for everything? Is that how morals come, unbidden, in the

> course of events, when you least expect them?)
> (*L&T*, p. 249)

There is 'time enough for everything' in the country because, as my discussion of Section I indicated, this is the time *outside* time, outside the concept of temporality which is produced in and by the narrative. Whereas the writer, in conveying his/her meaning, must articulate segments of narrated time, and bring the self into being in the narrative time which is always *past* in relation to the present time of the narrating self, K, as representative of *unconscious* meaning, has the potential to re-establish himself in the present moments of future *acts* of reading-as-narration, which are potentially infinite. In Derrida's words, K stands for that which enables the writer 'to think the present from time as difference,'[30] and so releases him/her from the attempt to bring the self into being in the narrative present. As protagonist in Coetzee's novel, K becomes an agent of change, rather than an item of exchange, and provides the means for talking about the future and about freedom which does not automatically translate this future into the past, and circumscribe this freedom in some kind of formula. K's time is that of an endless series of always supplementary journeys, and we see him, finally, planning another journey with another passenger, and with a destination that will mean satisfying desire in the same meagre way that his first needs were met, with milk, or water, from a teaspoon:

> And if the old man climbed out of the cart and stretched himself (things were gathering pace now) and looked at where the pump had been that the soldiers had blown up so that nothing should be left standing, and complained, saying 'What are we going to do about water?', he, Michael K, would produce a teaspoon from his pocket, a teaspoon and a long roll of string. He would clear the rubble from the mouth of the shaft, he would bend the handle of the teaspoon in a loop and tie the string to it, he would lower it down the shaft deep into

the earth, and when he brought it up there would be water in the bowl of the spoon; and in that way, he would say, one can live. (*L&T*, p. 250)

NOTES

1. In *Life & Times* Michael K is made to reflect that 'he was not a prisoner or a castaway, his life by the dam was not a sentence that he had to serve out' (*L&T*, p. 158), and a man whom he encounters says to him, 'This isn't jail. This isn't a life sentence. This is just a labour gang. It's peanuts' (*L&T*, p. 59)
2. Other notable examples in the South African context are the plays of Athol Fugard. *Out* of this context one thinks of a novel like Bernanos' *La Nouvelle Histoire de Mouchette*.
3. J.M. Coetzee, 'Time, Tense and Aspect in Kafka's "The Burrow", *MLN*, 96 (1981), 556–579. Henry Sussman, 'The Court as Text: Inversion, Supplanting, and Derangement in Kafka's *Der Proze*,' *PMLA*, 92, 1 (1977), 41–55. Dorrit Cohn, *Transparent Minds* (Princeton: Princeton University Press, 1978). Charles Bernheimer, *Flaubert and Kafka: Studies in Psychopoetic Structure* (Yale: Yale University Press, 1982).
4. The Dutch commentators on Joubert's text refer to the difficulty of establishing whether it is a biography or a novel. Despite the fact that the word 'novel' does not appear on the title page, and that the text is presented as a true story to which the writer has added nothing, Joubert says: En daarom is ek baie dankbaar . . . dat die boek nou as roman erken word. Met al die bohaai het dit amper al soos 'n stukkie politieke sensasionalisme begin lyk. Maar die politiek was nie voorop vir my toe ek geskryf het nie. Dit was die mens wat ek wou leer ken.'

   I am very grateful that the book is now recognized as a novel. With all the commotion, it was almost beginning to look like a piece of political sensationalism. But politics was not a priority for me when I was writing. It was the person I wanted to get to know. (Elsa Joubert, Rapport, 1 April 1979, cited by Janssen, Lijphart and van Ijzeren, p. 57. My translation from the Afrikaans.)

The implication here is that as a novel the text is not political; that is to say that it does not grant the writer an identity as a political activist in the way that a biography or a factual document might do.

5. *The Long Journey of Poppie Nongena*, which was serialized in a woman's magazine, provides a good example of this phenomenon, as the name *Poppie* has become a household word.

6. Gordimer's comment here may be compared with her claim, in 'The Essential Gesture', that 'the white writer's task as cultural worker is to raise the consciousness of white people, who, unlike himself, have not woken up'. In this article she says:

   'White writers who are 'only writers' are open to related reproach for 'stealing the lives of blacks' as good material. Their claim to this 'material' is the same as the black writers', at an important existential remove nobody would discount. Their essential gesture can be fulfilled only in the integrity Chekov demanded: 'to describe a situation so truthfully that the reader can no longer evade it'.' (pp. 14 and 15)

   'The Idea of Gardening', Gordimer's review of Coetzee's novel, apart from being the only piece of any length to have been written on *Life & Times* thus far, is useful in that it provides an example of 'automatized' reading: it tries to situate Coetzee's novel *within* the codes which the novel itself attempts to decode, providing an example of the kind of response which the novel anticipates and attempts to subvert. The effect of this subversion is evident in Gordimer's ultimate dissatisfaction with the novel, in her complaint that 'it denies the energy of the will to resist evil', and that in it 'Freedom is defined negatively: it is to be 'out of all the camps at the same time'. (p. 6)

7. Bernheimer's analysis of the function of the subject of the utterance is made in the context of a discussion of K's interview with Burgel, which is the passage from which my earlier quotation from *The Castle* is drawn, and the passage in which Kafka seems to come closest to explicitly self-reflexive commentary.

8. There is no equivalent verb form in English, the anonymous heterodiegetic narrator and past verb forms being the closest equivalent in terms of a mode of narration.

9. The process of construction which Barthes describes here may be compared with Elsa Joubert's decision not to use the tapes she had transcribed 'just as they were' because 'It was boring, and there was no connection or development in the events.' (see p. 269, this chapter.) Barthes betrays a desire for a 'zero degree' of

style which is not possible in the novel: all that can be done is for the narrator to make his/her presence explicit, and for the writer to make his/her intention and intervention explicit.

10. Käte Hamburger, *Die Logik der Dichtung*, cited by Bronzwaer, *Tense in the Novel*, note 21, p. 135.

11. Jefferson, p. 145, paraphrasing V.N. Voloshinov, *Marxism and the Philosophy of Language* (1930), trans. Matejka and Titunik (New York: Seminar Press), p. 156.

12. Jefferson points out that 'These indeterminate origins of free indirect speech could be used as support for Derrida's attack on what he calls the metaphysics of presence,' and that

    'As a certain kind of writing, free indirect speech certainly seems a pertinent example of the conception that Derrida is trying to put over, for the indeterminacy of its origins makes it impossible to decide whose mind or soul lies behind it, whether narrator or character is present in it. If this style prevents us from tracking down a mind behind it, from finding even an illusory inhabitant for it, then, for all its apparent gains in narrational realism, it must be regarded as being finally non-representational, as a product of literary writing' (pp. 145 and 146)

13. Sussman says 'The doorkeeper is only to the *Mann vom Lande* what Lawyer Huld, Titorelli, Block, and the priest are to K.: textual mediators' ('The Court as Text', p. 50).

14. Franz K. Stanzel also refers to this deviant use of the definite article. He says:

    '. . . another linguistic element which helps to reinforce the reflector-mode [as opposed to the teller-mode] is the repeated use of the definite article with objects that have not been mentioned beforehand in the text. Following G. Storms, W.J.M. Bronzwaer has called this deviation from the conventional cohesive ties in a text the 'familiarizing article.' The term seems aptly chosen because it suggests that the first mention of a thing, event or person already presupposes familiarity; this is justified only if they are looked at from a point of view of a reflector character, but not from the reader's angle of vision. Such an opening strategy induces in the reader immediate and complete empathy with the reflector-character and his 'here-and-now' in the fictional world. The reader senses that what he has not yet learned about the antecedents is contained or stored in the consciousness of the reflector-character and that he has to suspend his curiosity for the time being. By putting himself squarely in the place of the reflector-character, the reader hopes to retrieve in good time the information initially withheld from him'. (p. 11)

15. Roy Pascal claims that

> 'Kafka's parables, including those that, like 'Little fable', seem closest to the form of the fable, are concerned with spiritual attitudes and problems, not with practical morals; one might almost say, indeed, that viewed in relation to the ancient tradition of fable they strangely and alarmingly lack all concern for practical behaviour, for interpersonal and social obligations.' (pp. 144–145).

One might replace 'spiritual' here with 'metaphysical', and say that Kafka's (and Coetzee's) parables or fables are concerned with 'practical behaviour' and 'interpersonal obligations' only in so far as these are related to the act of writing and the process of subject constitution.

16. The neume is a term in church music for 'pure vocalization, forms of inarticulate song without speech' (*Of Grammatology*, p. 249).

17. According to Lacan, 'it is quite simply . . . as desire of the Other that man's desire finds form,' and 'It is precisely in his solitude that the desire of the little child has already become the desire of another [the mother], of an *alter ego* who dominates him and whose object of desire is henceforth his own affliction' (*Ecrits*, pp. 311 and 104).

18. Discussing Freud's concept of propping, Laplanche says:

> 'The phenomenon Freud describes is a leaning *of the drive*, the fact that emergent sexuality attaches itself to and is propped upon another process which is both similar and profoundly divergent: the sexual drive is propped upon a non-sexual, vital function . . . in the particular case first analyzed by Freud, the instinct is hunger and the function feeding.' (p. 16)

19. According to Ann Jefferson,

> 'For an item to qualify as *mise en abyme* in a text, it must first have points of analogy with the text as a whole, and, secondly it must, ontologically speaking, be embedded (*emboité*) in the spatio-temporal world of the text, existing both as an object within it and as a representation or mirror of it . . . . And, since it is the text itself which is represented by mise en abyme, the self-criticism resulting from this strategy will be very intense indeed'. (p. 195)

20. Derrida, *Of Grammatology*, p. 272, citing Kafka's *Journal* from *The Diaries of Franz Kafka* 1914–29 (New York, 1949), vol. 2, pp. 200–1.
21. In the interview with Folke Rhedin, Coetzee said: '. . . I am feeling a certain dissatisfaction, particularly with this fourth book with limitations of traditional form' (p. 10).
22. Elizabeth W. Bruss, Beautiful Theories p. 63, citing Edward Said, 'Contemporary Fiction and Criticism,' *Tri Quarterly*, No. 33 (Spring 1975), 154–55, who is citing and commenting upon Foucault's *The Archaeology of Knowledge*.
23. Talking about the symbolic struggle to the death between Master and Slave as an expression of the death instinct, Lacan says: 'It still remains to be decided which death, that which is brought by life or that which brings life' (*Ecrits*, p. 308; see my Chapter One, p. 35).
24. 'But the hands of one of the partners were already at K's throat, while the other thrust the knife into his heart and turned it there twice. With failing eyes K. could still see the two of them, cheek leaning against cheek, immediately before his face, watching the final act. 'Like a dog!' he said: it was as if he meant the shame of it to outlive him'. (Kafka, *The Trial*, p. 251)
25. A homodiegetic narrator is 'present as a character in the story he tells' (Genette, p. 245).
26. Bruss makes the point that, 'Although they may repeal our efforts to visualize or embody them, theoretical categories share the capacity of characters and images to . . . propel the discourse forward and collect its scattered energies into a momentary intensity' (p. 88).
27. 'Something that carries within itself the trace of a perennial alterity: the structure of the psyche, the structure of the sign. To this structure Derrida gives the name 'writing' (Spivak, Translator's Preface to *Of Grammatology*, p. xxxix).
28. According to Lacan,

    'The very delimitation of the 'erogenous zone' that the drive isolates from the metabolism of the function . . . is the result of a cut (*coupure*) expressed in the anatomical mark (*trait*) of a margin or border – lips, 'the enclosure of the teeth', the rim of the anus, the tip of the penis, the vagina . . .' (*Ecrits*, pp. 314–15).
29. Gordimer's response to the novel makes it clear that this is, indeed, one of the reader expectations related to this genre. Although she asks 'is there an idea of survival that can be realized

entirely outside a political doctrine? Is there a space that lies between camps?' her determination to derive a moral lesson from the novel leads her to read it as an ecologist's plea to save the earth: 'Beyond all creeds and moralities, this work of art asserts, there is only one: to keep the earth alive, and only one salvation, the survival that comes from her' ('The Idea of Gardening', p. 6)

). Derrida says: 'The present is that from which we believe we are able to think time, effacing the inverse necessity: to think the present from time as difference' (*Of Grammatology*, p. 166).

6 Foe

Coetzee's most recent novel, *Foe*, is a re-writing of Daniel Defoe's *Robinson Crusoe.* Or perhaps it would be more accurate to say that it is about the narrator, Susan Barton, and her attempt to re-write Defoe's novel. Returning to England after a fruitless search for her abducted daughter in South America, Susan Barton is castaway on an island inhabited by Cruso (sic) and Friday. After spending some months on Cruso's barren kingdom, she rescues both Cruso and Friday against their will when an English ship puts in at the island. Cruso dies at sea, and Susan and Friday eke out a living in London, meagrely provided for by Mr Foe, to whom she has sold her story. Much of the novel takes the form of letters addressed to Foe, in which Susan Barton argues for the truthful transcription of her island story, but in the latter sections of the novel the epistolary form is, significantly, abandoned.

Foe was published in September 1986, subsequent to the development of my argument concerning Coetzee's first four novels. The frame still fits, however, and insofar as Foe is allegorical, is concerned with the vicissitudes of a narrating self that is articulated largely in Lacanian terms, and, once again, constitutes criticism-as-fiction, Coetzee's project may be said to remain consistent. If the frame must be shifted or re-shaped, it is in terms of the object (or subject) of this criticism-as-fiction. Whereas the first four novels take as their starting point certain sub-genres of white South African writing, the critical activity of *Foe* operates within a far wider discursive arena. Indeed, the space of this arena would seem to be constituted by nothing less than the discourses of feminism, postcolonialism and postmodernism. And, while it is hardly possible to talk about either feminism, postcolonialism or postmodernism as though it could be contained within a single, homogeneous discourse, it is the virtue of Coetzee's criticism-as-fiction that it is able to avoid doing this, as the narrator occupies shifting positions that reproduce both the contradictions and conspiracies within and amongst these discourses. My own reading of the novel, my deciphering of the allegory, while it risks becoming reductive and too conclusive, is, at the same time, not conclusive enough, in that it omits much that the novel takes in. Having access to neither the economy nor the allusiveness of the novel, I find myself caught up in commentary's tedious repetition, as this is described by Foucault:

> whatever the techniques employed, commentary's only role is to say *finally*, what has silently been articulated *deep down*. It must – and the paradox is ever-changing yet inescapable – say, for the first time, what has already been said, and repeat tirelessly what was, nevertheless, never said. The infinite rippling of commentary is agitated from within by the dream of masked repetition: in the distance there is, perhaps, nothing other than what was there at the point of departure: simple recitation. Commentary averts the chance element of discourse by giving it its due: it gives us the opportunity to say something other than the text itself, but on condition that it is the text itself which is uttered and, in some ways, finalised. The open multiplicity, the fortuitousness, is transferred, by the principle of commentary, from what is liable to be said to the number, the form, the masks and the circumstances of repetition. The novelty lies no longer in what is said, but in its reappearance. ('The Discourse on Language', p. 221)

While in commentary repetition is a snare, a maze from which there is no escape, in *Foe*, as in the other novels, it functions positively as a strategy (see pp. 31–43 of my Chapter One). Re-writing, or repeating, Daniel Defoe's *Robinson Crusoe*, *Foe* occupies a site of numerous repetitions.[1] It is a literary palimpsest,[2] superimposed upon an already jumbled layering of marks, a jumble which makes the original marks barely legible. Occupying this well-worn scene of writing, Coetzee's novel does not engage primarily in a transvalorisation of the original text as this process is described by Gérard Genette in relation to Michel Tournier's *Vendredi, ou les limbes du Pacifique*:

> Transvalorisation: c'était ici un double mouvement de dévalorisation et de (contre-) valorisation portant sur les mêmes personnages . . . L'opposition entre Robinson Crusoé at Vendredi, en revanche, me semble plus univoque, parce que constamment *sérieuse*, et qu'entre le jeune sauvage et son bon maître anglais, industrieux et protestant, le parti de Defoe est manifeste, explicite et investi dans un processus d'intégration (de Vendredi au système axiologique de Robinson) qui est l'éducation de Vendredi par Robinson. La transvalorisation hypertextuelle, dans ce cas, consisterait à prendre, antithétiquement, le parti (des valeurs supposées) de Vendredi contre (celles de) Robinson, et de substituer en conséquence a l'éducation de Vendredi par Robinson une éducation, symétrique et inverse, de Robinson par Vendredi. (*Palimpsestes*, pp. 418–19)

> (Transvalorisation: here we have a double movement of 'devalorisation' and of '(contra-) valorisation' with respect to the same characters . . . . It seems, on the other hand, that the opposition between Robinson Cruso and Friday is more univocal, because constantly serious, and that, with respect to the young savage and his industrious and protestant English master, Defoe's preference is explicitly manifested and committed to a process of integration (of Friday into Robinson's 'axiological' system) which involves the education of Friday by Robinson. In this case, the hypertextual transvalorisation would consist in taking, antithetically, the side

> (of the supposed values) of Friday against (those of) Robinson, and consequently to substitute, for the education of Friday by Robinson, the symmetrical and opposite education of Robinson by Friday.) (my translation from the french.)

Rather than take up an oppositional stance in relation to the values manifest in *Robinson Crusoe*, *Foe* locates the discourse of Susan Barton within the discursive context whose genealogy may be traced back to Daniel Defoe, and to the historical moment of the emergence of his novels in the 18th century. Defoe is widely regarded as the father of the English novel, and, while his role as originator may be disputed, his particular role as writer in the 18th century does allow him to figure as Author or as representative of the Author function as this is delineated by Foucault in his paper 'What is an Author?' In this respect it is significant that the title of Coetzee's novel is not, as Tournier's is, a reversal of Defoe's title, but involves a re-inscription of the author's name, which, in lopping off the 'de' (added by Defoe himself), alerts us to the antagonistic relationship of this text to the Author as Foe. Asking 'What is an author's name?' and 'How does it function?' Foucault proposes that

> The author's name serves to characterize a certain mode of being of discourse: the fact that the discourse has an author's name, that one can say 'this was written by so-and-so' or 'so-and-so is its author', shows that this discourse is not ordinary everyday speech that merely comes and goes, not something that is immediately consumable. On the contrary, it is a speech that must be received in a certain mode and that, in a given culture, must receive a certain status . . . . As a result we could say that in a civilization like our own there are a certain number of discourses that are endowed with the 'author function,' while others are deprived of it. A private letter may well have a signer – it does not have an author; a contract may well have a guarantor – it does not have an author. An anonymous

> text posed on a wall probably has a writer – but not an author. The author function is therefore characteristic of the mode of existence, circulation, and functioning of certain discourses within a society ('What is an Author?' pp. 107–108).

Foucault goes on to say that 'discourses are objects of appropriation', and that the type of ownership from which they spring 'has always been subsequent to what one might call penal appropriation. Texts, books, and discourses really began to have authors . . . to the extent that authors became subject to punishment, that is, to the extent that discourses could be transgressive' (p. 108). Thus, Foucault claims, 'since the eighteenth century, the author has played the role of the regulator of the fictive, a role quite characteristic of our era of industrial and bourgeois society, of individualism and private property' (p. 119). Arrested on several occasions for his political writings, and, in the first half of the 18th century, producing novels that are concerned largely with the struggle for economic, and spiritual, independence of their protagonists, Daniel Defoe figures effectively as one of the early author-owners of discourse.

Clearly, one cannot separate the Author function from the texts in which it is manifested, and, at points, Coetzee's novel inevitably does produce a 'transvalorisation' of certain aspects of *Robinson Crusoe* and *Roxana*. I believe, however, that focussing upon the ways in which, first Susan Barton, and then the novel as a whole, challenge the Author function will prove a more fruitful critical strategy than would a back-to-back reading of Defoe's and Coetzee's novels.[3] Via Susan Barton and her relationships with the Captain, with Cruso, with Foe and with Friday, Coetzee constructs an intricately developing debate amongst the discourses of feminism, post-colonialism and postmodernism, producing an almost too-fertile ground for criticism. While I cannot hope to formulate adequately the diverse premises of what might be considered the three major contemporary discourses, what I will do here, as with the previous novels, is a form of criticism-as-pastiche, drawing together what I see as the relevant theoretical positions, and establishing their points of intersection in this novel.

I should, at the outset, establish how and why I am able to posit this intersection as useful, or even as possible. This is best done by locating the discursive projects of postcolonialism, feminism and postmodernism within the present historical moment, that is to say, within the context of postmodernity, of which all three must, in some sense, be considered both the enemy and the expression.[4] Frederic Jameson defines the postmodern condition as being inextricably linked to multinational capitalism, a system so totalising that it makes the achievement of critical distance impossible:

> However distinct those conceptions [radical conceptions about the nature of cultural politics] may have been – which range from slogans of negativity, opposition, and subversion to critique and reflexivity – they all shared a single, fundamentally spatial, presupposition, which may be resumed in the equally time-honoured formula of 'critical distance.' ('Postmodernism, or the Cultural Logic of Late Capitalism', p. 87)

According to Jameson, we are submerged in the new space of postmodernism, in which 'the prodigious new expansion of multinational capital ends up penetrating and colonizing those very pre-capitalist enclaves (Nature and the Unconscious) which offered extraterritorial and Archimedean footholds for critical effectivity', so that

> we all, in one way or another, dimly feel that not only punctual and local countercultural forms of cultural resistance and guerilla warfare, but also even overtly political interventions . . . are all somehow secretly disarmed and reabsorbed by a system of which they themselves might well be considered a part, since they can achieve no distance from it (ibid).

Within this context, the problem that arises for discourses that are in any sense oppositional is essentially a problem of representation, of finding a space from which to speak and to produce representations of the self which are not immediately subsumed by the system in which they emerge. It is possible to say that it is this spatial project that characterizes subversive feminist, postcolonial and postmodern discourses, a project which may also be described as the attempt to represent the unrepresentable. Thus, with regard to postmodernism, Lyotard says:

> The postmodern would be that which, in the modern, puts forward the unpresentable in presentation itself; that which denies itself the solace of good forms, the consensus of a taste which would make it possible to share collectively the nostalgia for the unattainable; that which searches for new presentations, not in order to enjoy them but in order to impart a stronger sense of the unpresentable. A post modern artist or writer is in the position of a philosopher: the text he writes, the work he produces are not in principle governed by pre-established rules, and they cannot be judged according to a determining judgement, by applying familiar categories to the text or to the work. Those rules and categories are what the work of art itself is looking for. The artist and the writer, then, are working without rules in order to formulate the rules of what *will have been done*. Hence the fact that work and text have the characters of an *event*; hence also, they always come too late for their author, or, what amounts to the same thing, their being put into work, their realization (*mise en oeuvre*) always begins too soon. *Post modern* would have to be understood according to the paradox of the future (*post*) anterior (*modo*). (p. 81)

It is more than merely an interesting coincidence that Alice Jardine, in her 'Introduction to Julia Kristeva's

"Women's Time" ', should begin by claiming that

> Julia Kristeva writes in a kind of 'future perfect' – a modality that implies neither that we are helpless before some inevitable destiny nor that we can somehow, given enough time and thought, engineer an ultimately perfect future. She often uses this term herself, particularly in reference to the poetic text; a literary text is always before or after its time (because of the negativity forcing the rejection of all theses) but also of its own time to the extent that it represents a certain linguistic and ideological configuration. In the following article, she evokes the future perfect to characterize a new social formation now in the process of rediscovering what part of it has forgotten. (p. 5)

This, too, we must recall, is the mode of representation of the Lacanian subject:

> I identify myself in language, but only by losing myself in it like an object. What is realized in my history is not the past definite of what was, since it is no more, or even the present perfect of what has been in what I am, but the future anterior of what I shall have been for what I am in the process of becoming. (*Ecrits*, p. 86; see my Introduction, p. 41)

While this is perhaps revelatory of the Hegelian sources of these three theorists, the shared temporal metaphor does imply a common attitude toward the problem of representation. This connection between postmodernism and feminism has been made by Craig Owens, who says:

> It is precisely at the legislative frontier between what can be represented and what cannot that the postmodernist operation is being staged – not in order to transcend representation, but in

order to expose that system of power that authorizes certain representations while blocking, prohibiting or invalidating others. Among those prohibited from Western representation, whose representations are denied all legitimacy, are women. Excluded from representation by its very structure, they return within it as a figure for – a representation of – the unrepresentable (Nature, Truth, the Sublime, etc.) . . . . In order to speak, to represent herself, a woman assumes a masculine position; perhaps this is why femininity is frequently associated with masquerade, with false representation, with simulation and seduction. Montrelay, in fact, identifies women as the 'ruin of representation': not only have they nothing to lose; their exteriority to Western representation exposes its limits.

> Here, we arrive at an apparent crossing of the feminist critique of patriarchy and the postmodernist critique of representation . . . ('The Discourse of Others: Feminists and Post modernism', p. 59)

And Simon During makes the connection between what he calls postmodern thought and postcolonialism in similar terms:

> We can, rather brutally, characterize postmodern thought . . . as that thought which refuses to turn the Other into the Same. Thus it provides a theoretical space for what postmodernity denies: otherness. Postmodern thought also recognizes, however, that the Other can never speak for itself *as* the Other . . . For me, perhaps eccentrically, post-colonialism is regarded as the need, in nations or groups which have been victims of imperialism, to achieve an identity uncontaminated by universalist or Eurocentric concepts and images. Here the argument becomes complex, since, clearly, for postmodernity (thought of as a cultural dominant) post-colonialism constitutes one of those

> Others which might derive hope and legitimation from the first aspect of post-modern thought, its refusal to turn the Other into the Same.
> As such it is threatened by the second moment in post-modern thought [its recognition that the Other can never speak for itself *as* the Other]. ('Post-modernism or post-colonialism today', p. 33)

What emerges from these perspectives is the danger, inherent in both feminism and postcolonialism, of an insistence upon the possibility of representing an *essential* difference, or a radical Otherness, upon the possibility of speaking *as* Other. Postmodern art seeks to avoid this danger, as, in Lyotard's words, 'it searches for new presentations . . . in order to impart a stronger sense of the unpresentable.' And in Coetzee's novels, which may be regarded as postmodern in this sense, it is the dramatization of the paradoxes of the Lacanian subject which provides a way around this danger. Thus, while his novels insist upon the existence of a 'secret' self, they recognize that this self has its genesis in the Other, that there can be no Other of the Other, no position outside discourse from which the self can be represented (see my Chapter One, p. 17, and Chapter Two, p. 116). The problem of speaking as Other, indeed, the notion of Otherness, needs to be re-examined from the point of view of feminism, postcolonialism and postmodernism. However, so as not to prolong this theoretical exposition in isolation from my reading of *Foe*, I will deal with these issues as they emerge in my discussion of Susan Barton's development as narrator.

The most significant displacement which takes place between Defoe's *Robinson Crusoe* and Coetzee's *Foe* is, of course, the use of a woman narrator, who tells Cruso's story in place of Crusoe himself.[5] However, my claim that Susan Barton's discourse is representative of certain positions in feminist discourse is based not only on this fact, but on the way in which Coetzee represents her relationships with the various men she encounters. I will, accordingly, explore each of these in some detail. There are, too, scattered allusions to certain seminal feminist works: perhaps the most obvious of these is Sandra Gilbert's and Susan Gubar's *The Madwoman in the Attic*, to which Susan Barton's repeated references to the attic as Foe's, and then her own, writing space seem to allude. And Susan Barton's name (which, she is made to claim, has been anglicized from the French, Berton) may be read as a combination of Sandra Gilbert and Susan Gubar. More important than these somewhat playful allusions is the palimpsestic nature of Coetzee's novel. Discussing the work of certain 18th and early 19th century American and English women, Gilbert and Gubar identify the palimpsest as a positive strategy in women's struggle for literary authority:

> Such writers . . . both participated in and – to use one of Harold Bloom's key terms – 'swerved' from the central sequences of male literary history, enacting a uniquely female process of revision and redefinition that necessarily caused them to seem 'odd.' At the same time, while they achieved essential authority by telling their own stories, these writers allayed their distinctively female anxieties of authorship by following Emily Dickinson's famous (and characteristically female) advice to 'Tell all the Truth but tell it slant.' In short, like the twentieth-century American poet H. D., who declared her aesthetic strategy by entitling one of her novels *Palimpsest*, women from Jane Austen and Mary Shelley to Emily Brontë and Emily Dickinson produced literary works that are in some sense palimpsestic, works whose surface designs conceal or obscure deeper, less accessible (and less socially acceptable) levels of meaning. Thus these authors managed the difficult task of achieving true female literary authority by simultaneously conforming to and subverting patriarchal literary standards. (*The Madwoman in the Attic*, p. 73)

While the palimpsest is, in some measure, the strategy adopted in all of Coetzee's novels, I will argue here that in *Foe* Coetzee is concerned precisely to deconstruct the claim to 'true female literary authority',[6] and to problematize the notion of concealed levels of meaning. Probing these deeper levels of meaning, Gilbert and Gubar go on to ask 'What is the secret message of literature by women, if there is a single secret message? What, in other words, have women got to hide?' (p. 75). And they answer this question by saying:

> what literary women have hidden or disguised is what each writer knows is in some sense her own story . . . . More specifically, however, the one plot that seems to be concealed in most of the nineteenth-century literature by women which will concern us here is in some sense a story of the woman writer's quest for her own story; it is the story, in other words, of the woman's quest for self-definition. (pp. 75–76)

Now the story that Susan Barton tells is precisely this: the story of how she attempts to tell her own story. It is possible to say that this is the story told in all of Coetzee's novels, and, recalling Coetzee's discussion of Barthes' claim that 'the field of writing . . . has today become nothing but writing itself' (see my Chapter One, p. 14), that this is the story told in much contemporary writing. *Foe* is made up of four sections, which mark the progression of Susan Barton and of the novel itself toward and beyond the achievement of Authorship. It will be the task of this chapter to trace the successive moments of these two interlocking tales. Section One tells of Susan Barton's stay on the island: it is, so to speak, Susan's retelling of the story of Robinson Crusoe. While this section provides the purest example of narrative in Susan's entire discourse, on an initial reading it is disturbing to encounter, quite early in the narrative, an unnamed *you*:

> I sat on the bare earth with my sore foot between my hands and rocked back and forth and sobbed like a child, while the stranger (who was of course the Cruso I told you of) gazed at me more as if I were a fish cast up by the waves than an unfortunate fellow-

creature. (*Foe*, p. 9)

It is not until the conclusion of this section that this *you* is specified as Foe:

> Do you think of me, Mr Foe, as Mrs Cruso or as a bold adventuress? Think what you may, it was I who shared Cruso's bed and closed Cruso's eyes, as it is I who have disposal of all that Cruso leaves behind, which is the story of his island (*Foe*, p. 45)

This narrative is, thus, addressed to Foe, as are the dated letters of Section Two. The epistolary form of these two sections means that Foe, as Author, is situated as *You* in the *I/You* relationship constituted by women's writing as speech act. He is destined to be the recipient of Susan's letters, or her story; he is her co-respondent, the Other, or the *sujet supposé savoir*, whose reponse, it is hoped, will constitute the truth of the speaking subject (see my Chapter One, p. 58). There are, however, no letters to Susan Barton in response from Foe, and it is the reader who intercepts these letters and has to adopt the recipient function, that is to say, who becomes the *You* that is addressed and must respond to the letters.[7] Adopting the recipient function, the reader colludes with Foe-as-Author, as s/he produces conditions of reception which must be seen as an integral part of the Author function as Foucault defines it, as an element in the realization of certain 'modes of circulation, valorization, attribution and appropriation of discourses' ('What is an Author' p. 117). While this is a negative view of the text – reader relationship, reducing the reader to merely a function of the Other which cannibalizes the narrating subject, it is possible to construct this relationship in more positive terms, as I have done in my Chapter One, where I point out that 'The letter, or the text, "subverts the polarity subjective/objective": in the same movement the text constitutes the reader and the reader constitutes the text, and it is this point of intersection that is the site of subversion, a subversion that must be described as potential rather than intentional' (p. 57). The danger resides in the text positing both sender and recipient in terms that are too rigidly defined as do Susan Barton's letters to Foe in the first two sections of the novel. In Section Three this rigid polarization between the *I* and the *You* breaks down, as Susan is made to say:

> 'In the beginning I thought I would tell you the story of the island and, being done with that, return to my former life. But now all my life grows to be story and there is nothing of my own left to me. I thought I was myself and this girl a creature from another order speaking words you made up for her. But now I am full of doubt. Nothing is left to me but doubt. I am doubt itself. Who is speaking me? Am I a phantom too? To what order do I belong? And you: who are you?' (*Foe*, p. 133)

Rather than leap ahead, however, let me begin with this story of the island. Within the story addressed to Foe, is the story of how Susan Barton arrived on the island, a story which she addresses to Cruso, saying 'Let me tell you my story . . . for I am sure you are wondering who I am and how I came to be here' (*Foe*, p. 10). Here she tells of how she set out to find her daughter, who 'was abducted and conveyed to the New World by an Englishman, a factor and agent in the carrying trade' (*Foe*, p. 10). This is perhaps an allegory of women's attempt to appropriate, or reappropriate, their own writing: in Section Three Foe tells a fable in which the daughter figures as the woman's story, or writing.[8] Or, linked to this, perhaps it is an allegory of the attempt to retrieve women from their representation as items of exchange in men's discourse, as, for example, at the conclusion of *Robinson Crusoe*:

> From thence I touch'd at the *Brasils*, from whence I sent a Bark, which I bought there, with more people to the Island, and in it, besides other Supplies, I sent seven Women, being such as I

> found proper for Service, or for wives as to such as as would take them: As to the *English* men, I promis'd them to send them some Women from *England*, with a good Cargoe of Necessaries, if they would apply themselves to Planting, which I afterwards perform'd. (p. 306)

Failing to find her daughter, Susan Barton embarks for Lisbon, but is castaway along with the murdered ship's captain, her lover. One may read this scene of mutiny and murder as representing the bourgeois political revolutions which undermined precapitalistic, preindustrial patriarchal relationships between rulers and subjects. In her paper 'Placing Women's History in History', Elizabeth Fox-Genovese points out that

> Patriarchy is not merely a relation between men and women, but one between men and other men. And patriarchy evokes not merely the practices of domination, but their representation and legitimation as well. (p. 22)

Thus despite men's rejection of traditional patriarchy, 'The early bourgeois societies sought to retain as many patriarchal vestiages as possible, at least with respect to the control of women and labour', so that 'a distinctive bourgeois paternalism indisputably persisted in a variety of forms in all capitalist societies' (Fox-Genovese, pp. 22 and 23). Ship's master, or patriarchal figure of authority, and women are cast away at the same historical moment, for

> Despite, or perhaps because of, their potential contributions to female independence and equality, bourgeois ideology and capitalist social relations both raised massive barriers to female individualism. Both marshalled a formidable combination of custom and modern science to justify women's subordination; both invited the alliance of men across class lines to sustain it. (Fox-Genovese, p. 22)

Notwithstanding these intitial barriers to *women's* individualism, it is precisely the bourgeois insistence upon individualism that produces contradictions within bourgeois ideology, and which ultimately makes it susceptible to penetration by women. Arguing against Gilbert and Gubar's conception of a monolithic patriarchal ideology, Toril Moi says:

> Feminists must be able to account for the paradoxically productive aspects of patriarchal ideology (the moments in which the ideology backfires on itself, as it were) as well as for its obvious oppressive implications if they are to answer the tricky question of how it is that some women manage to counter patriarchal strategies despite the odds stacked against them. In the nineteenth century, for instance, it would seem true to say that bourgeois patriarchy's predilection for liberal humanism as a 'legitimizing ideology' lent ammunition and arguments to the growing bourgeois feminist movement. If one held that the rights of the individual were sacred, it became increasingly difficult to argue that women's rights somehow were not. (p. 64)

Coetzee gives us an image of the captain which is reminiscent of Mary Shelley's image of Frankenstein and his monstrous creation heading for destruction in the icy wastes of the polar region:

> 'I dreamed of the murdered ship's-master. In my dream I saw him floating southward in his puny boat with the oars crossed on his breast and the ugly spike sticking out of his eye. The sea was tossed with huge waves, the wind howled, the rain beat down, yet the boat did not sink, but drifted slowly on toward the province of the iceberg, and would drift there, it seemed to me, caked in ice, till the day of our resurrection. He was a kindly man – let me say so now, lest I forget – who deserved a better end.' (*Foe*, p. 19)[9]

If Shelley's Frankenstein is read as representing man's attempt to become self-progenitor, to challenge God as maker, and women as makers of children,[10] then he is clearly related to Eugene Dawn, who claims that he is captain of his soul, and that 'We have the capacity to breed out of our own head' (*Dusklands*, p. 28; see my Chapter Two, p. 123). And *both* represent extremes of bourgeois individualism and of the ideology of separate spheres[11] (another of its legitimizing representations), extremes to which the image of the murdered captain appears to allude. In this single image are conflated allusions to several successive moments in the history of individualism, for the captain is dead, a handspike through his eye (*I*), suggesting that, while the bourgeois revolutions introduced the ideology of individualism, they, paradoxically, initiated a process which has lead to the *death* of the autonomous individual and of the unified subject (see my Chapter One, pp. 98–100). Susan Barton survives on the island, while the captain drifts off into the icy wastes of the Antarctic, leading us to ask whether women's writing, insofar as it is a manifestation of individualism, emerges as a *by-product* of bourgeois individualism and the ideology of separate spheres at a point in time when post-structuralist and post-Freudian representations of the self make it untenable.[12]

Susan Barton is cast up on Cruso's island, a supremely 'separate sphere'. The island has, predictably, been read by reviewers as representing the South African situation,[13] and while Cruso's kingdom may indeed function as a metaphor of Afrikaner Nationalism, it would seem that here, as in the other novels, Coetzee is concerned to place the South African situation within the context of certain dominant Western ideologies: he has said that he sees 'the South African situation as only one manifestation of a wider historical situation to do with colonialism, late colonialism, neo-colonialism' (Watson Interview, p. 23). Cruso's rule over his island kingdom represents a form of postcolonial nationalism become neo-colonialism,[14] as the new colonizer, asserting his independence from the mother country, repeats the modes of oppression of the original colonizer. As sole survivors of a wrecked slave ship, both Cruso and Friday are victims of the colonizing enterprise. Friday's tongue has been cut out, and Cruso does not attempt to communicate in alternative ways, preferring 'not to disturb his muteness', and using words 'only as the shortest way to subject [Friday] to [his] will' (*Foe*, p. 60).

Susan Barton's initial resistance to island life and to Cruso's ways means that the significance of her island sojourn and of her encounter with Cruso does not become fully apparent until Section Two, in which, as 'possessor' of Friday, she becomes heir to Cruso, and in which she recounts her nostalgia for the island:

> When I was on the island I longed only to be elsewhere, or, in the word I then used, to be saved. But now a longing stirs in me I never thought I would feel. I close my eyes and my soul takes leave of me, flying over the houses and streets, the woods and pastures, back to our old home, Cruso's and mine'. (*Foe*, p. 50)

From the time she arrives on the island Susan is preoccupied with two things, that is, with what she refers to as her immoderate desire to be saved (*Foe*, p. 36), and with Cruso's failure to set down a record of his stay on the island. These two preoccupations are closely related, for, as I have indicated in my chapter on *Life & Times of Michael K* (pp. 301–302), the desire to save oneself or another functions as a metaphor for the desire to translate the self or the other into writing. Susan Barton says:

> Cruso had no stories to tell of the life he had lived as a trader and planter before the shipwreck . . . . It was as though he wished his story to begin with his arrival on the island, and mine to begin with my arrival, and the story of us together to end on the island too'. (*Foe*, p. 34)

And, back in London, she complains to Friday:

> 'Does it not speak volumes that the first and only piece of furniture your master fashioned was a bed? How different would it not have been had he built a table and stool, and extended his ingenuity to the manufacture of ink and writing-tablets, and then sat down to keep an authentic journal of his exile day by day, which we might have brought back to England with us, and sold to a bookseller, and so saved ourselves this embroilement with Mr Foe!' (*Foe*, p. 82)

If we consider Susan Barton's preoccupation with turning Cruso's story to profit within the context of what Benedict Anderson, in his book, *Imagined Communities: Reflections on the Origin and Spread of Nationalism*, calls 'print capitalism', we see how it reflects a dilemma which is common to both women's writing and postcolonial writing, the dilemma I have already referred to as that of self-representation. Anderson points out that 'In a rather special sense, the book was the first modern style mass-produced commodity', and that as 'One of the earlier forms of capitalist enterprise, book-publishing felt all of capitalism's restless search for markets' (p. 38 and 41). It is this connection between publishing and capitalism that constitutes print capitalism, and print capitalism, Anderson argues, is one of the primary phenomena associated with the emergence of nationalism:

> the convergence of capitalism and print technology on the fatal diversity of human language created the possibility of a new form of imagined community, which in its basic morphology set the stage for the modern nation. (p. 49)

A sense of nationhood arises as books, and newspapers, provide representations of and for people who identify themselves in relation to an imagined community:

> the newspaper reader, observing exact replicas of his own paper being consumed by his subway,

> barbershop, or residential neighbours, is continually reassured that the imagined world is visibly rooted in everyday life . . . . [And] fiction seeps quietly and continuously into reality, creating that remarkable confidence of community in anonymity which is the hallmark of modern nations. (pp. 39–40)

This analysis clearly pertains to the emergence not only of a national identity, but also of women's identity in relation to an imagined community. Susan Barton's attempt to translate her island experience into book form suggests that the history of women's writing, like that of nationalism, is inextricably linked to the processes of print capitalism.

There is, however, a paradox inherent in this achievement of identity via self-representation in print, a paradox akin to that of the Lacanian subject, doomed to translate the self into Other through representation in language. Simon During, offering a critique of Anderson's argument, says:

> If one language can be translated into another, if there is no such thing as a dead language, what untranslatable residue remains to be the property solely of those who speak it? Its form, which cannot be communicated in – as one says – any other form. Yet an identity granted in terms of the signifier (which I use, as it is often used, as a figure for form as such) is an identity that necessarily cannot be communicated. It would seem to be written into the fate of nationalism as print-capitalism that national identity is conferred in the form of its own death warrant. (Postmodernism or post-colonialism today', pp. 43–44)

Thus Cruso, as postcolonial nationalist, cannot be 'saved' by Susan Barton: it is inevitable that he should die en route for England. (Friday, because he is speechless, survives as Susan's dependant, that is to say, as a figure in her speech.) Cruso's refusal to set down his story in writing must be read as a refusal of print capitalism, and it represents an extreme, and impossible, insistence upon an autonomous identity, of the kind that During has described in relation to postcolonialism:

> Post-colonialism then is the name for products of the ex-colonies' need for an identity granted not in terms of the colonial power, but in terms of themselves. It operates in modes similar to what Derrida in his early work on Husserl called 'pure auto-affection': 'the operation of hearing oneself speak.' Indeed, though difficult and belonging to another realm of discourse altogether, Derrida's remarks on hearing oneself speak are very pertinent here:
>
> > On the one hand, it (hearing oneself speak) operates within the medium of universality; what appears as signified therein must be idealities that are *idealiter* indefinitely repeatable or transmissible as the same. On the other hand, the subject can hear or speak to himself and be affected by the signifier he produces, without passing through an external detour, the world, the sphere of what is not 'his own.'
>
> The subject hears him/herself speak using signs that are universal. They belong to a language uttered not only by the self but by others. Yet the signifiers are uttered as 'his own'. To apply the argument in our context: the postcolonial self knows itself in universal terms, that is, in terms of the international centres, of a colonial past. Yet the images and texts it produces as 'its own' can affect it as if they have passed through no 'external detour', no world which is not their own. ('Postmodernism or Postcolonialism?' p. 369)

Not only does Cruso refuse to write, but he also resists Susan Barton's attempts at dialogue. She says:

> 'I would have told him more about myself too, about my quest for my stolen daughter, about the mutiny. But he asked nothing, gazing out instead into the setting sun, nodding to himself as though a voice spoke privately inside him that he was listening to.' (*Foe*, p. 13)

Postcolonialism defined in the above terms is obviously supported by the ideology of 'separate spheres', and it is Cruso's life-denying insistence upon separateness that most closely approximates Afrikaner nationalism and Apartheid. The way in which Afrikaner nationalism can be seen to be located outside a universally translatable discourse, at least metaphorically, is evident in Derrida's definition of Apartheid:

> At a time when *all* racisms on the face of the earth were condemned, it was in the world's face that the National party dared to campaign '*for the separate development of each race in the geographic zone assigned to it.*'
>
> Since then, no tongue has ever translated this name – as if all the languages of the world were defending themselves, shutting their mouths against a sinister incorporation of the thing by means of the word, as if all tongues were refusing to give an equivalent, refusing to let themselves be contaminated through the contagious hospitality of the word-for-word . . . .
>
> APARTHEID: by itself the word occupies the terrain like a concentration camp. System of partition, barbed wire, crowds of mapped out solitudes. Within the limits of this untranslatable idiom, a violent arrest of the mark, the glaring harshness of abstract essence (*heid*) seems to speculate in another regime of abstraction, that of confined separation. The word concentrates separation, raises it to another power, and sets separation itself *apart*: 'appartitionality', something like that. By isolating being apart in some sort of essence or

> hypostasis, the word corrupts it into a quasi-ontological segregation. At every point, like all racisms, it tends to pass segregation off as natural – and as the very law of the origin. ('Racism's Last Word', pp. 291–92)[15]

Cruso is not represented as being entirely without desire for a form of reciprocal recognition which will provide proof of his identity: expressed via the building of stone terraces on the barren island, his is a utopian desire projected into an anticipated future. When Susan Barton asks what he will plant his reply is:

> 'The planting is not for us . . . . We have nothing to plant – that is our misfortune . . . . The planting is reserved for those who come after us and have the foresight to bring seed. I only clear the ground for them. Clearing ground and piling stones is little enough, but it is better than sitting in idleness'. (*Foe*, p.33)

Here we find a combination of images used previously by Coetzee to refer to the act of writing as an expression of desire: the stones are reminiscent of Magda's attempts at communicating with the sky gods via messages constructed in stone, and the planting of seed recalls Michaels K's obsession with guarding, planting and nurturing his seeds as a metaphor of the process of writing (see pp. 202–203, Chap. 2 and pp. 292–295, Chap. 4). That Cruso's work of moving stones is meant to be viewed as the equivalent of writing is evident in a subsequent passage, in which Susan Barton complains to Friday:

> 'You thought that carrying stones was the hardest of labours. But when you see me at Mr Foe's desk making marks with the quill, think of each mark as a stone, and think of the paper as the island, and imagine that I must disperse the stones over the face of the island . . . ' (*Foe*, p. 87)

The utopian nature of Cruso's work may be compared to the utopian nature of recent attempts to inscribe femininity in discourse, commonly referred to as *l'écriture féminine*.[16] Similarly, Susan Barton's nostalgia for a form of self-present speech, represented by Cruso and his island location, may be read as reflecting a certain feminist desire for an auto-affective language: feminists such as Luce Irigaray advocate auto-erotism as an essentially liberatory writing practice:

> 'She' is infinitely other in herself. That is undoubtedly the reason she is called temperamental, incomprehensible, perturbed, capricious – not to mention her language in which 'she' goes off in all directions and in which 'he' is unable to discern the coherence of any meaning. Contradictory words seem a little crazy to the logic of reason, and inaudible for him who listens with ready-made grids, a code prepared in advance. In her statements – at least when she dares to speak out – *woman retouches herself constantly*. [my emphasis] (p. 103)

Despite this nostalgia, Susan Barton does not engage in the attempt to tell her story (and Cruso's) from the position of the island, but from London: her discourse is located, not on some postcolonial periphery, but at the centre of the colonizing culture. And here we come to Coetzee's second significant deviation from the 'original'. While Robinson Crusoe's position of supreme mastery can be achieved only in the impossible setting of island isolation, Susan Barton's attempts at a form of self-mastery, or Authority (through self-representation) must be negotiated from a position *within* society in order to have any validity. Coetzee takes care to depict her and Friday as being as much castaways in the heart of London as they were on the island: Susan Barton says:

> ' . . . the life we lead grows less and less distinct from the life we led on Cruso's island. Sometimes I wake up not knowing where I am. The world is full of islands, said Cruso once. His words ring

> truer every day.' (*Foe*, p. 71)

Foe, too, risks becoming a castaway as he goes into hiding from the bailiffs soon after Susan's arrival in London. She describes how a bailiff tells her of the Fleet, 'of how men have spent their lives there abandoned by their families, castaways in the very heart of the city' (*Foe*, p. 62). Even Foe, representative of the Author function, is subject to the Law and therefore cannot be regarded as an inviolate and monolithic centre of power and authority.

Susan Barton's nostalgia for island life is gradually supplanted by an increasing preoccupation with Friday, as the concern with Cruso's story is replaced by the desire to fathom Friday's story. The struggle with Foe for truthful representation of her story is largely articulated via the figure of Friday, making it difficult to discuss her relationship with either one of them in isolation from the other. Toward the end of Section One, Susan Barton tells of how the captain of the ship bringing her to England suggests that she offer her story to the booksellers, who 'will hire a man to set [her] story to rights, and put in a dash of colour, too, here and there'. In response to this she says: 'I would rather be the author of my story than have lies told about me . . . . If I cannot come forward, as author, and swear to the truth of my tale, what will be the worth of it?' (*Foe*, p. 40). She nevertheless approaches Foe, saying, 'I hoped that you might have a place for me, and for him [Friday] too, in your establishment' (*Foe*, p. 48). She is given money, and takes up lodgings with Friday, writing letters to Foe in which she begs him to return to her the substance she has lost:

> 'When I reflect on my story I seem to exist only as the one who came, the one who witnessed, the one who longed to be gone: a being without substance, a ghost beside the true body of Cruso . . . . Return to me the substance I have lost, Mr Foe: that is my entreaty. For though my story gives the truth, it does not give the substance of the truth.' (*Foe*, p. 51)

Asking for a place, Susan Barton, as woman writer, is seeking a place from which to speak from within the masculine establishment. She is, at this stage, entirely dependent upon Foe as Author, whom she hopes can render her presence (substance) by means of truthful representations of herself. However, once Foe has gone into hiding from the bailiffs, she must increasingly assume the burden of her story. She takes up residence in Foe's house and uses his writing materials:

> 'I have your table to sit at, your window to gaze through. I write with your pen on your paper, and when the sheets are completed they go into your chest. So your life continues to be lived, though you are gone.' (*Foe*, p. 65)

This appears to allude to the way in which women have been physically confined to men's houses (their father's or husband's) and metaphorically contained by men's texts. Gilbert and Gubar draw attention to this literal and figural confinement of women,[17] and entitle their section on Jane Austen 'Inside the House of Fiction: Jane Austen's Tenants of Possibility'. The crucial difference with Susan Barton's occupation of Foe's house is, of course, that it represents a deliberately adopted strategy, rather than a condition that is submitted to passively. It thus becomes the equivalent of the deconstructive strategy adopted by Coetzee's novels:

> The movements of deconstruction do not destroy structures from the outside. They are not possible and effective, nor can they take accurate aim, except by inhabiting those structures. Inhabiting them *in a certain way*, because one always inhabits and all the more when one does not suspect it. (Derrida, *Of Grammatology*, p. 24; see my Chapter One, p. 11)

Although Susan Barton continues to write dated letters to Foe from his house, she has no means of conveying these to him, and says: 'To whom am I writing? I blot the pages and toss them out of the window. Let who will read them' (*Foe*, p. 64). From this point on her letters come to be dominated by her preoccupation with Friday, making it necessary here to address the allegorical function of this preoccupation in relation to Susan Barton's role as woman writer. She says:

> 'Then there is the matter of Friday's tongue. On the island I accepted that I should never learn how Friday lost his tongue, as I accepted that I should never learn how the apes crossed the sea. But what we can accept in life we cannot accept in history. To tell my story and be silent on Friday's tongue is no better than offering a book for sale with pages in it quietly left empty. Yet the only tongue that can tell Friday's story is the tongue he has lost!' (*Foe*, p. 67)

As I have already indicated, Friday survives the journey from periphery to centre by virtue of his speechless condition and his consequent dependence upon Susan Barton: he becomes a figure in her speech, and her preoccupation with his lost tongue may be read as an allegory of the way in which the colonized subject has been appropriated by feminist discourse, an appropriation which has taken two dominant forms. The first of these is the metaphorical alignment of women and colonized subjects as victims of patriarchal oppression, which has deprived both groups of their natural language. This alignment is evident in statements such as the following:

> I was thus compelled to accept the 'otherness' of women within Western culture and to admit a set of hypotheses postulating the source of this alienation as our secondary or auxiliary status in society. I did not need to enter the vexed lists of comparison and contrast between novels by men and women to discover in women's novels a clear sense that we are outcasts in the land, that we have neither a

> homeland of our own nor an ethnic place within society. (Annis Pratt, p. 6) I consider women's literature as a specific category, not because of biology, but because it is, in a sense, the literature of the colonized. (Christiane Rochefort, 'The Privilege of Consciousness', cited by Showalter, p. 197) Feminists since the time of Mary Wollstonecraft have noted the analogies between women's position in a male-dominated society and that of underprivileged ethnic groups, particularly blacks, in a society ruled by whites. For an almost equally long time economic theorists have recognized that women in an industrial society have, economically speaking, much the same function as colonies: they provide the underpaid work force and the completely unpaid domestic labor which serve as the system's working base, and they are the consumers of its finished products . . . . The parallels between the situations of colonials, of underprivileged ethnic groups, and of women create parallel consequences. The extent of social and economic victimization suffered by each group or by individuals within groups may vary, but the consciousness of all takes on qualities universal among victims. (Gelpi, p. 269)

It is also evident in a work like Caryl Churchill's *Cloud Nine*, in which British imperialism in Africa and the figure of the black man are used to construct a somewhat facile approximation of women's oppression.[18] This metaphoric use of the figure of the colonized victim is continued in the equation of an authentic women's language with the possession of a mother tongue. Thus we find a collection of essays in feminist psychoanalytic interpretation titled *The (M)other Tongue* (ed. Garner, Kahane & Sprengnether), and Gilbert and Gubar talk about

> a dialectic of the sexes that centered on the crucial issue of woman's command of language as against language's command of woman, a dialectic that now directs our attention to women's historic efforts to come to terms with the urgent need for female literary authority through fantasies about the possession of a mother tongue. ('Sexual Linguistics: Gender, Language, Sexuality', p. 527)

Elaine Showalter is alert to the problems of positing a women's language in the form of a mother tongue, for although she makes the point that 'From a political perspective, there are interesting parallels between the feminist problem of a women's language and the recurring "language issue" in the general history of decolonization', she goes on to say that

> despite its unifying appeal, the concept of a women's language is riddled with difficulties. Unlike Welsh, Breton, Swahili, or Amharic, that is, languages of minority or colonized groups, there is no mother tongue, no genderlect spoken by the female population in a society, which differs significantly from the dominant language. (p. 192)

Summarizing all of this, it is possible to say that the colonized subject functions in women's writing as a figure of essential Otherness; it becomes the means of representing women's otherness to men and to men's language. I will pause here to clarify this term, the Other, which is used to signify different, but overlapping, concepts in various discourses. Feminism, insofar as it can be described as a unified discursive field, is characterized by women's reaction to their being passively positioned as Other in relation to men. Chandra Talpade Mohanty describes this process as follows:

> Discourses of Power-Knowledge usually operate through the formation of hierarchies. Hierarchical divisions work precisely in obliterating differences, reducing

> heterogeneities to structured and homogenized fields. The play of unappropriated differences is frozen into uneven and unequal oppositions. The 'Other' is created in this process – installed in this new economy, governed by power and privilege. An 'Other' (intellectual, political, racial, sexual) who is suppressed, ignored, made invisible, exploited, even feared not because s/he is inherently evil, or inferior, but because s/he is 'different'. Differences are thus congealed, their mobility fixed in hierarchical divisions of conceptual categories in which a valorized 'positive' term is positioned against a repressed or subordinate 'negative' term, e.g. Presence/Absence, Truth/Error, Same/Other, Identity/Difference, Male/Female, White/Black, etc. It is possible to perceive the operation of concrete ideological power structures in terms of a similar valorization of the characteristics of dominant groups, and a corresponding subordination or repression of the characteristics of oppressed groups – the dominant group being the locus of coherence – the Same, and the oppressed (the 'different' group) being the subordinate 'Other'. Difference thus gets transcribed with the notion of 'Otherness', taking on a hierarchical positionality. Both the Civil Liberties movement and the Women's Liberation Movement of the 1960s can be viewed as a recognition of and response to the location of Blacks and Women as the 'Other' in the dominant White/Male power structure. (p. 243)

Resisting this definition of themselves as 'Other', by means of which they are fixed in representations which are *unlike* men, but must be understood by means of *reference* to men, women have posited for themselves a form of *radical* Otherness. Thus Candace Lang says:

> It must be understood from the outset that the Other is not the Opposite. The opposite is but the Same inverted or reversed: a verbal contradiction, a negative image, a mirror-writing . . . easily

> recognized and restored to its reassuring familiarity. The opposite is a category of logical thought, which arranges the world in neat pairs of things and their contraries, of theses and antitheses, interdependent and mutually exclusive. But the Other is irreducibly, incorrigibly different; exceeding our logical categories, it escapes our apprehension. (p. 3)

She refers to the two fundamental forms of reaction to the threat of alterity, these being denial and assimilation, the latter being 'the practice of systematically reducing the Other to the Same – or more commonly, perhaps, to that reverse image of the Same which we have defined as the Opposite, in order to then dialectically incorporate it into familiar categories'. And she continues: 'We might imagine a third position in relation to the Other, one characterized neither by denial nor by recuperation: an attempt to think alterity as such, respecting its difference' (pp. 3–4).

Turning now to the Lacanian definition of the Other, to which attaches a complex constellation of meanings (see note 38, p. 146, my Chapter Two), we are obliged to recognize that we are inevitably Other to ourselves: we speak as Other, *re*presenting the self in language, and we desire as Other, so that even the unconscious is '*discours de l'Autre*' (see note 43, p. 147, my Chapter Two). Any form of *radical* Otherness must thus be located outside language, and for feminists who would insist upon sexual *difference*, upon an *essential* femininity, the difficulty arises when one considers that the child accedes to language, subjectivity, and to a gendered identity in the same movement. Through the threat of symbolic castration by the symbolic Father, the child recognizes that it cannot be the mother's complement, that is to say, the phallus, but becomes the one who either 'has the phallus or . . . does not have it, or . . . who can give or receive it in a full sexual relation' (Lemaire, p. 83; see my Chapter Three, p. 160). Neither boy nor girl can *be* the Phallus, and both experience symbolic castration, as even the boy, who has the phallus, is left with merely a substitute for his desire. For women, the problem arises out of the fact that gendered identity is achieved by means of reference to the phallus, and that men have responded to the symbolic castration by repressing it, and projecting it onto women. Because the boy, on the basis of sight, is perceived to have the phallus while the girl does not, anatomical difference comes to *figure* sexual difference. Pointing out that 'Any speaking being whatever must line up on one or other side of the divide' [Ladies or Gentlemen], and arguing that 'It is not, therefore, a question of philology and then the phallus . . . but of sexuality/the phallus *as* language', Jacqueline Rose says:

> Sexual difference is then assigned according to whether individual subjects do or do not possess the phallus, which means not that anatomical difference *is* sexual difference (the one as strictly deducible from the other), but that anatomical difference comes to *figure* sexual difference, that is, it becomes the sole representative of what that difference is allowed to be. It thus covers over the complexity of the child's early sexual life with a crude opposition in which that very complexity is refused or repressed. The phallus thus indicates the reduction of difference to an instance of visible perception, a *seeming* value. (p. 42)

The process described by Rose produces a form of sexual identity which is fantasmatic, in that it posits 'man' and 'woman' as fixed poles of a binary opposition, while in effect these identities cannot be regarded as in any way consistent. Thus Rose points out:

> Sexuality belongs in this area of instability played out in the register of demand and desire, each sex coming to stand, mythically and exclusively, for that which could satisfy and complete the other. . . . there is a tendency, when arguing for the pregiven nature of sexual difference, for the specificity of male and female drives, to lose sight of the more radical aspects of Freud's work on sexuality – his insistence on

> the disjunction between the sexual object and the sexual aim, his difficult challenge to the concept of perversion, and his demand that heterosexual object-choice be explained and not assumed (Freud, VII, 1905, pp. 144–46, note i, 1915). For Lacan, the 'vicissitudes' of the instinct ('instinct' was the original English translation for the German word 'trieb') cannot be understood as a deviation, accident or defence on the path to a normal heterosexuality which would ideally be secured. Rather the term 'vicissitude' indicates a fundamental difficulty inherent in human sexuality, which can be seen in the very concept of the drive. (p. 33)

Sexuality seen as a factor of the drive, and not the instinct, on which the drive is anaclitic,[19] can only be understood in terms of the representation to which it attaches. Centred around a lost object, the drive by definition cannot be satisfied: it always persists in excess of the particular object upon which it focuses, producing what Lacan calls *jouissance* (Rose, p. 34).

As a consequence of the privileging of sight and of the phallus, along with the failure of *jouissance* and the sense of loss or lack arising out of this, men have projected their lack onto women, while simultaneously disavowing this lack:

> In relation to the man, woman comes to stand for both difference and loss: 'On the one hand, the woman becomes, or is produced, precisely as what he is not, that is, sexual difference, and on the other, as what he has to renounce, that is, *jouissance*'.
>
> Within the phallic definition, the woman is constituted as 'not all', in so far as the phallic function rests on an exception (the 'not') which is assigned to her. Woman is excluded *by* the nature of words, meaning that the definition poses her as exclusion. Note that this is not the same thing as saying that woman is excluded *from* the nature of words, a misreading which leads to the recasting of

> the whole problem in terms of woman's place outside language, the idea that women might have of themselves an entirely different speech . . . .
>
> As negative to the man, woman becomes a total object of fantasy (or an object of total fantasy), elevated into the place of the Other and made to stand for its truth. (Rose, pp. 49–50, citing Lacan)[20]

Or, as Larysa Mykata, puts it:

> The other sex . . . functions as the radical Other, the locus of Truth, of Language, of the symbolic functions as well as that aspect of the figure of God that is ineffable – the sacred, the holy. Paradoxically woman is seen as, is represented as, what cannot be represented. Consequently, just as the unconscious is repressed, so too woman is 'repressed' – is an image that cannot speak. (p. 51)

Positing *themselves* as radically Other, or different, women are in danger of simply reversing the poles of the traditional binary opposition. Thus Christiane Makward points out that

> it is impossible to found in theory, to SAY, the feminine without reference to a mythological masculine (the mirror effect), Or without repeating masculine discourse on feminity (the echo effect). It is thus difficult . . . to define feminine creativity and writing without opposing them to 'the Other,' to describe them while dissociating them from the writer's sex. All of these difficulties are beginning to pall. The key words have lost their punch, they are used up, collapsing. We are emerging from a long period of intense ferment in feminist thinking, whose first stage in France was marked by an embracing of DIFFERENCE which unavoidably referred itself to the Other, and therefore to binary opposition. (p. 101)

There *is* a sense in which the construction of sexual difference in the process of subject constitution can be compared to the construction of racial difference, as Homi Bhabha indicates in his paper, 'Difference, Discrimination and the Discourse of Colonialism':

> To describe the racist discourse of colonial power as constructed around a 'boundary dispute' is not merely to pun the political with the psychoanalytic. It is the object of my talk today to suggest that the construction of the colonial subject in discourse, and the exercise of colonial power through discourse, demands an articulation of forms of difference – racial and sexual. Such an articulation becomes crucial if it is held that the body is always simultaneously inscribed in both the economy of pleasure and desire and the economy of discourse, domination and power. I do not wish to conflate, unproblematically, two forms of the marking – and splitting – of the subject nor to globalise two forms of representation. I want to suggest, however, that there is a theoretical space and a political space for such an *articulation* – in the sense in which that word itself denies an 'orginal' identity or a 'singularity' to objects of difference, sexual or racial. If such a view is taken . . . it follows that the epithets racial or sexual come to be seen as modes of differentiation, realised as multiple, cross-cutting determinations, polymorphous and perverse, always demanding a specific and strategic calculation of their effects. Such is, I believe, the moment of colonial discourse. (p. 194)

However, the danger for feminists of a simple alignment of women with an unspecified colonized subject is that it risks repeating, for the colonized subject, precisely the representations of women produced in and by men's discourse. Thus it is possible, in the passage cited from Larysa Mykata, to substitute 'the racially and/or linguistically other' for 'the other sex', and to say that *this* other, in a certain feminist discourse, is represented as what cannot be represented.[21] Racial or linguistic otherness, the possession of a mother tongue from which the colonized subject has been alienated by the colonizer's language, becomes a symbol of undifferentiated presence, of a form of primordial identity. Rose describes this quest for a primordial feminine identity as follows:

> The objective is to retrieve the woman from the dominance of the phallic term and from language at one and the same time. What this means is that femininity is assigned to a point of origin prior to the mark of symbolic difference and the law. The privileged relationship of women to that origin gives them access to an archaic form of expressivity outside the circuit of linguistic exchange.
>
> The point of origin is the maternal body, an undifferentiated space, and yet one in which the girl child recognises herself . . . . In the argument for a primordial femininity, it is clear that the relation between the mother and child is conceived of as dyadic and simply reflective (one to one – the girl child fully knows herself in the mother) which once again precludes the concept of desire. (p. 54)

Returning now to Susan Barton and her story, we find that the final letter of Section Two describes her journey to Bristol in quest of a ship which will take Friday back to Africa. She says to Friday:

> From Bristol ships sail to all corners of the globe, principally to the Americas but also to Africa, which was once your home. In Bristol we will seek out a ship to take you back to the land of your birth, or else to Brazil and the life of a freeman there.' (*Foe*, p. 101)

This attempt to return Friday to the land of his birth provides an allegorical representation of the way in which women have posited a primordial identity for themselves via the figure of the colonized subject. This allegorical reading of the journey to Bristol is endorsed by an incident which is introduced at this point: Susan Barton discovers the body of a newborn baby girl, whom, it seems, has been 'cast out' (as Susan was herself castaway) by the inhabitants of nearby cottages. Laying the body back in the ditch, Susan says:

> 'Try though I might, I could not put from my thoughts the little sleeper who would never awake, the pinched eyes that would never see the sky, the curled fingers that would never open. Who was the child but I, in another life?' (*Foe*, p. 105)

This dead girl child stands for 'a point of origin prior to the mark of symbolic difference and the law' (Rose, p. 54), and is the correlative of the unsullied self to which Susan would have Friday return. Although Susan Barton cannot finally bring herself to hand Friday over to some unscrupulous ship's captain, her assumption that it is possible to return Friday to his origins simply by placing him on a boat bound for Africa represents a denial of geographical, historical and linguistic specificity to the colonized subject. The 'difference' of the colonized subject is reduced to 'sameness' as it is posited with reference to white Western women.

Thus far I have considered only one of the forms which the feminist appropriation of the colonized subject assumes. The second form involves what Spivak refers to as 'an information retrieval approach' to 'Third world' subjects, usually women ('Three Women's Texts', p. 243). Spivak argues that

> To consider the Third World as distant cultures, exploited but with rich intact literary heritages waiting to be recovered, interpreted, and curricularized in English translation fosters the emergence of 'the Third World' as a signifier that allows us to forget that 'worlding,' even as it expands the empire of the literary discipline. (Ibid.)

She cautions feminists against reproducing the axioms of imperialism, and points out that:

> No perspective *critical* of imperialism can turn the Other into a self, because the project of imperialism has always already refracted what might have been absolutely Other into a domesticated Other that consolidates the imperialist self. ('Three Women's Texts', p. 253)

In another paper, titled 'Imperialism and Sexual Difference', Spivak claims that 'feminism within the social relations and institutions of the metropolis has something like a relationship with the fight for individualism in the upwardly class-mobile bourgeois cultural politics of the European nineteenth century' (p. 226). And, concluding this paper, she says that

> much so-called cross-cultural disciplinary practice, even when 'feminist', reproduces and forecloses colonialist structures: sanctioned ignorance, and a refusal of subject-status and therefore 'human'-ness; that an unexamined chromatism is not only no solution but belongs to the repertory of colonialist axiomatics. (p. 237)

That this practice is felt as such by the subjects, or objects, of investigation is evident from Lugones and Spelman's 'suggestions about how to do theory that is not imperialistic, ethnocentric, disrespectful,' written 'Problematically in the voice of a woman of color':

> Do commitments to 'the profession,' method, getting something published, getting tenure, lead us to talk and act in ways at odds with what we ourselves . . . would regard as ordinary, decent behavior? To what extent do we presuppose that really understanding another person or culture require our behaving in ways that are disrespectful, even violent? That is, to what extent do we presuppose that getting and/or

> publishing the requisite information requires or may require disregarding the wishes of others, lying to them, wresting information from them against their wills? Why and how do we think theorizing about others provides *understanding* of them?
>
> . . . .
>
> Another possible motive for engaging in this task is the motive of duty, 'out of obligation', because white/Anglos have done people of color wrong. Here again two considerations: coming into Hispano, Black, Native American worlds out of obligation puts white/Anglos in a morally self-righteous position that is inappropriate. You are active, we are passive. We become the vehicles of your own redemption. (pp. 580–81)

Susan Barton's act of 'saving' Friday from the island against his will, her desire to penetrate to the source of his story and to translate it into words, into a book that will be published, functions as an allegory of this particular feminist project. Witness how she justifies her actions to Friday:

> 'This is a book, Friday . . . In it is a story written by the renowned Mr Foe. You do not know the gentleman, but at this very moment he is engaged in writing another story, which is your story, and your master's, and mine. Mr Foe has not met you, but he knows of you, from what I have told him, using words. That is part of the magic of words. Through the medium of words I have given Mr Foe the particulars of you and Mr Cruso and of my year on the island and the years you and Mr Cruso spent there alone, as far as I can supply them; and all these particulars Mr Foe is weaving into a story which will make us famous throughout the land, and rich too . . . And I will give you your own copy of our book bound in leather, to take with you. I will show you how to trace your name in it, page after page, so that your children may see that their father is known in all parts of the world where books

> are read. Is writing not a fine thing, Friday? Are you not filled with joy to know that you will live forever, after a manner?' (*Foe*, p. 58)

As in *Life & Times of Michael K*, the project of self redemption is disguised as salvation of the inarticulate victim. Returning Friday to his own lost language is not viewed as an end in itself, for this language would have to be translated into words, and a story, comprehensive to the colonizer:

> 'So, watching his hand grip the spade, watching his eyes, I seek the first sign that he comprehends what I am attempting: not to have the beds cleared (I am sure you have a gardener), not even to save him from idleness, or for the sake of his health to bring him out of the darkness of his cellar, but to build a bridge of words over which, when one day it is grown sturdy enough, he may cross to the time before Cruso, the time before he lost his tongue, when he lived immersed in the prattle of words as unthinking as a fish in water; from where he may by steps return, as far as he is able, to the world of words in which you, Mr Foe, and I, and other people live.' (*Foe*, p. 60)

And here we find repeated the image of a fish in water, an image used by Coetzee in both *In the Heart of the Country* and *Waiting for the Barbarians* to refer to a condition of unselfconscious, unreflective existence, to a use of words which allows for self-present being, rather than the separation from self which is one of the conditions of knowledge. (See my Chapter 4, p. 242).

Shown in the process of becoming increasingly attached to Friday, Susan Barton is shown simultaneously in the process of rejecting a girl who claims to be her daughter, and whom Susan believes has been sent to her by Mr Foe. This girl, and the maid, Amy, who makes an appearance in Section III, are characters from Defoe's novel, *Roxana*. Susan denies that she is this girl's mother, answering the girl's question 'Who is my true mother then?' by saying:

> 'You are father-born. You have no mother. The pain you feel is the pain of lack, not the pain of loss. What you hope to regain in my person you have in truth never had.' (*Foe*, p. 91)

Rejecting this girl, Susan Barton is rejecting the script that has been given to women by men writers, a particularly negative script in this case, for Roxana exemplifies the worst aspects of capitalistic enterprise and individualism: she turns her own body into an item of exchange, and makes her fortune out of duplicitous relationships with men, having abandoned her children on the doorstep of an unwitting sister-in-law. Roxana seeks out her daughter in later life, but when this child attempts to expose the secret of the mother's identity, she is conveniently done away with by the maid, Amy, whom Roxana then rejects. It is a script of a woman's treachery and betrayal of her own kind, of the daughter and the maid, and Susan Barton's disavowal of this daughter must be read as a positive strategy on the part of women writers. However, one form of self-representation is rejected in favour of another, as Susan Barton's quest for the daughter is replaced by a fetishistic attachment to Friday. Concluding Section Two, she says:

> 'A woman may bear a child she does not want, and rear it without loving it, yet be ready to defend it with her life. Thus it has become, in a manner of speaking, between Friday and myself. I do not love him, but he is mine. That is why he remains in England. That is why he is here.' (*Foe*, p. 111)

The concept of the fetish is important here, for, as a substitute phallus, it describes a form of attachment which both acknowledges and disavows castration.[22] Homi Bhabha has described the stereotyping which occurs in colonial discourse in terms of the fetish: while difficult, his argument is extremely useful, in that it allows us to read women's attraction to the colonized subject as an example of the same kind of stereotyping:

There is both a structural and functional justification for reading the racial stereotype of colonial discourse in terms of fetishism . . . . Fetishism, as the disavowal of difference, is that repetitious scene around the problem of secondary castration. The recognition of sexual difference – as the pre-condition for the circulation of the chain of absence and presence in the realm of the Symbolic – is disavowed by the fixation on an object that masks that difference and restores an original presence. The *functional* link between the fixation of the fetish and the stereotype (or the stereotype as fetish) is even more relevant. For fetishism is always a 'play' or vacillation between the archaic affirmation of wholeness/similarity – in Freud's terms: 'All men have penises'; in ours 'all men have the same skin/race/culture, and the anxiety associated with lack and difference' – again, for Freud 'Some do not have penises'; for us 'Some *do not* have the same skin/race/culture'. Within discourse, the fetish represents the simultaneous play between metaphor as substitution (masking absence and difference) and metonymy (which contiguously registers the perceived lack). The fetish or stereotype gives access to an 'identity' which is predicated as much on mastery and pleasure as it is on anxiety and defence, for it is a form of multiple and contradictory belief in its recognition of difference and disavowal of it. This conflict of pleasure/unpleasure, mastery/defence, knowledge/disavowal, absence/presence, has a fundamental significance for colonial discourse. For the scene of fetishism is also the scene of the reactivation and repetition of primal fantasy – the subject's desire for a pure origin that is always threatened by its division, for the subject must be gendered to be engendered, to be spoken. The stereotype, then, as the primary point of subjectification in colonial discourse, for both coloniser and colonised, is the scene of a similar fantasy and defence – the desire for an originality which is again threatened by the

> differences of race, colour and culture. ('Difference, Discrimination and the Discourse of Colonialism', p. 202)

If women's attachment to their child is perceived as a fetish which disavows their mother's, and their own, lack of penis, and which denies the process of sexual differentiation though symbolic castration in language, then the attachment to the colonized subject can be described as a second-degree fetish; a substitute for a substitute. In feminist discourse, the aligment with the colonized subject, as I have argued, manifests a desire for a pure origin: the figural appropriation of the colonized subject is a paradoxical move by means of which absence – the *loss* of a native language – comes to stand for presence – the potential *possession* of a mother tongue; or, conversely, presence – that of the visibly and/or linguistically different colonized subject – symbolizes the loss or absence that is experienced as part of women's condition.

In Section III Susan Barton describes to Foe a scene in which her gaze is directed at Friday's genitals in a replication of the ethnocentric encounter with the racially other,[23] and of men's privileging of the phallus and of the faculty of sight. What Susan Barton describes is an unveiling ceremony:

> 'When I heard the humming that first morning and came to the door and was met with the spectacle of Friday at his dancing with his robes flying about him, I was so confounded that I gaped without shame at what had hitherto been veiled from me. For though I had seen Friday naked before, it had been only from a distance: on our island we had observed the decencies as far as we could, Friday not least of us.' (*Foe*, p. 119)

Now Lacan points out that the Phallus 'can play its role only when veiled, that is to say, as itself a sign of the latency with which any signifiable is struck, when it is raised (*aufgehoben*) to the function of signifier' (*Ecrits*, p. 288).[24] And in my Chapter Two, I indicate that the particular function of the

Phallus as signifier arises out of the fact that it is a presence which signifies an absence (p. 101). Unveiled, its 'phallacious' status becomes apparent: the presence of the phallus signifies the absence of full, immediate signification. In the case of the feminist appropriation of the colonized subject, the loss of a mother tongue becomes the equivalent of the absence of the phallus, that is to say, of the symbolic castration suffered by victims of patriarchal oppression. Citing Lacan, Mykyta makes the point that:

> What the male 'is looking for is not . . . the phallus . . . but precisely its absence.' In other words, what he is looking for is the sexual organ of the woman, the 'not-all,' that which cannot be seen. What takes the place of that which cannot be perceived in or of the Other is what Lacan designates as the *petit objet*, a 'symbol of lack, of the phallus in as much as it is lacking' – an object of phantasy and desire. This obscure object of desire is, of course, usually the woman. Instead of having a penis and being a subject, for man, woman as the object of desire, woman as a whole, as a veiled hole, becomes the phallus. And it is by seeing the woman as an object that does not speak or look that the man can believe he is approaching her when what he approaches is only the cause of his desire (for her). (p. 54)

Looking for the absence of the phallus in women, men project their own sense of loss, or lack, onto women, who become 'negatives' in relation to the 'positives' constituted by men, symbols of absence providing proof of men's presence. In the scene of unveiling described by Susan Barton, the parallel between this objectification of women by men and the objectification of the colonized subject by women is evident. Anticipating that Friday will have been castrated, Susan Barton looks for his penis as absence:

> 'I have told you of the abhorrence I felt when Cruso opened Friday's mouth to show me he had no

> tongue. What Cruso wanted me to see, what I averted my eyes from seeing, was the thick stub at the back of the mouth, which ever afterwards I pictured to myself wagging and straining under the sway of emotion as Friday tried to utter himself, like a worm cut in half contorting itself in death-throes. From that night on I had continually to fear that evidence of a yet more hideous mutilation might be thrust upon my sight.' (*Foe*, p. 119)

And she finds its present absence, or its absent presence: her failure to say whether the penis is present or absent maintains the equivocal status of the phallus:

> 'In the dance nothing was still and yet everything was still. The whirling robe was a scarlet bell settled upon Friday's shoulders and enclosing him; Friday was the dark pillar at its centre. What had been hidden from me was revealed. I saw; or, I should say, my eyes were open to what was present to them.
>
> 'I saw and believed I had seen, though afterwards I remembered Thomas, who also saw, but could not be brought to believe till he had put his hand in the wound.' (*Foe*, pp. 119–120)

Friday is the 'dark pillar' at the centre of the 'scarlet bell': his absent penis/tongue allows him to figure as the phallus for Susan Barton as woman writer; he becomes a fetishized substitute phallus which allows her to elude the fact of her own castration in language.[25]

It is necessary now to return to Susan Barton's argument with Foe concerning the presentation of her story in order to elaborate upon how this scene of unveiling, or recognition, functions in Coetzee's allegory of a certain development in women's writing. While in Section Two Susan begs Foe to return to her the substance she has lost, in Section Three she no longer values existence merely as a substantial body, saying that 'such a life is abject. It is the life of a thing. A whore used by men is used as a substantial body' (*Foe*, p. 126), and even going so far as to claim 'to no one, not even to you, do I own proof that I am a substantial being with a substantial history in the world' (*Foe*, p. 131). She no longer writes letters addressed to Foe, but seeks him out in his hiding place, so that Section Three takes the form of a narrative in which Foe is not the *You* upon whom Susan is dependent, but a *he* – that is to say, is reduced to the pronoun of non-person in her speech.[26] Despite this assertion of independence, she continues to engage in a debate with Foe, as she is made to realize when she says:

> 'Yet, in the same room as yourself at last, where I need surely not relate to you my every action – you have me under your eyes, you are not blind – I continue to describe and explain. Listen! I describe the dark staircase, the bare room, the curtained alcove, particulars a thousand times more familiar to you than to me; I tell of your looks and my looks, I relate your words and mine. Why do I speak, to whom do I speak, when there is no need to speak?' (*Foe*, p. 133)

In this section we witness Susan Barton's resistance, as woman writer, to the various arguments put forward by Foe, as Author. There is no resolution of the debate: argument and counter-argument are more or less evenly balanced, and it is difficult to detect any weighting given to one or the other. We sense that Susan must resist the positions offered by Foe only because the debate is articulated as a scene of seduction, with Foe 'like the patient spider who sits at the heart of his web waiting for his prey to come to him', or like a father confessor:

> 'When I first heard of you I was told you were a very secret man, a clergyman of sorts, who in the course of your work heard the darkest of confessions from the most desperate of penitents. I will not kneel before him like one of his gallow-birds, I vowed, with a mouth full of unspeakable confidences: I will say in plain terms what can be said and leave unsaid what

> cannot. Yet here I am pouring out my darkest secrets to you! You are like one of those notorious libertines whom women arm themselves against, but against whom they are at last powerless, his very notoriety being the seducer's shrewdest weapon.' (*Foe*, p. 120)

If we consider the role which Foucault sees confession playing in the translation of a potentially subversive sexuality into discourse, by means of which it is defused and controlled, the significance of Foe's portrayal as father confessor becomes apparent. Tracing the way in which 'the scope of the confession – the confession of the flesh – continually increased', Foucault says:

> Discourse . . . had to trace the meeting line of the body and the soul, following all its meanderings: beneath the surface of the sins, it would lay bare the unbroken nervure of the flesh. Under the authority of a language that had been carefully expurgated so that it was no longer directly named, sex was taken charge of, tracked down as it were, by a discourse that aimed to allow it no obscurity, no respite. ('The Repressive Hypothesis', p. 303)

The impetus amongst women writers has largely been toward self expression in defiance of patriarchal oppression and repression, an attitude implicit in Virginia Woolf's directive: 'All that we have ought to be expressed – mind and body – a process of incredible difficulty and danger'.[27] However, Foucault argues that it is precisely *via* translation into discourse, *via* confession, that repression occurs:

> Since the eighteenth century, sex has not ceased to provoke a kind of generalized discursive erethism. And these discourses on sex did not multiply apart from or against power, but in the very space and as the means of its exercise. Incitements to speak were orchestrated from all quarters, apparatuses everywhere for listening and recording, procedures for

> observing, questioning, and formulating. Sex was driven out of hiding and constrained to lead a discursive existence. ('The Repressive Hypothesis', p. 314)

Initially Susan Barton is represented as having an urgent desire to tell everything. She relates her story to Cruso, despite his lack of interest, and would relate it to Foe, to whom she says:

> 'Who but Cruso, who is no more, could truly tell you Cruso's story? I should have said less about him, more about myself. How, to begin with, did my daughter come to be lost, and how, following her, did I reach Bahia? How did I survive among strangers those two long years? Did I live only in a rooming-house, as I have said? Was Bahia an island in the ocean of the Brazilian forest, and my room a lonely island in Bahia?' (*Foe*, p. 51)

Her desire to tell the whole truth, to leave no gaps or absences in her story, causes her to lament: 'To tell my story and be silent on Friday's tongue is no better than offering a book for sale with pages in it quietly left empty' (*Foe*, p. 67). However, in Section Three, Susan resists Foe's attempts to discover more about Bahia. And when he wants to narrativize her story in five parts, 'the loss of the daughter, the quest for the daughter in Brazil; abandonment of the quest, and the adventure of the island; assumption of the quest by the daughter; and reunion of the daughter with her mother' (*Foe*, p. 117), Susan refuses, saying:

> 'As for Bahia . . . it is by choice that I say so little of it. The story I desire to be known by is the story of the island . . . . Once you proposed to supply a middle by inventing cannibals and pirates. These I would not accept because they were not the truth. Now you propose to reduce the island to an episode in the history of a woman in search of a lost

daughter. This too I reject.' (*Foe*, pp. 120–21)

This rejection follows her description of the unveiling scene, which, in this context, must be seen as a means of registering her new awareness of the value of silence, of secrecy, of gaps in the story. Thus the unveiling marks a recognition, on the part of Susan Barton, of how Friday figures in her story, of the nature of his loss, and of how his condition of silence differs from her own silence. She now refers to Friday's story as 'properly not a story but a puzzle or hole in the narrative' (*Foe*, p. 121), and admonishes Foe, saying:

> 'You err most tellingly in failing to distinguish between my silences and the silences of a being such as Friday. Friday has no command of words and therefore no defence against being re-shaped day by day in conformity with the desires of others . . . . No matter what he is to himself (is he anything to himself? – how can he tell us?), what he is to the world is what I make of him. Therefore the silence of Friday is a helpless silence. He is the child of his silence, a child unborn, a child waiting to be born that cannot be born. Whereas the silence I keep regarding Bahia and other matters is chosen and purposeful: it is my own silence.' (*Foe*, pp. 121–22)

This differentiation between silences recalls Foucault's argument that

> Silence itself – the things one declines to say, or is forbidden to name; the discretion that is required between different speakers – is less the absolute limit of discourse, the other side from which it is separated by a strict boundary, than an element that functions alongside the things said, with them and in relation to them within overall strategies. There is no binary division to be made between what one says and what one does not say; we must try to determine the different ways of not saying such things, how those who

> can and those who cannot speak of them are distributed, which type of discourse is authorized, or which form of discretion is required in either case. There is not one but many silences, and they are an integral part of the strategies that underlie and permeate discourses. ('The Repressive Hypothesis', pp. 309–10)

Susan Barton's silence is 'chosen and purposeful', it is a strategic silence, as she indicates when she says: 'It is still in my power to guide and amend. Above all, to withhold. By such means do I still endeavour to be father to my story' (*Foe*, p. 123). Her silences are significant, they are capable of signification, whereas Friday's silence is outside signfication. As radically Other, situated outside the language systems of the West, Friday cannot, in and of himself, make meaning within these systems. Thus, at the conclusion of this section, when Susan Barton refers to herself, her daughter and Foe, saying, 'We are all alive, we are all substantial, we are all in the same world' (*Foe*, p. 152), Foe reminds her that she has omitted Friday, who, significantly, is busy with his newly learned 'writing'. The substantiality Susan refers to is not a mark of physical, or bodily, existence in the world: it indicates, rather, the materiality of linguistic representations. Friday is *not* in the same world because he is not able to represent himself within the same signifying system.

Susan Barton, however, as a Western woman, does have speech: as Rose points out in the passage I have already cited, women are excluded *by* the nature of words, not *from* the nature of words, and are therefore not to be considered mute. As an alternative to a form of defiant self-expression, certain feminists have proposed a strategy of absolute silence. However, as Makward points out, this is no more viable a solution to the problem of women's speech:

> By means of an essentialist definition . . . woman is incapable of speaking as a woman; therefore, the most female course of action is to observe an hour of silence, or (if you have dramatic talent) to imitate the scream

> of Artaud at the Theatre du Vieux Colombier, by way of creating woman-speech. Obviously the problem is that by identifying discourse with power, and then rejecting both, women are resigning themselves to silence, and non-speech. The speech of the other will then swallow them up, will speak *for* them, and *instead* of them. *Nothing will have taken place but a displacement of the feminine.* (p. 100)

The problem for women, and indeed for all writers wishing to signal their otherness within phallic discourse, is thus a rhetorical one, a problem of how to point to a strategic silence *within* speech. Friday's muteness provides the means of figuring this silence for Susan Barton as woman writer; he represents the hole in her narrative, a hole which figures her own hole, that is to say, the absence of the phallus. In his paper on Achterberg's 'Ballade van de gasfitter', Coetzee refers to the sexual significance of the hole in Achterberg's poem in terms which are relevant to the point I am making here:

> The search of the masculine *I* for the hole in the house of the feminine *You* . . . I take to be a kind of bawdy side-show in parallel to the metaphysical drama I have been outlining, one that points again to the danger of *naming* the *You* as God or woman. (p. 288)

And in the footnote to this passage he cites Monique Wittig's *The Guérillères*:

> The women say . . . the language you [women] speak is made up of signs that rightly speaking designate what men have appropriated. Whatever they have not laid hands on . . . does not appear in the language you speak. This is apparent precisely in the intervals that your masters have not been able to fill with their words of proprietors and possessors, this can be found in the gaps, in all that which is not a continuation of

> *their* discourse, in the zero, the O, the perfect circle that you invent to imprison them and to overthrow them.[28]

By definition, these gaps, this I, arise *un*consciously, *in spite of* conscious speech; it is thus impossible to inscribe this hole intentionally, without at the same time filling it up with phallic discourse. All that is possible is a rhetorical gesture, which, in Susan Barton's story, as in Coetzee's novel, is accomplished via the figure of Friday.

If women are constrained to speak as Other, it must be recognized that this is a condition of speech itself. Susan Barton has to give up her desire to speak the truth of her presence, has to realize that, once women enter the realm of writing, claims for 'appropriate' representations of the self and for authorial control are not valid. When Foe introduces the daughter and the maid from *Roxana* into the room in which he and Susan Barton are talking, Susan responds by saying:

> 'But if these women are creatures of yours, visiting me at your instruction, speaking words you have prepared for them, then who am I and who indeed are you? I presented myself to you in words I knew to be my own – I slipped overboard, I began to swim, my hair floated about me, and so forth, you will remember the words – and for a long time afterwards, when I was writing those letters that were never read by you, and were later not sent, and at last not even written down, I continued to trust in my own authorship.
>
> . . . .
>
> In the beginning I thought I would tell you the story of the island and, being done with that, return to my former life. But now all my life grows to be story and there is nothing of my own left to me. I thought I was myself and this girl a creature from another order speaking words you made up for her. But now I am full of doubt. Nothing is left to me

but doubt. I am doubt itself.' (*Foe*, p. 133)

Foe's response, is to kiss Susan, who asks: 'Was this his reply – that he and I were man and woman, that man and woman are beyond words?' However, she goes on to say, 'If so it was a paltry reply, demonstration more than reply, one that would satisfy no philosopher' (*Foe*, p. 134), thus rejecting this essentialist definition of sexual difference, refusing Foe's insistence upon natural, physiological difference as *the* mark of difference between men and women. This is not to say that anatomical difference does not exist, but, as I have indicated, that a gendered identity is produced, not beyond words, but *in* words, which translate anatomical difference into a symbol of fixed and polarized sexual identity. Susan Barton is thus shown in the process of realizing that gendered identity, indeed, identity itself, is a factor of language, and thus that her own status within writing cannot be *essentially* different from that of the daughter and the maid from *Roxana*: she is neither more nor less 'real' or substantial than they are.

Foe's seduction of Susan Barton comes to a climax with a scene of mutual blood-sucking, a form of cannibalism in which each preys on the other in quest of a story.[29] This scene, along with the image of Foe as spider, waiting in silence to devour his prey, suggests that Susan's frequently expressed fear of cannibals (which merely repeats the white Western insistence upon cannibalism as the mark of difference between the self and the racially Other) is in effect a fear of being 'devoured', or overcome, by the Other. This is the same fear that Jacobus Coetzee expresses on his encounter with the 'savages' in the African interior:

> The relation of master and savage is a spatial one. The African highland is flat, the approach of the savage across space continuous. From the fringes of the horizon he approaches, growing to manhood beneath my eyes until he reaches the verge of that precarious zone in which, invulnerable to his weapons, I command his life. Across this annulus I behold him

> approach bearing the wilderness in his heart. On the far side he is nothing to me and I probably nothing to him. On the near side mutual fear will drive us to our little comedies of man and man, prospector and guide, benefactor and beneficiary, victim and assassin, teacher and pupil, father and child. He crosses it, however, in none of these characters but as representative of that out there which my eye once enfolded and ingested and which now promises to enfold, ingest, and project me through itself as a speck on a field which we may call annihilation or alternatively history. He threatens to have a history in which I shall be a term. Such is the material basis of the malady of the master's soul. (*Dusklands*, p. 86)

The bloodsucking is followed by an act of intercourse, in which Susan Barton reverses the conventional positions, and straddles Foe, saying: 'It is always a hard ride when the Muse pays her visits . . . . She must do whatever lies in her power to father her offspring' (*Foe*, p. 140). While she assumes the conventional role granted to women as Muse, at the same time she imitates the position of mastery, becoming father of her story. Earlier she has said:

> 'Do you know the story of the Muse, Mr Foe? The Muse is a woman, a goddess, who visits poets in the night and begets stories upon them . . . . When I wrote my memoir for you, and saw how like the island it was, under my pen, dull and vacant and without life, I wished there were such a being as a man-Muse, a youthful god who visited authoresses in the night and made their pens flow. But now I know better. The Muse is both goddess and begetter. I was intended not to be the mother of my story, but to beget it'. (*Foe*, p. 126)

Now Gilbert and Gubar open their first section of *The Madwoman in the Attic*, 'Toward a Feminist Poetics', with the question, 'Is the pen a metaphorical penis?' and go on to cite

Hopkins: ' "The artist's most essential quality", he declared, "is masterly execution, which is a kind of male gift, and especially marks off men from women, the begetting of one's thought on paper, on verse, or whatever the matter is" '.[30] They discuss Harold Bloom's analysis of literary history, which is conducted in terms of just such a metaphor of literary paternity:

> Applying Freudian structures to literary genealogies, Bloom has postulated that the dynamics of literary history arise from the artist's 'anxiety of influence,' his fear that he is not his own creator and that the works of his predecessors, existing before and beyond him, assume essential priority over his own writings. . . . Thus Bloom explains that a 'strong poet' must engage in heroic warfare with his 'precursor,' for, involved as he is in a literary Oedipal struggle, a man can only become a poet by somehow invalidating his poetic father.[31]

Pointing out that Bloom 'metaphorically defines the poetic process as a sexual encounter between a male poet and his female muse', they ask: 'Where, then, does the female poet fit in? Does she want to annihilate a 'forefather' or a 'foremother'? What if she can find no models, no precursors? Does she have a muse, and what is its sex?' (p. 47). Not only do Gilbert and Gubar commend Bloom's theory for bringing to the surface the hitherto *implicitly* patriarchal nature of literary history, but they go so far as to analyse certain moments in women's literary history in terms of this theory. Thus, in the passage I cited earlier, they talk about the way in which certain woman writers ' "swerved" from the central sequences of male literary history', and how these women achieved 'true female literary authority' by means of a palimpsestic aesthetic strategy. Their feminist poetics, like Susan Barton's straddling of Foe, simply seeks a reversal of positions, a supplanting of men's literary authority by women's literary authority, which in no way disturbs the notions of ownership and mastery they criticize so strongly. Susan Barton's ongoing argument with Foe and her attempt to (re)write *Robinson Crusoe* is the equivalent of Gilbert and Gubar's poetics, in that it involves the application of what have been identified as men's strategies to men's texts and a battle for authority with male authors. Susan Barton's sexual encounter with Foe represents the achievement of authority on the part of women writers, as she begets her story upon him, repeating the way in which men have engendered their stories upon the figure of woman.

Having successfully countered Foe's various arguments and strategies with respect to her own presentation, and having constructed for herself a position of authority, Susan Barton nevertheless continues to be seduced by Foe in relation to strategies for presenting Friday's story. Thus, immediately following this scene of sexual role reversal, Foe proceeds to reflect upon Friday and his story in terms that repeat the means by which women have traditionally been reduced to figuration in men's texts. He deciphers Friday's enigmatic ritual of casting petals upon the surface of the ocean in terms of Western mythology:

> 'You wrote of your man Friday paddling his boat into the seaweed. Those great beds of seaweed are the home of a beast called by mariners the *kraken* – have you heard of it? – which has arms as thick as a man's thigh and many yards long, and a beak like an eagle's. I picture the *kraken* lying on the floor of the sea, staring up through tangled fronds of weeds at the sky, its many arms furled about it, waiting. It is into that terrible orbit that Friday steers his fragile craft.' (*Foe*, p. 140)

And he appropriates this ritual as a means of talking about the Western writer's need to penetrate to the source of the self:

> 'Friday rows his log of wood across the dark pupil – or the dead socket – of an eye staring up at him from the floor of the sea. He rows across it and is

> safe. To us he leaves the task of descending into that eye. Otherwise, like him, we sail across the surface and come ashore none the wiser, and resume our old lives, and sleep without dreaming, like babes.' (*Foe*, p. 141)

Thus Friday is to become the (negative) mirror image of their 'darker selves', in the same way that 'woman' has been the figure onto which men have projected their dark unconscious desires. To this end Foe argues that they must 'make Friday's silence speak' (*Foe*, p. 142), and persuades Susan Barton to overcome Friday's lack of speech by teaching him to write. Susan's triumph over Foe, her assumption of the authority to engender her own story, is, however, *undermined* by the presence of Friday. There is a subtle deconstruction of the Master/Slave positions as Susan is made to speculate that Foe, Friday and herself are all in some sense slaves. Of Friday she says: 'If he was not a slave, was he nevertheless not the helpless captive of my desire to have our story told?' and she goes on to say: 'And might not Foe be a kind of captive too?' (*Foe*, pp. 150–51). She describes her own situation of slavery in terms of the story of the old man of the river:

> 'I am Sinbad of Persia and Friday is the tyrant riding on my shoulders. I walk with him, I eat with him, he watches me while I sleep. If I cannot be free of him I will stifle!' (*Foe*, p. 148)

Just as the authority, the self-assurance, of men has been disturbed by women, whose words and whose gaze have returned to confront men from the position of the Other, so the newly assumed authority of women is undermined by the representative of racial Otherness, Friday. Susan Barton's sense of entrapment by Friday is the equivalent of the situation described by Homi Bhabha in his Foreword to Franz Fanon's *Black Skins, White Masks*. Bhabha talks about

> the image of post-Englightenment man tethered to, *not* confronted by, his dark reflection, the shadow of

> colonized man, that splits his presence, distorts his outline, breaches his boundaries, repeats his action at a distance, disturbs and divides the very time of his being. This ambivalent identification of the racist world . . . turns on the idea of Man *as* his alienated image, not Self and Other but the 'Otherness' of the Self inscribed in the perverse palimpsest of colonial identity. (p. xiv)

Susan Barton cannot tolerate this splitting of her presence, this confrontation by the Other: when Friday produces a design of row upon row of eyes upon human feet, walking eyes, she demands that he give her the slate. When he disobeys, rubbing the slate clean, she draws back in disgust and cries out: 'Mr Foe, I must have my freedom! . . . It is becoming more than I can bear!' (*Foe*, p. 147). She would efface the gaze of the Other, would refuse the look which Friday turns upon her, de-centering her, displacing her from the position of authority.

In relation to Susan Barton, Friday, as colonized subject and racial Other, is, to use Bhabha's words, a 'perverse palimpsest' of a fixed and stable identity. Addressing a figure whom she assumes to be Foe, she finds that it is Friday, dressed in Foe's garb:

> But the man seated at the table was not Foe. It was Friday, with Foe's robes on his back and Foe's wig, filthy as a bird's nest, on his head. In his hand, poised over Foe's papers, he held a quill with a drop of black ink glistening at its tip. I gave a cry and sprang forward to snatch it away. (*Foe*, p. 151)

This is a scene of mimicry which contains and brings to a climax the preceding ones; scenes in which Friday dances in Foe's guild-master's robes and wig, in a trance which places him 'beyond human reach' (*Foe*, p. 92), and in which he masters Foe's flute only to play the same tune of six notes which he had played on his hand-crafted instrument on the island. Much recent theoretical debate has been articulated around the notion of mimicry, which has been used to describe both feminist and postcolonial writing strategies. Referring briefly, and therefore superficially, to this debate, I wish to use the notion of mimicry here to tie together what I see as overlapping concepts and strategies, not only in feminist and postcolonial discourse, but also in postmodern discourse. To begin with feminist discourse, then, Rose makes the point that 'Sexuality belongs for Lacan in the realm of masquerade . . . . For Lacan, masquerade is the very definition of 'femininity' precisely because it is constructed with reference to a male sign' (p. 43). Accepting the inevitability of feminine sexuality as masquerade, a certain feminist discourse has proposed a *deliberate* masquerade, or mimicry, as a strategy for displacing patriarchal authority. Toril Moi cites Luce Irigaray, who says:

> They [women] must not pretend to rival them [men] by constructing a logic of the feminine that again would take as its model the onto-theological. They must rather try to disentangle this question from the economy of the logos. They must therefore not pose it in the form 'What is woman?' They must, through repetition – interpretation of the way in which the feminine finds itself determined in discourse – as lack, default, or as mime and inverted reproduction of the subject – show that on the feminine side it is possible to *exceed* and *disturb* this logic.[32]

Moi offers the following commentary on Irigaray's strategy:

> Through her acceptance of what is in any case an ineluctable mimicry, Irigaray doubles it back on itself, thus raising the parasitism to the second power. hers is a theatrical staging of the mime: miming the miming imposed on woman, Irigaray's subtle specular move (her mimicry *mirrors* that of all women) intends to *undo* the effects of phallocentric discourse simply by *overdoing* them. Hers is a fundamentally paradoxical strategy that reflects that of the mystics:

> if the mystic's abject surrender becomes the moment of her liberation, Irigaray's undermining of patriarchy through the overmiming of its discourses may be the one way out of the straitjacket of phallocentrism. (p. 140)[33]

In the area of postcolonial discourse, Bhabha constructs mimicry in similar terms, as a translation of the inevitable into a subversive strategy. Referring to the title of Fanon's text, he suggests that 'from such ambivalent identification – *black skin, white masks* – it is possible . . . to redeem the pathos of cultural confusion into a strategy of cultural subversion' (Foreword to *Black Skins, White Masks*, p.xxii). In his paper, 'Of Mimicry and Man: The Ambivalence of Colonial Discourse', Bhabha analyses the dialectical movement of mimicry. As a form of surveillance or control of the colonized by the colonizer,

> colonial mimicry is the desire for a reformed, recognizable Other, as *a subject of difference that is almost the same, but not quite*. Which is to say, that the discourse of mimicry is constructed around an *ambivalence*; in order to be effective, mimicry must continually produce its slippage, its excess, its difference. The authority of that mode of colonial discourse that I have called mimicry is therefore stricken by an indeterminacy: mimicry emerges as the representation of a difference that is itself a process of disavowal. Mimicry is, thus, the sign of a double articulation; a complex strategy of reform, regulation, and discipline, which 'appropriates' the Other as it visualizes power. Mimicry is also the sign of the inappropriate, however, a difference or recalcitrance which coheres the dominant strategic function of colonial power, intensifies surveillance, and poses an immanent threat to both 'normalized' knowledges and disciplinary powers. (p. 126)

Bhabha goes on to argue that

> What emerges between mimesis and mimicry is a *writing*, a mode of representation, that marginalizes the monumentality of history, quite simply mocks it power to be a model, that power which supposedly makes it imitable. Mimicry *repeats* rather than *re-presents* . . . (p. 128)

and that 'the look of surveillance returns as the displacing gaze of the disciplined, where the observer becomes the observed and 'partial' representation rearticulates the whole notion of *identity* and alienates it from essence' (p. 129).

Certain crucial defining features arise out of these feminist and postcolonial articulations of the notion of mimicry, features which, in turn, suggest the link between mimicry and postmodernism's reponse to the conditions of postmodernity. Mimicry is a form of 'repetition-interpretation', it 'repeats rather than re-presents'. To re-present is to acknowledge an authority, a source, an originating presence; even if that authority is challenged, re-presentation sets the self up in rivalry to that authority, and thereby takes as its model what Irigaray calls the onto-theological mode of identification. While Susan Barton's occupation of Foe's writing space and reversal of positions in the sexual act is closer to mimesis, or re-presentation, than to mimicry, Friday, in his disregard of the status and function of Foe's guild-master's robes, and of Susan's attempts to teach him a new tune on the flute, comes closer to producing the effects of mimicry, or repetition. Referring to Gilles Deleuze's *Logique du Sens*, J Hillis Miller identifies two forms of repetition, which correspond to this distinction between re-presentation and repetition:

> What Deleuze calls 'Platonic' repetition is grounded in a solid archetypal model which is untouched by the effects of repetition. All the other examples are copies of this model. The assumption of such a world gives rise to the notion of metaphoric expression based on genuine participative similarity or even on identity . . .
>
> The other, Nietzschean mode of repetition posits

> a world based on difference. Each thing, this other theory would assume, is unique, intrinsically different from every other thing. Similarity arises against the background of this 'disparité du fond.' It is not a world of copies but of what Deleuze calls 'simulacra' or phantasms.' (*Fiction and Repetition*, p. 6)

Both the Nietzschean mode of repetition and the concept of mimicry refuse the possibility of an originating presence; what they produce is merely an infinite succession of displacements, not copies but simulacra. This introduces the first point of contact between the concept of mimicry and a certain construction of postmodernity, most notably that of Jean Baudrillard. Baudrillard defines postmodernity precisely in terms of repetition, of the simulacrum:

> Abstraction today is no longer that of the map, the double, the mirror or the concept. Simulation is no longer that of a territory, a referential being or a substance. It is the generation by models of a real without origin or reality: a hyperreal. The territory no longer precedes the map, nor survives it. Henceforth, it is the map that precedes the territory – PRECESSION OF SIMULACRA – it is the map that engenders the territory . . . (p. 2)

Without an original, there are only copies of copies. In these terms, the postmodern subject experiences the same sense of pre-fabricated identity as that articulated in feminist and postcolonial discourse. And this experience of identity, or lack of identity, approximates Lacan's description of the way in which the subject

> becomes[s] engaged in an ever-growing dispossession of that being of his, concerning which – by dint of sincere portraits which leave its idea no less incoherent, of rectifications that do not succeed in freeing its essence, of stays and defences that do not prevent his statue from tottering, of narcissistic

> embraces that become like a puff of air in animating it – he ends up by recognizing that this being has never been anything more than his construct in the imaginary and that this construct disappoints all his certitudes? For in this labour which he undertakes to reconstruct *for another*, he rediscovers the fundamental alienation that made him construct it *like* another, and which has always destined it to be taken from him *by another*. (*Ecrits*, p. 42; see also my Chapter One, p. 132)

Like mimicry, and like the Lacanian description of the process of subject constitution, Baudrillard's notion of simulation is

> opposed to representation. The latter starts from the principle that the sign and the real are equivalent (even if this equivalence is utopian, it is a fundamental axiom). Conversely, simulation starts from the *utopia* of this principle of equivalence, *from the radical negation of the sign as value*, from the sign as reversion and death sentence of every reference. Whereas representation tries to absorb simulation by interpreting it as false representation, simulation envelops the whole edifice of representation as itself a simulacrum. (p. 11)

Using the example of feigned and simulated illness, Baudrillard describes the effects of simulation:

> 'Someone who feigns an illness can simply go to bed and make believe he is ill. Someone who simulates an illness produces in himself some of the symptoms.' (Littre) Thus, feigning or dissimulating leaves the reality principle intact: the difference is always clear, it is only masked; whereas simulation threatens the difference between 'true' and 'false', between 'real' and 'imaginary'. Since the simulator produces 'true' symptoms, is he ill or not? (p. 5)

And this introduces the second point of contact between mimicry and postmodern writing strategies: the simulator and the mimic necessarily participate in the system whose terms they displace, as does the deconstructive critic, inhabiting the structures of prior discourses, operating from the inside. Operating from within involves a recognition that there can be no critical distance, which brings us back to Jameson, who, in commenting on the difference between parody and pastiche, also produces the opposition repetition/representation:

> Pastiche is, like parody, the imitation of a peculiar mask, speech in a dead language: but it is a neutral practice of such mimicry, without any of parody's ulterior motives, amputated of the satiric impulse, devoid of laughter and of any conviction that alongside the abnormal tongue you have momentarily borrowed, some healthy linguistic normality still exists. Pastiche is thus blank parody, a statue with blind eyeballs: it is to parody what that other interesting and historically original modern thing, the practice of a kind of blank irony, is to what Wayne Booth calls the 'stable ironies' of the 18th century. ('Postmodernism, or the Cultural Logic of Late Capitalism', p. 65)

Mimicry, repetition, simulation, pastiche, blank irony – in implying the equivalence of these things I can be accused of participating in the processes of postmodernity, which reduce difference to sameness. However, the orchestration of these overlapping constructions of repetition and representation allows me to point to the ways in which feminist, post colonial and postmodern discourses are, as I suggested earlier, articulated around the *crisis* of representation. At the same time, it provides the means of linking the strategies of these discourses to the strategies both exposed and practised in Coetzee's novels. Via this route, from mimicry to irony, we have come almost full circle to my description, in Chapter One, of Coetzee's novels as 'allegories of irony' (see pp. 43–

44). Allegory, too, can be added to our list of overlapping strategies. According to Owens, who analyzes what he calls 'the allegorical impulse' in postmodernism, allegory, like mimicry and simulation, does not recognize an originating presence, and participates in the order it denounces. Thus he says:

> Allegorical imagery is appropriated imagery; the allegorist does not invent images but confiscates them. He lays claim to the culturally significant, poses as its interpreter. And in his hands the image becomes something other (*allos* - other - *agoreuei* - to speak). He does not restore an original meaning that may have been lost or obscured; allegory is not hermeneutics. Rather, he adds another meaning to the image. If he adds, however, he does so only to replace: the allegorical meaning supplants an antecedent one; it is a supplement. ('The Allegorical Impulse', 1, p. 69)

And, referring to Cindy Sherman's film stills, which mimic images of women projected by the media, he points out that

> if mimicry is denounced in these images, it is nevertheless through mimetic strategies that this denunciation is made. We thus encounter once again the unavoidable necessity of participating in the very activity that is being denounced *precisely in order to denounce it*. ('The Allegorical Impulse', 2, p. 79)

Interestingly, since I set out at the beginning of this chapter by referring to the strategy of palimpsestic writing, Owens argues that 'In allegorical structure . . . one text is *read through* another, however fragmentary, intermittent, or chaotic their relationship may be; the paradigm for the allegorical work is thus the palimpsest' ('The Allegorical Impulse', 1, p. 69). Owens is, of course, talking about post-modern allegories, which take as their starting point, not some eternal truth, in the manner of *The Divine Comedy* or

The Pilgrim's Progress, but other texts or images. However, even the allegory as palimpsest, or as 'appropriative' mode, risks assuming proprietorship, and so positing its own 'truth' in relation to the work it allegorizes. Coetzee's novels avoid this risk by being, as it were, double-sided allegories, simultaneously producing allegorical readings of prior texts and self-deconstructive allegories of the process of their own writing and future readings. In Chapter One, having suggested the connection between psychoanalytic repetition and de Man's interpretation of irony, I argue that 'Allegory allows for narrative continuity between the separate moments of consciousness and provides a temporary resting place for the repetitive movement of irony', and that 'In Coetzee's novels, this resting place may be located between their allegorical readings of the texts of the tradition, and the allegorical writing of their own evocation of the response of the Other in a future of potential readings' (p. 43). If the palimpsest is to be allegorical in this sense, it must imply an awareness that it will in turn be effaced by another writing, that it participates in the inevitable displacements of supplementarity.

The final section of *Foe*, like the final section of *Life & Times of Michael K*, provides some provisional supplements, or, as it were, figures of supplementarity, as an unnamed narrator recounts the discovery of the bodies of Susan Barton, Foe and Friday. In Section Three, Foe argues that to penetrate to the heart, or eye(I), of Susan's story they must make Friday's silence speak, to which Susan replies

> 'But who will do it? . . . It is easy enough to lie in bed and say what must be done, but who will dive into the wreck? On the island I told Cruso it should be Friday, with a rope about his middle for safety. But if Friday cannot tell us what he sees, is Friday in my story any more than a figuring (or pre-figuring) of another diver?' (*Foe*, p. 142)

In the final section the narrator makes this descent into the wreck of the slave ship. Metaphor and imagery invoke Adrienne Rich's exploratory feminist writing, particularly the poem, 'Diving into the Wreck', and the article, 'When We Dead Awaken: Writing as Re-Vision', in which she says:

> For writers, and at this moment for women writers in particular, there is the challenge and promise of a whole new psychic geography to be explored. But there is also a difficult and dangerous walking on the ice, as we try to find language and images for a consciousness we are just coming into, and with little in the past to support us. (p. 91)

Taking into account the way in which the unconscious 'is not only that which must be read, but also, and primarily, that which reads',[34] this diving, as a metaphor of the descent into the underwater world of the unconscious, reveals only further scenes of sexual differentiation, scenes of the Oedipal triangle, in which the daughter waits outside the parents' door. The unconscious is structured like a language,[35] what we find there is not, as Rich's poem suggests, an androgynous being prior to differentiation, not some instinctual self, but merely ideational representatives of the same old situation:[36] father, mother, daughter. Hence the repetition that occurs in the final section (the opening line of which repeats the opening of Section Three: 'The staircase is dark and mean'), as the narrator describes three successive scenes of discovery, each of which figures the girl, Susan Barton, Foe, and Friday, and each of which represents the attempt to penetrate to a deeper level of the unconscious. If it is bodies that are found here, these bodies are not essential anatomical presences; we may be beneath the level of language as words, but we are still in the realm of signs:

> But this is not a place of words. Each syllable, as it comes out, is caught and filled with water and diffused. This is a place where bodies are their own signs. It is the home of Friday. (*Foe*, p. 157)

In the first scene of discovery, Foe and Susan Barton 'lie side by side in bed, not touching' (*Foe*, p. 153); in the second

'The couple in the bed lie face to face, her head in the crook of his arm' (*Foe*, p. 155). The face to face position of these bed partners suggests that each sex confronts and so displaces the other from a position of fixed identity and of mastery. These scenes of discovery thus figure a form of repetition, of the retroactive re-creation of the anticipatory effects of sexual history (see my Chapter One, p. 31), as the descent into an unconscious past produces images of a utopian future. They suggest a utopian vision of sexuality such as that described by Derrida in response to his own question: 'What if we were to approach . . . the area of a relationship to the other where the code of sexual marks would no longer be discriminating?':

> The relationship would not be a-sexual, far from it, but would be sexual otherwise: beyond the binary difference that governs the decorum of all codes, beyond the opposition feminine/masculine, beyond homosexuality and heterosexuality which come to the same thing. As I dream of saving the chance that this question offers, I would like to believe in the masses, this indeterminable number of blended voices, this mobile of non-identified sexual marks whose choreography can carry, divide, multiply the body of each 'individual', whether he be classified as 'man' or 'woman' according to the criteria of usage. ('Choreographies', p. 76)[37]

And the face to face position of Susan Barton and Foe functions as a metaphor of a kind of writing which approximates Kristeva's description of the literary avant-garde:

> . . . in a culture where the speaking subjects are conceived of as masters of their speech, they have what is called a 'phallic' position. The fragmentation of language in a text calls into question the very posture of this mastery. The [literary avant-garde] confronts this phallic position either to tranverse it or to deny it. The word 'traverse' implies that the subject experiences sexual difference, not as a fixed

> opposition ('man'/'woman'), but as a process of differentiation. The word 'deny' means that the subject constitutes a fetishistic shelter in order to avoid castration. Only the true great 'literary' achievements bear witness to a traversal, and therefore, to sexual differentiation. In this way, the subject of the writing speaks a *truth* proper to any speaking subject, a truth that the needs of production and reproduction censure. All speaking subjects have within themselves a certain bisexuality which is precisely the possibility to explore all the sources of signification, that which posits a meaning as well as that which multiplies, pulverizes, and finally revives it. ('Oscillation between Power and Denial', p. 165)

I have traced the path of a writing which 'denies' sexual differentiation, a writing in which men have used the figure of 'woman' and women have used the figure of the racially Other as a fetishistic shelter in order to avoid castration. Concluding my re-writing, as a woman, of *Coetzee's* re-writing of *women's* re-writing of *men's* writing of women, I wish to suggest that the final scene of this novel takes us *beyond* the elimination of bi-polar sexuality, toward an 'area of relationship to the other where the code of *racial* marks would no longer be discriminating'. In the closing scene, the unnamed, unsexed narrator lies face to face with Friday, replicating the face to face position of Susan and Foe, and offering a preview of a future in which a non-dialectical, manichean opposition between self and Other is replaced by a process of mutual differentiation. As Bhabha points out in his Foreword to Fanon:

> The place of the Other must not be imaged as Fanon sometimes suggests as a fixed phenomenological point, opposed to the self, that represents a culturally alien consciousness. The Other must be seen as the necessary negation of a primordial identity – cultural or psychic – that introduces the system of differentiation which enables the 'cultural' to be signified as

> a linguistic, symbolic, historic reality. If . . . the subject of desire is never simply a Myself, then the Other is never simply an *It-self*, a font of identity, truth, or misrecognition . . . . In the language of psychoanalysis, the Law of the Father or the paternal metaphor, again, cannot be taken at its word. It is a process of substitution and exchange that inscribes a normative, normalizing place for the subject; but that metaphoric access to identity is exactly the place of prohibition and repression, precisely a conflict of authority. (pp. xviii-xix)

A section of Foe's argument in Section Three is couched in similar terms. He says to Susan Barton:

> 'Let us confront our worst fear, which is that we have all of us been called into the world from a different order (which we have now forgotten) by a conjurer unknown to us . . . . Then I ask nevertheless: Have we thereby lost our freedom? Are you, for one, any less mistress of your life? Do we of necessity become puppets in a story whose end if invisible to us, and towards which we are marched like condemned felons? You and I know, in our different ways, how rambling an occupation writing is; and conjuring is surely much the same . . . . Have we cause to believe that the lives it is given us to live proceed with any more design than these whimsical adventures?' (*Foe*, p. 135)

In other words, if we are circumscribed by the Other, if there is no access to a position outside the Other, no possibility of radical Otherness, there is nevertheless the consolation that the system is not purposeful or planned, that the Other is not a font of identity or truth. It is thus susceptible to transgression, is indeed constituted by these transgressions (see my Chapter Two, p. 146, note 39). In Bhabha's words, the metaphoric access to identity is precisely a *conflict* of authority.

In Section Three, Foe proposes either of two attitudes toward writing, or authorship, both of which refer to writing's relationship to death. Illustrating the first, he tells of a condemned woman, who forestalls the moment of execution by means of a potentially infinite series of confessions;[38] illustrating the second, he tells of a woman who is content to die only once her daughter has been taken care of, claiming that all her executioners have left in her is the husk a butterfly leaves behind when it is born. To these examples Foe appends the comment: 'There are more ways than one of living eternally' (*Foe*, p. 125). Now these fables correspond to the examples given by Foucault in the paper 'What is an Author?' Foucault refers to the 'tradition exemplified by the Greek epic, which was intended to perpetuate the immortality of the hero: if he was willing to die young, it was so that his life, consecrated and magnified by death, might pass into immortality; the narrative then redeemed this accepted death' (p. 102). Alternatively, narrative becomes the means of eluding death, as in *The Thousand and One Nights*, in which 'one spoke, telling stories early into the morning, in order to forestall death, to postpone the day of reckoning that would silence the narrator' (Ibid.). Foucault goes on to point out that

> Our culture has metamorphosed this idea of narrative, or writing, as something designed to ward off death . . . . The work, which once had the duty of providing immortality, now possesses the right to kill, to be its author's murderer, as in the cases of Flaubert, Proust, and Kafka. That is not all, however: this relationship between writing and death is also manifested in the effacement of the writing subject's individual characteristics. Using all the contrivances that he sets up between himself and what he writes, the writing subject cancels out the signs of his particular individuality. As a result, the mark of the writer is reduced to nothing more than the singularity of absence; he must assume the role of dead man in the game of writing. (pp. 102–3)

This approximates the position of the Lacanian subject, confronted with the alienation of the self in the signifier, the death-in-life that is produced in discourse. However, as I have argued in Chapter One, the Lacanian death instinct describes a two-way process, involving both the recognition of this necessary death and its negation. Thus Lacan points out that

> the reader should recognize in the metaphor of the return to the inanimate (which Freud attaches to every living body) that margin beyond life that language gives to the human being by virtue of the fact that he speaks, and which is precisely that in which such a being places in the position of a signifier, not only those parts of his body that are exchangeable, but this body itself. (*Ecrits*, p. 301)

The margin beyond the death-in-life discourse is offered by the possibility of a retreat into the life-in-death of non-speech. Thus we have a dialectic of self-destruction and self-invention, which is precisely the movement that Coetzee's novel, via the figures of Susan Barton and Friday, once again traces.

Rejecting Foe's parables, Susan Barton resists a view of authorship as a means of redeeming or forestalling death, and insists, instead, upon her capacity to beget her own story, to bring herself into life. The final section of the novel evokes an altogether different notion of authorship, one which anticipates the *disappearance* of the author function, as does Foucault at the conclusion of his paper:

> All discourses, whatever their status, form, value, and whatever the treatment to which they would be subjected, would then develop in the anonymity of a murmur. We would no longer hear the questions that have been rehashed for so long: Who really spoke? Is it really he and not someone else? With what authenticity or originality? And what part of his deepest self did he express in his discourse? Instead, there would be other questions, like these: What are the modes of existence of this discourse? Where has it been used, how can it

> circulate, and who can appropriate it for himself? What are the places in it where there is room for possible subjects? Who can assume these various subject functions? (p. 119–20)

The final image is of Friday:

> This is a place where bodies are their own signs. It is the home of Friday.
>
> He turns and turns till he lies at full length, his face to my face. The skin is tight across his bones, his lips are drawn back. I pass a fingernail across his teeth, trying to find a way in.
>
> His mouth opens. From inside him comes a slow stream, without breath, without interruption. It flows up through his body and out upon me; it passes through the cabin, through the wreck; washing the cliffs and shores of the island, it runs northward and southward to the ends of the earth. Soft and cold, dark and unending, it beats against my eyelids, against the skin of my face. (*Foe*, p. 157)

This soft, unending stream beating against the narrator's face suggests the possibility of a relationship in which each of the subjects would be able to perceive the self through the gaze, or the speech, of the Other, recognizing the self to be simply an Other amongst Others. In this way the conclusion points us forward to a time when the slow stream might become an anonymous murmur, to a time when the insistence upon difference and the claim to authority might no longer be a politically necessary strategy, and when it might be possible, like Foucault, to ask: What difference does it make who is speaking?'

NOTES

1. In their paper, 'Colonialism, Racism and Representation', *Screen* 24, 2 (Mar–Apr 1983), Robert Stam and Louis Spence claim that 'Daniel Defoe glorified colonialism in *Robinson Crusoe*', and refer to several film revisions of Defoe's novel:

   > 'Bunuel's film version of the novel mocks Defoe's protagonist by haunting him with surrealist dreams, turning him into a transvestite, and making it singularly difficult for him to make rational sense out of the tenets of Christianity to an inquisitive Friday. The film *Man Friday* . . . reportedly tells the story from Friday's point of view. And in a recent Brazilian adaptation of the novel, black actor Grande Otelo subverts Defoe's classic by playing a Friday who refuses the coloniser's power to name, repeatedly telling the Englishman: '*Me* Crusoe, *You* Friday!' (p. 5)

   Gérard Genette, in his *Palimpsestes: La littérature au second degré* (Paris: Editions du Seuil, 1982), refers to the following revisions of *Robinson Crusoe*: Michel Tournier's *Vendredi ou les limbes du Pacifique* (1972); Jules Verne's *l'Ile Mystérieuse* (1874); Wyss's *Robinson suisse* (1813); Campe's *Robinson allemand* (1779); Jean Giraudoux's *Suzanne et le Pacifique* (1921); Catherine Woillez' *Robinson des demoiselles* (1835). Interestingly, the latter two have women Crusoes. According to Genette, *Robinson des demoiselles* involves 'une simple transposition au féminin due thème robinsonnien' (p. 345), while in *Suzanne*:

   > 'La leçon de ce Robinson femelle, ce n'est pas exactement, comme disait Baudelaire, que 'le femme est naturelle', mais plutôt – Suzanne n'est guère que le développement et l'illustration de ce paradoxe typique – que la nature est femme, et, comme telle, spontanément portée au luxe, et a l'artifice.' (p. 350)

   Genette concludes that the character Suzanne, insofar as she is a woman, is an anti-Robinson, but that in textual terms *Suzanne et le Pacifique* does not constitute an anti-*Robinson Crusoe*, that is to say, it does not finally subvert the values of Defoe's novel.
2. Alan Sheridan in note 56 to Lacan's 'Function and field of speech and language', *Ecrits* (p. 109), defines a palimpsest as 'a piece of parchment or other writing material from which the writing has been erased to make way for a new text'.
3. Such as the reading of Tournier's novel given by Margaret Sankey

in her paper, 'Meaning through Intertextuality: Isomorphism of Defoe's *Robinson Crusoe* and Tournier's *Vendredi ou les limbes du Pacifique*'.

4. What I have found to be some of the most valuable theoretical perspectives on postmodernism and postcolonialism have been produced by Simon During. In his paper, 'Post-modernism or post-colonialism today', he argues that 'it is just as rewarding to construe literary postmodernism as an enemy of postmodernity as to consider it as its expression and help meet', and that 'if there is something that may be called postmodern thought, it too works in ways that cannot be regarded as a mere expression of an underlying postmodernity' (p. 32).
5. Coetzee uses the spelling Cruso, which spelling will indicate here that the figure in *Foe* is being referred to, as opposed to Defoe's Crusoe.
6. Offering a critique of Gilbert and Gubar's notion of 'true female literary authority', Toril Moi draws attention to the way in which this notion is complicitous with the patriarchal ideology it purports to challenge: their book, she points out, 'never once questions the authority of the *female* author', a necessary step, for

   'if we are truly to reject the model of the author as God the Father of the text, it is surely not enough to reject the patriarchal ideology implied in the paternal metaphor. It is equally necessary to reject the *critical practice* it leads to, a critical practice that relies on the author as the transcendental signified of his or her text. For the patriarchal critic, the author is the source, origin and meaning of the text. It we are to undo this patriarchal practice of *authority*, we must take one further step and proclaim with Roland Barthes the death of the author.'
7. For this notion of the recipient function, I am indebted to Gayatri Chakravorty Spivak, who articulates this in relation to Mary Shelley's *Frankenstein*, which takes the form of letters addressed to the narrator's sister, Mary Saville. Spivak says:

   'Here the reader must read with Margaret Saville in the crucial sense that she must *intercept* the recipient-function, read the letters *as* recipient, in order for the novel to exist.'

   'Three Women's Texts and a Critique of Imperialism', p. 259.
8. Foe tells Susan Barton a story about a condemned woman who despairs because she can find no one to take charge of her infant daughter. When the gaoler and his wife agree to adopt the child she is content to die, saying: 'Now you may do with me as you

wish. For I have escaped your prison; all you have here is the husk of me', intending, as Foe explains, 'the husk that the butterfly leaves behind when it is born'. (*Foe*, p. 125)

9. Compare this with the images of Frankenstein's monster; images which both introduce him into the narrative and mark his exit at the conclusion of the narrative:

   'We perceived a low carriage, fixed on a sledge and drawn by dogs, pass on towards the north, at the distance of half a mile; a being which had the shape of a man, but apparently of gigantic stature, sat in the sledge and guided the dogs. We watched the rapid progress of the traveller with our telescopes until he was lost among the distant inequalities of the ice.'

   'He sprang from the cabin window as he said this, upon the ice raft which lay close to the vessel. He was soon borne away by the waves and lost in darkness and distance.'

10. A reading proposed by Spivak in her 'Three Women's Texts and a Critique of Imperialism': 'Frankenstein's apparent antagonist is God himself as Maker of Man, but his real competitor is also woman as the maker of children' (p. 255).

11. Elizabeth Fox-Genovese describes the functioning of the ideology of separate spheres as follows:

   'The concept of separate spheres has deep roots in the gender differentiation at the core of all world-views and social formations. Bourgeois society cannot, in this respect, be credited with inventing separate spheres, but it can be credited with promoting and generalizing the ideology of separate spheres as the custodian of displaced notions of hierarchy. It thus disembedded – to borrow, by analogy, from Karl Polanyi's discussion of the capitalist market – gender difference. Where traditionally this difference had figured in all explanations of the world as it is, the very fact of difference became an ideological justification for collective male and class dominance in a society that claimed to draw its identity from the freedom of individuals.' (p. 24)

12. Toril Moi criticizes Gilbert and Gubar's feminist aesthetics on the basis of their emphasis on the wholeness of the text and of the self:

   'Parallel to the wholeness of the text is the wholeness of the woman's self; the integrated humanist individual is the essence of all creativity. A fragmented conception of self or consciousness would seem to Gilbert and Gubar the same as a sick or dis-eased self. The good text is an organic whole, in spite of the sophisticated apparatus the authors of *The Madwoman in the Attic* bring to bear on the works they study.

But this emphasis on integrity and totality as an ideal for women's writing can be criticised precisely as a patriarchal or – more accurately – a phallic construct.' (p. 66)

13. Thus, for example, Harriett Gilbert says:

'The madness of Boer-style colonialism is certainly part of *Foe's* subject: besides his obvious position as master, Coetzee's Crusoe, unlike the original, refuses to rescue from the wreck of his ship any of those tools that might make his island more civilised; his energies are spent constructing terraces which, to Susan's baffled distress, obscure the natural beauty of the island and on which, besides, there is nothing to plant; and Crusoe desires neither rescue nor escape from this sterility, dying of something like a broken heart when the ship that eventually *does* turn up is three days away from Bristol.'

Harriett Gilbert, 'Island Stories,' rev. of *Foe* by J.M. Coetzee, in *The New Statesman*, 12 September 1986. Sandra Tatts argues:

Coetzee's altering of the original Crusoe story is a device, therefore I believe that this novel is again Coetzee's comment on South Africa and its people. Cruso's structure and control of his island is not unlike the rigorous example of the early South African settlers: tame the land, tame the black people, prepare a seedbed for posterity; building walls to enable a fortress mentality, monuments to the generations that follow. It is an isolationist mentality expressing suspicion and fear of intruders and rescuers, that is, foreigners. There is a need to resist and withstand change, poor communcation and a lot of misunderstanding. The physical description of the island is evocative of South Africa: flat table top rocky mountains, strong winds, semi-Karroo scrub.'

Sandra Tatts, rev. of *Foe* by J.M. Coetzee, on Jill Kitson's First Edition: Writing from a land apart, South Africa, ABC Radio, 20 November, 1986.

And André Brink says:

'Die eiland is bar; Cruso bestee sy tyd daaraan om eindelose klipterrasse te pak wat geen aardse doel dien nie – tensy daar ééndag iemand sou opdaag met saad wat in die droë beddings gesaai kan word. Cruso wil ook nie gered word nie: hy is volkome genoegsaam in sy botte heersersbestaan saam met sy slaaf (en naderhand met die vrou).

(Die parallele van hierdie skrikwekkende vereenvoudigde bestaan met 'n steriele politieke situasie soos dié in Suid Afrika, sal die leser wel nie ontgaan nie!)'

[The island is barren; Cruso spends his time constructing endless stone terraces which have no earthly use – unless one day someone should arrive with seed which could be planted in the dry beds. And Cruso does not want to be rescued: he is quite content with his dull ruler's existence, with his slave (and later with the woman).

(The parallels of this terrifyingly lonely existence with a sterile political situation such as that in South Africa will not escape the reader!)]

André Brink, 'J.M. Coetzee – roman steek effe af by voriges', rev. of J.M. Coetzee's *Foe* in *Rapport* (my translation).

14. Simon During points out that 'like Jameson, Lyotard sees post-colonial nationalism as not just archaic but dangerous. Post-colonial nationalism articulates itself in the 'narrative-mythic' which constructs an immutable cultural origin . . . and it projects a 'home' in which difference is suspended; its greatest modern exemplar is Nazism' ('Postmodernism or Post-colonialism Today,' P. 41).

15. During citing Jacques Derrida, 'Racism's Last Word,' trans. Peggy Kamuf, *Critical Inquiry*, 12 (Autumn 1985), 291–2. See also my Chapter Two, pp. 000, in which I cite Derrida on language and autoaffection.

16. Ann Rosalind Jones describes *l'écriture féminine* as 'a utopian ideal, an energizing myth rather than a model for how all women write or should write'. 'Writing the body: toward an understanding of *l'écriture féminine*', p. 96. And, in the same vein, Elaine Showalter says:

 'The concept of *écriture féminine*, the inscription of the female body and female difference in language and text, is a significant theoretical formulation in French feminist criticism, although it describes a Utopian possibility rather than a literary practice.'

 Elaine Showalter, 'Feminist Criticism in the Wilderness,' p. 185.

17. They say:

 'Literally, women like Dickinson, Brontë, and Rossetti were imprisoned in their homes, their father's houses; indeed, almost all nineteenth-century women were in some sense imprisoned in men's houses. Figuratively, such women were . . . locked into male texts, texts from which they could escape only through ingenuity and indirection. It is not surprising, then, that spatial imagery of enclosure and escape, elaborated with what frequently becomes obsessive intensity, characterizes much of their writing.' (*The Madwoman in the Attic*, p. 83)

18. In her introduction to *Cloud Nine* Caryl Churchill says:

    'When I came to write the play, I returned to an idea that had been touched on briefly in the workshop – the parallel between colonial and sexual oppression, which Genet calls 'the colonial or feminine mentality of interiorised repression'. So the first act of *Cloud Nine* takes place in Victorian Africa, where Clive, the white man, imposes his ideals on his family and the natives.'(p. 245).

    Having served Churchill's purpose in Act One, Joshua, the black man, is effectively marginalized, for he does not appear again in the play – the play ends in London in 1979, 'in the changing sexuality of our own time' (p. 246).

19. 'The entire instinct with its own 'source,' 'impetus,' 'aim,' and 'object,' . . . the instinct, kit and caboodle with its four factors, is in turn the source of a process which mimics, displaces, and denatures it: the drive.'

    Jean Laplanche, *Life and Death in Psychoanalysis*, p. 22; see my Chapter Three, p. 164.

20. Rose offers this as an explanation of Lacan's much debated statement: 'The woman does not exist'. She says: 'It means, not that women do not exist, but that her status as an absolute category and guarantor of fantasy (exactly *The* woman) is false'. (p. 48). I have, accordingly, used the plural, *women*, or *men* and the epithet *women's*, or *men's*, throughout this chapter. I have also avoided using the epithets *male* and *female*, because these imply a purely biological distinction. Toril Moi criticizes Gilbert and Gubar for their use of the epithet *female*, saying:

    'It has long been an established practice among most feminists to use 'feminine' (and 'masculine') to represent *social constructs* (patterns of sexuality and behaviour imposed by cultural and social norms), and to reserve 'female' and 'male' for the purely biological aspects of sexual difference. Thus 'feminine' represents nurture and 'female' nature in this usage. 'Femininity' is a cultural construct: one isn't born a woman, one becomes one, as Simone de Beauvoir puts it. Seen in this perspective, patriarchal oppression consists of imposing certain social standards of femininity on all biological women, in order precisely to make us believe that the chosen standards for 'femininity' are *natural.* Thus a woman who refuses to conform can be labelled both *unfeminine* and *unnatural.* It is in the patriarchal interest that these two terms (femininity and femaleness) stay thoroughly confused. Feminists, on the contrary, have to disentangle this confusion, and must therefore always insist that though women undoubtedly are *female*, this in no way guarantees that they will be *feminine*. This is equally true whether one defines femininity in the old patriarchal ways or in a new feminist way.' (p. 65)

I have avoided using the epithet *feminine* precisely in order to avoid the confusion between the old patriarchal and the new feminist usages of the term.

21. It is interesting that Tournier, too, uses the figure of Friday to represent what cannot be represented. Although his title, *Vendredi, ou les limbes du Pacifique*, would appear to make Friday central to this narrative, in the end Friday is effectively marginalized, having served the purpose of educating Crusoe into ways of being which are radically different to those of Western civilization. Friday leaves the island on a ship which calls there, and which conveniently provides Crusoe with a substitute for Friday in the form of a white-skinned, red-headed cabin boy, a narcissistic image of Crusoe himself. And as Gérard Genette points out:

> ' . . . dans ce livre intitulé *Vendredi*, la narration reste pour l'essentiel . . . focalisée sur Robinson. Cette apologie du bon sauvage est bien faite, comme toujours, par le civilisé, et l'auteur même ne s'y identifie nullement à Vendredi, mais bien à Robinson: un Robinson fasciné et finalement converti par Vendredi, mais qui demeure le foyer – je dirais volontiers le *maitre* du récit, et d'un récit qui raconte son histoire, non celle de Vendredi . . . Le véritable *Vendredi*, où Robinson serait vu, décrit et jugé par Vendredi, reste à écrire. Mais ce *Vendredi* – là, aucun Robinson – fût-il le mieux disposé – ne peut l'écrire.' (*Palimpsestes*, p. 424)

22. According to Freud, the fetish

> 'is not a substitute for any chance penis, but for a particular quite special penis that had been extremely important in early childhood but was afterwards lost. That is to say: it should normally have been given up, but the purpose of the fetish

precisely is to preserve it from being lost. To put it plainly: the fetish is a substitute for the woman's (mother's) phallus which the little boy once believed in and does not wish to forego – we know why.

....

In very subtle cases the fetish itself has become the vehicle both of denying and of asseverating the fact of castration.'

Sigmund Freud, *Fetishism*, in *The Standard Edition of the Complete Psychological Works of Sigmund Freud*, trans. James Strachey (London: Hogarth Press, 1957), V, pp. 199 and 203.

23. Discussing John Barrow's portrait of Bushmen, and comparing it with a passage from John Mandeville's *Travels* (circa 1350), Mary Louise Pratt says:

> 'The only trace of a face-to-face encounter, real or imagined, in this description is the fact that it begins with the body as seen/scene. Such portraits conventionally do so, commonly with the genitals as the crucial site/sight in the 'bodyscape' – as they are in Barrow's Bushmen portrait, where he devotes two full pages to the supposed genital peculiarities of Bushmen men and women.'

Mary Louise Pratt, 'Scratches on the Face of the Country; or, What Mr. Barrow saw in the Land of the Bushmen', *Critical Inquiry*, 12 (Autumn 1985), 120.

24. Neal Oxenhandler elaborates upon Lacan's metaphor of the unveiling ceremony in his paper 'The Horizons of Psycho-criticism'.

25. Homi Bhabha analyzes in similar terms the process by which 'forms of racial/cultural/historical otherness have been marginalised in theoretical texts committed to the articulation of *différance*, *signifiance*, in order, it is claimed, to reveal the limits of Western metaphysical discourse.' He concludes his discussion of this process by saying that:

> 'The place of otherness is fixed in the West as a subversion of Western metaphysics and is finally appropriated by the West as its limit-text, the Anti-West. This results in a disciplinary gaze upon difference that disavows the castrating and negating return of the look of the Other.' ('Difference, Discrimination and the Discourse of Colonialism,' pp. 194–5)

26. See my Chapter Five, p. 308 for a discussion of the use of pronouns in *Life & Times of Michael K* with reference to Benveniste's analysis of 'third person' pronouns.

27. Virginia Woolf, 'Speech, Manuscript Notes', *The Pargiters*, ed. Mitchell A. Leaska (London, 1978), cited by Showalter in 'Fem-

inist Criticism in the Wilderness', p. 193.

28. Coetzee, citing Monique Wittig, *The Guérillères*, trans. D. Le Vay (London: Pan, 1972), p. 23, in note 13, p. 296 of his 'Achterberg's "Ballade van de gasfitter" '. Coetzee adds: 'The O, the circle, the hole are symbols of that which male authoritarian language cannot appropriate.'

29. ' "And why should you be, as you put it, haunting me, Susan?' 'For your blood. Is that not why ghosts return: to drink the blood of the living?' . . .

    Instead of answering, Foe kissed me again, and in kissing gave such a sharp bite to my lip that I cried out and drew away. But he held me close and I felt him suck the wound. 'This is my manner of preying on the living," he murmured.' (*Foe*, p. 139)

30. *The Madwoman in the Attic*, p. 3. Gilbert and Gubar are quoting from *The Correspondence of Gerard Manley Hopkins and Richard Watson Dixon*, ed. C.C. Abbott (London: Oxford Univ. Press, 1935), p. 133.

31. *The Madwoman in the Attic*, pp. 46–47. Gilbert and Gubar are referring to Harold Bloom's *The Anxiety of Influence* (New York: Oxford University Press, 1973).

32. Toril Moi, p. 139, citing and translating Luce Irigaray, *Ce sexe qui n'est pas un* (Paris: Minuit, 1977), p. 75–6.

33. Moi criticizes Irigaray's *practice* in relation to her *theory* of mimicry, pointing out that when she offers a positive alternative to patriarchal constructions, 'The mimicry fails because it ceases to be perceived as such: it is no longer merely a mockery of the absurdities of the male, but a perfect reproduction of the logic of the Same'. (p. 142). Moi goes on to say that what Irigaray 'seems not to see is that sometimes a woman imitating male discourse *is* just a woman speaking like a man: Margaret Thatcher is a case in point. It is the *political context* of such mimicry that is surely always decisive' (p. 143).

34. Shoshana Felman, in 'Turning the Screw of Interpretation', makes the point that:

    'For Lacan, indeed, the unconscious is not only *that which must be read*, but also, and primarily, *that which reads*. Freud's discovery of the unconscious is the outcome of his *reading* of the hysterical discourse of his patients, i.e., of his being capable of reading in this hysterical discourse *his own unconscious*. The discovery of the unconscious is therefore Freud's discovery, within the discourse of the other, of what was actively reading within himself: his discovery, in other words, or his reading, of what was reading – in what was being read. The gist of Freud's discovery, for Lacan, thus consists not simply of the revelation of a new *meaning* – the unconscious – but of the *discovery of a new way of reading*.' (p. 118)

35. Lacan says that 'what the psychoanalytic experience discovers in the unconscious is the whole structure of language', and goes on to argue that 'the notion that the unconscious is merely the seat of the instincts will have to be rethought' (*Ecrits*, p. 147).

36. According to Freud:

    'We have reason to assume that there is a *primal repression*, a first phase of repression, which consists in the psychical (ideational) representative of the instinct being denied entry into the unconscious. With this a fixation is established, the representative in question persists unaltered from then onwards and the instinct remains attached to it.' (*Papers on Metapsychology*, Vol. XIV of the Standard Edition of the *Complete Psychological Works*, p. 148, cited by Anika Lemaire, pp. 153–4)

37. Jacques Derrida interviewed by Christine V. McDonald, 'Choreographies', DIACRITICS, 12, 2 (1982), 76. This passage is cited by Toril Moi at the conclusion of her Sexual/Textual Politics.

38. In his paper, 'Confession and Double Thoughts: Tolstoy, Rousseau, Dostoevsky', in *Comparative Literature*, 37, 3 (Summer 1985), Coetzee makes the point that the mode of fictional confession 'is already practiced by Defoe in the made-up confessions of sinners like Moll Flanders and Roxana; by our time, confessional fictions have come to constitute a subgenre of the novel in which problems of truth-telling and self-recognition, deception and self-deception, come to the forefront' (p. 194). Tracing a certain progression in Tolstoy's *The Kreutzer Sonata* and Rousseau's *Confessions*, Coetzee says:

    'A crime is confessed (murder, theft): a cause or reason or psychological origin is proposed to explain the crime; then a rereading of the confession yields a 'truer' explanation. The question we should ask now is: What must the response of the confessant be toward these or any other 'truer' corrections of his confession? The answer, it seems to me, is that to the extent that the new, 'deeper' truth is acknowledged as true, the response of the confessant must contain an element of shame. For either the confessant was aware of the deeper truth but was concealing it, in which case he was deceiving his confessor, or he was not aware of the deeper truth (though now he acknowledges it), in which case his competence as a confessant is in question: what was being offered as his secret, the coin of his confession, was not the real secret, was false coin, and a *de facto* deception has occurred, which is fresh cause for confession.' (pp. 213–14)

Appendix One

Ballad of the Gasfitter

1

You must have made your entries from the rear.
I glance into the houses from the street:
in windowfronts, between the curtains, out
of nothing You appear and reappear.

I pass, You vanish necessarily.
But I'm proved right by the next windowpane.
One Jansen lives there with his family –
as if You could escape me in this name.

It will not help. A door remains a door,
each with its steps, its mailbox, and its bell.
The apple-hawker lures You with his call.
A master-key is easy to procure.
Indeed I can quite freely step inside
as (at your service) gasfitter by trade.

2

Indoors with You, in daylight, on the job
disguised in workman's clothing, I wheel around
and see You standing. The walls turn to ground,
the ceiling slowly becomes a marble slab.

We grow murky in the fading light.
The room is bursting, won't take any more.
This can't go on. I drive the screws in tight.
As long as I confine myself to this chore

You and I can keep our incognito –
as long as I stay busy, bend or kneel
or lie flat on my belly trying to feel
what's wrong; all the while thinking, It's better so.

Dead silence by a hammer blow dispelled.
Death hush by which the hammer blows are healed.

3

Shall I punch the gaspipes full of holes? or burst
the water-main and flood the house? I spot
the trap here, look again to the fittings, thrust
the fallacy with all haste from my thoughts.

For later in the papers one would find:
'While practising his livelihood a fitter,
for reasons we have yet to comprehend
inhaled monoxide gas and met his end.
In the adjoining room a similar bitter

fate befell the owner of the dwelling.
She lay prostrate, one hand stretched out in falling.
In it was clutched a letter which began:
"However wide the world I come again."
It seems that she was overcome while reading.
Nothing suggests adulterous proceedings.'

4

At last the tiny leak is traced and sealed.
Slowly I bring together and pack my tools.
My legs have grown as heavy as lead tubes.
The sweat is trickling down my face in beads.

As if performing a superhuman feat
I turn with an explanatory wave
of the hand, but You are gone, and nothing save
the afternoon's declining light is left.

I pick my tray of tools up from the floor
and hoist it to my shoulder. In retreat
my footsteps raise a hollow song. The door
clicks shut behind me. The hubbub of the street
seems further off. The fog settles and thickens.
It seems that this time I have been mistaken.

5

But just as I am settling down at home
to eat my dinner I hear the telephone.
I pick it up and from the other end
comes, as if nothing has changed, a new command.

My supervisor. His voice is sharp, severe,
but a veiled gentler undertone comes through.
'My son, go to the same street tomorrow.
You know the interest that I take in you.'

Only a fool repeats an old mistake.
Best not to stay at home, but go and take
a look instead at the block of flats I see
rise sheer up from the ground across the way.
There, once I find the floor directory,
all will of itself become clear to me.

6

That night, however, I got to know no more
than that the concierge was asleep. Weary,
he had loosed the numbers from his memory
and lay there crumpled, head in arms. Absorbed

I stared in through the window. A soft wind
rustled through the grass where I stood outside:
and near to me, his duties pushed aside,
a living being who could have helped me find

my way out of this mess, if it had not
become so lonely and too dark for me
to think of whispering him awake. For he
would lose his head. Which would not do at all.
My supervisor's head would also fall then
then. No one heard me leave. Did he look up?

7

At daybreak I am on the road, my face
still blurred with sleepiness. Although somewhere

the final goal has taken up its place
the streets this first hour seem as free as air.

I feel a safety I have never known.
One of my superiors cycles by.
I greet him but he barely turns an eye.
Probably quarreled with his wife again.

Perhaps he is a bit suspicious meet-
ing me in suburbs of the city where
a fitter has no business. A young and heed-
less generation has arisen here
by other forms of light. I've been observed.
Therefore toward the city my steps are turned.

8

My last chance now approaches. Rows of white
pushbuttons, like teeth in a false denture, stand
fierce in their array defying my hand.
My fingers carry on a bitter fight.

As I stand there biting my nails I hear
The door spring suddenly open, and a maid
puts out the garbage can. I'd have remained
nonplussed forever had she not appeared.

But time is short. I turn to her and ask
in haste, Where is the hole? She points above
with vague derision as if to say, You're mad.
I know – so far gone that I pray to God.
The lift goes up toward the climax of
a job no fitter has ever yet pulled off.

9

The higher I ascend, the wider space
yawns between You and me. Life seems to be
enclosed in steel and nickel. Every
last rivet of this structure is in place.

There is no gas here. God is the hole, and pours
out his depths upon me to reveal
to a presumptuous fitter how much more
exalted he becomes with every floor.

Beneath me storey after storey falls.
I don't know where I must begin, or what.
Perhaps a last word will spring to mind
if I ask him what was the first cause.
A shock runs through my frame. I must get out.
I give it over. Be it as he finds.

10

Door after door swings open and a host
of men of every nation, race, and tongue
call out in chorus, 'You don't fool anyone!'
looking at me as if I were a ghost.

Is that the reason I've crept underground?
I descend the pit of glass toward the street
with a bag of dirty washing at my feet.
Up there one can still hear them scurry around.

For a while I hang about the neighborhood.
Past noon, I see. The rush hour has arrived.
School is over. Children run and yell
or prattle stories to their mothers. Bells
tinkle. Cars bellow past as if I had stood
for years and years upon this spot unmoved.

11

The gasworks spin upon their axleshaft.
Seeing my project utterly fallen to bits –
nothing, not even room for hope, was left –
and having, like a whipped dog, to turn tail –

a vacuum must have slipped into me then.
Up there there is no trade or craft that fits.
The children take each other's hands again:
as in remembered games they spin and wheel.

I set off for the office without waiting.
My supervisor himself comes to the door.
I yield myself to mild interrogation.
I need not make up stories any more.
Behind his glasses tears obscure his eyes.
He clasps my hand, collects himself, half-smiles.

12

The leaders of the Christian union call
the gas- and water-fitters into session
to say that one of them has been transgressing
the code of regulations binding all

by showing up with tools in hand wherever
he found himself, such action causing harm
to the body as a whole; wherefore they charge
that he who broke the rule confess his error.

For the first time in the history of the trade
the gas- and water-fitters fall to their knees
without a thought for leaks beneath the floor –
at one, fraternal, and amalgamate.
Then says the chairman, Go, and sin no more,
and they depart, well satisfied, at ease.

13

Years later, hair now white, we find the fitter
moved to an old men's home. Feeble of mind
he sits and pores over a city guide
spelling the names of streets out letter by letter.

Bed and board he shares with several brothers:
a postman, a broker's runner, and a plumber.
He often gets it in the ass from others
for only coming down to meals to grumble.

Provision has been made until he dies.
Health and funeral benefits reward
one's efforts towards charity; besides
they save him from being strangled by the warden.

Public Works has given him his lodgings.
Tobacco quid is his if he has longings.

14

In the end he closed his eyes for good.
His mouth, slumped open, was tied shut again.
Measured, he was found fit to be contained
in a regulation coffin, deal, six-foot.

And all of them came – people from the flat,
Jansen, the main, the supervisor – to bear
their final joint respects. Like mine, their wear
was sober: a dark suit, with cane and hat.

Once at the graveside no one made a sound.
With critical eye each stepped up to behold
the fitter slowly sink into the ground
as if still hoping to catch him in an error
not that he had to plug his final hole.
He rests with God. The earth covers him over.

Gerrit Achterberg, 'Ballade van de gasfitter' (1953), translated by J.M. Coetzee in his paper 'Achterberg's "Ballade van de gasfitter": The Mystery of I and You.'

Appendix Two

Waiting for the Barbarians

What are we waiting for all crowded in the forum?
 The Barbarians are to arrive today.
Within the Senate-house why is there such inaction?
The Senators making no laws what are they sitting there for?
 Because the Barbarians arrive today.
 What laws now should the Senators be making?
 When the Barbarians come they'll make the laws.

Why did our Emperor get up so early in the morning?
And at the greatest city gate why is he sitting there now,
Upon his throne, officially, why is he wearing his crown?
Because the Barbarians arrive today.
The Emperor is waiting to receive
Their Leader. And in fact he has prepared
To give him an address. On it he has
Written him down all sorts of names and titles.

Why have our two Consuls gone out, both of them, and the Praetors,
Today with their red togas on, with their embroidered togas?
Why are they wearing bracelets, and all those amethysts too,
And all those rings on their fingers with splendid flashing emeralds?
Why should they be carrying today their precious walking-sticks,
With silver knobs and golden tops so wonderfully carved?
Because the Barbarians will arrive today;
Things of this sort dazzle the Barbarians.

And why are the fine orators not come here as usual
To get their speeches off, to say what they have to say?
Because the Barbarians will be here today;
And they are bored with eloquence and speechmaking.

Why should this uneasiness begin all of a sudden,
And confusion. How serious people's faces have become.
Why are all the streets and squares emptying so quickly,
And everybody turning home again so full of thought?
Because night has fallen and the Barbarians have not come.
And some people have arrived from the frontier;
They said there are no Barbarians any more.

And now what will become of us without Barbarians? –
Those people were some sort of a solution.

C.P.Cavafy, 'Waiting for the Barbarians', in *The Poems of C.P. Cavafy*, trans. John Mavrogordato (London: Hogarth Press, 1951), p. 28.

References

Publications by J.M. Coetzee

Novels

Dusklands. Johannesburg: Ravan Press, 1974.

In the Heart of the Country. London: Secker & Warburg, 1977.

In the Heart of the Country. Johannesburg: Ravan Press, 1978.

Waiting for the Barbarians. 1980; rpt. Harmondsworth: Penguin Books, 1982.

Life & Times of Michael K. Johannesburg: Ravan Press, 1983.

Foe. London: Seckcr & Warburg, 1986.

Articles & Reviews

'Achterberg's "Ballade van de gasfitter": The Mystery of I and You.' *PMLA*, 92 (1977), 285–296.

'The Agentless Sentence as Rhetorical Device'. *Language and Style*, 13 (1980), 26–34.

'Blood, Flaw, Taint, Degeneration: The Case of Sarah Gertrude Millin'. *English Studies in Africa*, 23, No. 1 (1980), 41–58.

'Captain America in American Mythology'. *UCT Studies in English*, No. 6, (Oct 1976), pp. 33–39.

'Confession and Double Thoughts: Tolstoy, Rousseau, Dostoevsky'. *Comparative Literature*, 37, 3 (Summer 1985), 193–232.

'Farm Novel and *Plaasroman* in South Africa'. *English in Africa*, 13, 2 (October 1986), 1–19.

'The First Sentence of Yvonne Burgess's *The Strike*'. *English in Africa*, 3, No. 1, (1976), 47–48.

'The Great South African Novel'. *Leadership SA*, 2, No 4 (Summer 1983), 74–79.

'Idleness in South Africa'. *Social Dynamics*, 2 (1982), 1–12.

'Lineal Consciousness in the Farm Novels of C.M. van den Heever'. Association of University English Teachers of South Africa Conference, Cape Town. 3–5 July 1985.

'Man's Fate in the Novels of Alex la Guma'. *Studies in Black Literature*, 5, No. 1 (Spring 1974), 16–23.

'Nabokov's *Pale Fire* and the Primacy of Art'. *UCT Studies in English*, No. 5 (Oct 1974), pp. 1–7.

'A Note on Writing'. In, *Momentum: On Recent South African Writing.*

Ed. M.J. Daymond, J.U. Jacobs and M. Lenta. Pietermaritzburg: Univ. of Natal Press, 1984, pp. 11–13.
'Pauline Smith and the Afrikaans Language'. *English in Africa*, 8, No. 1 (1981). Rpt. in *Pauline Smith*. South African Literature No. 3. Ed. Dorothy Driver. Johannesburg: McGraw-Hill, 1983, pp. 198–205.
'A Poet in Prison'. Rev. of *The True Confessions of an Albino Terrorist* and *Mouroir* by Breyten Breytenbach. *Social Dynamics*, 11, 2 (December 1985), 72–75.
'Surreal Metaphors and Random Processes'. *Journal of Literary Semantics*, 8 (1979), 22–30.
'Time, Tense and Aspect in Kafka's "The Burrow" '. *MLN*, 96 (1981), 556–579.
'Triangular Structures of Desire in Advertising'. *Critical Arts: A Journal for Media Studies*, 1, No. 2 (June 1980), 34–41.
'Truth in Autobiography'. Inaugural Lecture, Univ. of Cape Town. 3 Oct. 1984.
'The White Man's Burden'. *Speak*, 1, No. 1 (Dec 1977), 4–7. Rpt. '"The Burden of Consciousness in Africa": Review of *The Guest*'. In, *Athol Fugard*. South African Literature, No. 1. Ed. Stephen Gray. Johannesburg: McGraw-Hill, 1982, pp. 96–100.

Other References

Anderson, Benedict. *Imagined Communities: Reflections on the Origin and Spread of Nationalism*. London: Verso, 1983.
Bakhtin, Mikhail. 'The word in the novel'. Trans. Ann Shukman. In, *Comparative Criticism: A Yearbook, II*. Ed. Elinor Shaffer. Cambridge: Cambridge Univ. Press, 1980, pp. 213–220.
Barthes, Roland. *The Pleasure of the Text*. Trans. Richard Miller. New York: Hill and Wang, 1975.
Roland Barthes. Trans. Richard Howard. New York: Hill and Wang, 1977.
S/Z: An Essay. Trans. Richard Miller. New York: Hill and Wang, 1974.
Writing Degree Zero. Trans. Annette Lavers and Colin Smith. London, 1967; rpt. New York: Hill and Wang, 1968.
Bataille, Georges. *Death and Sensuality: A Study of Eroticism and the Taboo*. Trans. anon. New York: Walker & Co., 1977.
Baudrillard, Jean. *Simulations*. Trans. Paul Foss, Paul Patton, Philip Beitchman. New York: Semiotext (e), 1983.

Belsey, Catherine. 'The Plurality of History'. In, 'The Text in Itself: A Symposium'. Southern Review, 17 (1984), 138–141.

Benveniste, Emile. *Problems in General Linguistics*. Trans. Mary Elizabeth Meek. Coral Gables: Univ. of Miami Press, 1971.

Bernheimer, Charles. *Flaubert and Kafka: Studies in Psycho-poetic Structure*. Yale: Yale Univ. Press, 1982.

Bersani, Leo. *A Future for Astyanax: Character and Desire in Literature*. Boston: Little, Brown & Company, 1976.

Bhabha, Homi K. 'Difference, Discrimination and the Discourse of Colonialism'. In, *The Politics of Theory*. Ed. Frances Barker. Colchester: Univ. of Essex Press, 1983, pp. 194–211.

Foreword: Remembering Fanon: Self, Psyche and the Colonial Condition. *Black Skins, White Masks*. By Frantz Fanon. Trans. Charles Lam Markham. London and Sydney: Pluto Press, 1986. pp. vii-xxvi.

'Of Mimicry and Man: The Ambivalence of Colonial Discourse'. October, 28 (Spring 1984), 125–133.

Brink, André. 'J.M. Coëtzee-roman steek effe af by voriges'. Rev. of *Foe* by J.M. Coetzee. *Rapport,* 26 October 1986, p. 36.

Bronzwaer, W.J.M. Tense in the Novel: *An Investigation of Some Potentialities of Linguistic Criticism*. Groningen: Wolters-Noordhoff, 1970.

Brooks, Peter. 'Freud's Masterplot'. *Yale French Studies*, 55/56 (1977), 280–300.

Bruss, Elizabeth W. *Beautiful Theories: The Spectacle of Discourse in Contemporary Criticism*. Baltimore: Johns Hopkins Univ. Press, 1982.

Cavafy, C.P. 'Waiting for the Barbarians'. Trans. John Mavrogordato. In, *The Poems of C.P. Cavafy*. London: Hogarth Press, 1951.

Churchill, Caryl. Introduction to *Cloud Nine*. In, *Plays: One*. London: Methuen, 1985, pp. 245–247.

Cixous, Hélène. 'The Character of "Character".' *New Literary History*, 5 (1974). 383–402.

Cohen, Philip. 'Mies is die Mies.' Rev. of, *In the Heart of the Country*, by J.M. Coetzee. *Speak*, 1, No. 3 (May/June 1978), 25–26.

Cohn, Dorrit. *Transparent Minds*. Princeton: Princeton Univ. Press, 1978.

Coward, Rosalind, and John Ellis. *Language and Materialism: Developments in Semiology and the Theory of the Subject*. London: Routledge & Kegan Paul, 1977.

Crewe, Jonathan. '*Dusklands*'. Rev. of *Dusklands* by J.M. Coetzee. Contrast, 9, No. 2 (1974), 90–95.

Culler, Jonathan. *The Pursuit of Signs*. London: Routledge & Kegan Paul, 1981.

Davis, Robert Con. 'Critical Introduction: The Discourse of the Father'. In, *The Fictional Father: Lacanian Readings of the Text*. Ed. Robert Con Davis. Amherst: Univ. of Massachusetts Press, 1981, pp. 3–12.

'Introduction: Lacan and Narration'. *MLN*, 98 (1983), 848–859.

Defoe, Daniel. *The Life and Strange Surprizing Adventures of Robinson Crusoe, of York, Mariner*. Ed. J. Donald Crowley. Oxford: Oxford Univ. Press, 1981.

Roxana: The Fortunate Mistress. Ed. Jane Jack. Oxford: Oxford Univ. Press, 1964.

de Man, Paul. 'The Rhetoric of Temporality'. In, *Interpretation: Theory and Practice*. Ed. Charles S. Singleton. Baltimore: John Hopkins Univ. Press, 1969, pp. 173–209.

Derrida, Jacques. 'Choreographies'. Interview with Christie V. McDonald. *Diacritics*, 12, 2 (1982), 66–76.

Of Grammatology. Trans. Gayatri Chakravorty Spivak. Baltimore: John Hopkins Univ. Press, 1976

'The Purveyor of Truth'. *Yale French Studies*, 52 (1975), 31–113.

'Racism's Last Word'. Trans. Peggy Kamuf. *Critical Inquiry*, 12 (Autumn 1985), 290–99.

du Plessis, Menàn. 'Towards a true materialism'. *Contrast*, 13, No. 4 (Dec 1981), 77–87.

Durand, Régis. 'The Anxiety of Performance'. *New Literary History*, 12 (1980), 167–176.

' "The Captive King": The Absent Father in Melville's Text'. In, *The Fictional Father: Lacanian Readings of the Text*. Ed. Robert Con Davis. Amherst: Univ. of Massachusetts Press, 1981, pp. 48–72.

'On *Aphanisis*: A Note on the Dramaturgy of the Subject in Narrative Analysis'. *MLN*, 98 (1983), 860–870.

During, Simon. 'Postmodernism or Postcolonialism?', *Landfall*, 39, 3 (Sept 1985), 366–380.

'Postmodernism or post-colonialism today'. *Textual Practice*, 1 (1987), 32–47.

Felman, Shoshana. 'Beyond Oedipus: The Specimen Story of Psychoanalysis'. *MLN*, 98 (1983), 1021–1053.

'To Open the Question'. *Yale French Studies*, 55–56 (1977), 5–10.

'The Originality of Jacques Lacan'. *Poetics Today*, 2, No 1b (Winter 1980/81), 45–57.

'Turning the Screw of Interpretation'. *Yale French Studies*, 55/56 (1977), 94–207.

Fineman, Joel. 'The structure of Allegorical Desire'. In, *Allegory and*

Representation. Selected Papers from the English Institute, New Series, No. 5. Ed. Stephen J. Greenblatt. Baltimore: John Hopkins Univ. Press, 1981, pp. 26–60.

Foucault, Michel. 'The Discourse on Language'. Trans. Rupert Swyer. *Social Science Information*, April 1971, pp. 7–30. Rpt. in *The Archaeology of Knowledge*. Trans. A.M. Sheridan Smith. New York: Pantheon, 1972, pp. 215–237.

'The Repressive Hypothesis'. In, *The History of Sexuality, Volume I: An Introduction*. Trans. Robert Hurley. Rpt. in *The Foucault Reader*. Ed. Paul Rabinow. New York: Pantheon, 1984, pp. 301–29

'What Is an Author?' Trans. Josué V. Harari. In *Textual Strategies: Perspectives in Post-Structuralist Criticism*. Ed. Josué V. Harari. Cornell Univ. Press, 1979, pp. 141–160. Rpt. in *The Foucault Reader* Ed. Paul Rabinow. New York: Pantheon, 1984, pp. 101–120.

Fox-Genovese, Elizabeth. 'Placing Women's History in History'. *New Left Review*, 133 (May–June 1982), 5–29.

Freud, Sigmund. *Beyond the Pleasure Principle*. In, *The Standard Edition of the Complete Psychological Works of Sigmund Freud*. Vol. XVIII. Trans. James Strachey. London: Hogarth Press, 1955. 7–64.

Fetishism. In, *The Standard Edition of the Complete Psychological Works of Sigmund Freud*. Vol. V. Trans. James Strachey. London: Hogarth Press, 1957, pp. 198–204.

'The Psychology of Women'. *New Introductory Lectures on Psycho-Analysis*, No. 24. Trans. W.J.H. Sprott. 1933; rpt. London: Hogarth Press, 1967, pp. 144–74.

Gallop, Jane. 'Lacan's "Mirror Stage": Where to Begin'. *Substance*, No. 37/38 (1983), pp. 118–128.

Garner, Shirley Nelson, Claire Kahane and Madelon Sprengnether. *The (M)other Tongue: Essays in Feminist Psychoanalytic Interpretation*. Ithaca: Cornell Univ. Press, 1985.

Gelpi, Barbara Charlesworth. 'A Common Language: The American Woman Poet'. In, *Shakespeare's Sisters: Feminist Essays on Women Poets*. Ed. Sandra M. Gilbert and Susan Gubar. Bloomington: Indiana Univ. Press, pp. 269–279.

Genette, Gérard. *Narrative Discourse*. Trans. Jane E. Lewin. Oxford: Basil Blackwell, 1980.

Palimpsestes: La Littérature au Second Degré. Paris: Editions du Seuil, 1982.

Gilbert, Harriett. 'Island Stories'. Rev. of *Foe* by J.M. Coetzee. *New Statesman*, 12 September, 1986.

Gilbert, Sandra M. and Susan Gubar. *The Madwoman in the Attic: The Woman Writer and the Nineteenth-Century Literary Imagination.* New Haven and London: Yale Univ. Press, 1979.

'Sexual Linguistics: Gender, Language, Sexuality'. *New Literary History*, 16, 3 (Spring 1985), 515–543.

Girard, René. *Deceit, Desire and the Novel: Self and Other in Literary Studies.* Trans. Yvonne Freccero. Baltimore: Johns Hopkins Univ. Press, 1965.

Violence and the Sacred. Trans. Patrick Gregory. Baltimore: John Hopkins Univ. Press, 1977.

Gordimer, Nadine. 'The Essential Gesture: Writers and Responsibility'. *The Age Monthly Review*, Dec 1984/Jan 1985, pp. 13–15. 'The Idea of Gardening'. Rev. of *Life & Times of Michael K* by J.M. Coetzee. The New York Review of Books, 2 Feb. 1984, pp. 3 and 6.

Gray, Stephen. *Southern African Literature: An Introduction.* Cape Town: David Philip, 1979.

Green, André. 'La déliaison'. *Littérature*, No. 3 (Oct 1971), pp. 33–52. Rpt. 'The Unbinding Process'. Trans. Lionel Duisit. *New Literary History*, 12, No. 1 (1980), 11–39.

Gussow, Mel. 'Novelist Syncopating History in *Ragtime*'. *New York Times*, 11 July 1975, p. 12.

Harris, H.S. Introduction to the *Difference* Essay. In, *The Difference Between Fichte's and Schelling's System of Philosophy.* G.W.F. Hegel. Trans. H.S. Harris and Walter Cerf. Albany: State Univ. of New York Press, 1977, pp. 1–75.

Harvey, C.J.D. *'Waiting for the Barbarians'. Standpunte*, 34, 4 (August 1981), 3–8.

Heath, Stephen. *The Nouveau Roman: A Study in the Practice of Writing.* London: Elek, 1972.

Hegel, G.W.F. Preface. *The Difference Between Fichte's and Schelling's System of Philosophy.* Trans. H.S. Harris and Walter Cerf. Albany: State Univ. of New York Press, 1977, pp. 79–83.

The Phenomenology of Mind. Trans. J.B. Baillie. London: Swan Sonnenschein & Co., 1910.

Hughes, H. Stuart. *Oswald Spengler: A Critical Estimate.* 1952; rpt. New York: Charles Scribner's Sons, 1962.

Ingarden, Roman. *Time and Modes of Being.* Trans. Helen R. Michejda. Springfield: Charles Thomas, 1964.

Irigaray, Luce. 'Ce sexe qui n'en est pas un'. *Ce sexe qui n'en est pas un.* Paris: Minuit, 1977. Trans. in *New French Feminisms: An Anthology.* Ed. Elaine Marks and Isabelle de Courtivron. Amherst: Univ. of Massachusetts Press, 1980, pp. 99–106.

Jacobson, Dan. Introduction. *The Story of an African Farm*. By Olive Schreiner. Gloucester, Mass.: Peter Smith, 1976.

James, Frederic. 'Imaginary and Symbolic in Lacan: Marxism, Psychoanalytic Criticism, and the Problem of the Subject.' *Yale French Studies*, 55/56 (1977), 338–395.

Postmodernism, or the Cultural Logic of Late Capitalism'. *New Left Review*, 147 (July–August 1984), 53–92.

Janssen, Irene, Truida Lijphart, and Barbara van Ijzeren. 'Over de vertelsituasie in *Die swerfjare van Poppie Nongena*.' *Standpunte*, 34, No. 3 (June 1981), 57–66.

Jardine, Alice. 'Introduction to Julia Kristeva's "Women's Time" '. *Signs: Journal of Women in Culture and Society*, 7, 2 (1981), 5–12

Jefferson, Ann. *The Nouveau Roman and the Poetics of Fiction*. Cambridge: Cambridge Univ. Press, 1980.

Johnson, Barbara. 'The Frame of Reference: Poe, Lacan, Derrida'. *Yale French Studies*, 55/56 (1977), 457–505.

Jones, Ann Rosalind. 'Writing the Body: toward an understanding of *l'écriture féminine*'. In, *Feminist Criticism and Social Change: Sex, Class and Race in Literature and Culture*. Ed. Judith Newton and Deborah Rosenfelt. New York: Methuen, 1985, pp. 86–101.

Kafka, Franz. 'The Burrow'. In, *Metamorphosis and Other Stories*. Trans. Willa and Edwin Muir. 1949; rpt. Harmondsworth: Penguin Books, 1961.

The Castle. Trans. Willa and Edwin Muir (and additional material trans. by Eithne Wilkins and Ernst Kaiser). 1930; rpt. Harmondsworth: Penguin Books, 1975.

'A Fasting Showman'. In, *Wedding Preparations in the Country and Other Stories*. Trans. Willa and Edwin Muir. 1949; rpt. Harmondsworth: Penguin Books, 1978.

The Trial. Trans. Willa and Edwin Muir. 1935; rpt. Harmondsworth: Penguin Books, 1953.

Knox-Shaw, Peter. '*Dusklands*: A Metaphysics of Violence'. *Commonwealth Novel in English*, 2, No. 1 (January 1983), 65–81.

Kojève, Alexandre. *Introduction to the Reading of Hegel*. Trans. James H. Nichols, Jr. Ed. Allan Bloom. New York: Basic Books, 1969.

Kristeva, Julia. 'Oscillation du "pouvoir" au "refus".' Interview with Xavière Gauthier. *Tel Quel*, (Summer 1974). Rpt. 'Oscillation between Power and Denial'. Trans. Marilyn A. August. In, *New French Feminisms: An Anthology*. Ed. Elaine Marks and Isabelle de Courtivron. Amherst: Univ. of Massachusetts Press, 1980, pp. 165–67.

*La Révolution du Langage Poétique: L'avantgarde à la fin du XIXe*

siècle: Lautréamont et Mallarmé. Paris: Editions du Seuil, 1974.

Kritzman, Lawrence D. 'Barthesian Free Play.' *Yale French Studies*, No. 66 (1984), pp. 189–210.

Lacan, Jacques. *Ecrits: A Selection*. Trans. Alan Sheridan. London: Tavistock Publications, 1977.

The Four Fundamental Concepts of Psycho-Analysis. Trans. Alan Sheridan. Ed. Jacques-Alain Miller. London: Hogarth Press, 1977.

'Seminar on the Purloined Letter'. *Yale French Studies*, 48 (1973), 39–72.

Lang, Candace. 'Aberrance in Criticism'. *Substance*, No. 41 (1983), 3–16.

Laplanche, Jean. *Life and Death in Psychoanalysis*. Trans. Jeffrey Mehlman. Baltimore: Johns Hopkins Univ. Press, 1976.

Lemaire, Anika. *Jacques Lacan*. Trans. David Macey. London: Routledge and Kegan Paul, 1977.

'Litcrit and the Novels of J.M. Coetzee'. Anonymous unpublished paper.

Lugones, Maria C. and Elizabeth V. Spelman. 'Have We Got a Theory For You!' *Women's Studies International Forum*, 6, 6 (1983), 573–581.

Lyons, John. *Semantics*. Vol. II. Cambridge: Cambridge Univ. Press, 1977.

Lyotard, Jean-Francois. 'Answering the Question: What Is Post-modernism?' Trans. Régis Durand. In, *The Postmodern Condition: A Report on Knowledge*. Trans. Geoff Bennington and Brian Massumi. Manchester: Manchester Univ. Press, 1984, pp. 71–82.

Maclennan, Don. '*Dusklands*'. In, *Perspectives on South African Fiction*. Ed. Sarah Christie, Geoffrey Hutchings and Don Maclennan. Johannesburg: Ad Donker, 1980, pp. 174–183.

Makward, Christiane. 'To Be or Not to Be . . . A Feminist Speaker'. Trans. Marlène Barsoum, Alice Jardin, and Hester Eisenstein. In, *The Future of Difference*. Ed. Hester Eisenstein and Alice Jardine. New Brunswick: Rutgers Univ. Press, 1985, pp. 95–105.

Mannoni, O. *Prospero and Caliban: The Psychology of Colonization*. Trans. Pamela Powesland. London: Methuen, 1956.

Marinelli, Peter V. *Pastoral*. Critical Idiom No. 15. London: Methuen, 1971.

Mendilow, A.A. *Time and the Novel*. 1952; rpt. New York: New Humanities Press, 1972.

Miller, J. Hillis. *Fiction and Repetition: Seven English Novels*. Cambridge, Massachusetts: Harvard Univ. Press, 1982. 'The Limits of Pluralism, III: The Critic as Host'. *Critical Inquiry*, 3 (1977),

439–447.

Mitchell, W.J.T. 'Editor's Note: On Narrative'. *Critical Inquiry*, 7 (Autumn 1980), 1–4.

Mohanty, Chandra Talpade. 'On Salvaging Difference: The Politics of Black Women's Studies'. Rev. of *All the Women Are White, All the Blacks Are Men, but Some of Us Are Brave: Black Women's Studies*, ed. Gloria T. Hull, Patricia Bell Scott and Barbara Smith. *Women's Studies Int. Forum*, 6, 2 (1983). 243–247.

Moi, Toril. *Sexual/Textual Politics: Feminist Literary Theory*. London: Methuen, 1985.

Mykata, Larysa. 'Lacan, Literature and the Look: Woman in the Eye of Psychoanalysis'. *Substance*, No. 39 (1983), 49–57.

Norris, Christopher. *Deconstruction: Theory and Practice.* New Accents. London: Methuen, 1982.

Owens, Craig. 'The Allegorical Impulse: Toward a Theory of Postmodernism'. Part 1. *October*, 12 (Spring 1980), 67–86.

'The Allegorical Impulse: Toward a Theory of Postmodernism.' Part 2. *October*, 13 (Summer 1980), 59–80.

'The Discourse of Others: Feminists and Postmodernism.' In, *Postmodern Culture*. Ed. Hal Foster. 1983; rpt. London and Sydney: Pluto Press, 1985, pp. 57–81.

Oxenhandler, Neal. 'The Horizons of Psychocriticism'. *New Literary History*, 14, 1 (Autumn 1982), 89–103.

Pascal, Roy. *Kafka's Narrators: A Study of His Stories and Sketches*. Cambridge: Cambridge Univ. Press, 1982.

Pratt, Annis. *Archetypal Patterns in Women's Fiction*. Sussex: Harvester Press, 1982.

Pratt, Mary Louise. 'Scratches on the Face of the Country; or, What Mr. Barrow Saw in the Land of the Bushmen'. *Critical Inquiry*, 12 (Autumn 1985), 119–43.

Rhedin, Folke. 'J.M. Coetzee'. Interview with J.M. Coetzee. *Kunapipi*, 6, 1 (1984) (6–11).

Rich, Adrienne. 'When We Dead Awaken: Writing as Re-Vision'. *College English*, 34, 1 (October 1972), 18–25. Rpt. in Adrienne Rich's *Poetry*. Ed. Barbara Charlesworth Gelpi and Albert Gelpi. New York: Norton, 1975, pp. 90–98.

Rich, Paul. 'Tradition and Revolt in South African Fiction: The Novels of André Brink, Nadine Gordimer and J.M. Coetzee.' *Journal of Southern African Studies*, 9, No. 1 (Oct 1982), 54–73.

Ricoeur, Paul. 'Narrative Time.' *Critical Inquiry*, 7 (1980), 169–190.

Robbe–Grillet, Alain. *For a New Novel: Essays on Fiction*. Trans. Richard Howard. New York: Grove Press Inc., 1965.

Roberts, Sheila. 'South African post-revolutionary fiction'. *Standpunte*, 35, 3 (June 1982), 44–51.

Rose, Jacqueline. Introduction II. *Feminine Sexuality: Jacques Lacan and the ecole freudienne*. Ed. Juliet Mitchell and Jacqueline Rose. London: Macmillan, 1982, pp. 27–57.

Sankey, Margaret. 'Meaning through Intertextuality: Isomorphism of Defoe's *Robinson Crusoe* and Tournier's *Vendredi ou les limbes du Pacifique*'. *Australian Journal of French Studies*, 18, 1 (1981), 77–88.

Schafer, Roy. 'Narration in the Psychoanalytic Dialogue'. *Critical Inquiry*, 7 (1980), 29–53.

Schleifer, Ronald. 'The Space and Dialogue of Desire: Lacan, Greimas, and Narrative Temporality'. *MLN*, 98 (1983), 871–890.

Schreiner, Olive. *The Story of An African Farm*. London, 1883; rpt. Gloucester, Mass.: Peter Smith, 1976.

Shelley, Mary. *Frankenstein, or The Modern Prometheus*. 1816; rpt. New York: Signet Classics, 1965.

Sheridan, Alan. Translator's Note. *Ecrits*. By Jacques Lacan. London: Tavistock Publications, 1977, note 113, p. 112.

Translator's Note. *The Four Fundamental Concepts of Psycho-Analysis*. By Jacques Lacan. Ed. Jacques-Alain Miller. London: Hogarth Press, p. 280.

Showalter, Elaine. 'Feminist Criticism in the Wilderness'. *Critical Inquiry*, 8 (Winter 1981).

Spivak, Gayatri Chakravorty. 'Imperialism and Sexual Difference'. *Oxford Literary Review*, Special Issue on Sexual Difference, 18, 1–2 (1986), 225–240.

'The Letter as Cutting Edge'. *Yale French Studies*, 55/56 (1977), 208–226.

'Three Women's Texts and a Critique of Imperialism'. *Critical Inquiry*, 12 (Autumn 1985), 243–261.

Translator's Preface. *Of Grammatology*. By Jacques Derrida. Baltimore: John Hopkins Univ. Press, 1976, pp. ix–lxxxvii.

Stam, Robert and Louis Spence. 'Colonialism, Racism and Representation.' *Screen*, 24, 2 (Mar–Apr 1983), 2–20.

Stanzel, Franz K. 'Teller-Characters and Reflector Characters in Narrative Theory'. *Poetics Today*, 2, 2 (Winter 1981), 5–15.

Sussman, Henry. 'The Court as Text: Inversion, Supplanting, and Derangement in Kafka's *Der Prozess*'. *PMLA*, 92 (1977), 41–55.

Tatts, Sandra. Rev. of *Foe* by J.M. Coetzee. In 'Writing from a land apart.' Ed. Jil Kitson. First Edition, ABC Radio, 20 November, 1986.

Thorold, Alan, and Richard Wicksteed. 'Grubbing for the ideological implications: A clash (more or less) with J.M. Coetzee.' Interview with J.M. Coetzee. *Sjambok*. A *Varsity* publication. S.R.C., University of Cape Town. No date.

Tournier, Michel. *Vendredi ou les limbes du Pacifique*. Paris: Gallimard, 1972.

Vaughan, Michael. 'Literature and Politics: Currents in South African Writing in the Seventies'. *Journal of Southern African Studies*, 9, No. 1 (Oct 1982), 118–138.

Voss, A.E. 'A Generic Approach to the South African Novel in English'. Association of University English Teachers of South Africa Conference, Cape Town. January 1977.

Watson, Stephen. 'The Liberal Ideology and Some English South African Novelists'. M.A. Diss. Univ. of Cape Town 1980.

'Speaking: J.M. Coetzee'. Interview with J.M. Coetzee. *Speak*, 1, No. 3 (May/June 1978), 21–24.

White Hayden. 'The Value of Narrativity in the Representation of Reality.' *Critical Inquiry*, 7 (1980), 5–27.

Wilhelm, Peter. Rev. of *Life & Times of Michael K*, by J.M. Coetzee. *Leadership SA*, 2, No. 4 (Summer 1983), 105.

Wilden, Anthony. 'Lacan and the Discourse of the Other'. In, *The Language of the Self*. By Jacques Lacan. Trans., Notes and Commentary by Anthony Wilden. Baltimore: Johns Hopkins Univ. Press, 1968.

Wood, W.J.B. '*Waiting for the Barbarians*: Two Sides of Imperial Rule and Some Related Considerations'. In *Momentum: On Recent South African Writing*. Ed. M.J. Daymond, J.U. Jacobs and M. Lenta. Pietermaritzburg: Univ. of Natal Press, 1984, pp. 129–140.

Articles on J.M. Coetzee not referred to in the text

Engle, Lars. 'Outrageous Meaning: The Fiction of J.M. Coetzee'. *The Threepenny Review, 6, 4 (Winter 1986), 5–7.*

Gilmer, Joan. 'The Motif of the Damaged Child in the Work of J.M. Coetzee'. In, *Momentum: On Recent South African Writing*. Ed. M.J. Daymond, J.U. Jacobs and M. Lenta, Pietermaritzburg: Univ. of Natal Press, 1984, pp. 107–120.

Kohler, P. 'Freeburghers, the Nama and the politics of the frontier tradition; an analysis of social relations in the second narrative of J.M. Coetzee's *Dusklands*: Towards an historiography of South African Literature'. *The Making of Class.* History Workshop. Univ. of the Witwatersrand. 9–14 February, 1987.

Martin, Richard G. 'Narrative, History, Ideology: A Study of *Waiting for the Barbarians* and *Burger's Daughter.*' *Ariel*, 17, 3 (July 1986), 3–21.

Olsen, Lance. 'The Presence of Absence: Coetzee's *Waiting for the Barbarians. Ariel*, 16, 2 (April 1985), 47–56.

Strauss, Peter. 'Coetzee's Idylls: The Ending of *In the Heart of the Country*:' In, *Momentum: On Recent South African Writing*. Ed. M.J. Daymond, J.U. Jacobs and M. Lenta, Pietermaritzburg: Univ. of Natal Press, 1984, pp. 121–28.

Watson, Stephen. 'Colonialism and the Novels of J.M. Coetzee'. *Research in African Literatures*, 17, 3 (Fall 1986), 370–392.

Zamora, Lois Parkinson. 'Allegories of power in the fiction of J.M. Coetzee'. *Journal of Literary Studies*, 2, 1 (March 1986), 1–14.

Russell Vandenbroucke

TRUTHS THE HAND CAN TOUCH

The Theatre of Athol Fugard

This is the first major study of the internationally acclaimed playwright Athol Fugard. Through numerous interviews with Fugard and his actors and associates, and drawing upon a wealth of source material, the author introduces Fugard and examines his plays closely and comprehensively. The book explores Fugard's craft as a writer and playwright, and the general shape of his life, primarily as it relates to his work. There is a condensed theatre history of the companies with which he has been associated. Most importantly, his work is placed within its intellectual and historical context, thereby suggesting why the plays have such reverberations and why Fugard is as important a playwright world-wide as any working today. This is an essential study for those who make theatre as well as for those who teach it, study it, and attend it.

308 pages, a paperbook

Ridley Beeton

FACETS OF OLIVE SCHREINER

A Manuscript Source-book

Olive Schreiner always had an effect on people – no-one who encountered her was afterwards neutral about her. She was adored or thoroughly loathed. In this collection of letters, diaries and other manuscript sources, Ridley Beeton integrates her warmth and arrogance, her anger and love, her brilliance and contrariness into a comprehensive portrait of Olive Schreiner the woman and writer. The emotional/intellectual entanglements with Karl Pearson, Edward Carpenter and Havelock Ellis are extensively covered. The facets presented are based on primary sources held at research centres, and are linked by notes which give further information about the people who influenced her, or under whose guidance she worked.

275 pages, a paperbook

Olive Schreiner

THE STORY OF AN AFRICAN FARM

The Story of an African Farm was first published in 1883, under the pseudonym Ralph Iron. Only later did it transpire that the author was actually a woman – Olive Schreiner. When the book first appeared it was received with mixed feelings by its Victorian readers, some of whom were shocked by the 'morality' of the author, and felt that it would have been better if the book had never been published. Schreiner's perseverance paid off, and today the novel, set on a farm in the Karoo, is considered important for South African literature, as the beginning of a national literary tradition. This new paperbook edition is introduced by Cherry Clayton.

281 pages, a paperbook

Olive Schreiner

THE WOMAN'S ROSE

The short stories and allegories in *The Woman's Rose* have been selected to provide a fuller and more varied picture of the achievement of Olive Schreiner, so often considered to be the one-book author of *The Story of an African Farm.* The pieces in this book offer an insight into nineteenth century feminism, which for the Victorians was a spiritual and educational revolution as opposed to the largely sexual one of today. Although the issues are different the principles are perhaps the same. Schreiner is of interest to the modern reader both as an example of historical conditioning and for her attempt to peer over the shoulders of her contemporaries into the future.

128 pages, a paperbook

Sarah Gertrude Millin

GOD'S STEPCHILDREN

First published in 1924, *God's Stepchildren* is no less relevant today. Miscegenation had long been a preoccupation of Sarah Gertrude Millin, and in this novel, the poignant story of segregation and people of mixed heritage, it is the dominant theme. The book begins in 1821 when Andrew Flood becomes a missionary in a remote section of the Cape Colony and, after failing to establish any spiritual contact with his Hottentot charges, marries one of them as a gesture of brotherhood. The marriage is a failure in all respects, and Sarah Gertrude Millin traces the lives of the next four generations, concentrating on one person in each, and emphasising their problems. These people question 'But is God himself not white?' and come to the final conclusion, 'Perhaps we brown people are his stepchildren.'

320 pages, a paperbook

Lionel Abrahams

THE CELIBACY OF FELIX GREENSPAN

Lionel Abrahams was born in Johannesburg in April 1928, and graduated with a BA degree from Wits. Before turning to writing, something he had always wanted to do, he edited various books, and with Walt Sanders, co-edited Donker's annual anthology of new local writing, *Quarry.* He also founded Renoster Books which published first volumes by Oswald Mtshali and Mongane Wally Serote. In 1975 a collection of his poems, *Thresholds of Tolerance* was published and in 1977, the year that *The Celibacy of Felix Greenspan* was first published, he was awarded half the Pringle Prize for creative writing. This book, a novel in 18 stories, describes the quest of Felix Greenspan, South African and Jewish, 'to know reality and to partake of life's fullness' in a way that has been described as 'liberating' and 'unexpected'.

190 pages, a paperbook